Praise for *Gabriel's Songbook*

What a wonderful book! Artistic ambition, first love, small-town Appalachian life, the image-obsessed machinations of the Nashville music industry: all ring so authentic, so true. Michael Amos Cody's first novel is gripping, poignant, and unforgettable.

—Jeff Mann, author of *Country*

Michael Amos Cody writes with a strong, authentic voice about the Appalachia I know. There is no posturing or exaggeration here. Instead, this is a book that strives after Hemingway's maxim to write one true sentence, and Cody does that without fail. *Gabriel's Songbook* is a novel full of heart and longing and it deserves its distinguished place on the shelf with some of the best stories of the region. I hope it is the first of many more books about Runion, North Carolina.

—Charles Dodd White, author of *A Shelter of Others* and *Lambs of Men*

In *Gabriel's Songbook*, Michael Amos Cody has created a living portrait of the artist as a wayward musician, whose talent carries him out into the world, and whose heart pulls him back toward his home in the mountains. I came to care for these characters so much I wished I could step into the book and warn Gabriel and Eliza of the perils ahead of them, or to sit in the audience and hear the searching songs Gabriel sings. Cody shows a care with how his characters speak, and how they interact with one another, that gives the novel both a poetic charge and a lived-in authenticity. *Gabriel's Songbook* resonates like a great ballad, a song of love and struggle that keeps chiming in the ears long after the final note is played.

—Jesse Graves, author of *Tennessee Landscape with Blighted Pine* and *Basin Ghosts*

Gabriel's Songbook is the story of a musician's journey from the hills of Appalachia to the grime and glamor of Nashville, and back home again. Equal parts gritty and lyrical, rock 'n' roll and old-time country, this is a novel that transports the reader deep into that age-old dream of making the big time, and shows us the beauty and pathos that lurks underneath.

Michael Amos Cody writes with the vivid clarity of one who has made it through the punishing Nashville grind and survived, and the passion of a true believer in the power and beauty of the music itself. Behind the glaring lights of Nashville, the late nights, seedy managers and bad deals, is a beautiful tale of redemption and a love story that will stick with you long after the novel is finished.

Cody is not just a wonderful writer but a top-notch musician and songwriter as well, and that musicality is in evidence on every page— from the heartfelt lyrics that occasionally punctuate the action, to simple moments like a haircut shared between estranged lovers. This is the best novel of the music business I've come across in a very long time.

—Mark D. Baumgartner, Editor, *Aethlon: The Journal of Sport Literature*

Gabriel's Songbook

Gabriel's Songbook

by
Michael Amos Cody

Pisgah Press
Asheville, NC   IP

Pisgah Press was established in 2011 to publish and promote works of quality offering original ideas and insight into the human condition and the world around us.

Copyright © 2017 Pisgah Press

Published by Pisgah Press, LLC
PO Box 9663, Asheville, NC 28815
www.pisgahpress.com

Book design: A. D. Reed, MyOwnEditor.com
Cover design by A. D. Reed & Michael Cody
Cover photo of the author at work by Ed Huskey.

Portions of Chapter 18 appeared under the title "To the Moon, Alice" in *Potpourri,* February/March 1993, and in *Potpourri Tenth Anniversary Issue* (1999). The story won *Potpourri*'s Nancy Pickard Fiction Award in 1994.

Library of Congress Cataloging-in-Publication Data
Cody, Michael A.
Gabriel's Songbook/Michael Amos Cody
Library of Congress Control Number: 2017946781

ISBN-13: 9781942016366
ISBN-10: 1942016360

First Edition
December 2017
Printed in the United States of America

For Leesa

&

In memory of jb ("George MacDougall")

Gabriel's Songbook

The Intro

Her name was Eliza Garrison, and she appeared at Runion High the first day of school my junior year. Nobody was surprised to see her there. Word had gotten around the high school grapevine, as it always did when some new athlete or pretty girl moved into town over the summer.

I was in love from the moment the principal escorted her through the door of Mrs. Tolley's homeroom. Short black hair. Silver-blue eyes. A cute nose and a dimpled chin. She wore a white sleeveless turtleneck, a short blue-jeans skirt and red flip-flops. Her toenails were painted a reddish brown. Her bare arms and legs were tan and looked soft and strong at the same time, and when she chose an empty desk—on the other side of the room from me—and put down her books, I saw a curve of breasts that made me more aware than I had ever been of the blood surging through my body. Despite a natural shyness inherited from my father, I maneuvered physically closer to Eliza in the other three classes we had together—across the aisle in one, behind her in another, even lab partner in a third.

I could work with that until the music made its move on her.

I sang in a band called Big Muddy, a staple for most of the local music functions that called for—or did not mind—a little loud rock and roll. I already knew that I was a livelier personality on stage than in person, and as I sat behind Eliza in Mr. Brown's science fiction class, after lunch on a nondescript midweek school day, I had an idea that one of Big Muddy's upcoming shows would be the start of something.

As it turned out, the first chance to play for the home crowd, Eliza included, did not come for two months. My bandmates were no longer schoolmates—Jonah, Stu, and Little graduated, Ezra quit—so we often traveled out of town on weekends. But in October Big Muddy was booked for the annual Runion River Festival and Dam Dance, held in Stackhouse Park.

I skipped school the day before and missed Runion High's Homecoming—the football game and the dance—to travel with Big Muddy to Cleveland, Tennessee, where the band played a private-school gig. We were back in Runion by dawn and met at Stackhouse Park after a few hours' sleep. When the equipment was set, the older guys crossed the Big Laurel Creek trestle to Chunn's Tavern for a few beers, Ezra disappeared as usual, and I sat on the stage and watched the bustle of the festival.

The sun was warm but not hot, and the sky was that deep clear October blue. Shadows stretched toward town. In the yellow autumn light, the burnt orange, red, and gold of the first fallen leaves lay strewn across cobblestone walks. Transistor radios created a tinny din of pop, country and gospel music. People laughed and talked while they arranged their wares for the evening's festivities. The air filled with the blended aroma of charcoal fires, hot apple cider from Avalon Orchards, baking bread, pepper-seasoned steak and onions, and chicken that had marinated long in vinegar, mustard and Tabasco.

I soaked this all in and then hopped down from the trailer and wandered around, speaking to several people I knew, including a couple of teachers who teased me about missing school the day before. Then I found my cousin Cutter—nicknamed after his own rendition as a two-year-old of his real name, Carter—under a pine tree with two of our friends, Wiley and Jay.

"We got trounced as usual," Cutter said. "Forty-two to six."

"Yeah," I said. "I saw that in the paper this morning. Who got Homecoming Queen?"

Cutter folded his hands together under his chin and rolled his eyes toward the sky.

"Our Lady of the Red Corvette. Who'd you expect?"

"You're right. Dumb question. How was the dance?"

"Well, it probably would've made a better story for the paper than the game did."

"No surprise there."

"Does every year," Wiley added.

"Anyhow," Jay cut in, "you guys weren't around, so we had that big-mouth deejay"—he went into his radio voice—"Dr. Disco Herb, from WILD-FM! Boring as hell."

"T.W. and Moose got hold of a jar of 'shine from old Bell-Eye," Wiley said.

"Yeah," Cutter said. "They ended up puking hot dogs all over the dance floor, and Loose Lucy slipped and fell in it."

"Good God, Gabe!" Jay said. "You should've seen her when she skated into it, arms and legs going ever'-which-a-way and trying to keep her balance before she finally went down."

"Sounds like her usual dance steps to me," I said and laughed.

"Really!" Cutter said. "Anyways, she put on her skimpy gym clothes out of her locker and burned her dress and unmentionables out in the parking lot. With all that homemade alcohol in them they went up like she'd been pissed on by the Sinclair dinosaur."

"Then Johnny and the Piney Ridge Bombers took turns driving her home," Jay added.

"So I really didn't miss anything unusual," I said.

"Nothing but Eliza." Cutter flashed his wicked grin at Wiley and Jay.

"Dear Eliza," Wiley said, touching his heart with fluttering fingertips.

"Sweet Eliza," Jay echoed, slowly sliding the zipper on his jeans down, then up.

"Who?" I asked. But of course I knew—and they knew I knew—who they were talking about.

"Come on, Gabe," Wiley said. "We all seen the drool shower your pig got when you and her were cutting it up in Mr. Raney's class."

"And how she bats her eyes at you, boy," Cutter said and punched me in the arm.

"Ah, the new girl," I said. "Now I know who you're talking about. She go down in the hot dog pool too?"

"No way, man," Wiley said. "I don't think her feet even touch the ground when she dances. O' course, she only danced with that little Billy Dean from Cosmetology."

"The rest of us guys was too scared of catching lump-jeans," Jay said.

I looked down at the ground, kicked at a little pine cone and grinned. The Homecoming Dance was the first big school social since Eliza moved to Runion, and my biggest fear had been that she would take up with somebody there while I was out of town with Big Muddy. Since that had not happened I thought I still might have first shot at her if she showed up at the Dam Dance. I imagined there would be others who, after a long Homecoming night with her filling their restless dreams, would find the courage to ask her to dance tonight. But I would be the one on stage. I saw myself come down from that high place to find her starry-eyed among the dancers. The sea of people would part and recede to the other sides of the world, and the two of us would stand alone together on the glittering shore of Heaven.

I was such a romantic young man.

The day took its sweet time fading, but finally the sun dropped behind the mountains across the river, leaving Stackhouse Park in the blue shadow of Piney Ridge. For a few minutes light stayed on Runion. Brassy brilliance reflected from the windows in town, and, higher up and all around, the wooded slopes glowed with the gold and rust of October. Directly behind Runion and its house-dotted hill, Lonesome Mountain stood lit like a bonfire. The shadow swelled. Twilight climbed the mountainsides to join the darkening purple of the eastern sky. The low lamps along the walks in Stackhouse Park stuttered and warmed to life and strings of tiny white bulbs in the trees appeared like a sudden waking of angels.

At last Runion's tower clock struck nine, and the stage lights came up.

For the next two hours, Stu and Ezra's guitars jangled and cried. Little's drums and Jonah's bass cracked and boomed and rumbled like thunder rolling across the sky above Runion and the French Broad River.

I sang. And for the first time—as I scanned the crowd in front of the stage in hopes of seeing Eliza's face turned up to me like a flower to the morning sun—the songs I sang became my own. I had not written them, but that night they were mine. I caught glimpses of the inspiration that had seeded them, felt their note-to-note and line-by-line creation, saw behind that creation a hundred alternate thoughts that could be fleshed out to create a hundred more songs. Ideas and hints of ideas rose to swirl around and through me like the glowing millers that with powdery wings danced in and out of the blue, red and yellow stage lights.

That evening, the journey through each song brought me—from different directions and always for only a moment—to the border of a shadowed place I sensed existed in the middle of the music, some otherplace where songs lived whole before they flowed from some songwriter's heart. I wanted to find and map that place, learn to shape my own notes and line my own words. But each glimpse was spectral and fleeting, escaping before I could discover whether the otherplace was in me or on stage with Big Muddy or somewhere high in the starry heavens.

At times during the dance, my mind was jolted out of these musings when I thought I had caught a glimpse of Eliza. But the crowd would wash one way or the other and she would be lost in the small sea of shiny faces.

Then, toward the end of the final set, while Jonah thanked the three hundred or so folks who had been gathered around the flatbed trailer all evening, I let my eyes wander over the crowd. Not listening to Jonah. Not seeing the people. Thinking only that Eliza was not there. Trying not to think that she was in some Asheville movie theater with Joe Powell or Paul King. But as Jonah was wrapping up, a sudden movement caught my attention, and my eyes focused.

Eliza waved again.

My first thought was that she must have just arrived. I could not believe I had missed her all night when now she stood out in that crowd as if she were a glowing, hovering angel bringing me a message from God Almighty.

I looked away from her long enough to glance at the set list taped to a stage monitor. Two more songs before the end of the Dam Dance. The next song was Big Muddy's homespun version of "Nights in White Satin"—always reserved for the last-chance-slow-dance.

When the intro started, Eliza did not leave the area in front of the stage. With a sweet smile for each boy, each man, each girlfriend, she stood in the middle of the dancers and refused every invitation and plea. She just stood there, a slight flush coloring her throat and cheeks as she watched me step to the microphone and sing the first verse.

I felt a heat in my own cheeks and knew they must be blazing red, knew everybody would notice. Still I stared at her and did not care who noticed what. But when I sang the refrain—"And I love you. Oh, how I love you"—I could not bear the intensity of our connection any longer and looked up and away just as light streaked east to west across the dark October sky.

Another followed. Then another and another. The next one seemed big enough to see the trail of flames and sparks it dragged behind. For a moment it flared brighter than the moon, its green-white glow ghosting Runion and the surrounding hills, its thousand-degree descent seemingly reflected in those pale blue eyes my star-struck gaze sought out again.

I finished the song's final refrain, but the band would be riffing for several minutes on the sensual rhythm for the benefit of the dancers. I turned to Little's drum riser and swallowed a quick swig of water and turned again and took three loping steps toward the front of the stage and jumped. I felt as if I hung in the air, a sprawl of faded jeans and denim shirt tinted yellow-purple above the blended colors of the footlights and backed by blackness and shooting stars.

"I've been looking for you all night," I yelled above the music.

Eliza smiled and said something too soft to be heard.

We both laughed and shook our heads. Then I held out my arms, standing in what I hoped was a formal dance posture, an invitation. She looked away for a moment, turned back and placed her right hand in my left. My fingers touched the wetness of her back. In the breeze off the river, I felt my own sweat soaking my shirt. I smelled her perfume, something of honeysuckle and musk. My arms were shaking, and I felt a shaking in her too.

Our dance began.

In the purity of that moment—filled with music and Eliza—I discovered a light. A guiding star, as I've always imagined it. Over the years, even in times when I felt most earth-bound, I kept sight of that star in the heavens. When I sat in some darkened room with my guitar in my arms, trying to fit words to music, it hovered above me like a muse invoked. And when I finally got a real stage and an audience made up of more than friends and family, it became a spotlight, or the spot-lit reflection of myself in some pretty woman's smiling eyes.

I followed that star. Not that I'm making any claims to being a wise man. I just followed it, without question, through a great wilderness and some of my wildest dreams.

Chapter 1
The Dead of Night

He wrecked around midnight on the winding Rocky Bluff section of North Carolina Highway 209-A. The narrow blacktop lay dusty in one particular curve where the guardrail happened to be down due to construction. A witness following him through the fog and dust and darkness said the car didn't jerk or swerve before it vaulted off the mountain road. It just kept straight when it should have turned and then disappeared into the tops of the pines that cling to the mountain's side.

The only thing the sheriff and paramedics found in one piece was his Martin guitar.

Less than forty-eight hours later, a three-legged stand of weathered gray tobacco sticks stood at the head of the mauve casket. On the stand, a burlap heart—straw-stuffed and twine-tied and frilled with sprays of dried wildflowers—framed a picture of Theodore James smiling and holding that guitar. More than three hundred floral arrangements—created in a flurry by the Posy Patch—lined the walls and swelled toward the ceiling behind the casket, their soft blues and reds, gentle yellows and purples and greens, blanched by the fluorescent lights overhead. Two hundred thirty-nine people signed the guest book by the door at the back of Ramsey's Chapel. Then in a solemn shuffling line, they passed by the flowers and the casket. At the smiling picture, the line turned sharply on itself, and everybody stopped to give teary or stony condolences to Aunt Myrtle and Bobbie James and the rest of the family standing by the front pew.

Delbert Gunter brought up the end of this mourning line. Fiddle and bow passed together from left hand to right and back while he fussed with the faded blue galluses that crossed his shoulders. Then he stood still and looked down at the body for a few breaths.

The room faded into silence.

He rubbed the belly of his overalls and turned from the casket. His glistening blue gaze fell to the row of Sunday-go-to-meeting shoes on the floor in front of the first pew, and he took the bow in his right hand, and with a flick of the other wrist, held the fiddle cradled on his left forearm.

Aunt Myrtle reached for a fresh tissue.

The old fiddler touched bow to string, and a variation of an old mountain melody cried for a moment before he hushed it with whispered lyrics he'd written himself—Uncle T's favorite song.

Mama serves biscuits and gravy at sunrise
And coffee to open our eyes.
The frost is a-coming, the gathering begins,
And you're missing harvest again. . . .

*   *   *

I slipped out of the heavy smells of tears, stale sweat and flowers and stepped into the cool air of the late May evening, walked half a block up Main Street, hid in a doorway and smoked.

A woman I didn't know came along the sidewalk from the direction of Ramsey's Funeral Home and stopped in front of my hiding place to dab her eyes with a balled-up tissue. Tall and graceful, she wore beige high heels, a cream-colored dress of soft-looking acrylic, several gold bracelets, gold earrings, and a long string of pearls looped at three lengths down over her breasts.

I cleared my throat.

"Oh," she said, stepping backward and stuffing the tissue into her purse. "I didn't see you."

"Sorry to startle you, ma'am," I said. "Twenty-one years old and still don't like my folks to see me smoking." I stepped out into the light and smiled, searching for something else to say. "Have you been to the visitation for Dr. James?" I assumed she had, but in Ramsey's Upper Room, another visitation was being held for a mountain woman from

Sodom Laurel.

"Yes, I was one of his first patients before I moved up to Virginia. And I saw him now and again when I was back visiting." She looked down and brushed a tiny moth from her left breast and then looked back at me. "He must've took care of that pretty smile."

"Yeah," I said, feeling my smile stretch wider for a moment and my cheeks flush. "But he was my uncle too. His sister Maggie is my mom."

"Oh, you poor dear." The woman touched my arm with long-nailed fingers. "I'm so sorry for y'all. I'm sure he was a wonderful uncle, and I know you'll miss him."

"Yes, ma'am." I dropped my cigarette on the sidewalk and ground it under foot.

She took her hand from my arm.

"Let me show you something." She reached into her purse and pulled out a photograph. "Come over here where you can see better."

I took the picture and turned it so that the blue-white glare from the streetlight overhead didn't overpower the creased and faded image.

In the background a half-cut field of tobacco flowed down the gentle slope of a hillside and spread out across the bottom land around a creek. To the front a young and shirtless Uncle T stood in that loose way he had, kissing a jar of what looked like ice water and draping a lean arm around the shoulders of a pretty blonde girl.

The picture had a dim inscription on the back: "Theodore James and Lacy, 1952."

"Is that you?" I asked.

"Yes," she said with the hint of a smile. "A long time ago."

She stood at my elbow, so close that I felt the warmth of her body on my back and the occasional brush of the wispy fabric of her dress on my arm. I smelled her flowery perfume and the gin on her breath.

Still sniffling, she took the picture from me.

"I was seventeen," she said as she gingerly slid the picture back into her purse and brought out the tissue again. "He had a Chevrolet and a guitar." She patted my shoulder, began soundless crying and turned away without another word.

"What happened?" I said after her.

She didn't turn or give any answer I heard. She hurried up the sidewalk, got into a white Lincoln and sped through the intersection of Main Street and Lonesome Mountain Drive, disappearing where the road bends sharply downward and right toward the hairpin curve that returns it to its course along the east bank of the French Broad River.

*   *   *

Two floors above Uncle T and the now silent chapel, I sat at our little kitchen table, bending over a blank sheet of paper, holding my guitar in my arms and trying to write. My tongue felt thick with whispered conversations and too many secret cigarettes. My ears rang with a sound like the echoed fluttering of mandolin strings. Before staring eyes that burned without tears, there was Uncle T—holding an arm around the proud shoulders of a country girl named Lacy; peering into my gaping mouthful of baby teeth, his sparse-haired head backlit by the greenish light that hung above; arriving in his red Mustang convertible and a loud plaid sportscoat at the Piney Ridge Methodist Church to marry Aunt Myrtle; sitting on the porch in his sleeveless white t-shirt and khaki pants, laughing so hard at family reminiscences and dirty jokes that he had to wipe the tears from his dark eyes; pulling out mandolin or guitar when visitors came to the old homeplace, still playing when they said good night.

My pencil scratched at the silent paper.

Music has always been my life

The bed squeaked as Eliza rolled over. Her dusty sleep-voice mumbled a few foreign-sounding words. The light dimmed as the refrigerator compressor kicked on. In the quiet of the apartment, the old appliance sounded as sputtering and reedy as a poorly played bassoon.

I put down my pencil and rubbed my face hard, trying to wipe away the sleep gathering like cobwebs around my eyes. I grabbed a pick off the table and strummed a few chords, reading what I'd written and humming quietly, trying to fit the words to some fragment of melody and rhythm.

Sometimes I'm up so late at night
'Cause it's hard to find the words that rhyme
And fit together right. . . .

The hands on the red rooster clock above the fridge crept past two-thirty.

My jaw hung slack. Eyelids drooped. Face felt like it might collapse onto my chest if I didn't cave in and get some sleep.

The bed squeaked again as Eliza shifted in her dream.

After we'd come upstairs, she stayed awake only long enough to get ready for bed and call her goodnight from the bedroom door.

Those days our lives were that way—different work, different schedules. The splitting wasn't violent, like that of a tree struck by lightning, but something subtle, almost unnoticeable, like a schoolhouse path that crosses a field and slowly forks toward two neighboring silent houses.

For maybe a year after our simple ceremony at Judge Davenport's mansion in Greenville, she'd adjusted her schedule to mine, working late on the nights I traveled, getting off in time to be in the audience when I played locally, coming home early when I was there waiting. Before another year passed we were making pretty good money for Runion folks—over five hundred dollars a week between us. But then she stopped coordinating schedules and began working late every night, asking whenever I brought it up if I remembered how tight money was when we started out—as if that beginning had been years and years before—and saying she couldn't stand the thought of its ever being like that again. I tried to understand her fear, but I'd never been able to dread something in the future that wasn't threatening me in the present.

I pushed back my chair and leaned my guitar against the wall, got up and took a Mountain Dew from the refrigerator and stood sipping it by the table. I read and reread what I'd written so far, wondering where to go with the next line.

This part, the writing of lyrics, I loved most of all about songwriting, even on this edge of exhaustion. The soul churning. The stirring up of memories and feelings and dreams. The strange sensation that I was a bystander watching as the page filled with these things put into words.

My old sense of the songs living whole in some otherplace always came back to me when I sat down to write.

I walked into the shadowy living room and stretched out on the couch, staring for a moment at the bluish light from the street below that hung on the ceiling in the foreshortened shape of windows. I rubbed my face hard again with both hands, yawned and released my breath in brief whispered grunts. Thoughts and images swirled, coalesced, dissolved—Uncle T and the new song, Eliza the beautiful and an unbroken guitar, life like treading water.

*   *   *

A door creaks open and then closed. The hollow sound of footsteps— the heavy booming tap of hard-soled shoes on the wooden stairs— reverberates in the stairwell.

Somebody's coming up.

The climber reaches the second landing, and I wait to hear the door there. Nothing.

Footsteps on the third set of stairs.

I can't think what time it is but know it's late. If somebody's looking for me or Eliza at this hour, it's bad news again. Bad news coming on stone feet. Slowly.

When death comes in the night, Mr. Ramsey and his helpers are in the building, laying out the body, but they move quickly for sleepy men, getting done whatever they need to so they can go home and crawl back in bed.

These steps are ponderous, in no hurry, carrying something heavy up the stairs, perhaps carrying something heavy up to put in the stockroom across the hall.

The footsteps sound on the third floor landing and stop. No labored breathing after the laborious climb. Only silence until grit grinds under heel, and whoever it is turns and comes slowly down the short hall. Stops between the door to the stockroom—where the vaults and caskets are kept—and the door to our apartment.

Empty silence again.

I wait to hear the stockroom door. Nothing.

So I wait to hear a knock on our door as loud and slow and reverberating as the footsteps.

Instead the doorknob whimpers, and the latch slides free.

I remember Eliza triple-checking the lock, just like every night, but the dim light of the hall spills into the living room as the door swings slowly open.

I stare wide-eyed at the ceiling. Frozen. Breathless.

Somebody in the hall, waiting in silence.

I try to lunge upright and face the door, but my movement is sluggish, as if I lie in deep water. I finally reach a drooping, defenseless sitting position just as the rhinestone-and-sequin-suited man struts into the room glittering in his own private spotlight.

Get up, Gabriel, *Uncle T says.*

We are outside. We turn left and walk up Back Street toward the north end of town.

I can't take my eyes off my uncle, can't understand if the dazzling light that dances off the suit comes from within the man or shines from somewhere else.

So different from the lightless flesh the family tearfully huddled around a few hours before. The still fingers that lay clean-scrubbed and folded together as if he were only napping between patients sparkle with rings and snap to some unheard rhythm. Gone is the dark blue suit Aunt Myrtle laid him out in. The boots that slap the sidewalk are made of phoenix skin. His pants are the blue of a September sky, and rhinestones line every seam. The dazzle on the shoulders and chest of the jacket is broken only by an intricate and dizzying pattern of embroidered roses blossoming at the end of greenery that climbs up the sleeves from the rhinestone-studded cuffs. His Stetson glows the same shadowy white of a full moon reflected off deep snow.

But it's his face that hypnotizes. The pale face, with its hint of bruises and its closed eyelids white as a catfish's belly, is tanned and smooth, with chiseled features and laughing eyes. Just like the face in the picture the woman, Lacy, held under the street light.

So, I come to see where you're at. Where you're headed.

Silence.

Gabriel James Tanner?

My uncle's tone and voice but my mother's words.

Music.

I speak with an open mouth. My tongue flicks and flattens and rolls, and the sounds are nonsense.

Forget making a living, Gabriel. Better and easier ways of doing that. Your music's alive?

I hesitate. Then more nonsense.

There's where you're thinking wrong, boy. Playing live is life for them songs. The writing in here—*a ringed finger points to my chest and then sweeps away to take in the mountains and one bright western star*—and the playing shoved way the hell out there somewhere ain't gonna cut it. All starts as one thing at the center—you—and radiates out like the wheel around the sun.

But nobody listens, I try to say. They talk and laugh and eat and get drunk.

Uncle T's dark eyes lose themselves in the shadow under the brim of his hat.

We're on Lonesome Mountain Drive.

Do people have to look at the sun to know it's there? To be warmed by it? To be turned brown by it? To have it feed 'em their whole damned life? No. But it's there all the same. They look up at it sooner or later. Now, you ain't gonna govern folks' night and day, but you've got a gift—

We're on Main Street.

Do you see?

Uncle T stops dead in his tracks on the corner in front of his dark office. Behind him, the sign painted on the glass door reads, "Dr. Theodore James, D.D.S." and below that, in the middle of a wreath of dried wild flowers, hangs a laminated copy of his obituary. But he doesn't look. He stares straight at me.

Then you'll have to leave Runion. Pack up and move to Nashville, New York, Los Angeles, somewhere you'll get noticed.

From me, moans that whine and complain.

Uncle T doesn't flinch.

From the time I heard my first Ernest Tubb record, I wanted to go to Nashville. See if I could make it big. Then there was Lacy, then dental school for a trade to fall back on—your Granny James talked me out of the girl and into the job. Then Myrtle and Bobbie and more until I learned to be happy making music whenever and wherever I could. You ain't like that. I can't see you banging your guitar at some old folks' home on Memorial Day and being happy about it.

Uncle T leans over the dental chair.

Open wide, Gabriel. Wider. Wider.

His fingers are in my mouth, working.

You can stay here and take whatever does or doesn't come—*he pauses and looks away from me and his work, his eyes finding the dark bedroom window on the third floor of Ramsey's Funeral Home*—or you can leave here. Leave her. Leave Eliza. Go somewhere your chances are better. There'll be some hard years. Some rainbows and guiding stars that'll just up and disappear when you think you're right ready to grab for it all.

I follow Uncle T's gaze up to the window of the room where my wife nestles in her solitary warmth. My arms and throat and jaw ache with the wide-open horror of some unspeakable loss, and my lungs fill with cold wind.

Choices voiced by the dead in the dead of night. On the empty and blue-lit streets of home. Beneath that window—

I stand speechless, watching while the glittering suit shimmers and disappears in the darkness down Stackhouse Park Riverwalk. A breeze picks up, and I feel rain on my cheek.

* * *

Eliza's wet kiss woke me, but she was rinsing out the coffee pot in the kitchen sink before I could get my eyes to stay open. Through the windows I saw that the sky was lost in the gray blank of a foggy morning.

"What time is it?"

She dried her hands and turned and looked up at the red rooster clock.

"It's a quarter after seven. I've got to go." She picked up her purse, checked it for her keys, came to the couch and kissed me lightly again. "Bye. I love you," she said and turned toward the door. "If I'm not at work too long tonight, I'll try to come hear you play a while. The

Portico, right?"

Then she was gone.

In the bedroom, I stripped and climbed under the covers. I could still feel pockets of her warmth, but most of the bed was cold.

* * *

That Saturday afternoon, Cutter was waiting for me when I pulled up to the back door of a club called the Study Hall, on Kingston Pike just off the campus of UT-Knoxville.

"Where the hell's Eliza?" he said, grunting her name as we butted chests.

"Where do you think? Somebody wanted to be made over for a date, and she can't say no."

"Well, she's gonna miss a hell of a party." Cutter pulled a small camera from his back pocket. "But we'll take pictures."

After we hauled my equipment into the club and set it up, we went for a walk around campus, but the longer we walked, the quieter I became. My mother had wanted this place for me before I got married. Now the campus buildings towered over me like monuments to a future I'd turned my back on. The girls I passed on the broad sidewalks had a casual ease about their dress and movements and conversation. The boys weren't much different, only louder. They were all around the same age as me and Eliza, but they seemed so much younger, so much more relaxed.

"What's got you all of a sudden?" Cutter asked as he unlocked his room in the frat house.

"I don't know," I said and sat down on one of the two beds in the room. I looked up at him.

He stood looking back, waiting.

"I guess I'm just wondering what all of this would've been like for me," I said. "You know." I stood again and gazed for a moment out the only window in the small square room, then looked down and mused over the clutter on Cutter's desk. "I've been thinking a lot lately that maybe it's what I should've done. Like we planned. . . ."

* * *

On the morning of the day Eliza and he married, his wake-up call was not a clock radio or his mother's worried voice or Eliza's on the telephone. It was Cutter's yanking open the bedroom door and diving on top of him.

"It's eight o'clock, slug," Cutter said. "I've cut school and got the old man's truck 'til one. Let's get rolling."

They traveled the hills and hollows around Runion most of the morning, picking up furniture and household goods his mother had been offered for the newlyweds. Gabriel checked off the items on the list she had made, navigating as Cutter drove.

They pulled around the corner onto Back Street a few minutes after eleven, Uart Clement's big, slat-sided livestock truck piled high with an apartment's worth of mismatched furnishings.

Cutter leaned over the wheel and looked up the brick back of Ramsey's Funeral Home.

"You say it's on the third floor?"

"Yeah, but it's a straight shot up."

"In an elevator, I hope."

"Yeah, right."

Inside the back door of the funeral home, dusty stairs rose up into the darkness in front of them. When Gabriel flipped a switch, a single, naked bulb lit on the top landing.

They shifted their armloads of smaller items and started up.

"I don't know, Gabe," Cutter said as they stood in the third-floor hallway while Gabriel dug the apartment key out of his pocket. "This is pretty creepy. I'm surprised Eliza went for it."

"Well, she hasn't actually seen it yet," Gabriel said, pushing the door open. "To be honest, she doesn't even know about it."

"At least you've got Mr. Ramsey's services right handy."

"That's something, I reckon. And he's already got a hundred-dollar deposit."

Inside the apartment, they both were drawn to the opposite wall, which was completely divided in the middle between floor and ceiling by a row of windows that brightened the room and gave a view of the tops of the buildings across Main Street, Stackhouse Park, the French Broad River and Piney Ridge.

"Well," Cutter said. "If you can get Eliza up here and across the living *room without her killing you, this view just might save your life."*

"You've got to admit it's a great little place to start out with. The mansion can come later."

Cutter made no comment. He still stood staring out the windows.

Then, "Geez, Gabe. I can't believe you're getting married on me. We had plans, buddy. UT-Knoxville, remember?"

"I know, I know. I didn't forget. I just didn't expect this marriage to come up so quick." Gabriel put a hand on his cousin's shoulder. "Look at it this way. You'll get all the girls if I'm not around."

"Climb up my leg and have a ball," he said and turned back to the door.

They wrestled the borrowed furniture up the long stairs and into the apartment, and it was after noon before they were in the truck again and driving to Eliza's to get her car.

"So, this is it," Cutter said as he wheeled onto Eliza's road. "You sure you're ready?"

"I don't know. I think it's gotten too close. Like being facedown in the grass and trying to see the whole world. Just too damn big to think about."

Cutter turned the truck around in the Garrison's driveway.

"Well, good luck. Be seeing you around, I guess."

Gabriel dropped from the cab to the ground.

"You know where I live." He watched Cutter and the big truck rumble back the way they had come.

He walked to the door and knocked. Nobody was home, and he was thankful for that. He barely knew the people who would that night become his in-laws. The keys were in Eliza's car, and, feeling for all the world like a thief, he drove it away. . . .

* * *

Almost three years had gone by since then, and here I was at UT at last.

"Geez, Gabe," Cutter said. "That's bullshit, and you know it. You're on a different road from the rest of us. Like the yellow brick road, cuz."

"Yeah, right."

"Well, if you only knew how many guys on this campus would give at least one nut to be doing what you're doing."

I laughed, touched my groin and winced.

"You've got the guitar thing and that stuff. And we'd all like to bed down with a beautiful babe every night without worrying about getting caught or getting her pregnant. School is school."

I still stood by the desk, going through the piles of books, listening to Cutter's homespun wisdom. A title caught my attention—*Memories, Dreams, Reflections.*

"These are all on psychology," I said. "I thought you were planning to be the next Howard Hughes."

"I switched majors at the first of this year," Cutter said. "It's the new me."

I looked at him and thought the devilish grin looked the same as it always had.

"What new you?"

"I told the business world to get fucked. I'm into social work now, cuz."

College hadn't changed Cutter's way of expressing himself, but something was surely different.

* * *

At eight o'clock, we went out and ate pizza with some of Cutter's fraternity brothers and their little sisters, and by ten I was standing on the Study Hall's small stage, tuning, getting ready to launch into my first set.

The place was already half full with Cutter's recruited audience, male and female, and more folks were arriving in ones, twos and threes. The waitress scooted around delivering sloshing pitchers of beer. A silent baseball game played on the TV above the bar. Balmy darkness nearly overpowered the neon signs and the single 60-watt light bulb hanging on a drop cord above my head. The air filled with the smell of cigarettes, perfume and spilled beer.

Cutter had told me Bruce Springsteen's music was the big thing on campus, so I stomped one-two-three-four on the hollow stage and banged into my version of "Hungry Heart."

Midway through the second set, when the club crowd was drunk enough to get up and dance to my acoustic guitar and the pounding of my boot heel, I let go. Everything worked together without thought. My voice rough in the microphone but howling or whispering at my command. Hands sweaty but locked on the guitar neck. I rolled into the third set without a break, playing for a solid two hours.

Suddenly it was one in the morning. The manager of the bar flipped on the house lights, and the show was over.

I collapsed into a chair beside Cutter and took a long draw on an ice-cold beer.

Faces I'd studied mid-song in the dim light appeared before me. Voices told me in slurred words that I sounded great. Some asked if I had tapes to sell. A guy with foggy glasses stuck a napkin and pen in front of me for an autograph. I spoke to each in a hoarse croak, and when they had gone, when only Cutter and I were left at the table, I downed my second beer and buried my face in a towel.

"Gabriel Tanner," a boggy-sounding voice said. "Fine stage name you've got there."

I wiped my face and looked up. But not too far up. The man standing in front of me seemed only about a foot taller than I was sitting down.

"What made me come down here tonight was that name," he said. "Where'd you get it?"

"From my folks," I said. "They gave it to me a long time ago."

The short man's face was round as a basketball. He had small brown eyes and a droopy dun mustache. His blue Hall & Oates t-shirt was stretched tight across a large middle-aged paunch, although the legs that dropped out of his big beige shorts were thin and knotty. He wore brown loafers with no coins in the tongues and no socks. An expensive-looking gold watch strained to circle his wrist, and three gold chains hung around his neck. His fine gray hair had been permed on small rods and topped his head like a poodleskin cap.

"I'll tell you what," he said. "That's quite a talent you got there." He extended one plump hand. "Mo Biggs is the name. Entertainment booking and management is the game."

"Nice to meet you, Mr. Biggs," I said, shaking his hand after I'd wiped my own on the thigh of my jeans.

"I'll tell you what," Biggs said, snorting. "Did you write any of that stuff you just played?"

"Yeah," I said. "Quite a bit of it."

"That song toward the end there, about some kind of magic. You write that?"

"It's one of my newer ones."

"I'll tell you what. That sounded like a hit to me. You ever thought about going to Nashville?"

I stood up.

"I've thought about it quite a lot lately, but I wouldn't know where to go or who to see."

Mo Biggs took a step closer.

"Well, Gabriel Tanner, it might be a fortunate thing for you and me both that I wandered in here tonight. I'll tell you what. I been making contacts right and left in Nashville the last couple of years. Maybe we can work something out so I can introduce you around down there. You got tapes?"

"Well, I've got some demos I've been recording at the radio station back home," I said. "But they're not really country."

"Listen here, buddy-ro, Nashville is getting ready to bust wide open. Country ain't gonna be the only music coming out of there before long. I predict in the next three years it'll be the music center of the goddamn world." Biggs snorted again. "I'll tell you what."

We walked out to the parking lot and exchanged telephone numbers, leaving Cutter to put the dust covers on my little PA system.

"A band of mine's playing a joint down in Old Town," Biggs said. "Let's go listen, and we can talk some."

"I'd like to, but I can't," I said. "Got a wife waiting home for me."

"Well then, I'll call you Monday," Biggs said and squeezed into his car. "This could be a good thing, Gabriel Tanner."

I nodded and waved and went around to the back door of the bar to help Cutter carry out the equipment.

"I'll tell you what," Cutter drawled, laughing as Biggs drove around the corner, gave us thumbs-up and disappeared down the street behind the Study Hall. "If I was you, cuz, I don't know if I'd trust that guy."

I lit a cigarette and smiled through the smoke.

"Well, I've got to do something soon," I said. "And I don't think I can do it by myself."

We carried out the two PA columns and monitor, the amp, the microphones and stands and cables, and then went to the bar to get my money.

"When can you come back?" the manager asked. "I've got a few dates open in July and August. They're yours if you'll play for the same pay."

I took the envelope and thumbed through the bills. Two hundred. Not bad for three hours.

"I walked out of the house and forgot my date book," I said as I stuffed the envelope in the back pocket of my jeans. "I'll call first of the week, and we'll see what we can do."

Cutter and I left by the back door.

"Why didn't you take those dates?" Cutter asked when the door closed behind us.

"What?"

"Come on, cuz. You know every date you've got open for the next three months. Didn't you get off on that crowd in there tonight?"

"Yeah, they were great," I said. "And I'll probably do the dates. But it's getting weird, Cutter. I loved it in there while I was playing, but the second a gig like that gets over, I want more."

"Then do the dates."

"I don't mean I want more of the same. I want bigger places. Bigger crowds. A band. Records in the record stores. Songs on the radio."

"Ain't you got to pay dues before all that?"

"I'm hoping my dues are about paid up," I said, rubbing the back of my neck. "I reckon I'm ready."

"Think you'll give that Biggs fellow a call?"

"I thought you just said you wouldn't trust him."

"And you just said you can't do it by yourself."

"That's right. But Knoxville ain't exactly the place I expected to get a boost from."

"Well, you ain't getting no boosts from Runion either."

I looked at Cutter. He suddenly looked tired, but I couldn't let him head back to his fraternity house just yet.

"I had the weirdest dream that night after Uncle T's funeral," I said.

"About meeting a fat man wrapped in gold chains?"

"Weirder than that. It was Uncle T in a rhinestone suit. He came up to the apartment and told me I had to leave Runion."

"What for?"

"For what we've just been talking about. To get out of this rut I'm in." I dug my keys out of my pocket. "Got an interpretation of that dream?"

"I do. Your subconscious is telling you to pack up your bags, throw the wife in the car and light out for the territory, Huckleberry."

"Easier said than done." I took a deep breath and looked up at the black-orange city sky. "You want a ride up to the frat house?"

"I'm thinking about calling on a lady friend of mine who ought to be just getting off work at the hospital," he said and flashed his old grin. "You be careful driving home through the mountains. Stay off Rocky Bluff."

"I will," I said and, weary to my bones, dropped into the car and drove away.

Chapter 2
Runion to Nashville

I drive a flat gray highway in billowing fog, naked and cold in the pale green glow of the dashboard. My gaze shifts between the lighted wall of mist I'm moving through, the radio dial and the silhouette framed in the rearview mirror.

Eliza sits in the back seat, nodding, sleeping, dreaming perhaps of traveling some other highway as she sways with curves that don't exist on this one.

The sermon on the radio is all stutter and static, and a flock of glistening signs flies at me out of the fog. But I receive no coherent message from the preacher, and the signs pass before I get a sense of the directions they give.

The road widens, begins to fork.

Eliza rouses and mumbles, Left.

Too late. Already in the right turn, bending west, I glance in the rearview mirror to apologize, to say that I'll turn around the first chance I get.

She's gone.

Deep in a valley ahead of me a city of light takes shape, its radiance thinning the mist.

My window is down, and the wind roars like a crowd of people.

They're waiting for me.

I hit the hazy web of cold blue light, still naked, beginning to shiver.

* * *

The music of the dream woke me, not the ghostly stutter from the radio but something felt instead of heard—a frenzied treble of excitement over a slow-moving bass of sadness.

I lay still for a moment, staring into the shadows of the bedroom, trying to grasp the essence of the dream before it faded. Then I rolled onto my back and turned to look for Eliza.

She lay breathing softly and staring into the darkness above us, and I realized I had only to feel her heat to know she was there. I tried to look closer without moving again, tried to see if she was crying. But no tears stretched in her eyes, no snuffles disturbed the quiet. I slid my hand under the covers and touched the warm smoothness of her hip. She didn't move at first. But then a hand lighted on mine for a moment, floated part way up my arm, and over to my belly.

We lay there, stroking each other for slow minutes. Then I rolled over onto her, and we made love. Without kissing. Without speaking. Raised over her, I opened my eyes and looked out the window and saw the snow—big-flaked March snow, falling so straight and thick that it looked like fog in the blue-white light of Main Street.

Afterwards I lay awake, and she slept.

Mo Biggs had been calling a lot since June. At first, after he approached me at The Study Hall, he called once a month. Then every couple of weeks. And now it seemed he was on the line every other day. He always responded the same way when I answered—"Gabriel Tanner," said slowly in a drawl born somewhere in South Carolina or Georgia, just my name followed by silence.

I wasn't often in the mood to talk, so I would let the silence hang there until I heard the nervous cough on the other end and Biggs got busy with whatever he had to say.

And Mo Biggs had plenty to say every time. Big news every time. He'd just come back from Nashville or just gotten off the telephone with Nashville, talked to so-and-so there about me, usually some so-and-so I'd never heard of. "Leave no stone unturned," he kept saying, pressing me to let him set up some meetings for the two of us.

My resistance was wearing down. I played the same circuit of lounges and coffeehouses and folksy dives that I'd been playing for more than three years, like running a delivery route, going to the same places with the same packages over and over again. Nashville, New

York, Los Angeles—these were my routes of escape. New York scared me. LA was so far from these mountains. It had to be Nashville.

*   *   *

On a Monday early in April, Eliza and I slept in. The night had been full of wind and fast-moving clouds, the stubborn stains left from a lamb-lion March. But the morning sky was a clean-washed blue. The nine o'clock sun shone brightly on the buildings across Main Street, on Stackhouse Park, the French Broad River and the still winter-brown slopes of Piney Ridge. A chilly breeze whispered and whistled its way through loose panes in the apartment windows.

We stayed under the covers, drowsily waiting as the heat came up.

That was the difficult thing about winter on the third floor of the funeral home. The heat for the entire building was controlled in the office on the second floor, and we had to wait for Mr. Ramsey to arrive and turn up the thermostat to a tolerable level for the living.

But finally we were out of bed. Eliza started a pot of coffee and went to wash her face, while I sat at the kitchen table, smelling the coffee and looking over lyrics I'd worked on the night before.

> *Her name was Lacy and she drove me crazy*
> *In the back of my first Chevrolet. . . .*

Most of the first verse captured the feeling I'd retained from the image of Uncle T and his archetypal country girl, but after that it slid seamlessly into a different story. Mine and Eliza's.

> *Young hearts get carried away and get married—*
> *What's right or wrong don't mean a thing. . . .*

*   *   *

They drove his parents' LTD to Greenville, South Carolina. Eliza navigated, using the map Judge Davenport's secretary, a Mrs. Gullick, had included with some paperwork they needed to have filled out by the time they arrived. Gabriel turned onto Palmetto Drive at twenty-five minutes after six, halfway hoping that they would not find Judge Davenport's residence and wondering if Eliza felt the same. He had tried to convince himself that this was no more than a very special date and that by some miracle—something akin to the Rapture—it would end with the two of them in bed, rings on their fingers and a piece of paper saying it wasn't a sin.

Above the entrance to the paved circular driveway of 70 Palmetto Drive, an arch of wrought iron spelled DAVENPORT against the fading blue sky. Four cars—all shiny and European except for one dull-orange Mercury Bobcat—lined the middle of the circle. The bricks of the house had been antiqued with whitewash, and the windows were winged with black shutters. A stone stairway led up to the massive front door, also black. And the whole was lit by spotlights on the front lawn.

"Well, let's do it," Gabriel said, looking in the rearview mirror and clipping on his navy-and-red-striped tie. He stood up out of the car and looked down to make sure no cigarette ash had blown back in the window onto his new white shirt or tan corduroys.

Eliza was out on her side, brushing the rear of her skirt with one hand, shading her eyes from the spotlights with the other and looking worried.

"You look beautiful," he said and patted his shirt pocket to be sure the rings were still there. He folded the papers Mrs. Gullick had sent and stuffed them in the pocket as well.

Judge Robert Davenport answered the door himself. He stood at least six-four, broad-shouldered and barrel-chested, hair a stone gray flecked with white and black.

"Miss Garrison and Mr. Tanner," he said offering a hand that swallowed Gabriel's whole. "Right on time. We're ready for you upstairs in the study."

Following the judge into that place of sparkling light and space, feeling Eliza's awe increasing in the grip she had on his hand, Gabriel tried to shake the image of the little apartment on the third floor of Ramsey's Funeral Home—the dim overhead fixtures, the mismatched furniture Cutter and he had filled it with that morning. The judge's antechamber was the size of the entire Runion apartment. French doors led to rooms *on either side, and hallways winged the summit of the elegant staircase.*

Judge Davenport guided them up into the right wing and down a wide hall to the last door on the left. Eliza and Gabriel, wide-eyed, followed him into the room.

Thick cream-colored carpet disappeared under richly padded leather chairs, a matching couch, and a large oak desk with two shiny golden green-shaded lamps. Beyond the desk, two large windows looked out over a terraced garden crowned by a blue-lit swimming pool. The walls on either side were covered top to bottom with full bookshelves.

And there were people in the room.

"Mr. Gabriel Tanner and Miss Elizabeth Garrison," Judge Davenport said. "This is my wife, Olivia. And our dinner guests, Dr. and Dr. Green, Frederick and Jeanette. They've agreed to serve as witnesses to your marriage. And Mrs. Gullick will serve as best man, maid of honor, and ring-bearer, if you choose to give rings."

They spoke their vows quietly, and in that immense house, in that luxurious study, in the company of strangers, they were pronounced husband and wife.

Afterwards they drove around Greenville, lost for a while. They passed hotels and motels, but they did not turn their heads to see if this place or that had a vacancy or offered a pool. They simply wandered through the city, trying to find their way north and home.

As he drove, Gabriel pictured the motel scenario. Registration card and key. Door opening to the smell of musty sheets and disinfectant. He swallowed hard, imagining the two of them on either side of the bed, the lights out and their backs to one another. They had never made love in a bed before. The back seat of the LTD, yes—Eliza, wearing only blouse and bra and socks, facing him and lowering herself onto his naked lap. But never in a bed. How would they decide which side to sleep on?

And he imagined them in their tiny apartment in Runion, putting sheets and pillowcases on their unmade bed, avoiding each other's eyes, undressing and crawling under the cool covers, jumping out of their sweaty skins when her father—despite the rings and the marriage certificate—shouldered his way though the bedroom door and bellowed her name.

He shook the image out of his head and wondered what she was thinking. *That night at the Dam Dance? The cool constriction of the new ring on her finger? The plushly carpeted halls of some comfortable future, with a circle drive in front and a swimming pool with gardens in back?*

They were going to live in a motley apartment above a funeral home, and she did not even know it yet. Was she just assuming that this night would end like any other with Gabriel dropping her off at her parents' house?

"Oh, God, where are we going to stay tonight?" she suddenly asked. "I just thought of that!"

He straightened in his seat and cleared his throat.

"Well, as a matter of fact, we've got our own place."

"What? Where?"

"Yeah, uh, I—me and Cutter, I mean—moved us in this morning. It's a third-floor place downtown in Runion. Lots of windows. You can see Main Street and Stackhouse Park and across the river to Piney Ridge. You're gonna love the view."

"Do we have furniture? I mean—"

"Sure. Sure. Everything. It's borrowed stuff. Doesn't match real well. But it'll do us for now. We've got a kitchen with a fridge and a stove. A bathroom. The bedroom and living room have new carpet. And the whole place has a new paint job."

"How much is this going to cost us?"

"A hundred a month."

"That doesn't sound bad." She sat quietly for the next few miles through the mountains and into Asheville.

Gabriel drove, waiting for the inevitable.

"It's funny," she said finally, "but I don't remember any apartment buildings in Runion."

"Well, yeah. It's not exactly in an apartment building. Just in a regular building on Main Street with this one apartment in it."

"Which building?"

"Mr. Ramsey's."

"What? Not the funeral home! Oh, no, Gabriel, no! You've got to be kidding."

When he responded with a nervous laugh, she did not speak for the rest of the ride home.

But once they were up the creaking steps, past the silent door to the room where the coffins and vaults stood, and into their own apartment, she seemed to feel better. She walked around and looked at everything, saying how much she liked this and what she could do to fix that.

He caught her in his arms and laughed into her hair, smelling the mix of fading perfume, shampoo, and salon chemicals. He pulled her closer and kissed her ear and then felt himself beginning to shake deep inside.

"I love you, Eliza," he said at last.

She did not answer, her soft body tense and trembling with silent, uncontrollable sobs. . . .

* * *

That night she cried in her sleep like the sound
Of the rock-a-bye breaking of boughs.

"Gabriel," she called over the splash of water running into the bathtub. "If you'll run down to Whitson's and get some eggs, I'll make us omelets."

When I got back to the apartment, she was just hanging up the telephone.

"Who was that?" I asked.

"That guy from Knoxville. What's his name?"

"Mo Biggs. His real name is Maurice, I think."

"He made me miss my bath." She took the grocery bag and stepped into the kitchen. "He told me he's been trying to get you to go to Nashville with him so he can introduce you to some people in the music business." She paused in unpacking the bag. "Why haven't you gone?"

"Well, first off, I don't much like the guy."

"But what if he can get your songs heard by somebody?"

"I didn't say I hadn't been tempted. I've thought a lot about Nashville ever since Uncle T died. He always wanted to take a shot at the music business."

"So, why don't you go? Maybe you ought to spend some time with Mr. Biggs. He might not be as bad as you think, you know?"

"That's possible, I reckon."

Eliza checked for broken eggs and set the carton on the counter by the stovetop. She turned on the burner, and the blue flame appeared with a pop like tiny thunder and danced in a jittery circle. She still wore her thick white socks and pink sweatpants. The hem of a white nightie with purple stripes hung out from under her pink sweatshirt. Her black hair was a tangle of night—parts of it flat with sleep, parts jagged and sticking straight out where she'd run her fingers through it.

"Gabriel," she said as she hovered over the stove, "He said he did his pitch—or something like that—to Billy Keith, and now he wants to meet you and hear some of your songs."

"Really?"

She looked at me as I stood leaning in the doorway of the kitchen, a clinical look, as if she were trying to decide if it was time to trim my hair. Then she turned back to the stove.

"You know," she said, "I've always thought some of your songs would be perfect for Billy Keith. Ellie plays his tapes a lot at work, and I can just hear him singing 'Rhymes' or 'Carry Me Away.' He's got such a nice voice."

"I wonder how Mo Biggs got in to see Billy Keith."

"He didn't say." She turned away from the beaten mixture of eggs, milk and cheese, and looked at me again. "Don't you think you could at least go meet with him?"

"With Biggs or Keith?"

"With Billy Keith, silly."

I stretched and yawned.

"If I go down there with Biggs and something good comes of it, I'm gonna feel obligated to him for helping."

"But just think of the chance to meet Billy Keith." She turned back to the stove and folded the omelet and slid it onto a plate and set it on the table. "I think you should give Biggs a chance. He sounds like he really believes he can do something for you."

"Maybe he can and maybe he can't," I said.

The kitchen was beginning to heat up, so she stripped off her sweatshirt and straightened her nightie. She poured herself another cup of coffee and took a quiet sip. Then she went back to stirring the other omelet, her breasts and upper arms trembling with the motion, her hips swiveling slightly.

"I can tell there's something you're not saying," she said. "What is it?"

I sat down at the table and started clearing away the fragments of my writing—two pencils, a pen, a spiral notebook, three guitar picks, a crumpled napkin from the Portico Lounge in Asheville with a couple of lines jotted on it. I pushed the desk lamp I kept on the table back against the wall and pulled my plate in front of me.

Eliza finished cooking the other omelet and stood holding her plate with both hands.

I reached for the pepper and cleared my throat.

"If something good happens in Nashville, I'm afraid it'd be too hard on us." I peppered my breakfast without looking at her. "I mean, it'd be tough. I don't have any clue about how quick I'd be making money. It might be weeks. Even months. I just don't know how the music business works. You wouldn't have any problem getting a job there, but it'd mean starting over."

She set down her plate and turned away and cut off the stove.

"Can't you live here and travel back and forth?"

"I don't know. Maybe. But if I wasn't making much of a living there for a while, and if I couldn't keep up with the gigs on my circuit here, I'd end up burning a bunch of money on gas and food and hotel rooms." I passed her the pepper as she pulled out her chair and sat down. "And if I got a contract to write songs for some publishing company, they might want me in the office writing nine to five, Monday through Friday."

"Well," she said. "In some ways, it couldn't be much less of a life together than we have now." The words seemed to squeeze through her throat as if they'd been growing big inside her for a long time. But when she continued, the strain was gone. "I still think you ought to at least go down there and see what happens. We can decide what to do when we know more about it."

She ate only a few bites more and was in the bathroom reheating her bathwater by the time my plate was clean.

I cleared the table, washed the dishes and then returned Mo Biggs's call.

He said Billy Keith would be spending the whole month of May and half of June in Nashville doing Fan Fair and finishing a new album.

We could make an appointment with him any time during that period.

Eliza came out of the bathroom with her hair wrapped in a towel and my black Bruce Springsteen t-shirt on.

"I called Mo Biggs back," I said. "We'll go meet Billy Keith in May."

"Good," she said and stepped into the bedroom and closed the door behind her.

* * *

It was midnight on a Sunday when I left Eliza and Runion sleeping and drove west through the mountains to meet Mo Biggs at a truck stop on the outskirts of Knoxville. At three in the morning Biggs said he was going to stop at the Crossville Waffle House for coffee.

We settled into a booth by the windows where we could keep an eye on his faded green Buick Electra. I lit a cigarette and stared past the parking lot into the night. Biggs rubbed his eyes for a full minute and then looked at the menu.

The waitress squeezed from behind the counter and came to our table. She pulled a tablet from a pocket in her yellow-and-red-striped apron and a pen from the netted red hair above her right ear.

"What can I get for y'all this morning?"

I ordered first, a large Mountain Dew and some buttered toast.

The waitress turned to Biggs.

"Well, let me see," Biggs said. "I'll tell you what. I think I'll have three eggs over easy, toast and jelly, bacon, a side order of sausage, and coffee with cream and sugar." He folded his menu and smiled as he handed it to the waitress. "Thank you," he said slowly, looking at the name tag on her breast, "Marge."

Marge smiled and leaned across Biggs's side of the table, and stuck our menus in a holder next to the window.

"I'll give this order to the cook and be back directly with your drinks."

"Large Marge smells like bacon," Biggs said as the waitress walked away. "Too bad we've got to be in Nashville so early. I'd have her for breakfast when she gets off."

"What time are we meeting Billy Keith?" I asked.

"He said he'd be at the Stage Deli around nine, and he'd need to be at the studio by ten." Biggs fingered the gold chains stretched around his neck. "You brought some tapes?"

"They're in my bag."

Marge came back with our drinks, and Biggs struck up a brief conversation with her about the nightlife in Crossville. I pretended to look out the window but watched the crude seduction scene reflected in the smoky glass.

"What's Keith got in mind for me?" I asked when the waitress left the table.

"Since you wouldn't never give me any tapes, not a damn thing yet," Biggs said. "All he's got on you is my description of what I've heard and seen you do. But I got him interested enough to give us some of his time."

"And if he likes what he hears?"

"From what I understand, he has his own publishing company. He's likely to sign you up to write for him. He'll probably do some demos on you and try to get you a record deal. I'll get us the best I can out of him."

"Speaking of that," I said and stopped and took a quick sip of my Mountain Dew. Then I tongued the drops out of my mustache and went on. "What is it you get out of all of this?"

Biggs pulled a folded document out of the inside breast pocket of his jacket and slid it across the table.

"Look this over," he said.

"What is it?"

Marge brought the three plates that held Biggs's order and then went back for my toast.

"Anything else I can get you boys?" she asked.

Biggs had already set to with a flurry of salting and peppering and pounding the bottom of the ketchup bottle.

I looked up at the shiny plump face.

"No, thanks."

"That's a management contract," Biggs said around the wad of food in his mouth when Marge was gone. "I plan to be your manager. That's what I get out of it. Look it over while I eat." He fell quiet except for the clinking of his knife and fork and the slurping of runny eggs and coffee.

I held the contract with the tips of my fingers and could feel in each fingertip my heart pounding against the warm paper.

At the top of the first page of the document were the words "Exclusive Manager's Contract." It was several long pages full of legal jargon, lettered headings and numbered paragraphs, repeated phrases that twisted and turned back on themselves so often that I kept losing my place. I bogged down on page three, struggling to make sense of a paragraph that read, "Inasmuch as Artist's services are unique and extraordinary, Artist acknowledges that Manager shall be entitled to equitable relief (in addition to all other available rights and remedies) to enforce provisions of this agreement. If for any reason Artist fails or refuses—"

"Here," Mo Biggs said.

I looked up and saw the three plates wiped clean and a pen shoved toward me.

"I borrowed it from Marge," he said.

"Shouldn't I get a lawyer to check this out?"

"Gabriel, it's just your standard management contract. I got it from a friend of mine in New York. It's a good contract. I use it all the time."

"This just seems a little weird." I felt naked and cold and lost. Something began to shiver deep inside me and found its way into my voice. "I just think I should talk to somebody about it first. Eliza ought to—"

"Your wife don't have a goddamn thing to do with this," Biggs said loud enough to make Marge and the cook and the two men at the counter turn. "This is between you and me. You sign contracts for your gigs without a lawyer all the time. Am I right?" He settled back in his seat, lit a cigar, and spoke more quietly. "If you don't sign it, I can't take you on to Nashville tonight. I can't take you there without some assurances that I'll be looked after for my part in it. Besides," he added with a puff of smoke and a smile, "I think we'll make a great team."

"You mean that if I don't sign this right here and now, you'll turn around and drive us back to Knoxville?"

"Shit, son. I'll have to. I'll tell you what. If you don't sign it, I can't represent you with Billy in the morning. We don't know him at all. He might try to take advantage of you by yourself. This is your assurance that somebody with experience'll be looking out for your interests. And since they'll be my interests too, you know I'll strike the best deal

I can." Another thick puff of smoke billowed across the table. "Look at it this way. If I'm gonna make a living on the twenty-five percent I make off you, then just think how good you're gonna live on the rest."

I worked the greasy pen into my palm, and closed my fingers around it.

"Hell," Biggs said. "Colonel Parker took fifty percent of Elvis and ran everything for him."

And Elvis died a recluse and a drug addict in a house with black windows.

"And Grossman did practically everything for Bob Dylan except wipe his ass."

I clicked the spring button at the top of the pen.

"You're getting me and my services cheap."

I touched the pen to the line just above where my name was typed on the last page.

Gabriel James Tanner.

"Sign it just like my secretary wrote it out there," Biggs said, pointing with a chubby finger.

I pictured myself riding back to Knoxville and then back to Runion, climbing the long steps up to the apartment, crawling into bed with Eliza just as the sun came up. She'd wake with a start and ask what had happened. What could I tell her?

I closed my eyes, thinking I ought to pray for direction, and against the red backs of my eyelids, Nashville and Billy Keith glowed like some kind of heaven seen through fiery fog. I drew a deep breath, opened my eyes, squinted at the paper in the harsh white light of the Waffle House, and scrawled my indecipherable signature on the dotted line.

*   *   *

During the rest of the trip west, as well as the two and a half hours we sat in the car outside the Stage Deli, I kept my face turned toward the window and pretended to sleep. I'd watched the stars hang silent and unreadable in the black sky, watched as sunrise slowly overtook us from behind, saw Eliza's face as it'd be in each moment of the growing light.

I heard again the scratchy sound the pen had made with every irretrievable stroke and knew I should've taken a stand and called her before signing Biggs's contract. But, at bottom, I'd been afraid my anxiety would be met by the same silence and stiffness that met me every time I'd talked to her over the last few weeks.

"There he is," Mo Biggs said at fifteen minutes after nine.

"What?" I sat up, trying to look disoriented. "What?" I said again and rubbed my eyes.

"That's Billy in the yellow Mercedes convertible," Biggs said, pointing. "Damn. A fucking 280 SL. He goes in style, don't he?"

Keith stepped out of the car and walked around it. He bent down into the passenger seat and straightened up again, put a brown cowboy hat on his head and threw a set of saddlebags over his shoulder. He looked different than he did on television or on his album covers. He was older and taller. Along with the hat, he wore a purple flannel shirt with angular Southwestern designs done in beige and light blue across the chest and shoulders, pressed jeans, and cowboy boots made of some creamy-colored leather. He didn't look around the parking lot, just turned and headed for the door of the deli, his walk an oddly waddling strut for somebody so tall.

Mo Biggs struggled out of the car.

"Hey!" he called as Keith reached the door of the restaurant. "What's for breakfast?"

Keith didn't turn around. He opened the door and disappeared into the building.

"He's used to not hearing people out in public," Biggs said as he motioned for me to follow and bounced across the parking lot.

"Two for breakfast?" the hostess asked when we walked through the door.

"We're meeting someone here," Biggs said. "Billy Keith."

"Oh," she said. "Is he expecting you?"

"Yeah, we're meeting with him." Biggs moved closer to the hostess, staring at her nametag.

The hostess stood her ground.

"If you'll give me your names, I'll be glad to tell him you're here."

"Well, Dana, are you like a secretary away from his office or something?" Biggs didn't wait for a reply. "It's Mo Biggs from Knoxville, bringing him a new star named Gabriel Tanner."

Dana looked at me over Biggs's head.

I shoved my hands in my pockets and turned and looked out the door.

She grabbed two menus, disappeared around a corner, and returned in less than a minute.

"Right this way, gentlemen."

"Mr. Mo," Keith said as he stood up and reached out to shake hands. "I got to admit I forgot you was coming. And this must be Gabriel." He shook my hand vigorously but a little loosely. "Pleased to meet you, son. Sit down, sit down."

I slid into the booth and Biggs squeezed in beside me. Keith sat in the center on the other side. A waitress named Kris, a tiny girl Keith addressed as "little darling," took our orders. Just outside the window, the Mercedes gleamed in the morning sun.

"Well, now," Keith said. "Where'd you fellows stay last night?"

"We drove down during the night," Biggs said. "Got here around six-thirty or so. We just sat out in the parking lot and waited for you."

Lots of lines weathered the singer's face, and they deepened when he smiled, which he did a lot while he and Biggs talked. His eyes were dark brown, slightly bulging, heavy-lidded. His ashy black hair hung down over his collar and was graying at the temples. His skin was deeply tanned and his fingernails neatly trimmed and clean. He wore a single gold chain around his neck and a large gold insignia ring on the middle finger of his right hand.

When Kris brought our orders, Keith slid against the window, directly across from me, to make room for the spread of plates that held Mo Biggs's breakfast.

"How old are you, son?" he asked.

"I turned twenty-two in March. On the eighth."

"You ever been to Nashville before?"

"Yeah. Once. I was seventeen and came with my uncle. He was a big country music fan."

"There's lots of those around, thank God," Keith said and began to eat....

* * *

That trip had been during one of the periodic "vacations" Theodore James took from his wife Myrtle. These separations never lasted for more than a month, but they worried his sister Maggie. There had never been a divorce in the James family, as far back as such things could be traced, and she wanted to keep it that way. Usually Theo came to her house and moved into the spare room, but on this occasion—late June in the summer between Gabriel's junior and senior years, the summer Eliza Garrison moved to town—he announced that he was going to Nashville. Maggie sent her son along, hoping that the responsibility of looking after his impressionable nephew would keep her brother out of trouble.

He rented an old school bus—nicknamed The Boiler—from a nomadic retiree he knew in Asheville. The thing had been hand-painted blue on the outside. Inside, the seats had been ripped out and replaced in the front half with easy chairs and a dinette set and in the rear with two sets of bunk beds, all bolted to the carpeted floor. The bus earned its nickname in more ways than one. It had no air conditioner, and it overheated every hundred miles if the water level in the radiator was not regularly checked.

Nine-thirty and a purple darkness had come to middle Tennessee by the time uncle and nephew arrived at Kuntry Kuzzins Kampin, some twelve miles east of Nashville. The woodsy campground sprawled around the southeast side of J. Percy Priest Lake. They checked in and were assigned a space and then rolled through the darkness under a canopy of trees, rolled for what seemed miles over pebbled dirt avenues named after country music legends. There were tents of various sizes here and there, but most of the spaces were occupied by little white vinyl or silver metal campers. Hickory smoke rose from grills. Several spaces were bordered and lit with strings of tiny plastic Chinese lanterns.

They found Space 116, a corner spot where Marty Robbins Drive and Patsy Cline Avenue dead-ended into one another, and Uncle T backed the Boiler into it.

Gabriel looked down past the other lots to the far end of Patsy Cline and saw a yellow light bulb shining on a wooden pier. Tawny light and shadows waltzed on the sleepy surface of the lake.

Bang! from the Boiler's tailpipe, and people in the glow of their grills and lanterns snapped to attention.

After showers, they pointed the Boiler toward town. Uncle T drove.

Gabriel sat in an easy chair and took in the view of the Music City skyline at night.

Gabriel thought it a thing of wonder. He knew that Bob Dylan at one time or another had recorded his songs somewhere under those lights. And Dan Fogelberg. And Jimmy Buffett. Merle Haggard and Larry Gatlin. He had just learned to play the Guild acoustic guitar his entire family had chipped in to surprise him with the Christmas before and had begun trying to write songs for Big Muddy. He could not help being shaken by a breathless chill at the sight of Nashville and the thought of all the music mixing beneath its lights.

They found a place to park the Boiler near the corner of Second Avenue North and Union Street, a couple of blocks from Printer's Alley. Uncle T grinned as he straightened his tie in the big rearview mirror, told Gabriel to behave himself and left the bus, walking up Union and fading quickly into the night and the music. Gabriel locked up, dropped the spare padlock key into his pocket and walked down Second toward what looked like the glow of more night life in progress.

He sat down on a gray bus stop bench at the corner of Fourth and Broadway and for a few minutes breathed in the cacophony of music and laughter and breaking glass that spilled from the door of each bar. Sitting there within sight of the old Ryman Auditorium and Tootsie's Orchid Lounge, although he did not attach much significance to those places then, he noticed that his heart was pounding like a kick drum and that he could not stop sweating.

Apart from the asphalt, the concrete and the streetlights, everything around him had more in common with the darkly radiant world of television than with Runion. Prostitutes in wild make-up, who looked dirtier and more dangerous than the ones in the detective shows, clicked by on stiletto heels, crossed the street and glittered on the opposite corner. Venereal bums, who had stains on their pants and might cover themselves with newspaper and sleep on this bench when Gabriel abandoned it, shuffled up and down the block, stopping anybody who met their stares. Young men with guitars awaited country music stardom on every corner, warbling songs about trucks and alcohol and mamas and cheating hearts, guitar cases opened at their feet. Grungy kids Gabriel's age or younger, looking both frightened and defiant, one moment weaved and bobbed through the starry-eyed sidewalk crowd like the children they were, the next disappeared into some black hole of a bar.

The light of flashing bulbs and colored neon splashed like water across the tinted glass and waxed bodies of passing cars, hurting his eyes. Garbled music and traffic and voices ebbed and echoed in and out of dark alleys, hammering his ears in waves. Suddenly, the street had a smell, too, a smell that stung his nose like the reek of urine on hot metal.

"Boy, get your lazy ass up off my bench, and gimme a goddamn cigarette!"

Gabriel turned where he had landed on the sidewalk.

The bum at first appeared to be an old man. But the matted hair and the dirty weathered face and hands created the illusion. He was not much older than Gabriel's brother Butler, not in his blue eyes at least. He took the two cigarettes Gabriel fumbled out of his flattened pack and quickly surrendered to him, stuck one behind his ear, sat down on the bench with a grunt and lit the other with a match from a crumpled book he fished out of his shirt pocket. He held the smoke in for so long that Gabriel thought he might have forgotten about breathing, but then it slowly began escaping from his mouth and nostrils, shrouding his head as if it seeped out of his ears and pores as well.

"See that little girl over there, boy?"

Gabriel followed the direction of the bum's slight nod and the gaze of his glaring eyes.

"You stay the hell away from her. Just stay the hell away. Got more fuckin' diseases than a pack of rats." He sniffed hard, gagged and spat on the sidewalk. "Might just have to get her before she gets me," he said in a quieter voice. "Got my record contract and all, you know. Now ain't no time to die for a piece of ass."

Gabriel's eyes and imagination left the pale girl.

"You've got a record contract?" he said but could not keep a tone of skepticism bordering on sarcasm out of his voice.

"Why, hell yes. You think I don't?" The bum sniffed hard again. "Ben Cartell's taking me into the studio next week." A wheezing cough. "Kill him if he don't. Kill you too, if you don't believe me." He laughed and gagged again, and spit splattered on the sidewalk between them. With a jerk he drew a ragged sleeve across his mouth. "You little shit."

Gabriel took a couple of steps back toward the curb, nervously trying to watch the bum and the traffic at the same time and wondering who Ben Cartell might be.

"Think I won't, goddamn it?" The bum made some grunting sounds in his throat and jerked his head toward the dark end of Broadway. "Down under them Cumberland bridges, either way from the end of the street there, I've killed many a bad girl." He began rocking back and forth on the bench, his hands gripping his knees. "Many a pussy little virgin like yourself. Strangled 'em. Dumped 'em in the river and laughed at the fuckin' splash."

He spoke the last word of this so distinctly, hissed the s-h so long and harshly that Gabriel saw the body smack the water, saw the bubbly white vortex created as a worn sneaker or a red pump disappeared beneath the dark surface, saw the ripples lap against the sand and stiff grass of the shore and the river slowly ebb to its normal flow.

Now every time the bum leaned forward, he nearly stood up.

"Gimme a dollar, boy."

Gabriel stood with his left hand in his pocket, protecting the money— two twenties and a ten his father had given him before the Boiler left Runion that morning. He looked up and down the street for a policeman and thought of Uncle T arriving like the cavalry.

The bum suddenly lurched to his feet.

"Gimme a goddamn dollar, boy, or I'll fuckin' kill you right here and now."

Gabriel whirled and ran, his hand pulled from his pocket and still clutching the thin fold of bills. He heard footsteps and curses and crazy laughter behind him. But the threatening sounds were soon drowned out by the wind passing his ears, the rubber slap of his solitary footsteps and the wild pounding of his heart.

He escaped into the Boiler and hid among furniture, watching the street. His heart rate began to drop back toward normal. His breathing slowed and deepened. Finally calm and cautiously feeling safe again, he lay down on a bunk, listening to the murmur of traffic and faint music floating.

The next thing he knew, Uncle T was shaking his shoulder with one hand and jangling a set of keys above his face with the other. His eyes were red and droopy, and he seemed unsteady on his feet. He had a rim-chewed drumstick between his teeth, and he was saying something about a driver's license.

"What?" Gabriel said, sitting up and rubbing his eyes.

Uncle T spat the drumstick into his hand and dropped it.

"Do you have your driver's license?" he said with the exaggerated articulation of the drunk.

Gabriel said that he did.

"Think you can drive this thing? It's a manual transmission, you know."

Gabriel took the keys and said he could if it was like Uncle Uart's farm truck. He got up from the bunk and followed Uncle T toward the front of the bus, excited and scared, like all young drivers, about the opportunity and responsibility to drive something new, something big—never mind that he would be driving through a bustling night in a strange city. When he settled into the driver's seat, Uncle T started down the steps of the bus.

"Where are you going?" Gabriel asked.

"I've got me a pretty little waitress coming on strong up at The Carousel," he slurred. "I'm gonna wait for her to get off work." He tried to wink but blinked both eyes as if something had nearly hit him in the face. "I'll catch up with you at the campground sometime tonight or in the morning."

"How do I get out of here?"

"There's Interstates in a ring around downtown," he said, making a circling motion with one hand. "Just follow anything that says east and has the number forty on it."

Then he was gone.

After a shaky start, Gabriel returned the Boiler back to its corner of Kuntry Kuzzins Kampin. When he cut the motor, the blast from the tailpipe echoed through the dark woods. Lights snapped on in some of the campers, and a few shaggy silhouettes peered into the night.

He tried to go to sleep on each of the beds in turn, but the interior of the bus was too hot. He went outside with a pillow and two blankets, climbed up onto the roof and bedded down.

At some point in the night, he dreamed himself struggling to run uphill along blue-gray sidewalks. Saxophone laughter rang out behind him. He

ran, not far but for a long time, and then banged into a blackness. A
doorway. "Gabriel?" his mother's voice called from somewhere. A hand
grabbed his collar. Another thrust itself down into his pocket. "No!"
somebody yelled, and he thought it must have been himself. He struggled
with the hands. His money fell free and shattered when it hit the street.
The pieces made grinding and popping noises like small rocks under tires
and then disappeared in the downtown wind.

He sat bolt upright at some sudden loud noise, like a horn or a scream.
Looking out over the front of the bus, down Marty Robbins Drive, he saw
a car disappear around a corner, heard it sling dry dirt and gravel as
it gunned down the road where the bathhouse stood. In a moment, it
came fishtailing back around the corner at the lake end of Patsy Cline
Avenue and then slid sideways to a stop in front of the Boiler. A door
flew open, and the dim light inside barely had time to come on before a
shadowy figure fell out of the car and scrambled to its feet. The driver was
a woman. A man with a blurry face sat twitching close beside her in the
front seat.

"Get the fuck out, Jimmy!" the woman screamed. "We're going down
to the lake! We're gonna kill somebody and leave her on your doorstep!"

Uncle T escaped into the Boiler before the screaming stopped, and the
car roared away in a cloud of red-lit dust.

Gabriel watched it out of sight and then fell back onto his pallet,
wondering what Uncle T had gotten into. He did not know what time
it was, but the half moon had been directly overhead when he had come
up and made his bed. Now it was in the misty trees, and everything felt
damp.

Sometime later the car came back and ground to a stop in another
swirling cloud of white and red glowing dust.

Groggy and feeling as if his body were stuffed with cotton, Gabriel
wondered if the wild woman might have just swept around the block once
and returned. But as the dust settled and the interior light came on again,
he saw that things were obviously different.

The man was driving now, his fingers flitting around the steering wheel
like moths around a streetlight. Both he and the woman appeared to be
naked and wet. She laughed wildly between screams for "Jimmy." Her
right arm waved in a snaky motion as if it moved to balance the weight

of something it could barely control. Her wet heavy breasts glistened and quaked with the motion.

Gabriel stared, unable to take his eyes off their naked flesh, until something caught and gleamed for a moment in the car's interior light. He saw the gun in her hand and flattened himself to the top of the bus. He thought of praying, but he could not close his eyes or turn away.

"We're back to get you, Jimmy!" she screamed. "Nobody's at the lake. Looks like you're elected! Come out, come out, wherever you are. We wanna play!"

Gabriel thought he felt the Boiler shiver, but all around the old bus silence hung in thick folds of darkness like a drawn stage curtain in an abandoned theater.

The woman pushed the gun out the window of the car, and the burning tongue of the powder burst licked at the darkness.

Gabriel felt the explosion in his back teeth. For a second he thought he might roll off the top of the bus to put the Boiler between himself and the madwoman, but just then he saw another car roll slowly around the curve into Patsy Cline.

The man driving the crazy naked lady slammed on the gas, spinning away down Marty Robbins and around the opposite corner. Two more gunshots rang out before her screaming laughter faded into the night.

The oncoming car crept alongside the row of campers, many of which were now lit. Patrol lights sat darkly on its top. It seemed about to stop beside the Boiler but continued past.

Gabriel lay awake a long time. As much as he fought to hold it, the image of her breasts grew shadowed and mysterious while the glowing curve of her neck and shoulders hung before his eyes. The noise of the one close shot rang in his ears. These troubled his dreams until he felt the light spray of rain in his hair and heard Uncle T's groggy morning voice.

"There you are," he said, squinting against the bright gray morning and the drizzle. "What say we go home to the mountains?"

Theodore James never left Aunt Myrtle again as long as he lived.

The experience stayed with Gabriel, too. But what he remembered most was not what he expected—not the bum on Broadway, not the drive alone back to the campground and not the bare-breasted heroin addicts. What he remembered most from that one-night stand in Nashville were *the lights of that city on the hill and the music in that hot and humid and bright air. . . .*

*   *   *

"The tourists come here in droves," Billy Keith was telling Mo Biggs. Both had finished eating. "They walk around Music Row until they fall up from heat stroke, and then they go home and tell their friends they saw my house or caught a glimpse of Barbara Mandrell going by in a limousine." He sipped his coffee for a moment and looked at me. "Did you bring me a tape?"

"I've got some I recorded at the radio station back home," I said. "They're just me playing guitar and singing."

"That's what I like." Keith smiled again and winked. "Can't stand production that gets in the way of hearing a good song."

We finished breakfast and went outside. Above us the sun was getting hot, the sky changing from the blue of early morning toward a hazy white.

Keith looked up and squinted and then looked at me.

"I've got to run back out to the farm and get something I forgot. What say you grab your tapes and ride with me, son?" He turned to Biggs. "I like having just the artist with me when I listen to tapes. Managers make too much noise."

"I won't say a word," Biggs said.

"Well, for sure you were plenty quiet when breakfast was in front of you." He let go a wheezy laugh and slapped Biggs on the back. "Do you know where Bullet Recording Studio is?"

Biggs's lips pursed for a moment and then relaxed. He said he'd seen the sign.

"You meet us there in an hour," Keith said as he dropped his saddle bags behind the driver's seat of the yellow Mercedes. "If anybody asks what you're doing, just tell 'em you're waiting for BK. Now, don't say Billy Keith or they'll call up a crew and throw you out on your ass. All right?"

When Keith pulled out onto Twenty-First Avenue, he took the cassette I offered him and plugged it into the player. He turned the volume up so loud that the hiss of the blank tape at the beginning could be heard even with the car's top down.

Every time a line or an image or a vocal section I was particularly proud of went by, Keith would look at me, smile and wink. He listened twice to the four songs as we flew past the edges of the city and broke out into the rolling farmland to the south. When "Carry Me Away" finished for the second time, he popped the tape out and turned off the radio. He drove fast, looking straight ahead.

"When I first met Mr. Mo, he told me he's your manager," Keith said above the wind that whipped our shirts and blew our hair from behind. "That a fact?"

I said I guessed it was.

He continued to stare straight ahead.

"Too bad," he said after a moment. "So far, I don't like the man. I can tell he's the pushy sort."

My chest felt as if Mo Biggs were sitting on it.

"But I like your music," Keith said.

"Thanks."

"How long you got left on the contract?"

"I'll have to ask," I said, embarrassed as soon as the words were out of my mouth. "I mean, I'll have to check and see the exact date it runs out."

"Well, I can deal with Mr. Mo. Or work around him." He looked at me, his heavy eyelids almost completely closed against the wind and the bright sunshine. "I'm afraid you don't look much like what Nashville's after these days. Too much mountain man, not enough drugstore cowboy. But we can always change all that. If the four songs I just heard say anything to me, it's that you're a strong writer for a kid just come out of the hills. You sing good too. We can work on your image till we all drop dead, and it ain't gonna do a damn bit of good if you can't write or sing."

After a succession of side roads, he finally wheeled the Mercedes into an almost hidden driveway, and we rolled along with green overhead and dust underneath. Left of the shady lane, a pasture swept up the hillside toward a line of trees. Five sleek horses stood watching, and Keith waved at them. Down the slope to the right, a few head of cattle circled a small pond at the edge of another stand of woods.

The farmhouse sat on the back side of a low hill, facing south. It was a two-story place, smaller than I'd expected. No wings or columns. A tin roof and a wrap-around porch.

He pulled the Mercedes up to the right side of the house, scattering scratching chickens. When he killed the engine the only sounds were the excited clucking of the hens and the tinkling of several crystal wind chimes that hung along the eaves of the covered porch and in the tree above the chicken yard.

"Nice place," I said.

"I like it. It's quiet and private. Tried to fix it so it reminded me of a place I used to know north of Dallas." He got out of the car. "Be back in two shakes."

I lit a cigarette and looked over what I could see of the farm.

Eliza would love this place.

Alternate images of her moved like shadows in my mind. One moment the shadow danced in a joyful frenzy. The next it stood absolutely still, and I couldn't tell if she faced me or turned her back. I closed my eyes and presented that shadowed figure with the range of possibilities Billy Keith might represent, watching for some reaction. She didn't move, so I shook her off and pulled my notebook from the shoulder bag I carried the tapes in and read again the last thing I'd written.

Lacy, Lacy,
Let me dry your tears.
I know you're wondering if I'm gonna leave you.
Put away those fears. . . .

Keith came from the rear of the house. He was smiling and empty-handed.

"Forget what you came for?" I asked.

"What? No," he laughed. "I didn't come out here for nothing. Just wanted to get you away from Mr. Mo for a little while. I took a piss and got on the phone to one of my lawyers. He's gonna draw up a little agreement between you and me. And I want you to slip me a copy of your management contract as soon as you can so I can see if there's any way to get shed of it."

The words jumbled like a train wreck in my mind.

"We'll start out with having you write for my new publishing company. Then we'll see about a production and recording thing."

"That sounds great." I stared out over the farm, wanting to ask questions, but I didn't understand enough about the music business to know where to begin. And I was afraid that a bunch of questions might jinx it somehow.

"What's that there on your notebook?"

I looked over and saw him sitting with his hand on the ignition key, his head cocked at an angle to read the lyrics scrawled on the notebook in my lap.

"New song?" he asked after a long moment. He looked from the page to me and back again.

"It's the draft of a lyric. Don't have any music for it yet."

He fired up the engine and spun the tires in the dirt and sparse gravel.

"You got a guitar in Biggs's car?"

"Sure."

"All right. I'll set you up in a quiet corner of the studio, and you can go to town, putting music to that sucker. Get it done by the end of the day, and I'll have my musicians record it tonight before they leave."

"You're not serious," I said.

"Oh, hell yes I am."

At Bullet Studios less than an hour later, Keith settled me in a vacant upstairs office.

"Coffee's down in the lobby if you feel the need." He winked and closed the door.

I'd heard in the first line of the refrain of "Lacy" the tune of an old mountain ballad called "Little Nellie." My mother often sang that song on her knees in the garden or sitting on the back porch sorting laundry. Uncle T sometimes hummed a few bars as he leaned over me during my annual checkup. Delbert Gunter or one of the family groups was sure to sing it most any given Saturday in Stackhouse Park. All afternoon I worked with melodic variations of the old song, fitting these and the sparks of original melody they struck in my imagination to the lyrics of "Lacy."

Billy Keith and Mo Biggs each looked around proudly and smiled when they heard the finished version, and I thrilled at the thought of what I'd done.

"Let's go put on the feed bags, boys," Keith said. "We'll record that on full stomachs."

When we walked back into the studio after supper, the engineer handed Keith a legal folder.

"Ah, good," he said. "Mr. Mo, read over this publishing contract." He gave the folder to Biggs. "I've got a check for a two-thousand-dollar advance if he signs."

Biggs took the folder and, without even opening it, turned to me.

"Sign it," he said, slapping the folder flat against my chest.

I just stood looking down at him for a moment.

Trapped again.

But now the thought of going home to Eliza with two thousand dollars in my shirt pocket made the situation seem a little more tolerable.

The contract was with Franklin Music and several pages longer than the one I'd signed with Mo Biggs less than twenty-four hours before. I looked over the first few paragraphs, understanding only enough to know that I'd be paid five hundred dollars a month for a period of five years. I made more than that now on my circuit of lounges and coffeehouses, but this would be for just staying home and writing. So I flipped to the last page and walked over to where Biggs and Keith were standing and talking with the engineer.

"Turn around," I said to Biggs.

I put the contract against his wide back and signed my name on the last page—*Gabriel James Tanner*—dotting my "i" with a sharp jab that ripped through the paper and made Biggs flinch and grunt.

Chapter 3
Words and Notes

Gray January light drained into the apartment from a rainy Sunday afternoon. The television was on, the sound turned down. A tape rolled in the cassette player, the one with the three songs—"Lacy," "First Love" and "Carry Me Away"—I'd recorded in Nashville when I met Billy Keith in May.

Eliza sat on the couch, reading the Sunday paper by the weak light that fell through the steamy windows. She wore the black sweat suit and pink leg-warmers I'd given her for Christmas. Her thick black hair was pulled back in a short ponytail. She chewed her bottom lip as she read.

I sat at the kitchen table, alternately watching her and writing a note to accompany some new songs I was sending to Billy Keith's Nashville home. And listening to the music from the stereo too. I liked the way the two slow songs—"Carry Me Away" and "Lacy"—had turned out. There was a simple grace about them. But "First Love" lacked the power I'd intended when I wrote it. Keith hadn't let me cut loose on the vocal like I wanted to, and the synthesized string section washed all the drive out of the track.

The experience still amazed me. On my first trip to Nashville as a music business hopeful, I'd wound up in a recording studio, being produced by Billy Keith and working with musicians who could play a song through perfectly after hearing it only one time. Mo Biggs and I had stayed in Nashville for three nights, and each night after the musicians finished with the daily tracking for Billy's album, the star paid them to stay and record one of my tunes. "Lacy" had been first and everybody's favorite. On the third night, after the musicians went home, Billy and a scarecrow-thin, red-bearded engineer named George MacDougall worked in the studio until sunup to record my final vocals for all three tracks. Biggs spent most of that night laid out in the middle of the lobby floor, snoring so loudly that my microphone picked him up more than once. By the time I finished singing, I was pumped full of caffeine, and I whirled around the control room in foolish excitement while Billy and George laughed.

After another breakfast at the Stage Deli, he handed Mo Biggs two copies of my contract with Franklin Music and a check for two thousand dollars. He gave me his home address so I could send new songs to him. Then he said he would be in touch, fell into his Mercedes and drove away.

Back on I-40 and heading east, I'd fallen asleep to my own music playing on the deck in Mo's car. When I awoke in Knoxville three hours later, he was still listening to the tape.

Mo deposited the two thousand dollar check and wrote me one for half that amount, claiming the other half for his percentage plus expenses. Billy's check immediately bounced, and Mo's voice sounded so strained and angry over the telephone that I thought he would have a heart attack. But everything was soon set aright, with Billy blaming his bank for the problem.

A month after I was back in Runion, a check for $375 had arrived from Mo Biggs, along with a note explaining that Franklin Music would be sending my monthly draw to him in Knoxville.

"Here's one," Eliza said from the couch.

"One what?"

"A house. I've been sitting here looking through the paper for houses in Asheville. Here's one we might be able to afford. This says it's got two bedrooms and a bath, a sunken den with a fireplace, hardwood floors, 1325 square feet, and one acre of land with a pond. It's at the end of a cul-de-sac. Doesn't that sound just perfect?"

"Well, I guess so."

"And it's on the south side of town too. I've heard that's a good place to buy right now. Can you go look at it with me tomorrow?"

"No, I've gotta go to Knoxville and meet with Mo and play some banquet he booked me for."

"Oh, okay. I think I'll just go look at it myself."

I got up from the table, drew a glass of water from the tap and went into the living room. I sat down sideways on the end of the couch, drinking and looking out through the wall of windows.

It wasn't even five o'clock yet, but the street lights of Runion were already stuttering to life. At the top of the hill the town's only traffic signal blinked yellow. Beyond the roofs on the other side of Main Street, beyond Stackhouse Park and the French Broad, mist hung like a tattered white shawl across the blue-brown swells and darkening hollows of Piney Ridge. Nobody moved on the sidewalks below, and it was only now and then that a car rumbled slowly up or down the street.

"Eliza," I said.

"Gabriel, don't say it." She didn't look at me. Her hands clinched at the edges of the paper.

The sound of blank tape hissed from the speakers of the stereo.

"Honey, we've got to talk about what we're gonna do. We've hardly brought it up since—"

"No!" The word exploded out of her like a balloon popping. "I know you want to move to Nashville, but I can't leave."

"Why? What makes you say that? Look, we can find a place where my monthly money'll take care of the rent and some of the bills. You'll find a job and be booked solid in no time. It's a bigger city than Asheville. We'll find you the best salon. By the time our savings run out you'll be making—"

"Oh, Gabriel, it isn't the money. I think we could make it. I really do." The struggle to round up her thoughts and force them into words was deeply etched in her forehead. "It's other things now."

"What other things?"

She let her head fall onto the back of the couch and stared at the ceiling. After a long stretch of silence, she drew a quick breath and held it for a moment.

"It's my people," she said. "Some of them left the best hairdressers in Asheville, even left my boss, because they wanted me to do their hair. They tell me every appointment how much they love me. How much they love what I do for them."

"Well, you're the best. It shouldn't surprise you. But you're not obligated to them for what they say about your work. You'll have the same experience in—"

"Gabriel. I don't want the same experience. I want the same people." Her knuckles whitened as she tightened her grip on the newspaper. "And our families. What about them?"

"People grow up and leave home all the time. Dad left Montana. Your folks came here from West Virginia. What's the difference?" But I felt the same way she did about leaving them. I knew I'd miss them and Runion and the mountains. If we argued that point, my dream was over. "It's not like we'll never see them again. We can come home as much as you want to."

Her profile grew soft in the gray light. A tear slipped from the corner of her eye, a twinkling drop that disappeared into the darkness of her hair. Another pulsed along the same trail. She remained quiet, only sniffling from time to time or drawing her breath and holding it to stifle a sob.

She had her career made from the day she started working, but it was something she could do anywhere. I had to go to Nashville. The more these thoughts stumbled over one another in my mind, the more anger built up like fire inside me. I didn't feel like comforting her.

"Is there somebody else?" The question was out of my mouth almost before it loomed in my mind, out with a cutting edge even sharper than the anger I felt.

"Oh, Gabriel," Eliza sobbed and jumped up from the couch. "Just go to hell!" With the sound of crying squeezing past some chokehold on her throat, she ran into the bedroom. The door slammed, and there was the shriek of squeaky bedsprings.

I propped my elbow on one raised knee and cupped my bearded chin in my palm and sat where I was, listening to her cry as the corners of the apartment filled with a visible darkness.

A train coming upriver from Hot Springs bellowed in the dusk, and the lights in the naked trees of Stackhouse Park came on as if in answer.

I couldn't see the train passing, but I could hear it. I listened to the clack and roar of it and followed with my eyes the deserted cobblestone walks of the park. My gaze finally came to rest on the basketball court, where once I'd sat alone on a flatbed trailer, surrounded by the instruments and amplifiers of Big Muddy, filled with the fervent hope that Eliza would make it to the Dam Dance.

After that hope had been realized—she'd come, and we'd danced—I croaked the words of "I Saw Her Standing There," the last song of the night. . . .

* * *

She stood with Cutter and waited, nibbling at her right thumbnail and smiling, her body twisting slightly back and forth in time with the music As Little pushed the beat, the dancers became feverish, the dancing riotous.

Gabriel felt famous. He sensed how it would be to stand between a band and an audience and sing a song he had written for Eliza, and he wondered how she might react to seeing him touch a faceless mass of people with feelings he felt for her alone.

While he stared at her and sang, these thoughts tumbling through his mind, a flashing light above her head caught his attention. Beyond the asphalt and the little midway between booths and sparkling trees, one of the low lamps along the walkway to Runion had suddenly started to blink steadily.

The boxcars crossed one by one between Gabriel and the light. He had not heard the warning whistle or the rumble of the engine as the train approached town, had not seen the passing of the headlight powerful enough to carve a tunnel of day into the mountain night. With everything whirling around his senses—Eliza, the swirl of light and movement, the white noise of the crowd, the high-speed roar of the band—only the persistent out-of-place flashing of the walkway light that, like a sound from the waking world seeping slowly into a sleeper's dream, alerted him to the passing of that dark and silent train.

The thought struck him that life could pass a person by like that, and if he wasn't on the lookout, he would never even know. . . .

* * *

When the phone rang at mid-morning a few days later, I answered it expecting the usual "Gabriel Tanner" from Mo Biggs.

"Gabriel," the bright voice said. "How are you, my boy?"

"Hey, I'm fine," I said, recognizing Billy Keith's voice. "How are you?"

"Son, I've been so busy I ain't had time to wipe my ass."

I laughed. "But that's good, right?"

"Yeah. Great. How's the little wife?"

"She's fine, a big fan of yours. I hope you get to meet her someday."

"I reckon that'll be pretty soon. I'm about ready for you here."

I'd been waiting eight months to hear those words. But now that they actually tickled my ear, I wished I hadn't heard them. Eliza had hardly spoken to me all week. She worked late, came home and fell asleep on the couch, then got up early every morning and left before I could get awake.

"Your new songs have been a-knocking me out," Billy was saying. "It's gonna be great to get in the studio with 'em."

"I'm glad you like the stuff. Have you booked studio time yet?"

"It ain't gonna be till the first of May. Spring's busy here. We'll cut three or four more tracks and then get back at it around the end of the summer before—"

"Can't I just stay here until the times you need me?"

"Well, I need you here to work closer with you on your writing. And you need to get around town a little, meet some other writers. You gotta make yourself available in this here crazy business. It's a out-of-sight-out-of-mind town."

"I know asking about it sounds bad, but—"

"Hell, son, don't worry about it. You're gonna do great."

I started to pace the floor.

"Can I live there on $375 a month?"

"Oh hell yeah. I've bought a building with an apartment in it. You can live there for nothing." He suddenly stopped short. "Are you afraid the little woman won't be able to get a job?"

"No, it's not that." My jaw tightened and wouldn't relax. "I'm afraid she won't come at all."

I told him how Eliza reacted to any mention of moving to Nashville, told him of the fight we'd had the Sunday evening before.

"Son," Billy interrupted. "I ain't gonna be the cause of a divorce here, no matter how great I think you're gonna do."

"Well, I don't think—"

"See if you can work it out. If you can't, we'll just call the whole thing off. I'll keep the publishing rights on what songs you've sent me, and you don't have to pay back the money I've sent you. We'll call it square at that." He suggested some things to tell Eliza, things that might reassure her or change her mind. "Good luck, son," he said. "Hope I'll be seeing you in May."

* * *

Through February, March and April, Eliza left for work earlier and stayed later than ever. She brought home over five hundred dollars a week and spent almost none of it. On Mondays she got up and left the house with the Sunday paper's housing section stuffed in her purse and spent the day with real estate agents, came home after dark and fell asleep.

At the same time, I accepted any gig that offered itself, as long as there was money involved—from the regular club dates to weddings, ladies club luncheons to office parties. When I got home I'd let Eliza stay on the couch until the small hours of the morning when I finished writing. Then I'd try to get her to come to bed.

Sometimes she came, but most of the time she didn't.

Sundays were the only times we spent together. Family days. No talk of buying a house in Asheville, no talk of moving to Nashville. After lunch or supper, we cuddled up on the Garrisons' or my folks' couch, and nobody seemed to notice that we hardly spoke a word to each other.

I tried all the assurances Billy Keith had armed me with—more money in the Nashville salons, places with famous clienteles, the free apartment in his office building. She didn't seem to care. I thought at first that maybe the music had lost its hold on her, but my tapes covered the passenger seat of her car and one was always in the deck. Nights when I came home late from a gig to find her curled up on the couch, the stereo would be on and one would be in the player.

And then it was May.

I was leaving on a Wednesday. That Tuesday morning I called Billy and told him that I'd be there but that things didn't look good for a permanent move.

"Well, son," he said, "come on down, and we'll record this session. If she don't change her mind, you can go back home and I can pitch the songs around town here."

She came home a little early that night, and we walked up the street to the Runion Pizzeria.

The spring air was clean and filled with the smell of growing things. Large pots of flowers sat on the sidewalk, their new blooms deepening in reds, oranges and yellows with the coming of night.

After we slid into our booth, we chatted a little about her day and whose hair she'd done, the gossip that'd been passed to her about people I didn't know, what songs I might record in Nashville, when I'd be back in Runion. But when Pam brought our pizza, we ate without talking.

Back outside and wandering with her toward Stackhouse Park Riverwalk, I was still trying to decide which of the latest songs I hoped Billy would record.

"That song, 'Lacy,'" Eliza said. "Parts of it I know you wrote about me."

"Well, you're in there somewhere, I guess," I said and tried to smile. "The part about going parking and getting married has a lot to do with us. It's a mountain boy and a pretty girl. Just a story."

I thought she might take my arm, but she shoved her hands into the back pockets of her jeans.

"What story would you write now?"

I stopped in the middle of the brick walk.

"What do you mean?"

"Well, that girl's crying, and you're telling her you'll never leave. How would you end it now?"

"The same way," I said. "I'd end it the exact same way."

She took a few steps down the Riverwalk and then turned.

"What about your contracts?"

"I've already talked to Billy about you not wanting to move—"

"Oh, so they'll say it's my fault," she said.

"What does it matter," I said. "It'll be okay."

"What about Mo Biggs? Won't you get in trouble with him?"

"I don't know. And I really don't care. When I get back from this trip to Nashville, I'll find a real job around here somewhere or in Asheville, if we move there. And I'll be home all the time."

Although it wasn't completely dark yet, the setting sun had given over its work to the blue-white street lights. Flowers so vibrantly colored at sunset had taken on various shades of lavender-gray.

"You know," I said. "All this time I thought you wanted me to go."

"I do if that'll make you happy. But I don't care if you become some big star. Your music doesn't have to be on the radio for me to love it."

"I know you love the music—"

A car passed along Main Street, and a horn blew. Neither of us looked.

"—but I can't make a living on your love."

A black tear streaked down her cheek, and she began walking quickly back up the hill toward Main Street.

I went after her, caught her arm and whirled her around, stopping her on the corner by the door that'd once been the entrance to Uncle T's dental office.

"Eliza, listen. I want to be a star. I admit it. And I can't do it here, so I have to go to Nashville. You know, out-of-sight-out-of-mind. I know I said I'd stay. And I will. But I really want to go."

"Then go," she said. "Ever since this whole thing started—"

"What?" I said.

"You never sing for me anymore. I miss—"

"That's bullshit, Eliza. You're never home or awake long enough for me to."

She wrapped her arms around herself.

"I'm going in," she said. "It's getting chilly out here."

We made love later, but I don't think anything was forgiven on either side.

In the morning she kissed me awake and told me good-bye. She stopped in the doorway of the bedroom and stood with her back to me, digging in her purse for her keys.

"When did you say you'd be back?"

"Saturday or Sunday," I said, yawning. "I don't know exactly. I'll call you."

* * *

It was five-thirty in the afternoon when Mo Biggs and I arrived at Bullet. The front doors were locked, so we rang the buzzer.

Engineer George MacDougall came hopping around the corner into the lobby and waved.

"Hey, guys," he said when he opened the door. "BK called and said to tell you he's going to be a little late."

"Big fucking surprise," Biggs said.

"The musicians should be here in about an hour," George said as he closed Bullet's front door behind us. "The session starts at seven."

"Let's go get a bite before they get here," Biggs said.

"I'd love to, man, but I've got to get everything ready. All the mics still have to be set up."

"I think I'll get my guitar out of the car and stay here with George," I said. "I'll get something later out of the machines upstairs. You go on, Mo. Try to relax a little."

"Man, he's an uptight dude," George said when Biggs was gone and I was standing my guitar in a corner of the darkened control room.

"Too uptight," I said.

While George moved quickly around the studio setting up the microphones, I sat in Billy Keith's chair and stared at the control board. It was nearly as long as the room was wide and looked like a miniature of some vast metropolis. The whole thing broken into segments like city blocks. The grid of streets between the channels. The buildings represented by knobs and buttons of various shapes. The tiny trios of red and green and yellow lights. I was as afraid to touch that thing as I would've been to walk naked through Manhattan at two o'clock in the morning.

Through the window on the other side of the control board, I could make out the contours of the grand piano. I stepped through the thick doors to the room where George worked and then through the entrance to the keyboard room. I'd never had a chance to play an instrument like this, and I touched the keys gently, one at a time, listening to the richness of the low notes, the clarity of the highs.

I'd written only one song on piano. The music came to me on a Sunday a few weeks before as I tinkered with my mother's old upright. When I got back to the apartment that evening, I transposed the chord progression for the guitar so I could write lyrics to it, but it remained a piano song.

I sat down on the padded black bench, got my fingers in position on the keyboard, found the sustain pedal with my right foot and began to play.

Babe, I'd like to find a way to tell you how I feel,
Some way to assure you that this love of mine is real.
But I've tried and tried so hard my head is spinning like a wheel,
And I just can't find the words.

Eliza appeared before me in the darkness, a tiny dancer turning on top of the piano like a ballerina on a music box. She wore faded blue jeans with a hole in the left knee, a white sweatshirt with RUNION HIGH on it in black block letters. As she came around to face me her expression was the same as that night years ago when I was seventeen and jumped from the stage at the Dam Dance and took her in my arms.

If I were a poet, I could write it down
In perfect rhymes that sound the way that love should sound,
Romantic lines to make you see the lover through the clown. . . .

She turned in the doorway and fumbled in her purse for her keys, her body haloed by the glow of early morning light in the living room.

But I just can't find the words. . . .

She sat on the orange couch, wearing her black sweat suit, holding the crumpled newspaper in her lap. Her head rested on the back of the couch, her face in profile, one glistening track of wetness between the corner of her eye and the dark line of her hair.

"God-a-mighty, that's nice!"

My hands sprung from the keyboard like startled cats, and I whirled around on the bench.

Billy Keith stood there with a smile spread across his face, a brown cowboy hat in his hands, his white athletic shoes shifting in excited agitation.

I felt my face turning red.

"Thanks," I said.

"Absolutely beautiful, son," he said, putting a hand on my shoulder. "Just great. Why haven't I heard that one yet?"

"It's fairly new. And I didn't have a piano to record it on when I finished it."

"Well, it's gonna get the treatment now. I already know where the band'll come in and what I want the strings to sound like. It'll tear the women up when we're done with it." He laughed and turned back toward the main part of the studio. "Damn near tore me up just like that."

With something like a grin as wide as Billy's spreading on my face, I stood up and followed him out of the piano room, leaving Eliza to fade into the darkness.

*   *   *

Billy moved among the musicians like a coach in the locker room before a big game. He talked quietly to each of them in turn and then gradually grew louder, talking and telling stories to the whole group.

Biggs, back from dinner and cleaning his teeth with a toothpick, stood at the edge of the circle of musicians and gear, stone-faced at first but now shaking with laughter at Billy's tales.

George still worked frantically, positioning the microphones he'd hooked up, distributing headphones, running back and forth between the control room and the musicians to check sounds and adjust mic placement.

I stayed in the control room, watching the activity through a wide window and eating a microwave burrito from a vending machine on the second floor.

Through the soundproof glass the scene of laughter and setting-up passed in near silence. The musicians for this session didn't look at all like Billy's long-haired band that recorded "Lacy" and the other two songs the year before. A businessman on guitar. A librarian on piano. A middle-aged singles-bar Romeo on drums. A fundamentalist preacher on bass.

Finally Billy motioned for me, and I got my guitar out of its case in the corner and took it into the studio, carrying it in my arms as if it were my lover.

"Folks," Billy said, "this is Gabriel Tanner. We'll be recording his songs tonight and the next couple of days. And this here"—he nodded toward Biggs—"is Gabriel's manager, Mo Biggs." He clapped his hands, rubbed them together, and turned to me. "My boy, let's start with something up-tempo to get us going. How about that little thing in A? 'Some Kind of Magic'?"

The musicians didn't even watch me as I played the song through. They simply sat in their folding chairs, pencils flying over notebooks.

"Okay," Billy said. "Let's hear a little drum thing at the start like Holly's 'Peggy Sue.'"

The drummer nodded.

"How about some kind of breakdown after that second refrain?" the guitar player said. "Build into a solo from there."

"Okay," Keith said. "If the drum thing from the beginning works, we can go back to that for the breakdown."

"It's going to get monotonous," the piano player said, pushing his round-framed glasses back to the bridge of his nose. "I feel a half-step modulation into the solo would be an appropriate change."

"All right," Billy said, "but let's make it a whole step."

The musicians took their places.

Billy Keith, Mo Biggs and George MacDougall moved back into the control room.

Under stairs that led down from a second-floor balcony, George had put together a vocal booth made up of three padded wood-framed partitions and the black-curtained studio wall. A large microphone the size of a sledgehammer head hung from a stand in the middle of the booth. Each of the partitions had a window in it. To my left I could see the drummer and the bass player, in front the guitar player and the sliding glass door that led into the piano room, and to the right the control room.

When the musicians put on their headphones, I did the same and positioned myself in front of the microphone, listening while they ran through different versions of the intro.

"Okay, guys, just one second for me." George's voice came over the headphones and seemed to speak in the middle of my head. Billy and Biggs could be heard mumbling in the background. "Okay, guys" George said again, "tape's rolling."

The drummer counted off the song and broke into a sixteenth-note roll on his floor tom. Two bars of that and the others entered, and for a moment it sounded like a record already on the radio. But the music suddenly stopped, and the musicians immediately began fidgeting.

"That's where you're gonna come in, son," Billy said, leaning over the talkback mic on the control board and smiling toward my booth.

The musicians settled and readied themselves for another start.

"Tape's rolling," George said.

After the third time through the song, Billy leaned over the talkback again and said, "I think that's a keeper. Y'all come on in and listen."

* * *

Biggs drove me to the Hall of Fame Motel on Division Street. He'd booked us a room there while he was out getting supper.

It was after midnight, after one in the morning in Runion, when I got settled and tried to call Eliza. I lost count of the times it rang before I finally hung up.

"Did she move out on you?" Biggs asked with a laugh.

"What? No," I said. "She goes and stays with her folks sometimes when I'm out of town. If you saw where we live, you'd understand." I looked at my watch. "It's too late to call her over there."

I knew the apartment spooked her when I wasn't around. She hadn't even stayed there the second night of our at-home honeymoon. . . .

* * *

The morning after they were married, her wet kiss on his cheek awakened him.

She was fully dressed.

"Can you take me over to my house? I need to get my car."

"Where are you going?" he asked. "What time is it?"

"It's a quarter 'til seven, and I've got to go to work. Will you take me to my car?"

"Oh, yeah." He sat up on the side of the bed, squinting, trying to clear his head. "No, wait. Your car's parked over by the trees across Back Street.

Cutter took me to get it yesterday."

"Where are my keys?"

"I think they're in the living room somewhere. Maybe on one of the window sills."

She kissed him again and walked out of the bedroom.

"My last appointment's at four, so I'll probably be home around six. Will you be here?"

"No. I'll be gone to Waynesville by then. I'm playing at some restaurant. But I won't be too late. Midnight or so."

He heard her keys jingle. The door opened and closed, and her quick footsteps echoed down the long flight of stairs.

That night the manager of the restaurant offered him an extra twenty dollars to play another two hours. There was no phone in the apartment yet, so he could not get word to Eliza.

At two in the morning he bounced up the stairs with his guitar. A note hung from a nail on the door. When he saw it, his knees buckled slightly, and he stumbled into the hallway wall.

She's gone, he thought. Already gone.

But the note read only that she had gotten scared, that she had run home to get the rest of her clothes, that she would see him in the morning and make their first breakfast together. . . .

* * *

Over the years the notes had shown up less and less often the braver she got, and now I felt bad about being gone and having not called early enough to catch and reassure her.

Almost as soon as the lights were out, a steady snore began in the other bed. It was quiet enough at first, but it grew louder with every breath Biggs took.

After half an hour of trying to go to sleep, first with a pillow over my head and then with my fingers in my ears, I pulled the covers off my bed, moved the table and chairs away from their corner, put a pillow on the floor under the air conditioner at the window and went to sleep at last, lulled by the constant hum, a white noise that almost drowned out Mo Biggs's cavernous snoring.

*　*　*

I stand among long black curtains with the microphone hanging in front of me. Above, the curtains reach into a dark infinity and the feet of them billow and flap around me with the constant rush of the traffic. Music from every car radio twists and blends in Doppler effect.

Magic ... taking control of me ... write it down in perfect rhymes ... maybe there's a magic ... some kind of magic in ... the words.

The wind-wake of a truck separates two curtains.

A street corner.

A man in a glittering cowboy suit plays guitar and sings, his guitar case open on the sidewalk in front of him. But his lyrics, his music, are lost in the din between.

Uncle T!

The musicians glare.

Pay attention, boy.

That's where you're gonna come in, son.

Son.

Just before the flapping curtain stills and the opening is lost, a black-haired girl dances past a row of windows three floors above the sidewalk and then disappears.

Eliza, listen.

*　*　*

The next two days we were in the studio by ten in the morning. We recorded three songs by six o'clock each evening, doing most of the instrumental overdubs as we went along. Billy let the musicians go home at that point and then took me, Biggs and George out to dinner. After that, the four of us returned to the studio and worked on my vocal tracks until midnight or later.

Each night slipped by without my hearing Eliza's voice. Calling her crossed my mind at various times during the day, but then the guitar player might lay down a great lead track or Billy might launch into some story, and I would forget. I played around with the grand piano several times during breaks, but her image never appeared to dance on top of it again. Sometimes when it was late and I was still in the vocal booth singing the songs over and over to make sure every note and word worked for Billy, the lyrics made me ache for her.

When I finished my vocals on the last night, Biggs retired to the lobby floor, George went to work on the rough mixes and Billy and I talked quietly at the back of the control room.

"I've had three different lawyers look at the contract you signed with Mr. Mo," he said. "They tell me it don't look good."

"What does that mean?"

"Well, it means the thing is tight on you, son. Whether you know it or not, he's basically took control of your life. And you can't do nothing for the next nine years without him saying it's all right." He downed a shot glass of bourbon and wiped his mouth with his fingers. "At the same time the thing's loose on him, and there ain't nothing he can do that'll put him in breach of it."

"But what if I don't move to Nashville? What if I just get out of the music business?"

"Son, you can't get out of the music business if he don't want you to. I know we talked about calling it even after tonight, but that son of a bitch can make you move if he's of a mind to."

"You've got to be kidding," I said.

"And even if you could quit and go get some other job, you still wouldn't be shed of owing him his twenty-five percent of whatever you made. Hell, son, you could dig ditches or be the damn president, and he'd still be able to sue if you didn't cut him in."

"Shit."

"We're in it waist deep," Billy said. He lit a cigarette and handed it to me and lit another for himself. After a long drag and a slow exhalation, he went on. "Fortunately, I've dealt with these situations before."

"Really?"

"Sure. Things like this ain't so uncommon in this business as you might think. But it's gonna depend on you staying close to me. You'll have to move to Nashville, with or without your wife."

"I can't do that," I said. "She won't come, and I can't come without her."

"Well, just pretend for a minute that she will," he said. "All right. Mr. Mo's got you by the balls without me. But here's the thing. The publishing contract is between me and you. His name ain't on it. What I want to do is go ahead and sign you to a production contract for the recording part. That'll be directly between me and you too. What that's gonna do is make all your business my business as far as songs and records go. He's still gonna get his money, but we can keep his fat ass out of the loop."

"That's gonna piss him off."

"It would me too. I'd fight it like hell. But he ain't that experienced. Maybe he'll just give up the ghost. At any rate, everything will go between the two of us, and he'll just have to open his pocketbook and see if anything falls in it." Billy snuffed his cigarette out in the nearly full ashtray and blew smoke through his nose. "I wouldn't tell Mr. Mo nothing about you maybe not moving to Nashville. Just go on home and talk your wife into it."

The next morning Biggs and I loaded the Buick and left for Knoxville. On the way we listened to the rough mixes George had made of the eight songs that'd been recorded over the three days—"Some Kind of Magic," "I Just Can't Find the Words," "Fiesta," "Take Me in Your Arms," "Rhymes," "Girl, It's You," "Somebody Somewhere," and "Half Moon Magic."

As the last song ended, Biggs pushed the button to rewind the tape.

"This morning when you were in the can before we left the studio, BK told me he wanted to offer us a production deal."

"Really?" I said.

"That's one step short of the record deal we wanted. He said we'll record some more of your songs, pick enough for a first album, and then he'll take it to the record company."

"Which one?"

"He'll probably start with Warner Brothers since that's who he's with. But he can take it anywhere he wants to."

"Some of these songs sound a little too slick for me," I said. "There's not a good acoustic guitar track in the lot."

"Well, I'll tell you what. I can't imagine things turning out any better for us, what with me negotiating publishing and production deals right out of the box. I told him to make it so that the publishing and production contracts end at the same time. I didn't think he'd agree, but he did. So when these contracts are ready to expire, we can threaten to leave. We'll have him right where we want him. He'll let us do your music our way just to keep hold of us."

The tape finished rewinding and started playing again.

I turned and looked out the window, wishing we'd hurry up and get to Knoxville.

* * *

A few hours later I rolled slowly into Runion, and the town looked small and drab in the four o'clock stillness of Saturday afternoon. I dreaded standing in that apartment, looking down on the empty streets, arguing with Eliza about moving.

I swung around to park on Back Street.

Her car wasn't there.

I slung my bag over my shoulder, grabbed my guitar and labored up the long flight of stairs, trying to think of something funny to say when I called her at her folk's place.

I topped the stairs and looked down the short hall.

There was the familiar sight of one of her notes on the door.

I let the bag slide off my shoulder and leaned my guitar against the wall, pulled the note from the door and, as always, stood to read her round and fluid handwriting under the single bare bulb that hung suspended from the ceiling by a dusty cord.

Dear Gabriel,

I love you. But I can't move to Nashville. I'm sorry. I can't help it. I rented a place in Asheville. Nobody in Runion knows where it is yet, not even Mama and Daddy. I know you can follow me there from work, but I don't want you to.

I took half of the bank account. You can have the

rest. This lawyer who's a client of mine will take care of the legal stuff. She'll send the papers to your mom and dad's address.

Gabriel, this hurts. I've been thinking about it for a long time. I know I should have talked to you, but I just couldn't find a way to start. Things have got so hard between us, the way we work and all.

Please, don't try to find me. I'll end up hating myself if you stay, and you'll end up hating me, too (if you don't already). Get rid of the apartment stuff, and get back to Nashville as quick as you can.

I'm sorry. I love you.

Eliza

P.S. Write a song for me sometimes. I'll be listening.

Chapter 4
Dancing on Air

This is how I pictured it. I'd be sitting in the guest chair at the side of David Letterman's desk or lounging on a couch in my home outside Nashville and chatting with somebody like Barbara Walters. Near the end of the interview, I'd look straight into the camera and tell Eliza the day and time I'd be back to get her. And on that day, at the appointed hour, I'd arrive at the salon or wherever she lived, unfolding from the back of a long black limousine or stepping down from a shiny silver tour bus just as the air brakes hissed.

Meanwhile I lived in Billy Keith's building on the corner of Eighteenth Avenue and South Street, an old two-story brick house that had been converted into office space. Double glass doors led from the concrete porch into the receptionist's area, where a twenty-four-year-old chain-smoking redhead named Kate reigned over the activity that daily swirled through the first-floor offices of Billy's publishing, production and farming interests. A thickly carpeted staircase with a gate at the bottom mounted the wall left of Kate's cluttered desk. The right side of the second floor was Billy's office, the left side my apartment.

At night I was alone in the building. The place surrounded me with even more deathly quiet than had the apartment above the funeral home. Without the extra money to buy or rent a television, I budgeted five dollars a week for paperbacks from a used bookstore in Hillsboro Village, often filling the quiet nights with the voices of Hawthorne and Fitzgerald, Shakespeare and Joyce, Tolkien and McMurtry. I listened to music—Springsteen, Roxy Music, Hoyt Axton, Dallas Holm, Kate Bush, Aaron Copland, Nanci Griffith, Don Williams, Bruce Cockburn, Jean-Pierre Rampal. When the mood to write came over me, I strapped on one my guitars—my old Guild or Uncle T's Martin that Aunt Myrtle gave me the night before I left Runion—and climbed up and down the dark steps for hours, covering every square inch of the building that was open to me. Singing, thinking, writing, singing, rewriting, singing.

When I finally lay down, Eliza stirred inside me, a transient ache that moved beneath my skin. Sometimes, certain I'd felt her touch my chest or back, I awoke with a start and searched the darkness of the bed in a sleepy daze. Then I'd get up and dress and plod the nighttime sidewalks. Again she'd be there, her fingers laced with mine, her footsteps the echo of my own in the quiet and empty spaces.

* * *

I awoke one April morning to the hammering and beeping of Kate's typewriter. Whenever she let up, I heard the laughter and conversation of Frank Long and John Withers, the office guys, standing around the coffee maker as they did every morning, pumping up for work and laying bets on whether or not Billy would show up that day.

I showered and dressed, planning to run a few errands and then meet engineer George MacDougall for lunch.

"I'm bringing a guy named Lukas Carroll along to meet you," George had said when he telephoned the night before.

"Who's that?"

"He plays piano and guitar, and he's got a studio in his house. I think you guys might hit it off."

I was winding my way downstairs when the telephone started ringing in my apartment. Even though it'd been almost a year now, my breath stuck in my chest every time I heard that sound. So I ran back up the stairs and fumbled with my keys, finally getting the door open on the fourth ring.

"Hello?"

"What's up, Gabe?"

I immediately recognized the booming radio voice of Jay Wheeler, who, along with Wiley Fastenau, Cutter, and me, made up an almost inseparable quartet of friends at Runion High School. He'd begun working afternoons at Runion's 500 watt WHMM—Where Hits Make Memories!—as soon as he turned sixteen. Since graduation he'd worked himself into the midday shift. We all figured the place would be his one of these days. Jay had recorded those first radio station demos for me, the first songs of mine that Billy Keith had heard.

"Hey, Jay," I said. "Not much going on here, man. How are things at home?"

"Fine, fine," he said. "We got 'Lacy' in today."

"What?"

"The 45 at least."

"You're kidding!"

"I've got it right here on my turntable, ready to go. Anything you want to say to the folks back home before I de-butt it?"

I sat down in the bay window and started playing with the tangle I'd worked into the phone cord during the last few calls I'd received.

"Will you call my mom real quick and tell her to listen?"

"Already did. Hold on."

I heard Jay flipping switches and listened while he read a spot for Whitson's Green Grocer.

"Okay, Runion," Jay said, his voice tinny and distant over the telephone line. "Ol' Jay's got a big surprise coming up for you right after the latest headlines from UPI, your local weather and sports. Stay tuned." The UPI newscaster's voice droned in the background, and Jay came back on the line. "So, anything you want to say?"

"I'm a total blank."

"Didn't you know it was coming out today?"

"I hadn't heard a word."

"Well, well. I just thought you were shocked that our one-seat shit shack got it in." Jay flipped more switches. "I'm gonna go ahead and play the record right now. You get your little thoughts in order and call me back this afternoon, say around two my time. We'll do an interview."

"Okay. Thanks, Jay. Talk to you then."

I stepped out the door of the apartment and called down to Kate.

"If BK checks in, I need to talk to him."

Soon after I got back from lunch, UPS delivered two boxes of the "Lacy" 45s.

I sat on the couch, holding one of the small black records. The label was royal blue. At the top in sky blue, the words "Stallion Records" circled the head and billowing mane of a white horse. My name was on the label twice—once in blocked white letters as the recording artist, once in tiny letters under "Lacy" as the songwriter. It was the version released to the radio stations, and the same song and label were on the other side too.

I called Jay and did the interview, turning the record over in my hands the whole time, amazed.

I got an excited call from Mom and then put in a call to Cutter in Knoxville. I started to try Eliza at Masterworks, but before I could pick up the receiver and dial her number, the telephone rang.

"Gabby, how are you?" Billy Keith said. "Kate said you needed to talk to me."

"She didn't tell you what?"

"No, she just said to call."

"'Lacy' came out at the radio stations today?"

"It did?" The telephone line hissed for a second as if the call were coming from far away. "What day is it?" Billy asked.

"It's Friday. The 22nd."

"Well, I guess that's right then," Billy said. "We set it up when I was in New York last month. Just forgot to tell you, son, plain and simple."

"Why did it come out to country stations? I'm not a country act."

"We decided to blanket pop, AC, and country with this first single. Ain't nothing wrong with picking up some airtime on any station where we can get added."

"Okay. When's the album coming out?"

"I'm sure it's three weeks or so, somewhere around the middle of May. I'd need to look at my papers. I'll let you know."

"Is there anything I should be doing? Do I need to get a band together?"

"No, hell, you need the hassle of dealing with a band about as much as you need that damn manager of yours." The scrape of a cigarette lighter sounded over the telephone, followed by Billy's heavy exhalation. "But here's what you can do. I've got some independent promotion men lined up to help out the label boys. I'll get you a list of radio stations, and starting Monday, you can just go to calling 'em to see if they got the record in and if they'll listen to it."

"Okay."

"If you hear from Mr. Mo, don't talk to him about it. Gotta run, son. See you soon."

I hadn't heard from Mo Biggs in a couple of months. While little was happening through February, March and the first of April, he'd quit calling and quit showing up every few days to check on things. Billy's plan to cut the manager out of the loop seemed to be working.

But not long after the reviews of "Lacy" began hitting the trades, Biggs was in my life day and night, heralded by either a ringing telephone or the banging of a handful of keys on the glass of the double doors downstairs at night when the office was closed. He knew Billy was trying to squeeze him out. He threatened legal action against anybody he could drag into court over the matter, and he demanded that I act as his spy and report on everything that went on in Billy Keith's offices.

I said I'd keep my eyes open. And hated myself for it. I still believed what Billy had said—Mo Biggs would be a stumbling block, a liability. But that didn't make it any easier when Biggs sat on the couch in the apartment, eaten up with frustration and heartburn, huffing and puffing after the climb up the stairs, wiping the sweat off his reddened round face, wringing his white hands, complaining about getting screwed. A time or two this scene almost drove me to tell him I was in on the plot to make him quit, but even the guilt I felt couldn't convince me to forgive the unfairness of the management contract and the awkward position he had put me in that early morning at the Crossville Waffle House. I hung on to what I'd heard Billy say time and time again— "Don't worry. It's just business. Happens all the time."

*   *   *

Stallion Records arranged for me to lip-sync "Lacy" during a May appearance on *Dancing on Air*, a live afternoon dance show from Philadelphia, with a regular cast of kids from all over the city and an audience made up of viewers throughout Pennsylvania and New Jersey.

The day before, Kate took me shopping for new clothes.

"What do you think about this, Gabriel?" She stepped aside to show me what she'd laid together on a table in Castner Knott's men's department.

I turned away from the clearance rack of flannel shirts and studied the ensemble—a raw silk jacket, a slick and colorful silk shirt with a vaguely Mexican-looking print and designer jeans.

"The Mexican lounge lizard, eh, muchacha?" I smiled and turned back to the sale shirts.

"I'm serious. Turn around and look again."

I turned and looked at her.

"This is exactly what my boss and yours told me to get for you," she said.

"You're kidding." I looked at the clothes again. "Kate, I've never worn anything like that before in my life."

"Welcome to your afterlife," she said, pulling a credit card from her purse.

Before we left the mall she also picked out a pair of short boots made from a soft cream-colored leather and a belt that matched them.

"Now for a hair cut," Kate said when we were back in the car.

"What?"

"You're going on TV, Gabriel, and you haven't had a hair cut since I've known you."

"Yeah, and I'm not getting one."

"Your boss—"

"I don't care what our boss says, Kate. I'm wearing the clothes he wants, but I'm not letting anybody else touch my hair."

"What do you mean by 'anybody else'?" she said as I drove up the ramp toward I-65.

I made a big deal of checking my mirrors as I merged into the southbound lanes, cleared my throat a couple of times, then lit a cigarette.

"Well?" she said. "That ponytail's gone way down over your collar."

"I trim my own hair." I didn't know what would come out of her mouth. Maybe something along the lines of *Looks like it* or *I can tell.* No matter what it was, I knew it would have a laugh behind it.

"It won't hurt," she said and chuckled. "I've already made an appointment at Leota's on Seventeenth. It's where I go."

"I trim my own hair," I said again and fixed my attention on driving so much that she didn't say another word.

Back at the office, I carried the bags up to my apartment, grumbling just loud enough to be sure Kate heard me.

"I haven't matched this much since Mom used to dress me for Easter."

When everybody left the office for the day, I went out and bought a six-pack of Dos Equis. I returned to the apartment and drank three of the beers very quickly. While they took effect, I unpacked the outfit and put it on. Then I laid one of the "Lacy" 45s on the turntable, set the REPEAT button, shouldered the Martin and planted myself in front of the mirror in the bedroom.

When the music started, I dipped my right knee and nearly fell into the bedside table, blaming it on the beer. I tried my left, swaying it from side to side, and thought I looked like I was shaking an embarrassing accident down the leg of my pants. A swivel of my hips and instead of the Elvis-the-pelvis look I expected, I got my own father trying to dance.

"You're in deep shit," I said to the mirror, wishing I'd taken Eliza dancing more often and let her teach me the secrets of fluid movement to music.

I discovered a smooth groove between my neck and shoulders and thought that looked okay, but I kept losing the rhythm every few bars. I gave up on my body and concentrated on my lips, trying to sing the song exactly with the record, exaggerating my facial expressions and the movement of my mouth and jaws for a stronger visual effect. As that felt more and more familiar I closed my eyes and mimicked the mental picture I held of myself on stage. When I peeked at the mirror again, I thought I looked more comfortable, but then self-consciousness turned me back into an unoiled tin man.

I put my guitar down and turned off the music, stripped off the clothes and threw them on the bed. Then I quickly downed the other three beers.

Naked and buzzing, I sat down at the piano and fumbled over the keys until I found a chord progression and a hint of melody to slow my racing heart and bring some order to my swirling mind.

After a few minutes of trying various voicings for the chords, of humming melody and variation, I held down the sustain pedal and let a jazzy cluster of notes ring and picked up my pen.

Off and running—
Up and coming morning in the east. . . .

The sluggishness of my drunken piano hands annoyed me, so I reached for my Guild. The strings under my fingers and the hollow body of wood against my belly felt more natural, and the lyrics and music rose out of me like breath. At the piano, I couldn't think of anything but the right blacks and whites, but with my old acoustic guitar in my arms, my mind was free.

I pictured her sleeping while I wrote, pictured the shape of her lying on her side with her back to the light that fell through the open bedroom door. The scene changed. She swirled her skirt and laughed as she bopped across a lighted floor, dancing rings around some dark partner. Then she was in bed again, writhing and moaning under the weight and thrust of that same dark figure. As I flailed the guitar, the man turned toward the light. It was me.

Too obsessed,
I came out west and found a place to hide.
You took a lover,
Then another, never satisfied.
People say
It's such a shame to see your appetite,
And to see me chase the sun
And end up running into lonely nights.
I look at that star again and see you as a queen—
Standing in your blue dress, girl, you'll always be
The best I've ever seen.

At three o'clock in the morning, I sat in the bay window, and played the song into a small tape recorder. Then I picked up the jumbled pile of new clothes from the bed and laid them out on the back of the couch and turned off the lights.

Just before sleep overcame me, I pulled the wedding band from my finger and dropped it in the drawer of the bedside table.

*   *   *

The next morning Kate told me I looked awful and drove me to the airport. At the gate she handed me spending money from Billy and put me on the plane.

Jack Widmark, a music marketing consultant working with Stallion Records, picked me up at the Philadelphia airport and drove me to the suburban studios of WPHL-17. Widmark was older than most men I'd met in the music business, graying but trim, his judge-like bearing betrayed only by a wide smile.

"We'll meet my wife and have something to eat when the show is over," he said as he held the front door of the studio open for me and my guitar.

During a commercial break, I was directed to a small stage and stool to one side of where *Dancing on Air*'s host and producer Hal Legesse coached the kids on the setup of the performance sequence. Now and then a girl or two in the crowd of dancers looked my way and smiled.

The kids all ran to gather around me when the commercial ended. They whooped and hollered and clapped their hands so that I could hardly hear the music start.

We all did the best we could. These kids were used to dancing to "Maneater," "Baby, Come to Me" and "Billie Jean," not string-laden adaptations of old Appalachian ballads. One young couple even tried something like a waltz, and I focused my attention on them at first. They were dressed neatly, and every hair was in place. Although they smiled a lot, their movements were self-conscious and awkward. Their faces shone with the nervous sweat and oil that's the curse of teenagers. Watching, I realized how much like them Eliza and I must have looked that night at the Dam Dance. It wasn't the image of us in that moment that'd always been in my head, but it was probably the truer picture. Embarrassed, wondering what other romanticized tableaus of our life together weren't as perfect as I'd imagined them to be, I turned away from the couple and focused on the music.

I tried to charge my performance with every ounce of the energy that surged through me whenever I performed for real. Without microphone or amplifier I began to bang the chords and belt out the lyrics, paying attention to the music above my head only enough to keep my lips in sync.

But it didn't work. It was all a contrivance, as stagy as a scene in a cheesy musical.

The forest glade. Enter a lover inspired to song. Sudden swell of violins.

As a camera rolled through the group of kids who danced in front of me, I smiled broadly at the image of string sections in concert black lined up on tree limbs like roosting crows.

* * *

Jack and Roberta Widmark, Hal Legesse and Hal's mother Antonia sat around me at a table in an Italian restaurant not far from the television studio. Hal related some of the favorable comments the kids on the show had about me—that I seemed comfortable and made them feel the same, that they liked my sense of humor when they swirled around me at the end of the show, that they liked the sound of the song and wished they could've heard it a little better.

"Are you married, young man?" Antonia Legesse broke in.

I glanced down at the naked ring finger of my left hand, at the pale depression still visible on my skin. I laid the hand in my lap.

"No, ma'am, I'm not," I said.

"You should be," Antonia Legesse said. "My Hal, he's not married too." She took another swirl of spaghetti into her mouth and kept talking. "Hal says you make beautiful music, no? You should have a wife. Make music to her. At night. Make mood for her. Make love with her. None of this running around the country. You be a lover, no?" She laughed and raised her eyebrows.

I blushed under Antonia's Legesse's smiling gaze, and the rest of the table laughed.

* * *

"You've generally got about six weeks," Jack Widmark said that night over coffee.

I sat with Roberta and him at the kitchen table in the cabin they owned in the Delaware Valley countryside north of Philadelphia.

The windows were open, as were the French doors that led outside to a deck. A light breeze wandered in and out of the room, carrying with it the sounds of crickets and frogs and now and then the haunting call of an owl or the swish of a car passing far out on the two-lane.

"If you can't get enough adds from the reporting stations to get 'Lacy' on the charts by then, you're through with it. The record's dead in the water."

"It's been four weeks already," I said. "Can't I do something to make it happen?"

"You're the artist. That means a lot to some stations, some of the smaller ones. But you're a new name. The bigger ones still aren't going to give you anything. They've got to have promo men they trust, got to have their egos stroked, got to have their perks. Billy knows." Jack got up and poured himself another cup of coffee. "Do you see him often?"

"Well, not really. I know he's not touring much anymore, but he's rarely ever around. I think I've only seen him twice since the record came out."

"I was afraid of that." Widmark set his coffee down and picked up Roberta's cup and mine and refilled them. "I think the man's a little flighty. Talented but flighty. A good ear for music, but not much head for business."

"I like him," Roberta said, leaning across the table toward me. "He's funny. But, being married to Jack, I've met a lot of people in the music business, and Billy's one that I can't figure out. He talks a good game, but I just don't know." She lifted her face and smiled when her husband set the fresh cup of coffee in front of her.

"He's in that gray area between creativity and business savvy," Widmark said. "His kind sometimes has trouble crossing that line with any grace."

"I'm almost afraid to ask this," I said. "Billy told me the album would be out by now, but it's not. Is there a problem?"

Jack Widmark took a long sip from his coffee cup.

"Stallion put it off for a couple of weeks. There was a meeting Monday. Billy was there. He didn't tell you that either?"

"No."

"Well, he should have." Jack rubbed his eyes and looked at the clock. "Damn, it's two in the morning already."

"What should he have told me?" I said.

"There are two ideas on the table at Stallion right now. One is to continue with the present setup and do the album release in the middle of June. 'Lacy' hasn't made the charts, but they feel like it's gotten enough response to go ahead. The other idea is for the company to go public, sell stock, raise enough capital to break away from Warner Brothers and function on its own. If that happens, the album will be shelved until the changeover is complete. It could take a while. A year even."

I didn't breathe. It was all I could do to keep my face from twisting like my gut. As uncomfortable as I'd felt during my *Dancing on Air* performance, I wanted to keep rolling, to build a career. If "Lacy" didn't hit, I wanted another single out, another show to do, an album, a band, a tour.

"Which way do you think it's gonna go?" I said finally.

"Right now I'm afraid they might go the public route. It's a new company, and the board is still too excited about being in business. They don't have a love for the music yet." Widmark rapped his knuckles twice on the table. "Billy should have told you."

"Gabriel, I want to tell you something," Roberta said. "I've listened to your tape almost every day since Jack brought it home. It's wonderful music."

"Thanks."

"You don't need to be involved with business people. It'll hurt you. It'll hurt your creativity. You need to be taken care of by someone who sees what you are and what you can do. Someone who can make it all happen. I know that sounds vague, but Jack and I were talking about it last night."

I shifted in my chair and wrapped my hands around the warm cup in front of me.

"Billy is moving from one career to the next," Roberta went on after a sip of coffee. "He's carrying you, hoping to get you into a position where you'll be able to carry him. But the music business is shaky ground. If he falls, he might take you down with him before you even get started."

"We're not saying you shouldn't work with him," Jack said. "I love the guy. I really do. And he did a creative job producing your album. But as soon as you get the chance, you need to separate yourself from him a bit. Look for a business person you can put between yourself and Billy."

There was already somebody between Billy and me, but I was sure that Mo Biggs wasn't what Jack had in mind.

The coffee fought an uphill battle against the clock. Yawns went around the table like a peace pipe. Finally, the Widmarks said goodnight and went upstairs.

I climbed up to the loft that looked out over the richly decorated living room. As I undressed, my mind tumbled backwards through the conversation about Billy Keith and the record company. I wasn't shocked by what the Widmarks had said. More than once during my first year in Nashville, I'd felt some of what they'd put into words. What shocked me was realizing that the chaos my life suddenly seemed to be in wasn't going to keep me awake. I was tired. As tired as I'd ever been.

Eliza was there as I lay down. The familiar ache she'd become. I smelled her perfume—its blend of honeysuckle and musk—on the breeze that moved in and out of the cabin's open windows. And yet as sleepy and tired as I was, I lay awake a long time, breathing deeply and listening to the rush of the stream that passed beside the deck at the back of the house.

* * *

Beyond the dirty strand of sand, the dunes are hotels, rising above the breeze-bent beach grass and swimming pools. The sky to the west—gray. The hotels jutting against it are only a more concrete shade of the same. The windswept table umbrellas and the glittering aqua pools, the patchy brown sand, and my peach-white skin—gray.

The warm water of the ocean laps around my ankles, playfully as it comes in, but as it returns, it swirls under my bare heels and tries to steal my footing.

Water runs farther up the beach and returns, foaming around my feet with an agitation akin to malice. My heels sink, waiting for solid ground. I stumble backward, turn and take a couple of steps into the water to regain my balance, and stop, frozen.

All the gray water is leaving, rushing to join the uprising in the east. From north to south, farther even than the curve of the earth should reveal, gray water is pulling itself into the gray sky.

I sprint south along the beach. Feet pound on the packed wet sand. Heart pounds in my throat.

Out of breath, I stop and look toward the line of hotels. Beyond to the mountains. And back to the ocean.

The wave lifts its head into the clouds and begins to crest.

I stand and stare, waiting for my body to be broken by the crash and borne by the surge, washed up on the shores of home.

Chapter 5
Eliza, Listen

On the dark paneled wall above the black cowboy hat hung eight gold records and several ASCAP songwriting awards, all dated between 1968 and 1977.

Beneath the hat sat Billy Keith, his hair graying faster, his paunch drooping over his belt buckle. Bags hung under his pale blue eyes, but his skin had been deeply tanned during a recent vacation to Acapulco. He looked both rested and bone tired at once as he leaned back and rubbed his eyes, swiveled in his chair, and threw his ostrich-skin boots up on the right-hand side of his oak desk's top and crossed his ankles.

"Well, Gabby," he said, "I guess you figured out Stallion ain't gonna release our album. They got newer projects they're more excited about right now."

I sat in one of the straight-backed wooden chairs in front of the desk.

"Well, I've kind of been hoping the stuff wouldn't be released," I said. I saw Keith's expression change but somehow couldn't tell if it hardened or softened. "The music on the radio's changed a lot since we did the Lacy sessions."

"Keep in mind now, son, you been hearing it enough to get tired of it. It'd be fresh to them that never heard it before."

I slid up to the edge of my chair and sat with fists on knees.

"A lot's changed for me too"—*sit easy, unclench fists*—"since I wrote those songs."

The telephone rang.

He took the call and chatted with somebody for ten minutes about things he wanted done around the farm. When he hung up he sat and shuffled through some papers in his briefcase.

"Son, I know this is a big disappointment to you. And I know what you gave up to be here. But we got a couple more years on your contracts, and I want to use 'em right. There's still time."

I shifted in my seat again. I had a batch of new songs I'd been working on only at night and not playing for anybody in the office. They were the best things I'd ever written. On another level in comparison with the older stuff. It seemed to me that if I could just get out of my contracts with Keith and Biggs, I'd be on my way. All I needed was some downtime to get the new songs recorded. Then I could use the new demo to land a new deal. Lukas Carroll, the musician George MacDougall had introduced me to a year and a half before, had offered to help record the new material over the holidays. It was late November, and no business would get done on Music Row before January or February. Time enough. It would all fall together if I could just talk my way out of the contracts.

"You remember in October when everybody was out at the Opryland Hotel," Billy said. "I met up with some folks from CBS, mostly New York boys down here for a laugh at the hillbillies. But they was investigating the club scene pretty serious, looking at some of the Nashville rock acts they been hearing about." He stopped and lit a cigarette. "Well, son, I got to drinking with 'em, and we all ended up down here at the office one night late. Played your stuff for 'em. They loved hell out of it."

"Where was I?" I said. "I don't remember you bringing people by."

"I don't know. Your car wasn't out back. I remember looking for it."

I'd been out a lot in October. At the Songbird Cafe some. Or jamming at Lukas's house. One long weekend I'd gone home to see the fall colors on Lonesome Mountain. I suspected Keith was lying, but I always suspected that in those days. With so many big plans and promises turning out to seem like just words in the man's mouth, disbelief had become a means of self-preservation.

"Since then," he said, "I got us a deal lined up with Chaz Wontall, direct with CBS and none of this Stallion shit in the mix."

"You mean CBS as in Columbia and Epic?" I said.

"You bet, son. Direct. They want us to get in the studio middle of

February. I got Bullet booked already."

I couldn't be sure if what I felt was my feet taking leave of the floor at the thought of seeing my name listed along with those on the label's roster—Dylan, Springsteen, Joel, Jackson—or the floor dropping from under me at the thought of staying under contract to Billy Keith.

I coughed and scratched my chin through black whiskers, pulled out a cigarette and lit it. Blue smoke curled into my face, and I turned away quickly, slamming my eyes shut against the sting.

"You got some new songs you ain't played me, I imagine," Billy said.

I still had my face turned away.

"Yeah," I said, all the nights of secrecy now in vain with that single word. "I've been working on some new things."

* * *

"You'd be crazy not to stick around and see what happens," Lukas said. "If it works, it works. If it doesn't, you'll write some more tunes and break away then."

"Well," I said. "But—"

"Meanwhile, we put the band together after the first of the year and get that part rolling."

We sat in the spare bedroom that he had converted to a home recording studio. We'd been working on a new song I'd finished writing that morning, the two of us playing or programming all the instruments.

Lukas took off his round-framed glasses, rubbed his eyes and yawned. Then he slouched, propped an elbow on the arm of his chair and smoked.

A yellow and white cat named Puppy curled in his lap, purring steadily. Bones, a German shepherd, lay by his chair with its head on its front paws, its brown eyes scanning the room. The theme song for *The Tonight Show* floated down the hall from the den, where Cassie, Lukas's wife, had been watching the ten o'clock news.

"You'd be crazy not to," Lukas said again, pulling his straight blond hair from behind his shoulders and laying it along the side of his neck.

I sat chin in hand, swirling the short beard with my palm.

"You're right," I said. "I just hate the thought of recording another album and then seeing it shot down like the last one." I sipped a beer that had become a little warm. "Doesn't matter now anyway. I already told him I've got new songs. He's anxious to hear them."

Lukas took a last slow drag from his cigarette and mashed the butt out in the ashtray.

"Well, I'm anxious to hear this tune one more time and take the wife to bed." He swiveled in his chair, hit PLAY and leaned back.

The music started.

Lonely footsteps play the sidewalk
Like a drum in the midnight still. . . .

"I think we should add some kind of synth part right here," Lukas said over the music that followed the first chorus. "I'll see if I can come up with something in the morning when I'm fresh."

I nodded.

So I go stumbling down memory lane,
Past the old school to that vacant lot,
Where once our engines ran hot,
And we kissed by the light of the radio. . . .

"I love the way the drums build right here into the bridge," I said loudly as the second chorus ended. "How about some kind of choral pad to build with it?"

Lukas scratched out a memo on his notebook and then practiced fading the end of the song.

I sat still, listening for the last words.

Eliza, listen to your heart. . . .

With the music faded and the tape machine turned off, we looked at each other, grinned and lit more cigarettes.

"She must be something," Lukas said from the lighted porch as I walked across the yard to my little white Pinto.

I turned.

"Who?"

"Eliza. The girl in the song. That's your wife back in North Carolina, right?"

"Ex-wife, now. The divorce went through last June." I looked away from Lukas and up at the clear winter stars. "But, yeah, she's something all right. Best I've ever seen." I zipped my coat and pushed my hands into the pockets.

"'Best I've ever seen,'" Lukas repeated. "Sounds like a song to me."

"Done and done it. I'll play it for you in the morning."

"Yeah, man. Maybe we'll record it."

"It might be a little too personal," I said. "I was naked when I wrote it."

Lukas laughed and wiped a hand over his eyes.

"I hope you don't have to sing it like that."

"Only emotionally."

"Drive safe, man," Lukas said and went back in the house.

I stood in the dark yard. Above me, the brightest stars cut through the Nashville aura. One I always looked for hovered in the east above the tree line at the end of Lukas's street. I hummed warm breath that billowed in the early December air, then sang softly as I walked across the frosty grass to my car.

Somewhere you
Can see it too, and I'm wishing I was where you are.
Though I can't bridge the years and miles laid in between,
I have learned with every step that you are still
The best I've ever seen.

* * *

Three days before Christmas and home in the mountains for the holiday, I sat at the kitchen table and drank coffee with Dad. Mom was there as well but in constant motion between the cabinets and the refrigerator, the oven and the sink.

The air in the room was warm around us and filled with the aroma of fudge and baking cookies. The windows had steamed over, and the colored lights outside shone like a kaleidoscope in the condensation on the panes.

Dad got up and grabbed the coffee pot and refilled our cups.

I felt the new warmth work its way through the mug and into my hands.

"When are Butler and Patty coming home?" I asked.

"Tomorrow afternoon," Dad said. "Butler's got his office party tonight and a Christmas cantata to sing at church in the morning. They'll probably get out of Statesville right after. That'll put 'em here about two, I reckon."

"Gabe," Mom said, "the new songs you sent us last week are just beautiful. You and Lukas—is that his name? It sounds like you boys work well together." She paused, her hands hovering above a blob of orange-white dough that sat on the table between Dad and me. "But I'd give anything if you had Eliza down there so the words wouldn't be so sad."

"Now, Maggie," Dad said. "He don't want to hear that right now." He lit a cigarette and tossed the match in an ashtray on a shelf by the table. "Besides, he ain't the one that left."

"It's okay, Mom," I said. "Don't worry about it. Things are getting better." I took a sip of coffee. "Next year I'm gonna write happy songs. It'll be my New Year's resolution."

On her next pass by the table, Mom bent and kissed my father through the coarse ginger-gray hair on the top of his head. Then she reached down and patted me on the shoulder.

Dad sipped his coffee and cleared his throat.

"Do you ever see Ezra MacRae down there in Nashville?"

I made a sound that was half grunt, half laugh.

"I've seen him a couple of times," I said. "He called me one night not long after he moved to town. Wanted to come over and jam some. I gave him directions, but a couple of hours later he called and said he needed help. He'd made a few wrong turns and hit another car head on at a four-way intersection all the way on the other side of town. By the time I found him, the police had gone, and he was under this one street light with about six or seven rough looking characters all around him." I paused when I heard Mom's breath catch. Then I grinned at Dad and went on. "Ezra was slapping hands and singing 'Under the Boardwalk,' drunk as he could be."

Dad laughed, and Mom shook her head.

"I've seen him a time or two since, and he's always in about the same shape."

"Poor Sarah," Mom said. "Don't you know Ephraim is so ashamed."

"Sounds just like a preacher's kid to me, Maggie," Dad said. "They all gotta act that way for awhile. He'll pull out of it one of these days."

"I hope so."

I bent my head toward the coffee cup and cleared my throat.

"Just so we can get all of this out of the way now," I said without looking up, "have you heard anything from Eliza?"

"She called in August, on my birthday," Mom said. "But we didn't talk long." She stood at a counter, dropping dollops of the dough onto a cookie sheet and pressing a whole pecan into the center of each one. "She asked about you."

"What about her folks? Do you ever see them at all?"

Dad blew smoke out his nose.

"We ran into 'em in the mall a couple weeks ago. They didn't have much to say." He snuffed out his cigarette. "I swear, I can't tell if those folks're shy or conceited. Or maybe they're just embarrassed. I don't know."

"Gabe," Mom said with a look at my father, "this is the only time I'll mention it while you're home, but I just think you ought to hear this."

"Hear what?"

"Myrtle still goes to Eliza and gets her hair done every week. She thinks Eliza's dating somebody." She smoothed the raven black hair at her temples with the insides of her wrists and blew air, more from relief, it seemed, than from the warmth of her work.

I gently pushed the coffee cup away and stood up.

"I think I'll go see if Cutter's home yet," I said.

*　*　*

Cutter and I slipped across the state line into Tennessee, bought two six-packs of beer and turned back toward Runion, taking the slow way over narrow mountain roads, drinking and talking.

"So you're leaving Knoxville after just six and a half years," I said. "What's next?"

"Well, I've finally got my damned master's, and I start work here in the county in February."

I sucked down the remainder of my beer, dropped the empty bottle back into the bag along with Cutter's, and pulled out two more for us.

"Are you serious?"

"Yep. Hard to believe, ain't it?"

"What'll you be doing?"

"My favorite thing is domestic squabbles," Cutter said with a grunt as he twisted off another top. He took a long drink and then wiped his mouth on his sleeve. "Just kidding, cuz. Hell, I'll be doing I don't know what all. But me and Rendy are excited about it."

"When am I going to meet this girl?"

"Who said it was a girl?"

I laughed.

"You're right. Pretty presumptuous on my part."

"She'll be coming up on Christmas Eve."

We rode awhile in silence, sipping beers.

"Let's go check out Santa Claus's trailer," I said.

"It's not there anymore," Cutter said.

"Really? What happened to it?"

"Pop said a fire gutted it back in the fall. Gunther's living in your old apartment. He gave up his wrecker service and digs graves for old man Ramsey now."

"Well, there's another legend gone up in smoke."

"Sucks, don't it?"

We rode with the radio turned down low, and the beer bottles slowly emptied. . . .

*   *   *

He had taken Eliza to see Santa Claus's trailer on a Saturday night during her first Christmas in Runion. She was leaving the next day after church to visit her grandparents in West Virginia for the holidays, and they had eaten at the Pizzeria and exchanged gifts.

"What's that?" she said when they were back in his parents' LTD and he mentioned Gunther Gosnell's yearly spectacle.

"I can't really describe it. You'll just have to wait and see."

They dropped down the hill at the south end of Main Street, turned right onto the bridge and crossed the French Broad River. On the other side, they wound slowly through the hairpin curves that climbed toward Piney Ridge.

Falling away below them, the river glowed. Everything reflected in the water—the white lights in the trees of Stackhouse Park, the street lights of Runion and its bustle of red-lit, green-lit, blue-lit decorations, the houses with all their festive trimmings.

"Oh, Gabriel, that's so pretty from over here."

He smiled and rounded the last climbing curve and slipped into the darkness of Piney Ridge.

"I don't think I've ever been this way," Eliza said.

"Not much reason to come over here if you don't live on the Ridge or in Spring Creek. Mom and Dad like it for Sunday drives. Take that road to the left back there, just before we passed the church, and Cutter lives up in there. So does my Uncle T, the town dentist."

After two miles or so of winding along the top of the ridge, the road descended into a backwoods blackness.

"Get ready," he said as the third in a succession of hairpin turns approached.

She put her hand on his thigh and leaned a little toward the windshield.

They emerged from the curve, and suddenly, on the hillside just above the next deep twist in the road, there appeared such a confusion of light that it was difficult to focus on at first.

Her grip tightened on his leg, and a whispered whistle escaped between her lips.

When they were near enough, he slowed the car to a crawl and turned off the headlights. The uproar of brilliance directly in front of them first seemed amorphous, like something from a dream. It gradually shaped itself into a swirling galaxy of whites, reds, greens, blues, yellows, oranges, purples and pinks. Then the trailer emerged from the center, its every angle and edge, every window and both doors, lined with tiny glowing bulbs. As they drew closer, the swirling galaxy metamorphosed to a spider's web that spread across the ground for at least twenty-five feet in every direction from the trailer. Each tree and bush and blade of grass within that perimeter seemed wound with colored lights. All over the yard, like creatures and debris caught in the web of brightness, were Nativity scenes, miniatures of Santa and his reindeer, groups of round-mouthed ceramic carolers gathered under old-fashioned street lamps with snow painted on top, giant candy canes, piles of gift-wrapped boxes and angels. The inside of the trailer appeared dark except for the lighted Christmas tree in one window.

"My gosh," Eliza said, "who lives here?"

"The guy's name is Gunther Gosnell. He runs the cheapest wrecker service in the county. One time he pulled Cutter's car up a ten-foot creek bank and only charged him three dollars. And on a Sunday at that. Dad says he's a little addled. Used to be some kind of wrestler or boxer or something."

"Can you imagine the light bill?" she said and laughed.

He turned on the high-beams and accelerated through the curve in front of the trailer. The sudden force pressed Eliza's body against him. He turned around in the next wide spot and raced back up the hill.

When they reached the top and the road leveled out along the ridge, he turned on the radio just in time to hear the deejay announce the nine o'clock news. He turned off the radio and wiped sweaty palms on his jeans. He started to speak but was stopped by the dry lump in his throat and the feeling that he could not judge how loud his voice would have to be to make himself heard over the pounding of his heart, the noisy rush of blood around his ears, the roar of butterfly wings flapping in his gut.

"We've still got a couple of hours. Do you want to stop?" To his surprise, his voice did not boom as the words rushed out but whispered like hissing fire.

"What?"

He cleared his throat.

"We've got a couple of hours. Do you want to drive into Asheville and back?"

"I don't mind stopping if you want to."

The spot he had been looking for suddenly opened up to the right. He slammed on the brakes and spun the steering wheel. Eliza lurched forward and then almost landed in his lap. With a terse squeal from the tires the car skidded to a stop and sat sideways in the road, facing the Piney Ridge Holiness Tabernacle and the cemetery rising up the hill behind it. The murmur of the engine was the only sound until he recovered his wits.

"Sorry," he said.

Eliza quickly struggled back into the seat, brushing a hand over the front of her sweater and looking around.

"What're we doing here?" she asked.

"You said you wanted to stop. This is a place the Piney Ridge Bombers told me about. Cutter's used it before."

"What? Are we just going to park right out where everybody can see us?"

"Well, no. There's a little driveway that goes all the way around back of the church."

"By that graveyard?"

"It'll be okay. Nobody'll see us back there."

She did not say any more, so he took her silence as consent. He turned off the headlights again and drove slowly into the moonlit parking lot, white gravel popping and grinding beneath the tires. Behind the church, he stopped the car and reached down with his left hand and pushed the button that electronically moved the front seat as far forward as it would go. Then he switched off the ignition.

The quarter moon had just risen and glowed in the cobalt blue sky like the snowy-white flesh of heaven revealed through a rip in the dark fabric of night. Its light glinted off the granite of the newer tombstones, and its reflection was framed in the one tall window at the back of the church.

They climbed out his door and took off their coats and threw them in the front seat. He pulled his shirt tail from his pants as Eliza ducked into the back seat. She slid all the way across and sat with her back against the opposite door, facing away from most of the graveyard. He slid in after her, closed the door quietly, turned and leaned back against her.

The car filled with moonlight. The pearly air grew heavy with the delicious aroma of her perfume—honeysuckle and musk. His body and mind filled with the warm softness of her at his back—the swell of breasts, the rise and fall of breathing.

She wrapped her arms around his neck and played her hands across his chest.

Feeling he could move only slowly, as if immersed in a baptistery of cold air and moonlight, he raised up and turned toward her. He could not speak, could not force enough air out from his chest even to whisper. A clamp seemed to tighten at the sides of his throat, choking the flow of blood to his brain, damming his saliva so that his swallowing moved like sand through an hourglass.

She curled the right side of her lower lip into her mouth and bit it lightly and looked out the back window across the white gravel to the part of the hillside cemetery that curved toward the trees by the side of the road.

He tried to imagine himself beyond her quietness, tried to hear her soft voice telling him what to do. But the wash of heavenly light and breath carried no messages from her.

He was on his own.

He stretched his left hand behind her, slid it under her sweater and touched her bare back.

She twisted the waves of black hair at his collar around the fingers of her left hand.

He moved his right hand to her belly, where it lay trembling like a man who finally finds the beach after swimming beyond his capacity. Then without looking at her face, he slowly lifted her sweater—up past her navel, up across the smooth tightness of the naked plain above, up over the lacy bra, the shadowed and mystical cleft—and pushed its folds into the wells of her arms.

He stopped. His eyes seemed to shiver and dance as he took in all this new beauty at once. He felt for a moment that he could not breathe, then realized he simply had not breathed.

Suddenly, with a cold finger, she discovered the skin behind the waist of his blue jeans. As if she had touched his belly with an electric wire, he buckled in the middle just as she leaned forward to kiss him.

His headbutt bloodied her nose.

"Ow!"

"Oh, shit! I'm sorry!"

She covered her nose with both hands.

"Get my purse, quick!"

He dove halfway into the front seat, grabbed her purse, and swung it around to her as he sat back. She yanked it open and pulled out a handful of tissue, wadded it up and stuck it under her nose.

"God, Eliza, I'm so sorry." He pulled her sweater back down and smoothed it, ran a shaking hand over his hair and watched her.

"It's okay," she said after a moment. "It really didn't hurt. Just the shock mostly, you know?"

"It's the last thing I expected," he said as he leaned again into the front seat and grabbed their coats. "That's for sure."

When he sat back, he could tell by her eyes that she smiled behind her hand. She laid her head back and shifted the tissue to find a clean portion of the wad. He lifted her legs and pulled them across his lap, then covered them with the coats. Her left hand found the hair at his collar again.

"You could write a funny song about this," she whispered and closed her eyes. In a few moments she took the tissue away from her nose.

Except for their breathing, they fell as quiet as the moonlight that hovered around the dusty dashboard.

He saw the dappled tissue drop to the floor. Under the coats, his fingertips traced feathery circles on the worn knees of her jeans. He squirmed to find a comfortable way to sit with the stiffness still pushing at his zipper, embarrassment buzzing around his ears like a gnat. He felt her legs slowly take on the heaviness of sleep. The desire to start over with the touching ached in his hands, but he didn't move.

They both fell asleep.

But he bolted upright and Eliza screamed when the flashlight banged on the window and then glared through the frosted glass.

Blue light whirled around their heads, across the windows and bricks of the church, the tombstones and trees on the hillside.

His hand shook as he opened the door.

The misty breath and the wrinkled, unshaven face of Deputy "Daggnabbit" Boyce leaned in.

"Morning, Gabe," he said. "That Miss Eliza in there with you?" The old lawman always spoke with a slow drawl, the crinkle of a knowing smile at the corners of his mouth. He had been given his nickname years ago by

Uncle T's generation. Anytime he caught a group of two or more boys up to mischief, the first words out of his mouth were "Daggnabbit, boys, . . ." Four different sheriffs had deputized him, and almost everybody in town felt as if they had known him since they could walk.

"What time is it, Daggnabbit?" Gabriel said, his head felt filled with goose down. He looked at Eliza.

She sat with her right hand over her eyes.

"Well, if you'd've left here about fifteen minutes ago, you might've made it up Walnut Road before your mama's rooster woke up."

Gabriel turned back to see if Deputy Boyce appeared to be telling the truth.

He did.

"Oh, shit," Eliza and Gabriel said together.

"Yeah, I'll say," the lawman chuckled. "Mrs. Garrison and Maggie been on the phone and on my ass since one o'clock this morning." Deputy Boyce began to pace slowly back and forth beside the car, his heavy steps making grinding and clicking noises in the loose gravel. "Had a helluva time finding y'all." He pulled the front door open. "I'm ready for some fresh coffee, so if y'all don't mind now." He made a herding motion with his flashlight.

They slid out the back door and dove back in the front. Gabriel cranked the ignition and revved the motor up too high. Eliza began a strange laugh and was somehow stuck in the middle of putting on her coat.

"A might cold tonight to be sleeping outside practically, ain't it?" the deputy droned on. "But I guess two bodies help."

"Oh, my gosh," Eliza said.

Deputy Boyce leaned down to look in at them.

"I been through Stackhouse Park, out to the high school twice, up the creek to the Suddy Hole pull-off, and here y'all are on the P-Ridge side of the river, hid between church and graveyard." He turned his head to the left and right and raised up to look over the roof of the car and bent back down. "Mighty quiet here, for sure. I'll have to remember this spot next time it's warm enough to get the Honeycutt sisters to venture out of a night."

"Are we free to go?" Gabriel said.

Deputy Boyce sighed.

"Yeah, I reckon. Just stay awake on the way home and keep a light foot. You're too late to make up for lost time. Don't kill yourself trying. I'll be coming right along behind you."

Just as they had begun the winding descent from Piney Ridge down to the French Broad River, the golden pink blush stretching above the eastern skyline had become centered with the first brilliant sliver of the rising sun. . . .

*   *   *

"What about Eliza?" Cutter said suddenly, bringing me back to the night, the warm bottle in my hand and the beer buzz in my head. "You heard from her?"

"Watch out for Deputy Boyce around this curve," I said. "Used to be a favorite spot of his."

"Okay," Cutter said and slammed his foot down on the gas.

Chapter 6
Resolutions

Early on the day after Christmas, the door to my bedroom creaked open.

"Gabe," my mother called softly. "There's a phone call for you. It's Mr. Biggs's office."

When I picked up the receiver from the kitchen counter, the voice in my ear was that of Sandy Jo, the secretary at Biggs Time Entertainment.

"Hold, please, for Mr. Mo Biggs," she said.

A beep sounded, and then I was listening to James Brown's "Papa's Got a Brand New Bag."

The flatness of Sandy Jo's voice, the abruptness of her tone, surprised me. When I used to call Biggs more often, she was always talkative, chatting on and on as if I'd called her instead of her boss.

"Gabriel Tanner, I'll tell you what," Mo Biggs said when he finally came on the line. "Come by my office on your way back to Nashville. I want to talk at you." Then he hung up without setting a day and time, as if he would be there whenever I came.

* * *

I stopped at Biggs's Knoxville office early in the afternoon on New Year's Eve. A little table in the back room held a loaded pizza, a bag of ice and some soft drinks, paper plates and a roll of paper towels.

Mo Biggs picked up two slices together and twisted the stringy cheese with his fingers to break it away from the rest of the pizza.

"I'll tell you what," he said, leaving the back room and motioning me into one of the red velvet chairs in front of the desk. "I got a interesting call from somebody a few days before Christmas. I ain't gonna tell you who it was. Somebody big. Don't ask me how he got my name. I know it wasn't you or Keith since y'all have disowned me for some reason or another."

I started to protest, but the look on Biggs's face stopped me.

Despite its fleshy roundness, the manager's face seemed drawn, its usual ruddiness a bloated ochre. His fingernails shown white when he lifted the pizza to his mouth.

"But I don't care about that right now," he continued, looking down at me from his high chair. "The fact is that this guy called me and not you or that horse thief you hooked up with. Me. I'm the one this big dog called. Let that be a lesson in where your loyalty ought to lay."

I sunk a little deeper into the bright red chair, thinking that my butt couldn't be more than three inches from the floor.

"This guy heard your music one night a couple of months back when he was hanging out in Nashville with Keith and some guys from CBS. He wants you to write for him. Said he used a lawyer to approach BK about buying you and your publishing, but the son of a bitch wouldn't sell. He found out about me somehow and called me up. I sent him copies of the contracts you signed."

So, among all the lies and half-truths I'd convinced myself Keith dealt in, the story of the night spent with men from CBS turned out to be true. And if that actually happened, then maybe the deal to record an album for CBS might be on the up and up as well.

"I'll tell you what," Biggs continued, chewing large bites of pizza as he talked. "He called right back and shamed me for letting you sign something like that. He said the only way you'll get out of Keith's back pocket is to file bankruptcy. Chapter 7 or 11 or 13. Don't remember which right now. But it don't matter. What it'll do is cancel all your personal contracts, including mine. That's why I ain't gonna tell you this big dog's name till you file and then re-sign with me."

Biggs dropped from his chair, went into the back and came out with another plate of pizza.

"Weird, ain't it? By contract, I got the power to tell you what to do, and here I am telling you to break your contract with me." He laughed and shook all over, and for a moment his face took on some of its familiar ruddy tint. Then he turned serious again and began to raise his voice.

"Listen to me, boy. This man is big stuff, and I ain't gonna let you screw it up for me. I'm tired of being jerked around." He pulled a business card from under his telephone and pushed it across his imitation oak desk. "Here's the name and address of a bankruptcy attorney in Nashville. You got an appointment with him a week from Wednesday at two p.m. Show up, or you'll be hearing from my lawyer about breach of contract. Now take the damn card and get the hell out of here."

I took the card from Biggs's pale fingers and, without looking at it, dropped it in my shirt pocket. I heaved myself up from the deep chair and left the room without a word.

"Happy fucking New Year, Gabriel Tanner," Biggs called out around a mouthful of pizza. "And cut that damn ponytail!"

At the front door I paused and looked at Sandy Jo.

She sat with her head down, her hands flitting through the contents of a drawer in her desk.

I stood for a moment, holding the door partway open.

Cold air rustled the fern separating her desk from the wall, but she didn't look up.

I took the card from my pocket, handling it again without looking at it, and tossed it onto her desk, where it slid across and into her lap.

Still she didn't look up.

I pushed the door hard with both hands, and it flew open with a metallic screech of hinges and then a bang against the outside wall. I tried to jump out of the way as the door bounced back, but it caught my heel. I somehow ended up on my butt in the parking lot, leaning back on elbows scraped by cold asphalt and looking at the window of Biggs Time Entertainment.

Behind the sheer red curtains, Sandy Jo sat half hidden by the fern. She was looking at me now.

*   *   *

Red-faced with embarrassment and burning inside and out with anger, I found my way back to I-40 West, and when I reached the Kingston exit I could see relatively straight and became aware again of the world around me.

By the time I stopped in Cookeville for a late lunch before driving the last leg to Nashville, I had decided two things. First, I wasn't going to file bankruptcy just to get out of one bad situation and into another that might be better but easily might not. I had to figure out a way to find faith in Billy Keith again and, at the same time, convince him to let Mo Biggs back in the game. Biggs was more accessible, so I would begin by repairing that relationship first. Then I would figure out what Keith was up to and what he was not, what he was capable of accomplishing on my behalf and what he was not. Jack Widmark had told me to find somebody who could handle my business for me, which I now understood would have to be somebody who could handle Billy Keith for as long as I remained involved with him. That somebody, it had occurred to me around Exit 320, could actually be Mo Biggs, if I gave him a chance.

Second, although I knew I had no head for business, I wanted to believe that I had a heart for people. Behind Biggs's demands and behavior lurked a lot of hurt. I was the cause of much of it. I had conspired with Keith, and Biggs knew. My anger when leaving his place was the anger of a prideful young man caught in the wrong, a young man not to be trusted. I hadn't even noticed I'd become that, and once I took notice, I didn't like it. As inept as I thought Biggs had been in handling the contracts with Keith, I suddenly understood that he was just as inexperienced as I was. Just as overwhelmed and just as excited. Except as the manager, the one who was supposed to know what he was doing, he tried to cover his inexperience and excitement with a façade of bravado. He failed, looking inept and silly. But I remembered how, after those first recording sessions, he listened to the songs all the way back to Knoxville, while I pretended to sleep in the passenger seat. He trusted himself—his ear, his faith in the music, his devotion to the idea of star-making. And he trusted me to be in this with him, which now I knew to be his only real mistake.

I sat in the Cookeville Wendy's and swallowed this embarrassing knowledge along with the final bite of my hot 'n' juicy half-pound double burger.

New Year's Eve had me thinking in terms of resolutions, so I resolved that tomorrow, in the new light of New Year's day, I would think better of Keith and call Biggs to try to repair a trust betrayed or figure out how to begin again.

I continued toward Nashville with the last full belly of the year and the promise of a better frame of mind than I'd managed in weeks.

*   *   *

Lukas and Cassie invited me over for a New Year's Eve celebration. I arrived early and went into the studio with Lukas and George MacDougall to hear the final mixes of the new songs.

"I've asked some potential band members over tonight," Lukas said. "I'll introduce you to them without saying that we're looking for players. You just get a feel for their personalities and see if you like them or not. The drummer's name is Reggie, and the lead guitarist is Hayes. I'm not going to tell you who the bass player is."

By nine-thirty the house was full of people, most of them musicians or songwriters or connected to the music business in some way. Cowboy hats and spiked hair, boots and sneakers, leather skirts and jeans and pant suits. Everybody was between twenty-five and thirty-five, and not one Nashville native among them. A loud and laughing crowd, but nobody drank much except me.

Cassie had small tables with board games and decks of cards set up in almost every room of the house. Music poured into the hall from the studio. Rented movies blared from the television in the den.

I stayed close to Lukas and George. They introduced me to everybody who came in, but I forgot the names of all except the ones Lukas had mentioned beforehand. Most of the guests came in couples, and I wondered what Eliza might be doing tonight, shuddering more than once to think of her dancing the night away in the arms of a stranger that wasn't me.

Reggie looked like he might play anything but drums. He was tall and thin, and his hand when I shook it felt like little more than fragile bones wrapped in soft skin. His voice was high pitched and raspy and quiet, but his laugh was loud and full.

Hayes, on the other hand, could be heard all over the house. He'd come to town from Chicago six months earlier and was moonlighting as a car salesman while he tried to break into the music scene. He never stopped talking, but he was funny and ingratiating. Everybody seemed to like him once they got past the volume and speed of his delivery.

At a quarter of eleven the doorbell rang for the last time that evening—at least the last time I remember. Lukas went out to answer it.

Everybody'd gathered in the living room to await the dropping of the apple into Times Square. That took place according to Eastern Standard Time, and all that would be left to do afterwards was wait for the anti-climactic moment when midnight brought 1985 to those of us living on Nashville time.

Lukas returned from answering the door.

"Hey, people," he said, stepping to one side as he entered the living room. "This is Yvonne Moon. She just moved to town from Dallas. Yvonne, I'll let everybody introduce themselves to you."

She immediately seemed at ease in the crowd, taking a seat in the middle of the floor and joining in on a conversation.

She had the strong, high cheekbones of a model, without the sunken cheeks. Large green eyes, wide smile, dimpled chin. The hands that moved constantly while she talked appeared strong as a man's—if not as large—and yet elegant, with short, perfectly manicured nails. But the most striking thing about her was her hair—cascading ringlets of auburn that flowed down the sides of her neck and onto her breasts and spilled down across her shoulders to the middle of her back.

"Gabriel," she said later, introducing herself and taking my hand in hers as Nashville time moved toward midnight. "That's like the archangel, isn't it? Lukas has been telling me about you, and he gave me a tape of some of your music." She squeezed my hand a little tighter. "I love your songs."

I forced myself to turn away from her as Lukas and Cassie came in from the kitchen with trays of drinks and party favors.

"Let's get ready to bring in our new year," Cassie said. "Everybody take a party hat, a noise maker and a glass of champagne."

Lukas began the countdown of the last fifteen seconds of 1984, and all the guests at the party quickly joined in.

All except two.

Yvonne looked me directly in the eyes as the count hit five, four, three—

"I play bass," she said.

*   *   *

We lay side by side in the dark, on our backs in the floor of her apartment, still wearing our clothes and party hats and listening to Roxy Music's *Avalon*.

As the windows grayed, the room took shape and spun slowly in the first light of New Year's Day. Her furniture sat at odd angles, looking as if it had been trying to arrange itself while she was out and froze when we stumbled through the door. On the floor along the base of the bare walls, unpacked boxes waited for the settling-in. The stereo stood in one corner, its back to the room so that its lights didn't spoil our darkness, and in the opposite corner, a Yamaha amp sat with a sleek black bass guitar leaned against it.

As the piano-and-percussion groove of "To Turn You On" began to fade, Yvonne rolled up on her elbow, leaned over me, kissed me hard on the lips.

My body locked.

She kissed me again.

I lay still, my eyes closed, my mind twirling, my heart pounding.

A third kiss.

This time I kissed back, opening my eyes and looking up into hers.

Roxy's ethereal "True to Life" filled the room while together we rolled over the floor, our heads bumping the legs of furniture, our feet and knees knocking over boxes.

Yvonne kissed hard, bit and sucked my lower lip. Sometimes she sat on my belly and bent over me, pinning me flat on my back while spirals of her long auburn hair fell around my head and chest like jungle foliage thick with night and heat. Sometimes she nibbled my neck and earlobes from behind, her small breasts pressing the flesh beneath my shoulder blades.

"True to Life" faded, and "Tara" began.

I tried to match her athletic intensity, but it was so alien next to the memory of the only passion I'd known. With Eliza, making out had been intense too, but in a different way. This amount of energy might be spent over the course of an hour, not during one song and a short instrumental lasting only five minutes and forty-nine seconds altogether. Passion with Eliza, even those rare times when it became hurried and desperate, was soft and fleshy. Now every stab of knee or elbow told me I was into something different here.

When the distant saxophone and oceanic synths of "Tara" stopped, so did the wallowing, and we once again lay side by side on our backs in the floor.

"Oh, shit," Yvonne said, rubbing her eyes. Her breathing was quick and shallow. "Where the hell did that come from?"

I didn't answer for a moment, just lay staring at the spinning ceiling, my hands rising and falling on my chest like boats on a stormy sea.

"You better be a damn good bass player," I said at last.

*   *   *

I left Yvonne brushing her teeth in the bathroom and drove carefully toward the Music Row area and my apartment on Eighteenth Avenue. I was anxious to shower and crawl into bed, hoping I could ward off the ghost of the New Year's Eve drunk and avoid a vague feeling of shame that had nothing to do with alcohol. The dull sky appeared to have a slight hangover as well, and the streets around me lay gray and empty.

"Whence this shame?" I said aloud, glancing at the rearview mirror to be certain I was as alone on Hillsborough Road as I thought I was.

Part of it, I knew, came from Yvonne's kisses—still on my lips— and the feel of the two of us pressed together and rolling across her apartment floor like wrestlers. Since that night at the Runion Dam Dance, Eliza had been the only love of my waking and dreaming hours, and I'd always been sure the palpable empty space inside me would be there until the day she filled it again. But now the space felt less impermeable, and something—new feelings for Yvonne or maybe just the idea that the space wasn't necessarily Eliza's alone—had begun to seep into it. I felt a little ashamed.

And yet my betrayal of Eliza wasn't the only source of this sense of shame.

Aside from the noise of New Year's Eve and the overnight spent getting to know Yvonne through listening to music together, the voice of Mo Biggs muttered on and on like a nagging faucet drip—*Happy fucking New Year, Gabriel Tanner.* I remembered my Cookeville Wendy's resolution from yesterday, after the ugly meeting with Biggs in Knoxville. In the new light of New Year's Day, I felt ashamed of myself for the call I had to make and for what I had to say when I made it.

At eight-thirty in the morning I passed through the double doors of Billy Keith's quiet office building and slowly climbed the stairs to my apartment. Sunup's wild passion with Yvonne hadn't led to lovemaking, and the build-up without the release, together with my sudden fixation on shame, had left me both tense and tired. I decided it was too early to make the call to Knoxville, so I could shower and sleep first.

I stood at the apartment door, sleepy-eyed, fumbling with my keys.

Inside, the telephone rang, and with Eliza on my mind—with Eliza threatening to slip from my mind—I just knew she was calling to reclaim me. By the second ring, I was in.

"Hello?"

Tinny silence on the other end.

"Hello?" I said again.

Nothing.

I started to hang up, but then I thought I heard something—a stifled giggle, maybe, or a sob.

"Hello?"

"Gabriel?" a girl's voice croaked.

"Yeah. Eliza?"

The line fell silent again for one long moment.

"It's Sandy Jo," she said at last. "In Knoxville."

I closed my eyes and massaged the bridge of my nose.

"Hey, happy New Year, Sandy Jo," I said, remembering how she looked at me yesterday as I sprawled in the parking lot outside her office window, remembering my resolution about Mo Biggs and deciding that she should also be included in the repair work to be begun today. "Are you okay?"

Are you drunk?

"No."

"What's the matter?"

She snuffled twice and exhaled.

"Mo passed away last night," she said then with surprising composure.

Something shorted in my brain, and a sudden loud ringing began in my ears. I couldn't hear anything else for a moment, and my head swam so that I thought I was going to be sick. I reached for the wall and held myself up.

"He had a heart attack, I think," Sandy Jo said. These words blew away the fragments of her self-possession, and she began to sob loudly and uncontrollably.

I stayed on the line, unable to speak, and allowed her her tears. My mind filled with what felt like electric fizzles and pops, as if whatever had snapped in me was trying to reconnect without success.

She finally calmed down.

"He spent the night here last night. With me, you know?" She sniffled loudly again. "Well, about four this morning he woke me up and asked if I had any bicarbonate of soda. Said he ate too much pizza yesterday and had the heartburn real bad."

I managed a grunt.

"I didn't even know what that was, but I went into the bathroom to see what I could find. And then I heard him make this loud noise, you know, like a snore. And I said to myself, 'Why, he's done gone back to sleep.'" She seemed building up to nervously chatty now. The light scrape of a cigarette lighter sounded through the line, followed by an exhalation thick with smoke. "Anyway," she said, "I found something for him and went back to the bed, and, there he was purple in the face, and the rest of him was so pale. The rescue squad said he must've had a massive coronary."

The only mental picture of Mo I could conjure was from the day before, when we were at odds in his office. I glanced around my apartment for a picture of him that might replace the one in my head, but I didn't have one. Not one.

"I didn't think he looked all that good when I saw him yesterday," I said at last.

"He's been looking like that for a while now," she said.

We talked for an hour. Mostly she talked. About how Biggs had promised to take her to Nashville and make her a star. How she'd soon take my place as his top priority. Then about her having to find another job, the possibility of looking for one in Nashville with the experience and contacts she'd gained working for Biggs. In the end, she was laughing a little and sounding more in control of herself.

"Do you have some place you can go?" I asked. "Don't stay there today."

"Oh, I won't, believe you me. I'm going to my mother's."

I stripped in the living room, letting Sandy Jo talk. My resolution to heal things with Mo and forge some kind of working friendship slipped into an abyss and was gone. I felt it drain away. I wanted to remember him with a lump in my throat and tears in my eyes, but all the sadness I could muster wallowed in my own regret, not in his loss. Everything I'd ever felt about Biggs was tainted to some degree with suspicion, tension, anger, plain dislike. Now, on the surface and as deep as I could fathom, tired as I was, I felt only a strange mixture of embarrassed relief and aching guilt.

I was trying to stretch the phone cord far enough into the bathroom to grab hold of my tooth brush when I noticed she wasn't talking anymore.

"Gabriel?" she said in a moment.

"What? I'm sorry, Sandy Jo. I'm really tired. Did you ask me something?"

"He was in the nude."

"Come again?"

"Mo was nude when they came. I couldn't dress him. Do you reckon they'll think he died in the middle of sex and maybe charge me with manslaughter or something? I've seen that on TV maybe." She was beginning to yawn. "Lord, wouldn't it be awful to be found dead in the nude?"

"I've got to get some sleep, Sandy Jo, and you should too." I felt I ought to say more. "You were a good friend to him, and I'm sorry that I wasn't. Keep in touch, okay?"

I brushed my teeth and peed the last of New Year's Eve's beer and champagne.

* * *

A cold bulk lies beside me in the bed. A chill radiates from it.

I glance beneath the sheet and glimpse two bodies, white and naked and nearly touching. Sparse dark hairs on bloodless and flaccid chests and bellies. Knobby knees. Toes tenting the sheet that settles back over our forms.

We are not fully covered like the dead in their winding sheets. I turn my head to see his discolored face. Purpled with a choking rage. I feel in my hands the memory or anticipation of that fleshy throat.

And then I am astraddle him, the sheet slipping from my shoulders and sliding in slow motion down my back to gather on his belly. My fingers dig deep for the windpipe, to reopen the passageway for breath— deep for the carotid arteries, to reanimate the congealed blood.

Suddenly a flood of faceless people surrounds the bed, murmuring and accusing, not understanding.

You killed him!—*from one growling throat.*

* * *

I jolted awake to find myself on my knees in the middle of the bed, sweating and breathing hard, the bedclothes twisted around my arms and waist and thighs.

The room was bright with New Year's Day.

I shut my eyes against the light and bent forward and pressed my forehead into the pillow.

The residue of the dream lingered—the breathless panic of being caught in a compromising position, of a last chance lost beyond recovery.

When my breathing evened, I raised up from the pillow and sat back on my calves, staring for a few moments through the window at the empty back alley. I climbed out of bed and in the kitchen downed two Mexican beers, brushed my teeth once more and, remembering what Sandy Jo said about how Mo was found, slipped on a clean pair of underwear and climbed into bed again.

In the new light of New Year's Day, everything got still and stayed that way for a long time.

Chapter 7
The Songbird

On a blistering Sunday afternoon in the gut of August, I sat in the musty cool of the Songbird Cafe, awaiting my turn to mount the tiny stage and audition for a spot on one of the nightclub's legendary Monday Writers' Night shows. I tried to blame my sweaty palms and dry mouth on the fact that I hadn't performed alone on stage in three years, but I knew I could at that moment play for a packed house in any lounge or coffeehouse on my old circuit and not even flinch. No, the fluttery feeling in my stomach and hands was brought on by the spirit of the Songbird itself, by the ghosts of greatness who had filled this room with their legendary music—Roger Miller, Kris Kristofferson, Willie Nelson, Harlan Howard, Dolly Parton, Harvey McDibb, Townes Van Zandt, Bob McDill, Jerry Jeff Walker, Guy Clark, Rodney Crowell, Nanci Griffith.

And on and on to Gabriel Tanner.

I smoked and sipped ice water, checked my tuning a third time, and glanced around the room. Although I'd lost count of the evenings spent here over the last three years, this was the first time I'd seen the inside of the place in the light of day.

The room that seemed so romantic and promising at night when the music was playing—the smoky globes on its lights, its shiny wooden bar, the wall behind its stage that was filled with autographs of the stars who'd made the Songbird famous—looked dull and worn and faded, like a thirty-year-old snapshot. Dark corners that at night gave the impression of being deep, of hiding mysterious and important people, were lit and made ordinary by the sunshine that reflected from buildings and parked cars on the other side of Twenty-First Avenue.

There were nineteen other people in the club for the auditions, probably a little over half of them songwriters, I guessed. Some, like me, sat alone with a guitar, while others sat with two or three extra musicians brought along either to beef up the sound of their songs or to bolster their courage—probably both. Now and then somebody strummed a quiet chord. The buzz of low conversation mixed with a slight hum and hiss coming from the PA system.

I turned at the sound of glass clinking behind the bar.

Mason Queenan, the manager of the Songbird, who earlier let the line of songwriters into the club and offered us ice water and soft drinks and then disappeared through a swinging door to the left of the bar, had suddenly reappeared and was fixing himself a drink. He wore a Hawaiian shirt that looked several sizes too big for him and khaki shorts that hung almost to his knees. His sandy brown hair was cut short and combed straight back. He looked up, and the light from the large front window reflected off his round-framed glasses.

"Anyone want another round before we start?" he asked.

When he finished the refills, he strolled up to the front of the room and handed a pen and a piece of paper to a blond girl sitting at one of the front tables.

"While this sign-up sheet gets passed around," he said, "I'm going to tell you a little about what we'll be doing here today. As you all probably know, our Monday Writers' Night showcases new writers, with the added attraction of an established writer who headlines each of the shows. These auditions aren't about whether or not you'll be scheduled on a show, but they give me the chance to see what I've got so I can balance the shows between more and less experienced writers."

The front door squeaked open, and a tall young woman struggled to maneuver her guitar case into the room. Her straight shoulder-length black hair caught the brilliant light outside and reflected it in rainbow colors like the feathers of a raven. Once inside, she stood near the door with her sunglasses on, looking lost.

"Sorry I'm late," she said with a wide grin, her face turned toward nobody in particular.

"That's okay, Tara," Mason Queenan said, smiling. "When your eyes adjust, there's a sign-up sheet going around. Get on it." He turned back to the room. "Now. I'll call names at random from the list. Come up and play me your best two songs. If you can stay until we're finished, I'll be able to tell you what night you'll be on the show."

The girl who had come in late brought him the sign-up sheet and took the perfect seat, where I could see her face and watch her without seeming to stare.

"Those of you who have to leave, do so quietly," Queenan said, scanning the list in his hand. "You can call in the next day or two and talk to somebody on the staff. The schedule will be by the phone. Finally, whatever night you're supposed to play, you'll need to be here by eight forty-five at the latest." He took a sip from his drink. "So, let's get started with, uh ... Martin Brown?"

I listened to the first part of each song the writers before me played. Most of the tunes were hard county fare—twangy and nasal tales about good love gone bad and illicit love gone good, Mama in the garden and outlaws on the run. Some were folksy stories about growing up in this town or that. Two or three were pop tunes—wistful remembrances of young love, complete with all the stock phrases and images heard up and down Casey Kasem's *American Top 40*. The rest of the time I spent stealing glances at the girl Mason Queenan had called Tara.

She sat very straight in her chair a couple of tables to my left, still with her sunglasses on, her guitar across her lap. She never turned her face away from the stage when somebody was performing. Her forehead creased slightly as she concentrated on the songs about love or death. Below the diminutive nose that curved up a little at the end, her full lips spread into a gleaming model's smile at every cute play on words. She pulled together the length of her shiny black hair and held it up off her slender neck and sat like that for the longest time.

In breathless increments, I traced the profile of her figure down to her trim waist.

So much like Eliza. Dark hair. Pale skin. Soft—

"Let's hear from Gabriel Tanner," Mason Queenan said.

I slung the strap across my shoulders and, holding the guitar tightly against my side, weaved my way through the small round tables to the stage. I adjusted the microphone and cleared my throat, searching for something to say as an introduction.

"My songs are a little different," I said and immediately wished I hadn't. I felt my face redden. "Anyway," I said and punched out the staccato rock rhythm of "Siren, Sing."

I hear the lonely voice calling from the distant hills,
And in the mist of a dream I run, to you I run . . .

I tried to hold eye contact with the small audience of songwriters but found myself looking past the faces and tables and chairs to the sparkling glasses that hung above the bar. My voice cracked, and my mouth dried. I closed my eyes and pretended it was that warm, blustery Saturday in the beginning of March when I'd sat with my guitar on the front steps of Billy Keith's office building and tried to capture in this song something I'd felt while reading Homer.

In the process of the writing, I'd thought Eliza far from my mind—she'd never been one to sing much, especially when I was listening. I'd hoped that the story of Odysseus and the Sirens would help me begin writing something that moved away from her. But in the first line, the voice that called to me from the hills was hers, and the more I looked, the more I found her hidden all through the lyrics. Even her absence was a kind of presence, and the reality that she wasn't calling to me from anywhere anymore colored the song and my performance.

Siren, sing to me,
And I will follow your voice.
Though I be lost at sea,
Still I have no other choice . . .

My smoky rasp sent these words leaping from my lips like souls from a burning building, escaping the pain hot on their heels. I ended the song with light touches on the guitar strings and a whispery voice and then stood holding my breath in the moment of roaring silence that followed.

Then everybody began clapping loudly.

I released my breath so hard that it popped in the microphone, and my face reddened again.

The small crowd reacted the same to the second song—"Best I've Ever Seen"—a moment like stunned silence and then loud applause and whistles.

I stepped off the stage and kept my eyes on the floor as I made my way to my seat.

"Very, very nice," Mason Queenan said from beside the stage. He stood quietly for a moment, staring at me, and then went on with the auditions. "Jimmy Austin?"

The beautiful latecomer was last to perform—Tara Southerland was the name Queenan called. She stepped on stage and took off her sunglasses and turned around to face the microphone.

Her eyes captivated me. They were just a shade off electric blue, leaning slightly toward aquamarine; an illusion created by contact lenses, I knew, but I couldn't look away from them. And through every bar of her two songs, those rare gems—set in alabaster, framed in ebony—never left me. While others in the club began to squirm in their seats, glancing back and forth between her and me, her gaze never broke down, and I never flinched.

* * *

"Let's see, Gabriel," Mason Queenan said, looking over the schedule he'd been scribbling as each songwriter auditioned. "Well, I know this is a long while off, but I'd like to have you do the show on September twenty-third."

"Okay," I said. "If you think that's best."

"We're going to have Harvey McDibb that night."

"You're kidding."

"He only does this for me once every two or three years, and I want you to meet him and let him hear your songs." Queenan pulled a jangling jumble of keys from his pocket, raised a section of the bar and walked through. "It'll be a packed house. Lots of industry folks, people who need to hear you."

"I appreciate that," I said. "I'd wait a year to play on the same show as Harvey McDibb."

Queenan started for the door, and I picked up my guitar and followed.

"Are you working with anyone in town?" Queenan asked.

"Well, sort of. I have a publishing and production deal with Billy Keith. There's not much happening with it though."

The club owner wrinkled his nose.

"How'd you get thrown in with Billy Keith?"

"It's a long and sad story." I put a hand on the door and looked at the empty Sunday afternoon outside. "Through a former friend of mine."

"I'm not surprised it's a former friend," Mason Queenan said. "Anyone that would hook you up with Billy Keith." He jangled his keys again. "Well, say hello the next time you're in, okay?"

I stepped out into the bright late afternoon sunlight and stood looking up and down the street for a moment.

Tara Southerland.

Then I sighed and shook my head and walked to my car.

* * *

I sat on the floor of the apartment, leaning back against the couch, watching the last red-gold light of the day fade from Music Row. When the color was gone, I downed the last of my third beer, heaved myself up from the floor, and dialed Yvonne's number.

"Hello?" The voice on the other end sounded thick and unfamiliar.

"Yvonne?"

"Oh, Gabriel, it's you."

"You sound like something stuck to the bottom of a pig farmer's shoe."

"Fuck you," she said tightly. There was the click of a cigarette lighter. "I feel bad enough without comments like that."

"Sorry. What's the problem?"

"Me and Thor got skunked by a bottle of something last night. He ended up staying." She exhaled smoke and then fell into a brief fit of coughing. "Geez, I can't even remember what it was we were drinking," she said in an even raspier voice.

"Thor's the guy that works with you at the record store?"

"Yeah," she said, yawning. "He's got the look but not the balls, you know? He's like a clinging vine or something. I kicked his ass out first thing this morning." She took another long drag on her cigarette. "I don't think I'll be seeing him anymore."

"How're you gonna pull that off?"

"I thought I told you."

"Told me what?"

"I must've just meant to call you and then thought I had."

"What?"

"I'm quitting the store," she said. "I got a job as a teacher's aide up at Whites Creek High."

"Really?" I said.

"School starts two weeks from tomorrow. I've got some things to do there next week, but it won't really get going for me until the kids come in."

"How'd you get into that?"

"I double majored in Psychology and Education back at North Texas. Of course, the only thing I told you guys about was the bands I played in." She blew the smoke of another long drag into the receiver and fell into another fit of coughing. "Sorry," she wheezed. "Oh, I feel like shit."

"Well, I was going to ask if you wanted to go out and get drunk, but maybe you'd better not. Wanna go to Dalt's and get something to eat."

"Oh no, I can't eat. Don't even mention it. I just feel like going to bed."

"Well, that's okay," I said.

"But listen, next Sunday's my last one without school the next day. Let's do dinner and a movie and my place after, okay?"

"Sounds like a date," I said and told her good-bye and hung up.

I flipped open the phone book and turned the pages until my finger landed on the name "Southerland T K." I dialed the number, cleared my throat and swallowed hard.

"Hello?" a female voice answered.

"Hi, is this Tara Southerland?"

"Who's this?"

"It's Gabriel Tanner. I saw you today down at the Songbird."

"Oh, sure. How are you? I really loved your songs."

"Thanks very much." I cleared my throat again. "Look, I was wondering if you'd like to go out to eat or something some time. Maybe talk about songwriting?"

"I'm sorry," she said, "but I'm seeing someone. I guess I'd better not."

"Well, darn," I said, feeling my face redden. "I just really enjoyed listening to you today."

"Well, thanks, Gabriel," she said. "That's sweet. I'll see you at the Songbird some time, okay?"

I hung up the receiver, closed the telephone book and went to the refrigerator for another beer.

* * *

Three hours before I was due at the Songbird, I telephoned Billy Keith. As usual the first ring was stopped short, and the tinny recording of his voice came on the line.

"Uh, BK, it's me," I said after the beep. "Tonight's my night at the Songbird. Just wanted to remind you. Harvey McDibb's the headliner. I've got a couple of new songs I'm going to try out. I hope you'll come hear them. Show starts at nine, but I'll be there early if you want to come in and have a cup. It seems like forever since I talked to you in person. Bye."

At nine o'clock, I sat at the Songbird's bar, alone in the crowd.

Tara Southerland had smiled and waved when she arrived, but she didn't come over and speak to me. She sat at a table in the middle of the room with Cy Popham—in A&R at Polygram Records—and Harvey McDibb. All three leaned their heads close together over the table, talking and drinking.

I tried to find something or somebody else to fix my attention on, but my eyes kept wandering to her—to her and Harvey McDibb. In the end, I turned my back to the crowd and sat watching the reflections of stage lights and movements in the glasses that hung from a rack above the blond barmaid.

"Ready?" The voice sounded in my ear just as the hand touched my shoulder.

I turned enough to see Mason Queenan.

"Am I on first?"

"No," he said. "Actually, you're after the break, just before Harvey.

I'm only checking. You look a little tense."

"Yeah, well, you know," I said and grinned into another sip of the beer.

Mason patted me on the back.

"You'll do fine," he said. "Just don't drink so much that you forget your lyrics."

While the first two writers performed, Cy Popham and Harvey McDibb passed the time with a constant stream of talk and drink. The rumbled murmur of Popham's deep voice grated like a hum from the speaker system. McDibb's strained whisper blended with the amplified rake of pick over guitar strings. Finally, during the third writer's second song, Mason made his way to the table and leaned in between the two men for a moment and then walked away, patting McDibb on the shoulder as he went and leaving a quiet table behind him.

The night progressed with the usual songs about partying the country way, dead mothers missed, loving and cheating in love, and the various forms of misunderstanding that come between women and men. But almost every writer seemed to have at least one good song in which the emotion rang true or the humor hit home or the melody was sweet.

I worked my way through two more beers and studiously watched the stage over the heads of Tara Southerland, Cy Popham, and Harvey McDibb. I felt myself playing the jealous man, the stricken courtly lover. But whenever Tara turned from the nervous writer on stage to her companions, my attention gravitated toward her profile. She was like a star in the little universe of that room, and I was her farthest, coldest satellite, swinging away in the darkness.

Popham took her with him when he left at the beginning of the break.

The waitress delivered two drinks to the table, and with one in each hand, McDibb rose stiffly and disappeared through a narrow door to the left of the stage.

Almost an hour later, after the break and two more writers, I stood under the lights without saying a word and checked my tuning, my eyes scanning the crowd from beneath lowered brows.

Several faces looked familiar in the glow of the lights, but I couldn't place them or give them names. Mason stood back in the shadows with the sound man. McDibb stood leaning against the door he'd disappeared through earlier.

My concentrated picking at the strings evolved into a chord progression, and I stepped up to the microphone.

I must have dreamed myself a shackled ghost,
And to you I was bound—
The spirit of Valentino, following you around.
But you knew I would never hurt you;
Maybe that's why you never cared.
Had I become wild and dangerous,
Would you have beckoned me upstairs?

When I finished my third song, loud applause filled the Songbird. Mason appeared beside me, caught my arm and leaned close to my ear.

"Plan to stay late with us," he said above the applause. Then into the microphone for the crowd, "Gabriel Tanner, ladies and gentlemen, Gabriel Tanner!"

I packed my guitar away and headed for the bar through the tangle of legs and handshakes and stares. I heard Mason introducing McDibb as I waited for another beer. When the cold bottle was in my hand, I turned back toward the stage.

Harvey McDibb sat on a stool, weaving slightly. His thick white hair glowed the blended color of the stage lights—mostly yellow, with highlights of purple and green. The harsh light darkened the lines that framed his mouth, creased his forehead and feathered the corners of his eyes. His eyelids drooped, and in spite of the yellowish light, the whites of his eyes shone dull and red. His fingers stumbled through runs up the neck, fell clutching at chords.

"Oh shit," he said with a weak smile. "I'm fuckin' drunk."

The crowd laughed, and I winced.

"Come on, Harvey," I whispered.

McDibb opened his eyes wide and drew a deep breath that whistled in the microphone.

"Can't call a damn song to mind," he said. "Yell one out."

"'TV Heroes,'" somebody said from the left side of the room.

The song had been a recent number one hit for The Highwaymen.

"Yeah," somebody said from the other side of the room.

"Hmm, a new one?" McDibb slurred. "Damn hard. Damn hard. But I'll give it a try."

He got a firm grip on the opening E, strummed it a time or two and eased into a breezy Tex-Mex rhythm.

Hey-hey, Tonto, what do you say?
Let's try something different today.
What would you think if maybe we robbed a train?

"Fuck that," he growled as his left hand fell completely off the neck of the guitar and swung at his side. "Give me something else. Something old, goddammit!"

The room was quiet for a moment.

"'Common Girl,'" a voice as slurred as McDibb's said.

"Hell, that's more like it." The old songwriter almost laughed. "Played and heard that one enough I ought to be able—" He coughed loudly into the microphone and found the opening chords.

In the redneck backwoods country of Tennessee
Her folks met one Friday at the grocery.
Banging carts and falling cigarette cartons shook their world,
And led to the birth of a common girl . . .

McDibb started more songs than he finished, but he seemed to sober slightly over the next half hour. The sobering brought with it a mellow ending.

"Thank you, folks, and thanks to Mason," McDibb said. "I always enjoy myself here at the Songbird." He drew a gentle breath and closed his eyes. "But Casper's dancing slow against the mountains, and winter's coming on. I'll see you again in a couple of years."

The crowd cleared out, and I sat nervously drumming my fingers on a table.

"Gabriel Tanner," Mason said as he pulled out two chairs, "meet Harvey McDibb."

I stood slightly and shook hands with the man.

McDibb grunted as he sat down heavily, still gripping my hand and nearly pulling me across the table. Then he let go and turned to Mason.

"Business always good as it was tonight?"

"Pretty close to it," Mason said. "It's always best when you come to town, but as long as I can keep finding writers like Gabriel in the meantime, I'll do okay."

McDibb's eyes were red again, and he looked at me for a moment, not smiling and not frowning.

"Tanner. That your real name?"

"Yessir, it is. I got it from my—"

"Go home, boy," the old songwriter slurred. "Just go home. You got no damn business here." The last word faded into a growl. "Mason says you're working with Billy Keith. That right?"

I didn't move. My insides began to tighten from stomach to throat.

"Shed him like water off a fucking duck's back," McDibb said. He turned again to Mason. "Billy's fun to play with but a son of a bitch to work with. You know that."

"He's been pretty good to me," I said.

McDibb waved his thick left hand in my direction but didn't look at me.

"Recording this boy? Making an artist out of him? Bullshit. You know that, Mason."

Mason's eyes widened behind his glasses.

"North Carolina, Mason says." McDibb looked at me again and blinked hard. "Go back to your mountains, boy. Not to that heart-breaking little bitch you sing about, but to your mountains." Spittle popped from his lips and foam formed at the corners of his mouth. "You're a good writer. A damn good writer. But this town'll pick at you 'til you're nothing but a pile of bleached bones." He changed his voice to a gruff mocking whine. "We need a hit, Tanner. Minimum three hundred dates this year, Tanner. Kiss this DJ's ass, Tanner." He planted his hands on the table and pushed himself to his feet.

Mason stood up awkwardly, his eyes still wide, his mouth open to speak. But he said nothing.

I felt a tightening around my own eyes. I leaned forward to stand

and nearly lunged across the table to wrestle the old man to the floor. Instead I took hold of the handle of my guitar case and stood up, glanced once at Mason, turned and headed for the door.

"If you're a real writer," Harvey McDibb said from behind me, "this town'll kill that part of you. Why do you think I live in Wyoming?"

I turned when I got clear of the tables and stood staring. Curses boiled in my chest, ready to spew. But some kind of stranglehold—too much confusion or anger, too much mountain-folk reserve, too much Christian-Southern-gentlemanly manners—silenced me. So I turned again and pushed open the door and stumbled out into the warm air of the September night.

Chapter 8
Rain on the River

Around the first of the year, Chaz Wontall left CBS to work with another company, taking with him most of the A&R staff that had been behind my project. The new album I'd recorded with Billy Keith during October and November couldn't fly through CBS's system without them, so it died. When I asked why we couldn't follow Wontall and the others to the new label, Billy said he'd already looked into that and found out they were going after the urban dance market and my music didn't fit.

Billy made one last push to get something to happen, spending the middle two weeks of March in New York—"Making the rounds with our stuff," he said. He took with him pictures of us in the recording studio that had already appeared in *Billboard*, camera-ready artwork for the album's cover, liner notes and a storyboard for the video of "Best I've Ever Seen."

But nothing happened. Another disappointment for me, another failure for Billy Keith.

Next thing I knew, he'd booked ten April days in a Nashville studio called The Platinum Mine and was set to begin working with Bobby Dale Cogburn, a country act in whom several Music Row labels were rumored to be interested.

On the morning of the first session, he was in his office early, and at 9:45, as he was leaving for the studio, he knocked on my door to tell me to drop by "the Mine" around lunch time. He was having Bobby Dale record a country version of one my newer songs, "Thunder and Lightning," and he wanted me there to help out with any ideas I had as the tracks were recorded.

I skipped out on the lunch invitation and walked into the control room at around half past one.

After shaking my hand, Billy leaned back in the producer's seat and watched as George MacDougall tinkered with some buttons on the board. A couple of the same musicians I recorded my first sessions with sat on the other side of the glass, along with two guys I'd never seen—a fiddler and a steel guitar player. To the left of them, in a booth adjacent to the piano room, Bobby Dale stood in a pool of light with the microphone hanging above him and listened to Billy's easy drawl in his headphones, watching, I knew, through the window for every wink and smile that told him he was doing just fine.

Keith was cutting corners.

I'd wondered when I found out he was recording at The Platinum Mine, despite its name a shabby place compared to Bullet. But I knew it for sure as soon as George started the tape rolling and my recording of "Thunder and Lightning" blasted through the speakers.

They didn't do a country version of my song that afternoon. Not from scratch anyway. They erased my voice from the existing track and replaced it with Bobby Dale's twang. They changed the bass and lead guitar and added flourishes from the fiddle and wails from the steel. But it wasn't until Billy decided—almost as an afterthought—to drop my driving acoustic guitar track in favor of a country shuffle from the lead player's electric that the thievery was complete.

"That's a take," Billy said. "Come on in and listen, boys."

There was a twinkle in the new kid's eyes as George's rough mix of the song played through, and the face beneath his cowboy hat was split by a usurper's wide grin.

I had the door halfway open when Keith finally turned to look at me. "What do you think, Gabby?"

"Sounds like a hit," I said and headed out for the bar at Brown's Diner.

*   *   *

On the first Saturday night in May, Lonesome Star rocked MacArthur's. Smoke curled around the red, yellow, blue and white lights that hung overhead at the front of the stage. The nearest people, visible in the blended light, jerked their heads back and forth in rhythm or swayed from side to side. Some of our regulars plugged their ears with their fingers to hear the lyrics better and sang along. Knotted groups smoked and drank but still moved, their faces a blur at the edge of the lights. The larger part of the capacity crowd bounced in darkness, silhouetted against the glowing screens of the video games lining the wall at the back of the club.

Tonight's packed house had been a long time coming. The band and I had been playing at MacArthur's and other clubs around town for eight months, on off nights in the beginning, but finally gathering enough of a following to play a weekend night or two. Now it was every weekend, and if not in Nashville, then somewhere else close by—Bowling Green or Murfreesboro or Chattanooga.

Lukas's hands moved back and forth from the blacks and whites of his keyboard stack to his sweat-soaked blond hair. Hayes chunked out the seething guitar rhythm, seeming barely able to hold back until the time he could cut loose on his solo. Reggie pounded his drums, slinging sweat from his brow, screaming the high background vocals. Locked beat for beat with him, Yvonne fingered her bass, her swirling auburn mane spilling across half her face, her large green eyes always on me.

I stomped my right foot, but my boot connected only with the pounding drum. The flesh and bone of my thighs and hips vibrated sympathetically with the velvet-gloved touch of the bass. The electric guitar and keyboards whirled around me like hawks and doves. My old acoustic guitar—the Guild now with a pickup mounted in the bridge but still the same old friend I'd discovered by the tree one distant Christmas morning—felt as much a part of me as my hair and teeth.

It's a river of pain and laughter,
Of life and love so sweet,
Running with tears and wine and blood,
From a trickle to a flood in a heart beat.

My mother had said Eliza was dating somebody seriously now. I tried to picture her with an unfamiliar man, but I couldn't. I'd seen her only with me, the gay hairdressers she worked with, the men of her family and mine. I pictured her standing in a doorway—her wrist hooked on the edge of the door, her head tilted sideways and leaning on the back of her hand, her dark bangs falling lightly across her moonlit forehead, the glint of her blue eyes shadowed by the wisps of hair. She'd be watching a figure standing in the darkness outside the door. Who would he be? What would she call him?

At two o'clock in the morning, the second show long over and the crowd gone, I sat at a small round table, rubbing my knuckles in my eyes and trying to come back to life long enough to finish the cold beer Yvonne brought me from the bar.

She sat across the table.

The rest of the band had packed up and headed home, and the only other people left were the bartender and one of the waitresses.

"You sounded great tonight," Yvonne said. "Sang your butt off."

"Thanks," I said, yawning. "It was a great crowd to play for." I looked at her out of the corner of my eye as I turned the bottle up, sucked out the last of the beer and set the bottle on the table. "That new bass rig you've got really brings out how well you play. Sometimes I nearly lost what I was doing while I listened to you."

"It's clean. I can't imagine how I ever got by without it."

"Probably on your looks," I said.

She laughed.

"Either you're drunk or this light's ruining your eyes."

"I'm not completely sober, but my eyes are perfect," I said and stood up. "Come on. I'll drive you home."

Along the way I pulled into an all night drive-thru to get some ice water.

There was another car in front of us at the service window, and two people in the back seat were making out wildly, their hands at times running through each other's hair and at other times disappearing out of sight, their faces never apart.

I sat with Yvonne beside me and watched in silence.

"Get a room," she said and laughed.

When I had my ice water, I settled the cup between my thighs and pulled back onto the almost deserted street.

"Gabriel," Yvonne said. "When I'm thirty, will you ask me to marry you?"

"What?" The street blurred in front of me as her words blared in my mind. "What?" I said again and turned to look at her.

She looked at me without a smirk of sarcasm or the hint of a joking smile.

"Yvonne, you're only twenty-three," I said. "What goes on over the next seven years?"

"Oh, just enjoy life, you know? So many places and things I want to see and do. But I should be finished by the time I'm thirty." She looked out the window toward the darkened shops along West End Avenue. "And besides, I figure you'll be over that woman back in North Carolina by then."

"What woman?"

"Get real, Gabriel. I know the words to your songs."

I cleared my throat and switched lanes for the upcoming turn into Yvonne's neighborhood.

"That ended years ago," I said. "I haven't seen her since."

"Will you tell me what happened?"

"I had to come to Nashville, and she wouldn't come with me. So we ended it."

"Bullshit," Yvonne said and punched me in the arm.

* * *

Early the next morning, I called information for Area Code 704 in North Carolina.

"What city, please?"

"Asheville."

"Can I help you?"

"The number for Eliza Garrison."

I could hear the operator breathing as she pecked on a keyboard.

"I'm sorry, sir," she said, "but I don't have a listing for anyone by that name."

"Oh, okay." I started to hang up, but then, "How about Eliza Tanner? T-A-N-N-E-R."

Again, pecking on a keyboard.

"Sir, I have an Elizabeth Tanner," the operator said.

"That'd be it."

"Thank you. Wait one moment, please."

A computer voice came on the line and gave me the number.

I broke the connection and called without writing it down.

"Yeah?" The man's voice was overloud, angry-sounding and slurred with sleep.

I hung up.

*   *   *

Five years.

Nothing but boxes and boxes of master tapes lined up on a shelf in the storage vault at Bullet, nothing but pages and pages of lyrics stuffed into a drawer in the filing cabinet behind Kate's desk.

Billy Keith and I had been friends out on the farm, mentor and student in the office, co-creators in the studio, co-conspirators, I believed, in the death of Mo Biggs. But a silence had grown between us as real as the silence of Biggs's grave in Knoxville's Old Gray Cemetery, a silence that hung in the emptiness of the landing at the top of the staircase, my dusty apartment behind one door, his glittering wall of old awards behind the other.

June 1986. Billy and I were finished. The five-year contracts between us had expired on the 18th of May. I remembered that day in 1981 and the anxious twist in my gut as Mo Biggs pushed me into contracts with him and Billy Keith. But I also remembered the excitement and hope, the way my star seemed to be in the control room at Bullet, shining on the three of us and close enough to touch. As George MacDougall worked on a headphone mix of "Lacy," the song visible at that moment in dancing LED meters on the muted soundboard, I signed my name by studio starlight.

To what end?

Friendship and work with Mo had fallen apart, leaving him angry and bitter, broken for no reason and, finally, dead. He lay beyond amends, and I was left fractured in a way that refused to heal. Friendship and work with Billy had fallen apart, leaving him no less distant than he'd been for most of the years I'd known him. He was now in the studio with the next man, another singer, and I was five years older, mired in distrust of my judgment, my gift and my dream. My marriage to Eliza had fallen apart, leaving her far away in another life with another man, the next man. She was now more mystery and mirage to me than real woman, and yet for almost five years I'd looked for her in every potential lover who crossed my path and mourned her loss in song after song after song.

Five years.

To what end?

I'd seen a lawyer to make sure the break would be clean. At my request, she wrote Billy a letter to confirm the expiration of the contract. I signed and mailed it.

I lay on the bed in my apartment, clothes still on from a late night of drinking and packing. Earlier, I'd heard Billy come in. Now my heart raced as I heard Kate flirting with the mailman, heard her slicing open an edge of each envelope, heard the rustle of paper as she pulled out the contents. I knew when she opened my letter, knew by the pause that was longer than when the envelope contained a bill or a royalty statement. I heard the wheels on her chair squeak, heard her feet on the stairs and then her quick quiet rap on Billy's door.

My telephone rang two minutes later.

"Gabby," Billy said in his most smiling voice. "Got your letter, son. You didn't have to pay a lawyer to do that. Could've just come into the office and pointed it out to me."

"Yeah, well, you've been busy with your new star and all. I just wanted something we could both keep on file."

"I certainly do appreciate you looking out for me, my boy. Hell, I ain't had time to even wipe my ass in weeks."

How many times had my telephone repeated that expression? It'd been funny the first time I heard it, and I'd laughed at it almost every time since.

"Gabby?" Billy said.

"Oh, I understand," I said.

"When I get Bobby Dale situated in the studio, I'll go to my lawyer's and get some new contracts put together real quick like. Meet me for lunch down at the deli. Say around two?"

"Okay."

I hung up the receiver, unplugged the telephone and moved quietly around the apartment, finishing packing and stacking boxes neatly by the door.

* * *

The day was hot and gray around me, stuffy already, like the doldrums of July or August. The still air in the parking lot held a mixture of food smells and garbage, peat, the flowering of late Spring.

I waited in the shade of an oak growing next to the alley behind Stage Deli, sitting on the hood of my car and smoking, watching the people in the booths by the windows of the restaurant.

The silence of forks and knives against their plates, the pantomime of their conversations and laughter, made me think of the people as unreal, as bodies empty of souls, going through the motions of living. It reminded me of something, something it took a few moments to remember. A train passing along the tracks between Runion and Stackhouse Park, a train thundering unheard through the mountain night, thundering silently past a celebration in progress. The Dam Dance—my ears filled with music and my eyes with Eliza while a train passed by, so unstoppable yet so easily missed.

I licked my lips, took a deep breath and continued to wait.

When Keith's yellow Mercedes pulled into the parking space beside me, I hopped down from my car, opened the heavy passenger door and dropped into the seat.

He didn't turn off the engine.

"Hey," I said. "I don't feel much like eating."

Keith squirmed in his seat and straightened his back, both hands still on the wheel.

"Sure," he said.

The air conditioner roared like a wind tunnel, now and then pulling in the outside smells.

"This is hard as hell," I said.

He looked straight ahead. Deep lines cut his face, dark under the brim of his cowboy hat. His eyes were red, and the lids seemed to droop a little more than usual.

"I know, son," he said.

"I think maybe it's time I tried something else."

"I figured."

He didn't seem to have any papers from his lawyer, so the speech I'd worked out didn't fit the moment. Something in the hunch of his shoulders said he didn't need or want to hear it.

"I'll have my stuff out of the apartment by this evening."

"Don't worry about it, son. There ain't no rush." He turned and looked at me for the first time since I got in the car. "What about when your record comes out? Where you gonna be? We'll need to negotiate something then."

"I don't know. I've been looking around for a place to rent. In the meantime, I'll stay with George or Lukas. Kate will know when I find something."

"Fine. That'll be just fine." His right hand slid off the steering wheel and floated, open, toward me. "Been a pleasure, son."

"Same here," I said. "Thanks for everything." I released my steady grip on his hand and opened the door. When I was out, I leaned back down and said, "Come hear the band when you get a chance."

"I'll try to make time. Heard good things about it." He eased the car into gear. "Keep in touch, son. Let's get together and have a cup now and again."

"Sounds good. I'd like that."

I let the door close with a solid thud, then stood and watched the car roll slowly away down the alley, feeling the old man's eyes watching me in the rearview mirror.

When the Mercedes turned at the cross street and disappeared, I looked up at the white sky. There was a lightness inside me, an emptiness like a vacuum, and I began my wait for the future to rush thundering in to fill it.

Chapter 9
Nashville Scenes

The Songbird crowd listened in pin-drop silence as I slid through transition chords and took up the second verse.

Every true heart has the dream of flying
Without fear of falling.
We stand on this ledge in answer
To love's higher calling.
Gold to blue to gray
To black with night and rain—
It's always the same big sky,
And every inch is ours to fly.

As I felt the energy in the room sharpen, directing both me and my listeners into the refrain, I was glad that the Harvey McDibb episode hadn't dampened Mason Queenan's enthusiasm for my music. We talked a lot those days, Mason and I, especially since Billy Keith was out of my professional picture. The owner of the Songbird knew about songwriting and had a good ear for what rang true in a lyric.

To the bridge!

When real life seems to steal the dream,
Don't let it break your heart,
Though these bodies tight to this earth cling.
We can still lean back in laughter—
We can still take to the sky,
'Cause these hearts have earned their wings.

When Mason asked me to fill a Saturday night cancellation, I jumped at the chance, glad that Lonesome Star's increasingly busy schedule was open on that date. Playing solo at the Songbird gave me opportunities I didn't get playing with the band at MacArthur's or somewhere out of town. The opportunity to reach a new audience, for one. Some of the developing group of Lonesome Star satellites followed me into this intimate little venue, but many of the faces lit by the candles on the tables and the reflection of the stage lights were at best vaguely familiar or else completely new to me. The opportunity to experiment with my songs was another gift from the Songbird. With no set band arrangement to worry about, I explored a different range of emotions and textures in Lonesome Star songs, and I tried out pieces the band didn't play.

For the attentive ears in this audience, I played "Soul Mates," a new song built around what had now become an old theme of mine. The lyric was based on a dream I'd had back in early March when the jonquils trespassed the calendar's border between winter and spring to herald the quickening of the world. In the dream I could fly. The flying was as real to me as the sound of my voice in the Songbird's speakers, the feel of the strings beneath the press of my calloused fingertips, the close warmth of the bodies and breaths in this listening room. I flew low, keeping under a dark and sagging belly of rain clouds. Surprise and excitement teased my breath away by the moment. But I wasn't afraid. Even though I knew the voice of reason, still nestled under the covers in my new apartment on Sixteenth Avenue, said in dreamy tones that I would fall, I couldn't hear it. And because I couldn't hear it, I wasn't afraid. That's partly the case, at least.

What really thrilled me about the flying was my shadow. Eliza was my shadow, my shadow in spite of the darkness. She floated beneath me, looking up as I looked down. She rose when I passed over Lonesome Mountain, rose so close that I could almost touch her. Almost. She fell far away when for a moment I sailed out over some still body of water. She danced up and down and side to side when I returned to the rolling hills of Tennessee. But when I crash-landed in the alley behind the Stage Deli, she was gone.

*   *   *

"Wonderful as usual," Mason said when I joined him at a table opposite the door through which the friendly crowd slowly disappeared into the night.

"Thanks," I said, both to him and to the tall waitress who brought me the cold beer.

"I think you won some new fans tonight," he said. "And I think you turned some of your regulars on to something they haven't heard before." He smiled and waved at a couple just rising from their table. "I'll bet some of them are going to want to hear a solo or two at the next Lonesome Star gig."

I smiled and pulled long and hard at my beer.

"I know you don't like to hear this," Mason said, raising a hand to get the waitress's attention and then pointing a finger at my already nearly empty bottle to tell her to have another ready, "but there's something in your solo performances that the band just can't—" He stopped, then rushed ahead. "It's a good band, don't get me wrong. It's even great sometimes, but there's something magical that happens when it's just you and the guitar."

"Thanks," I said again, not sure how to take these compliments. I fumbled a cigarette out of my pack just as the waitress brought the second beer. I flinched when her lighter suddenly appeared lit in front of my face. "Thanks again," I said and released the first draw of smoke. "Keep the cold ones coming."

"I'd like to see you doing this kind of thing a lot more often," Mason said.

"I don't know. Good as it felt tonight, I feel rusty on the solo thing. And I always think I can do better than I'm able."

"Geez, Gabriel, how can you think that? You were awesome tonight. Your voice never sounded better. You attacked those songs. You worked the room. Wonderful stuff."

I drew on the cigarette to hide my smile and then blew smoke at the ceiling.

"It's just that I'm really kind of in love with the band right now," I said. "The voice and the songs are developing because of it."

My friend gave me a narrow look.

"Are you sure it's the band you're in love with?"

I tapped ashes into the tray on the table next to ours.

"What do you mean?" I said.

"Whenever I see you and Yvonne together, I can't help but think that there's something between the two of you."

"No," I said. "Not really."

"What about that song you sang tonight? The new one about Broadway?"

"'Broadway Café?'"

"Yeah. Something about that brought Yvonne to mind. I don't know what it was."

I tipped down the last of the second beer. "Broadway Café" ran quickly through my mind, and I could see what Mason meant. The setting of the second verse—nights alive with neon and the young lions playing it cool at some all-night juke joint—admittedly had something in it of the late-night rambles Yvonne and I often took together.

At a table near the music,
I had an arm around you and a song on my mind. . . .

"Am I right?" Mason said. "Does your attachment to the band have anything to do with an attachment to Yvonne?"

"Maybe," I said and smiled a different smile this time. "We've had our moments, but nothing has really happened. Whatever's there remains in the shadows at this point."

"Just be careful. Tension like that makes for great energy on stage, but who knows what might happen if it gets out of control. If you really want the band to hang together—"

I laughed.

"This sounds so serious," I said. "Too serious for this time of night."

"Why didn't she come out this evening?"

"I don't know if I told her about it. They were all excited about a Saturday night off."

"Maybe she had other plans," Mason said with a shrug and an exaggerated grin.

That had crossed my mind, I guess, and I wondered if I'd ignored the possibility that I might care what she was up to tonight—or any other night when we weren't together.

"Do you know something I don't?" I asked. As soon as the words were out of my mouth, I realized that I didn't really want to know. I somehow didn't feel up to knowing. So I tried to redirect before he answered. "Anyway, the beer and the hour are working me over, and I'm not sure where this conversation is going."

Mason leaned slightly toward me and lowered his voice.

"I want to—" he said and stopped as the tall waitress set down my third beer and turned away. Then, "The band might not last forever, and I want to manage you, Gabriel," he finished. "I really think we could go far. Acoustic music is on the verge of a big upswing."

"Mason."

"What! Come on, Gabriel. You've known for a long time that I want to be your manager. This could be really great. There are some good acoustic music labels on the rise out there. If we go for it now, when the upswing really kicks in, we'll be sitting pretty."

I sighed smoke and looked out the window. I could almost see how the conversation came around to this point but was too tired and distracted to follow the step-by-step progression.

"I had a manager once," I said, turning back to him. "I doubt you ever knew."

"No, I didn't know that."

"He was this guy from Knoxville. Mo Biggs. Apart from the fact that he believed in me, he seemed practically useless. He started off bad, or so Billy Keith told me, but I've been thinking lately that he was just as inexperienced as I was."

"There are lots of bad ones out there. But good ones too."

"The thing is, I don't know if Mo was really bad or not." I reached over to the table next to ours and tapped the ashes from my cigarette and took two deep pulls on my beer. "Anyway, I didn't give him the chance to see what he could do."

"What do you mean?"

I smiled, took another pull on the beer.

"I killed him," I said.

Mason almost laughed.

"No, really, I did," I said and took one last drag from my cigarette.

"At least I believe I had a hand in it. It was Keith's idea."

The laughter beneath the surface of Mason's face faded suddenly.

"I don't understand. What are you trying to say?"

"Well, it's a long story for this time of night, but I'll give you the short of it." I crushed out my cigarette, drew the beer down to one remaining swig and told the story of how I'd met Mo Biggs, how he'd brought me to Nashville, how Billy Keith had devised a way to keep Biggs out of the picture as much as possible, how Biggs had died. I guess Mason could see that I felt like a criminal, but he didn't seem to sense the depth of my regret.

"That's quite a story," he said when I finished. "But you're forgetting one thing. I'm not this Mo Biggs, and I'm certainly not Billy Keith." He grabbed the waitress's arm as she started past and held it.

"I know, Mason, I know. But so far I've got a lousy track record for trying to develop friendships out of business relationships. I like you too much to get into bed with you." I looked up at the waitress and saw an eyebrow arch. "Professionally speaking, of course."

The eyebrow rose even higher.

I gave up, and Mason laughed.

"Never mind," I said. "I'll put the idea in the background and mull it over."

"I'd like a beer now, please," Mason said to the waitress and released her arm. He looked at me for a moment. "Be careful with Yvonne, okay?"

* * *

I'd been back in my apartment long enough to make sure there weren't any messages, strip off my sweat-stiffened clothes and brush my teeth before the telephone rang.

Yvonne had been on my mind since I left the Songbird, and even though the night was approaching the wee small hours, I felt ready to hear her smoky Texas purr when I picked up the receiver, sat down on the side of the bed and said hello.

No response, but I could hear the distant sound of music and a crowd in the background.

"Hello?" I said again.

"Hey," she said and stopped.

I knew the voice. But it sounded so out of place in my ear that somehow my mind refused to recognize it, refused also to allow my own voice to respond.

"It's Eliza," she said and stopped again.

"Eliza," I said.

"Believe it or not," she said. "Can you come and get me?"

"What?" I stood quickly and turned to the darkened window. The reflection I saw didn't seem to be me. It wasn't shaking as I felt I was suddenly shaking.

"Gabriel?"

"What? Where are you?"

"I'm someplace called Lonnie's on Printers Alley. Do you know where it is?"

"I know where Printers Alley is," I said. "What are you doing there?"

"Please, just come and get me," she said.

"Okay," I said. "I'll be there in—"

She hung up.

I lay the receiver in its cradle and stood looking at the window's reflection of my naked body. I could have used a shower. But she was out there in the city and wanted me, needed me. I wished that I hadn't stayed so long talking with Mason, that I'd left as soon as the gig was over and come back here to get cleaned up.

After all the years of longing and dreaming, how was it that I hadn't felt her presence?

How about a hat? My hair was wild with sweat and humidity. Maybe I could slick it back and pull it into a ponytail. What would she think of that look? She'd hate it, I was pretty sure. But maybe the time had come for her to cut it, cut it once and for all and come home with me. At least I'd brushed my teeth. Clothes. This was neither the Johnny Carson nor Barbara Walters scenario I'd rehearsed. So how did I picture myself dressed when meeting my wife for the first time since she was actually my wife? Same old Gabriel in jeans and a flannel shirt? Billy Keith's south-of-the-border creation? Leather and t-shirt?

Wait a minute. How many years? Five and counting.

A shock ran through me when I came back to the moment and saw my reflection still standing naked in the window.

Aware again of my mission, I moved quickly around the place. I put on a pair of jeans and a long-sleeved Bruce Cockburn tour shirt, brushed my hair without slicking it and pulled it back in a ponytail, stepped into a pair of white sneakers and capped the ensemble with a rumpled Indiana Jones hat. Butterflies had already whirled my gut into knots, so without a parting glance in the mirror to make things worse, I grabbed my car keys and left the apartment.

I parked in a loading zone on Fourth Avenue North, just steps away from Church Street, stumbled out of the car and turned right around the corner. Ahead of me hung the Printers Alley sign that spanned Church. I angled downward and left across the street and entered the brick passageway. Before me appeared a dingy carnival scene—swirling with weaving head-down drunks, floating faces and lights upon lights; blaring with laughter and breaking glass and a blend of country music, show tunes and lounge jazz. I glanced up and saw that Lonnie's Western Room was just there on my left, spilling unsteady light and muffled karaoke out into the Alley.

A man in red western shirt and faded blue jeans sat on a stool by the door. His head was slightly bowed, and a black cowboy hat covered his eyes. His paunch pushed hard against the front of his shirt, and a cigarette burned between the ring finger and pinky of his right hand, the way I sometimes held my own cigarettes when I was playing guitar. The heels of his cowboy boots were hooked into the bottom rungs of the stool. Beside him on the wall, a sign read,

LONNIE'S WESTERN ROOM

featuring

SPECIAL GUESTS

LIVE ENTERTAINMENT

OPEN

6 P.M. – 7 A.M.

7 DAYS A WEEK

I stood frozen on the brick pavement for a long moment and almost didn't recognize Eliza when she stepped through that doorway.

Her hair, always straight and black no matter what length, was curly and red and short enough to leave her white neck exposed. Her makeup was like nothing I'd ever seen her wear, either in quantity or design— almost like something from a *Star Trek* episode. A pale and shimmering gold glowed like Egyptian finery to highlight her silver-blue eyes. Her cheeks held a light flush, and her lips were drawn perfectly in dark red. She wore a black top beneath a gold lamé jacket. Although her shoulders were padded almost like a football player's, her legs were sleek in shiny skin-tight black pants. She wobbled slightly on stiletto heels.

I took her in at a glance, but had no time to pass judgment before she saw me. I'm sure her own first glance did the same work, but apart from the hair, she wasn't seeing anything much different from what she'd seen when we were last together. In that awkward moment when we stumbled toward an embrace, I couldn't read her judgment behind the mask of make-up.

"It's good to see you," she said in my ear. "Thanks for coming to get me."

I wanted to say something, but I didn't know what. My tongue suddenly seemed as mired and as dumb as an old oak root.

She pushed me back and held my arms in her hands, and I felt the same startled sensation I'd always felt when I saw the light play in her eyes.

"I've got to get out of here, okay?" she said.

"Okay."

Then I noticed a man in a cowboy hat standing and watching us from just inside the doorway of Lonnie's. He was tall and thin, like most Nashville cowboys, and his body language brought to mind a live electric wire. Beneath the brim of his hat, his eyes shown in shadow and his face held a smoldering threat. I looked away, back to Eliza.

She turned as if to glance over her shoulder but stopped herself and moved closer to me.

"Where are you parked?"

I looked from her face to the doorway.

The man was gone.

"Around the corner here," I said and ushered her out of Printers Alley.

She took off almost at a jog once she got the direction of the car, and

I had to pick up my pace to stay with her. I unlocked her side, but she stood holding her door open and looking in the direction of the Alley until I had my side opened.

"Who was the guy back there?" I asked as we settled into our seats and closed and locked the doors. It wasn't the only question in my mind, but it was the one that found its way out first.

"How the hell should I know?" she said and turned to look out the back window of the car. "He's been following me since we left the Stockyard steak place." She turned back around and fastened her seat belt. "Just some creep, I guess."

"Since who left the Stockyard?"

"What?"

"You said 'we.'"

"Oh, my friends that I work with."

"Are we leaving them behind?"

"Hell no! They left me behind," she said. "That's why I had to call you."

"Well," I said, "as long as you had to call me and didn't want to, I guess we're okay."

I felt her look at me for a moment and then turn to look ahead as we pulled out onto Fourth and headed down toward Broadway.

"I didn't mean it that way, Gabriel. I'm sorry."

"Okay," I said, trying to adjust the windshield defroster. "First tell me where we're going and then tell me how you came to be here in my car this fine June morning."

"I need you to take me to the Opryland Hotel," she said. "We've been at a hair show there this weekend."

"Briley Parkway," I said, trying to think of the longest possible route there. "Didn't you used to go to one of those in Myrtle Beach every year?"

"We did until last year when one of the girls ended up in jail for a night. That place makes a lot of money on little sting operations, you know? It's like Pigeon Forge that way."

I turned right onto Broadway.

I knew what she was talking about. . . .

*   *   *

One January, after their second Christmas together, they decided to go to Pigeon Forge in Tennessee for a couple of nights. On their first evening, they went to a popular seafood restaurant. He couldn't find a parking space in the main lot, but out behind the restaurant was a little diner that was all dark. Several NO PARKING signs were visible in the windows of the diner, but he thought parking there would be no problem with the diner closed. But when they came out after their meal, the lights in the diner were on, the open sign was in the window and their car was loaded onto a tow truck. The driver charged them $80.00 to lower and release their car, half of which they guessed went to the old lady watching the proceedings from the window of her diner. . . .

*   *   *

I always wished we'd gone in and tried to order something from the menu, to see if she was really open.

"So when did you come to town?" I asked.

"Thursday."

"Why didn't you call? You could've come to hear me play tonight instead of—"

"It's what all the girls wanted to do," she said. "To go out to these Nashville places."

I turned right on Eighth Avenue North.

"Where did you play?" she asked.

"At the Songbird over in Hillsborough Village."

"I've heard of that place. I think one of the girls mentioned it, but the people at the hotel sent us to the Stockyard."

"So where are all these other people you were with?"

"Oh, I can't wait to get hold of them," she said. "They left me in that awful place back there on purpose. I went to the restroom, and they just took my purse with them and left."

"Why?"

"I'm thinking about pressing charges," she said and snorted a tight-lipped laugh.

I remembered that sound and the powerful tension that always drove it.

"Why did they leave you?"

She didn't say anything for a moment as we turned right onto Charlotte Avenue and started making our way toward Main Street and Gallatin Pike.

"We'd been drinking, especially at that last place. You almost had to drink a lot to stand it in there with people like—" She stopped and watched the walls of the city go by for a moment.

"Like the guy behind you back there?"

"Yes, people like that," she said. "Anyway, I maybe had too much and let it slip about you. A lot of the girls I work with now don't know anything about you and me. They know about you, of course. They've heard 'Lacy' on the radio. But they don't know about us. So anyway, they were all excited and asking why I didn't call you up and get you to come join us."

She fell silent as we crossed over the Cumberland River.

"I wouldn't have been able—"

"I know that," she said. "That's what I told them. That you were a musician and you were sure to be somewhere working. But they just waited for me to go to the restroom and made their plan. We were paid up and ready to go, and they took my purse and my money. All they left me was a couple of coins and a napkin that said, 'your purse is with us! call gabriel!'"

"That's pretty irresponsible," I said. "I might have been playing some place out of town."

"And I guess they just assumed I had your number," she said. "I'm glad you were in the book."

"You ought to have my number," I said.

"I should, I guess," she said.

Then I heard in my head the sleepy voice of a man—"Yeah?" I wanted to ask her who he was, ask her if he was a man like the one in the doorway of Lonnie's or something else, something more. But I didn't really want to know, not just yet anyway, and pushed him out of my mind.

I drove northeast on an almost deserted Gallatin Pike, feeling her heat radiating from where she sat quietly looking out the window. In spite of that heat, I found it difficult to believe that I was inside a living, breathing moment, that I could pinch myself until I bruised and still not wake up in my Sixteenth Avenue bedroom. The smell of her same perfume, faded as it was at this hour, kept giving me small shocks of memory—the taste of her kiss, the thick richness of her hair, the feel of her fingers in mine, the ring of her laughter in our small apartment above the funeral home. I somehow made the ramp onto Briley Parkway and then the McGavock Pike exit and found myself approaching the Opryland Hotel's front entrance.

Eliza cleared her throat, the first sound she'd made in several minutes.

"Go right and park over there," she said, pointing. "We'll go in the entrance on this end and walk through the greenhouse."

We met no one as we followed a pathway through the cavernous atrium. I had been in it before when a harpist was playing, but at this hour, the echo of water trickling and splashing was the only sound. Eliza walked beside me, drifting closer now, then further away, then so close again that our arms touched.

Behind a small waterfall, we turned without word or warning into each other's embrace and kissed, not a wild Friday-night-in-the-back-seat kiss but one that was rich with warmth and passion. It began that way, at least, then tapered off in confusion. When we finally drew apart, we simply turned and continued walking—still without words—through the greenery and toward the hotel's main lobby.

Few guests still stirred in the wide corridors. Behind the long check-in desk, a couple of clerks busied themselves at small computer screens. A handful of crisply dressed housekeepers—male and female—worked sleepily. They vacuumed the carpets. They wiped down the several couches, chairs and small tables that created intimate areas in the large space. They sifted ashtrays clean and stamped the white sand. They shined mirrors.

Eliza led me into the convention area. Once out of sight of the hotel personnel, she pushed through a door and drew me into a room that had been partitioned off from a larger banquet space. She found the lights and turned them on.

Forty or fifty chairs sat in rows facing the newly lighted front portion of the room. A platform was raised there, a black styling chair in its center.

"Do you want to take your shirt off?" Eliza said.

"What?"

"You'll itch if you don't."

She was looking in the trays and drawers of two roll-abouts that had been pushed to the sides of the stage.

"It's for coming to get me," she said. "And because it looks bad."

She looked at me for a moment, then down at the floor as she tied the apron she'd put on. She picked up a couple of silver clips and a black comb and stuffed them in an apron pocket.

"Come back here," she said and disappeared between the curtains behind the stage area.

I followed and found her standing at a makeshift shampoo station.

"Are you leaving the shirt on?"

I shook my hair from its tie, looped the tie loosely around my thumb, and pulled the Cockburn shirt off over my head. At the same time, I sucked in my belly and expanded my chest—without being obvious about it, I hoped. I was softer in the middle than my image in the mirror those months before we separated, but my shoulders and chest had broadened. Again, I couldn't read her judgment in the look she gave me.

"Lay back," she said when I had eased myself down onto the shampoo chair.

I lay back as she turned on the water to warm. When I had settled my neck into the cradle on the rim of the black bowl, she put the warm water to my hair. Just as I began to relax, she turned off the water and I heard shampoo squirt into her palm. Then her fingers were in my hair, working up a lather.

I closed my eyes, remembering the slide of her palms, the scratch of her fingernails on my scalp, her breath high on my forehead, her breasts in motion above me as she worked. . . .

* * *

They had been dating only a few weeks the first time she cut his hair. It was a Sunday afternoon in November, and they were at her family's house. Her mother and brother were away with their church, and her father snored in front of a football game. A thrill ran through Gabriel as he took off his shirt in the warmth of the kitchen. And another at the cool touch of her fingers on his skin. Both of them were filled with nervous laughter that they tried to keep quiet so as not to wake her father. . . .

* * *

"What are you smiling about?"

Her voice jolted me back to the moment.

"I was thinking about the first time you cut my hair," I said.

"Was that the time I nearly cut your ear off?"

I laughed.

"It wasn't as bad as all that," I said.

"Maybe you didn't think so," she said, "but I was mortified! I don't know that I'd ever seen so much blood!"

"Well, it did look bad," I said. "But your dad's expre—"

The water came on again, and she began to rinse. Her hands and arms circled my head, and to rinse the back down near my neck, she lifted me until my face felt the heat of her breasts.

Then the water was off and a towel was around my head and she was helping me back to a sitting position.

"What were you saying?" she said.

"I don't remember." I stood up and moved with her through the curtains to the styling chair. As I sat down, I said, "Won't you get in trouble using this stuff?"

Eliza quickly wrapped me up in a styling cape.

"The hotel might not like it if they catch us," she said as she worked the towel all over my head. "But as far as this equipment goes, it's all for my use."

"Really?" I said. "You're the star of the show?"

"Sort of, I guess." She started to comb out the ends of my hair with quick short pulls. "In this room anyway. I'm what you call a platform artist."

"Very cool, Eliza," I said. "How long have you been doing that?"

"This is just the third time. I've done it in Myrtle Beach and Norfolk before here."

"Wow, you're like a rock star," I said. I winced as she worked at a tough tangle. "So, what is a platform artist?"

She sprayed my hair with something off the roll-about and with a few more strokes finished combing it out.

"I offer classes that people take," she said. "Mostly precision cuts, but I do some color and perms too."

"People come in and watch you work?"

"My picture's on the brochure and everything," she said. She stood with her scissors loaded on the fingers of her right hand and a comb in her left. The heels of both hands rested on my shoulders. She seemed as if she was beginning to sober up. "They want me to go national."

"Who does?"

"My bosses and a bunch of the product people."

"What would that mean?"

"Same thing, you know? Only in New York and Miami and Las Vegas. Places like that."

"That really is like a rock star," I said. I watched as she started combing through my hair again, now and then pulling it up between her fingers and looking at it. "Are you gonna do it?"

"I don't know," she said. "I doubt it."

"Well, why not?"

"It just doesn't make any sense to me, you know? I mean, I make good money, and I get to go home at night and sleep in my own bed. And I get to see my family and friends whenever I want to. I like that."

"But you might like the other too," I said. "For a while, at least."

"Maybe," she said. "But I've learned enough about it, and I don't think so."

We fell silent. I closed my eyes and felt the movement of her work in my hair and the heat of her body on my back. Spinning me this way and that, she combed and fluffed and combed and snipped.

This moment felt part dream, part memory, not at all real and present. In the dreams of my days and nights, I'd found pictures of our reunion. But the kiss under the waterfall, the sound of her voice and her touch were the only familiar elements. The Opryland Hotel and this wee-hours rendezvous—from Printers Alley to the scissors and comb—were completely unexpected.

"I've done these nasty ends," she said suddenly. "But you could lose all this length."

I could feel her working my ponytail into the position where one cut of the scissors would separate it from me. I could picture myself at home with her without this hair, but when I tried to picture myself without it on dreamed stages in New York or Dallas or San Francisco, even real ones in Murfreesboro or Bowling Green or Murray, I couldn't.

"Are you ready?" she said. She stood with my hair in her hand, her scissors poised.

I couldn't see her, but I could feel the tension that pulsed through her to me and back and forth between. This certainly was a singular moment, but it didn't feel like the right moment. The players were right, but the time and place seemed all wrong.

"Not yet," I said. "Just the ends, I guess."

She held on to my hair almost like the kid that won't let go when you say, "I give" or "uncle," but then she released her grip on the ponytail and arranged the way my hair fell across my shoulders.

"Well, then I guess we're finished here," she said.

And yet for several long minutes—or so it seemed—she pulled parts of my hair in different directions, checking, weighing, judging. When she moved around in front of the chair, a single glance was enough to tell that she was looking at a head of hair and no longer at me. Now she was behind me again, measuring and fluffing. A periodic crisp snip sounded from her scissors, but the room was otherwise quiet until with a loud rip of Velcro she took off my cape with a flourish, like a magician unveiling an empty box where moments before rabbits had been sitting and twitching with nerves.

"That does it," she said and began brushing loose cuttings off the back of the chair and the front of her apron.

While she returned apron, comb and clips to the roll-about, I stood up and put my shirt on again. When she moved the roll-about back to its place, I found a small broom and swept up the hair. She looked around as if to make sure that all was in place for the next day, and I pulled my hair back into the ponytail again, feeling a live wire somewhere deep in my belly and unsure what would happen next.

"What time's your first show tomorrow?" I asked.

"I go home tomorrow," she said. "The show's over. We'll pack up in the morning and leave."

When the lights were out, we stood in the deserted hallway, neither looking at the other.

"Are you tired?" I asked.

"Very."

"Well, can I walk you to your door?"

"We haven't done much catching up."

"No."

"I look a lot different. Did you notice?"

"Of course I did," I said. "I almost didn't recognize you when you came out of Lonnie's." In my mind I saw again the man who had been behind her and heard again the man who had answered her telephone. "You look great."

"So do you."

"But not much different."

"No, not a lot."

She turned, and we walked together along the hallway, back toward the main lobby.

"'Lacy' sounded good on the radio," she said, "the few times I heard it."

"Thanks," I said. "I wish the album could've been released. It was pretty good."

"What happened?"

We wandered aimlessly through various common areas of the hotel, and I told her about Stallion Records and the idea they had to take their business to a higher level just as they should have been releasing my album. I told her how the changeover took a long time and how by the time it was finished Stallion had new projects that they were more excited about releasing. But I didn't feel like telling her that something equally as unspectacular had happened to another entire album recorded for Columbia Records.

"I'm sorry that happened," she said.

"Well, I've got a lot of new stuff now."

"Maybe I'll hear it sometime."

"Maybe," I said. "I hope so." I searched for a way into what I wanted to say, what I wanted to know. "Next time I'm home we could get together and I could play some for you."

"No, Gabriel," she said. "No."

We stopped on the edge of the main lobby, and in the corner of my eye, I saw her arms crook at the elbows and her fingers spread wide the way they did when she was tense, angry, adamant. The suddenness of it almost took me by surprise, but somewhere in my gut I felt a flash of understanding and knew what was coming.

"You can't come to see me without coming home," she said.

That wasn't what I was expecting.

"What do you mean by that?"

"I'm living with someone," she said without hesitation, as if she'd been waiting for the right moment to say it just as I'd been waiting for the right moment to ask. "His name is Kevin, and I met him at a concert."

"Well," I said. "That's it. I called you one morning awhile back, and some guy answered. I guess I was hoping he was a one-night-stand or something."

"Go to hell, Gabriel," she said. "Is that what you think of me?"

"I don't know what to think, Eliza," I said. "You come to town without letting me know. You kiss me in the atrium. You—"

"I was drunk."

"Whatever. You tell me about this Kevin fellow, but you say I can come see you if I come home." I knew I was getting louder, but I couldn't help it. "What the hell does that mean?"

"It doesn't mean anything here," she said. "But if you come home—"

"There you are, baby doll!" The man's gruff voice sounded like the sudden roar of a dangerous animal in the lobby. "I knew a classy chick like you'd be here, baby!"

Eliza and I turned to see the cowboy from Lonnie's rise up from a couch and come toward us with long weaving strides.

"Baby, it took me a couple more beers, baby doll," he said, "but I got here, baby."

I glanced over to the front desk and saw one of the workers with a telephone to her ear and her eyes on the scene taking shape in front of her.

She's calling hotel security on this guy, I thought, but almost at once I realized that she had probably already been on the telephone calling them about me.

The cowboy was upon us now.

I saw his jaw clench and moved to get between Eliza and him, but when I tried to get a hold on him it was like wrestling with a charged fire hose. Skinny as the cowboy seemed, he was all hard bone and muscle. My weight advantage quickly lost ground to his strength and drunken intensity, and before I knew what had happened, I was stumbling backwards over one of the lobby couches. I lost sight of Eliza and fell in a thrashing heap. I could see a tall plant and a lamp falling in my wake, and I could hear the screaming—not Eliza's screaming but the cowboy's. I clawed my way up to where I could see what was happening.

Eliza stood over the downed dude, filling his face with an unrelenting stream of pepper spray or mace, and the security guys were coming up fast from the front doors, their jingling creaking sprint silhouetted by the first light of dawn.

* * *

The folks at the front desk had seen it all, and hotel security had taken the situation in hand, followed quickly by housekeeping. The suffering cowboy had been removed from the lobby to be picked up by the police and escorted to either jail or the emergency room. Where he'd fallen, the carpet was already being cleaned before the questions were finished. Where I'd fallen, all was being set right again. The hotel intended to press charges against the cowboy and needed Eliza's statement, so they took her away. I was asked to leave the premises immediately if I was not a guest.

The sun was up before I got back to my apartment. I hadn't seen the place in this early light before, and it didn't look like home. All of the angles and shadows seemed wrong. I took off my clothes and, on this Sunday morning in this foreign place, once again stood in front of the bedroom window. But this time I saw not my own naked reflection but the roof of the single-level apartments next door, the shaded alley off to the right, a deserted Sixteenth Avenue off to the left, and a hint of the Nashville skyline in the distance through the trees.

I stood there in front of the bedroom window with Eliza's last words ringing in my head—"But if you come home," she'd said. I couldn't shake the feeling that I'd missed some opportunity in the way things played out in that lobby. The feeling was like when the elevator doors quietly open and close on your floor and you're still standing there lost in some thought.

At that moment I realized that she had seen me without my wedding band, and I wondered what she had thought. Then I realized that I hadn't noticed if she still wore hers.

Probably not.

I crawled into bed, grabbed the telephone from the bedside table and set it beside my pillow, certain that she wouldn't leave town without calling.

Chapter 10
On Tour

On the night Eliza remarried, the reflection of the Harvest Moon stretched and danced on the waters of the Tennessee River. The Chattanooga skyline—etched in shadow and light against the afterglow of sunset—stood over the dock and the riverboat and the line of people quickly boarding. The wind carried the first thrilling chill of autumn across the lower deck of the *Chickamauga Queen*, carried it back to front across the stage set up starboard side.

The crowd swirled in, drinking and dancing to the canned music that thumped from the sound system. Some took seats at the tables around the dance floor, waiting for the paddle wheel and the band to get their evening under way. Others—mostly couples who seemed joined at shoulder, hip and thigh—drifted to the two decks above and leaned on the rails with their faces close together. They waited like that, looking out over the silvery tide toward the fading east bank, seemingly lost in the grand romance of the boat and the darkening river.

And later on the night Eliza remarried, I chipped a tooth on the silver weave of the microphone during "Best I've Ever Seen," and toward the end of the song, when a waitress scooted by the front of the stage and set a paper cup of beer there for me, I kicked it into the dancers, drawing threatening looks from a couple of big-chested men and sending their big-breasted women shivering toward the ladies' room.

During Hayes's lead break in "Driving Wheel," I disappeared from the stage, leaving Lukas to sing the bridge and the final refrain.

I go driving to outrun what I feel—
I guess I'll die behind this driving wheel.

As the long instrumental ending rolled on, Reggie's amplified "Earth to Gabriel" reached me in the stern of the third deck where I stood downing a beer and watching the paddle wheel churn mud and moonlight. But I didn't return to the stage, and the band took an early break.

I thought of that October night ten years before, of the mansion and the tall gray judge, our first halting steps together into the apartment above Ramsey's crying rooms. Would she remember these things in the company of another man on another wedding night?

According to Mom, via Aunt Myrtle, who had rushed home with the news from her Friday standing appointment, Eliza and the man she was marrying had gone to Greenville too. She'd be embarrassed if she walked into the courthouse to find Judge Davenport waiting to perform the ceremony. I imagined her covering her face with her hands and running out of the building in tears.

I'd vented my feelings on Yvonne the entire trip to Chattanooga, ignoring her one minute, lashing out at her for no reason the next. Lukas, Reggie, and Hayes stayed out of my way, but she wouldn't. And the worse I treated her, the closer she clung to me.

She drank as much as I did during the breaks. Not something she usually tried to do. But her performance didn't suffer. During the songs, she stood with her eyes closed, her baggy white shirt rolling in the breeze, her body swaying under the influence of the vodka and the boat and the music.

By the last set the pounding rhythms of the band and the dancers' feet broke away the edges of my pain and anger. I watched Yvonne and moved close to her during the instrumental sections, at first afraid she might topple off the stage, at length attempting to make her the surrogate object of the words I sang. But even though the brittle fragments of bitterness had worked their way out through the tips of my fingers and been shattered on the vibrating strings of my guitar, Eliza was still too much with me. She stood waiting behind some word or image in every song, stepping in front of Yvonne and shadowing me to the end of the lyric.

I thought of it as something merciful when the *Chickamauga Queen* returned to the dock and the gig ended.

I guided Yvonne to a seat out of the way, got her some coffee and gave her my jacket and silently helped the guys pack the equipment off the boat and into the trailer.

Hayes had reserved rooms across the state line at the Nite-Lite Motel in Ringold, Georgia. On this small tour—Atlanta the next night, then on to Tallahassee, Florida, and Tuscaloosa, Alabama—two double rooms had been figured into the traveling budget. Lukas, Reggie, and Hayes, the married members of the band, would share one, each taking a night on the cot we carried with us. Yvonne and I would share the other.

When we closed the door to our room and dropped our bags on the floor, she threw her arms around my neck and kissed me.

"My sad hero," she said, her words still slurred. "What the hell's been wrong with you today?"

I walked her backward to the nearest bed.

"Not this one," she said. "The one by the window."

I took her to the foot of it and gently pulled her arms from around my neck and eased her down until she was sitting on the edge.

"Eliza got married this afternoon."

"Then don't you think it's time you got over her?" She blinked in slow motion and twirled a finger in one long curl of her auburn hair. She drew the curly strand across her cheek, took it between her lips, and slowly began undoing my belt buckle.

"Yvonne," I said, taking hold of her hands.

"But we fuck on stage every night," she said. "Naked emotions,"— she began to work at the buckle again—"sweat, rhythm. All that's missing is the skin." The last of this trailed away in a whisper as she stopped working with the buckle and turned toward the window. She pushed the ringlets of her bangs away from her eyes, sniffed and let her hands drop to her lap. "It smells a little musty in here. Would you turn on the air conditioner?"

I flipped the switch and closed the curtains.

"You do the bathroom first," she said. "I'm sure you remember how long women take to get ready for bed."

When I came out of the bathroom, the curtains were open again, and the lights were off.

Through the window I could see a school on a little knoll next to the motel. Amber lights lined the boundaries of the playground and stood guard at regular intervals around the building itself.

All that light spilled across Yvonne's naked body. She lay motionless on her back on the side of the bed nearest the window, her hands resting on her breasts, her face turned away.

Thinking she must be asleep, I ran my thumbs inside the waistband of my boxers and tugged them upward a little and looked at her for a long time.

The way she dressed—in clothes not only baggy but much too big—her body had taken on a quality of mystery for me. I remembered the feel of it through her clothes as we rolled around the floor of her apartment that New Year's Day morning and wondered about it sometimes on stage or late at night. She was even leaner than I'd imagined. In the dim light, she looked surprisingly lithe and athletic.

When I'd stared too long, I stepped to the head of the other bed and turned down the covers.

"Gabriel?" she said. "I'm not drunk."

I sighed and sat down on the edge of her bed.

She turned and looked at me, her face half lit by the distant amber light, half hidden in motel shadows. She was wide awake, and her gaze was steady.

I lay back and rested my head on the warm firmness of her thigh.

She rolled slowly toward me, onto her side, hooked the crook of her right leg under my chin. She held me like that—held me tight. Then she moved my left arm up and bent it over her hip, out of her way. Her taut body curled close to mine, her small breasts embracing the soft flesh of my side, the heat of her face moving down across my belly.

* * *

Two nights later we sat naked on the tiny balcony of our third floor motel room in Tallahassee, Florida, sharing a cigarette and watching the thin traffic pass beneath the blue-white lights lining I-10. We'd brought towels out to wrap ourselves in, but the air was warm so we tossed them back inside. Our faces and chests still glistened with sweat from the rough tangle of another bout of lovemaking.

Yvonne curled into the white plastic chair with her knees pulled up under her chin and her arms crossed in front of her shins. She exhaled a puff of smoke over the railing and watched it float toward the thick air above the Interstate.

"Whoever says the third time's a charm is right," she said and handed the cigarette across the round glass-topped table between us.

I sprawled loosely in the other chair, like a wet towel somebody had spread to dry. I chuckled and took the cigarette, my eyes locked on the body that'd been all over me in the darkness of the room. I inhaled a final drag and dropped the glowing butt into the empty beer can on the table.

"Well," I said and paused to watch an eighteen wheeler roaring westbound beneath us. "Do you think you're in love?"

"Yes," she said and lay her forehead on her knees. "But not with you."

Her answer crashed into me, creating a wave of both anger and relief, startling but somehow completely failing to surprise. I didn't say anything at first. I lit another cigarette and handed it to her, then lit one for myself.

"Who is he?" I said finally. "Is it Thor again?"

"Hell no, it's not Thor," she said and raised her head and slung her hair away from her face. "I haven't even seen him since I quit the record store."

"Who then?"

"You don't know him."

"Who is it?"

She sighed and shook her head.

"His name's Swede Weaver."

I looked at her for a moment and then turned away.

"Cool name," I said.

"You son of a bitch. Why'd you have to go and drag love into this?" She reached across the table and slapped the back of my head. "I was having such a good time."

I didn't know if I loved her or not, but I hadn't suspected that what I felt might not matter to her or that the passion and lust we'd burned with the last three nights had little chance of becoming anything more.

"So, if this guy's back in Nashville," I said, turning to look at her again, "what in the hell have we been doing since Ringold?"

Her mouth dropped open.

"We've been having a beautiful fucking time, don't you think? Fun without guilt, you know? No worries. No responsibilities. No commitments other than being friends and making music."

She leaned back in her chair and stretched. With her arms straight above her head and her fingers locked, she popped her knuckles. The movement lifted her breasts. Her legs strained toward the wrought iron railing of the balcony, the muscles taking on sleek shadows of definition.

I crossed my legs and coughed.

"Tell me about him," I said.

Yvonne threw her cigarette over the railing and blew smoke after it.

"Well, he's got this wavy hair that he bleaches white and wears in a ponytail. It's disgusting, I know, but it hasn't bothered me that much yet. Blue eyes, a little mustache, and a pouty smile."

"Doesn't sound like your usual graveyard type, Yvonne."

"Do you want to hear this or not?"

"Sorry," I said and uncrossed my legs and stretched out again.

"He's a pretty big guy," she said. "I'd say about two or three inches taller than you and about forty pounds heavier. But he's not fat, just thick and solid."

"Geez, Yvonne. You'll be squashed."

"He's beautiful, Gabriel. His face, I mean. The way he's shaped. Outside of that, I can't say what the attraction is."

I sat up straight.

"Where'd you meet him?"

She stood up and shook her hair loose from her back.

"He's a wrestler, and I met him at school."

I chuckled and shook my head.

"Surely you're not dating one of the students at the high school."

"He's not a wrestler like that." She leaned the small of her back against the railing and stood silhouetted by the lights of I-10. "He's like a professional. You know, a ring with ropes around it, a bell, theme music."

"Even worse," I said and shook my head. "And how did you meet this guy?"

"Well, like I told you, I met him at the school, but he's not a student," she said and laughed. "My principal called me up a few weeks ago and asked if I would come sell chances on the door prizes at a fund-raising thing they were having at the gym that Saturday night." She spat toward the corner of the balcony. "The band wasn't playing for some reason, so I said I would. And when I got there was the first I knew about it being wrestling matches." She paused a moment, looking, it seemed to me, at her reflection in the balcony's sliding glass door. "My daddy used to watch that stuff in Dallas all the time. It was a pretty big thing around there, you know?"

"I used to watch it on TV with my grandfather when I was little," I said. "I remember when the lady wrestlers came on he'd call out to the kitchen, 'Come quick, Sadie, see what's on the box!' My grandmother would rush into the room and then stand there with her hands on her hips and say, 'Them girls ought to be lawed, wallowing around like that in next to nothing.' He got the biggest kick out of that."

"There were two ugly bitches wrestling that night," Yvonne said and turned and stared toward the other side of the Interstate for a moment. "Anyway, Swede came in before the crowd showed up. He even bought the first chance from me." She sat back down and nibbled at a thumb nail. "When I sold out of tickets for the drawings, I started for the door, but instead of leaving, I sat down on the bottom row of the bleachers to watch for a little while, and it was wild as hell! The matches and how the crowd reacted? So Roman!"

I lit two more cigarettes for us.

"Anyway, Swede was in the third match. The announcer rang this loud-as-hell cowbell over a microphone, and here came Swede out of the girls' locker room, wearing this jacket with sequins and rhinestones all over it, like something a tourist would buy down on Music Row."

"I'm guessing the girls' locker room is where the villains and the nobodies dress."

"Get screwed, Gabriel." She drew her thighs up against herself again "Anyway, this plain-looking guy came out of the boys' side. A real old-timer, it looked like. But he was good as hell. He twisted Swede up like a rag doll into these gnarly positions. Lord, Gabriel, my breath would

catch, and I couldn't fucking breathe until that old guy let him go."
She stood up quickly and bent over with her elbows on the railing.
Somewhere below, a car horn blew, but she didn't look or jump back
out of the light. "He was limping pretty bad when he was dressed and
came back by me. Shit, I couldn't blame him. I felt sorry for him losing
like he did. I wanted to make him feel better."

I thought I should remind her that it was all fake, but I didn't. As I
listened, a painless ache, the feel of something old and empty, started
growing in my chest. It spread up into my throat, and then it fell into
my crotch, forked and seeped down the insides of my thighs.

Yvonne kept talking.

"I followed him outside, and the only thing I could think of to say
was that I was sorry he didn't win. Pretty weak, huh?" She looked at me
and looked away again. "When he turned on me and grunted, I said
pretty damn fast that I meant I was sorry he didn't win a door prize for
his ticket. Like, 'I mean, I'm sorry you didn't win a door prize,' I said."
She took a deep drag of her cigarette and then dropped this one only
half smoked into the beer can. "I avoided the subject of what happened
in the ring. He seemed kind of wounded in a way I can sort of relate to,
but I really don't understand what pushed me toward him."

"Must've been the sequins and rhinestones," I said.

I thought she'd cuss or slap me again, but she didn't.

"Anyway," she said, her voice suddenly sounding weary, "we talked
beside his truck for a few minutes and then went over to the Shoney's
on Trinity Lane." She looked down at her hands, drew a deep breath
and released it slowly. "We've been together ever since."

"So," I said, forcing myself to stand up against the railing beside her.
"I've got two questions." I put my hand on her shoulder and turned her
around to face me. "Why have we been doing what we've been doing?
That's still the first one. And is this guy going to try to kill me when we
get back to Nashville?"

Yvonne laughed—a wheezy, musical sound, like an accordion—and
the energy returned to her voice.

"I'll answer question number two first, if I may. No, he's not going
to try to kill you because he's never going to know. This is a road thing,
between friends. And question number one?" She leaned close to me

and bit me lightly on the chest. "Like I said, it's a good time. And I think I've always wanted to since that New Year's morning. Maybe we both just needed that first time, and these last two have sort of been like aftershocks."

The night in Ringold began for me with bitter thoughts of revenge on Eliza. But within minutes, maybe even seconds, it'd turned sweet in its own rough way. I loved the feel of Yvonne's small body covering me. And in those moments, when I lay pinned beneath her, I loved the way my memories left me alone.

"So, it's back to separate lives when we get home?" I said.

"Definitely." She slid her arms under mine and pulled herself close to me. "But can we put one more quarter in the machine before then?"

I bent and picked her up, carried her carefully back into the room and threw her on the bed.

*   *   *

When the last chord of our mini-tour was struck in Tuscaloosa and the applause had faded away, the band collapsed into the chairs around one table, all of us dreading the teardown and loadout and the overnight drive back to Nashville.

"I think one more night of this heave-ho crap would kill me," Lukas said.

"You're Gabriel, right?" a waitress said as she leaned over my shoulder and set a beer in front of me. "These are from a Mr. Townshend at the bar." In addition to the beer she handed me a napkin folded in half.

"Thanks," I said, raising one eyebrow to glance at Lukas. I unfolded the napkin—"Chuck Townshend, Muscle Shoals Productions"—and passed the note around the table.

"I've heard that name," Reggie said.

Hayes nodded.

"Me, too."

"Well," I said. "Let me check this out." I pushed back my chair and stood up, letting my hand play across Yvonne's shoulders as I walked from the table.

Two men remained at the bar, but one was no more than a thick body in a sweaty flannel shirt slumped against the wall at the end.

"Mr. Townshend?" I said to the other man.

"Yep," Chuck Townshend said.

Even sitting down, he was tall and thin. With the low heels of his hiking boots hooked into the bottom footrest on the barstool, he seemed folded like a cardboard cutout.

"Pull up a stool, Mr. Tanner," he said.

I set the beer Townshend had sent me on the bar and climbed up on a stool.

"You're down from Muscle Shoals, I take it."

"That's right. I'm down here and drunk." He dug his fingers into the wiry gray hair on the top of his head and scratched hard. "I was in town to check out another band and heard you were here." He took off his glasses, laid them on the bar and rubbed his face with both hands. "Just a coincidence, really."

"You've heard of the band before?" I asked. "In Muscle Shoals?"

He let one foot drop to the floor with a thud.

"I called you over here to talk about music, but I've let that pretty barmaid get me too damn drunk." He pulled out his wallet and started digging through it.

I looked over at the band's table and saw that the four of them were looking back at me. I shrugged.

"Here we are." Townshend pulled out a business card and handed it to me. "Write your name and number on the back of that." His other foot hit the floor while I wrote, and he rose from the stool.

I handed the card back to him.

"Good show," he said and dropped the card in his shirt pocket. "I'll call you." He pushed off the bar and weaved his way out the door.

*   *   *

The sun was up by the time we rolled into Nashville. After we returned the big equipment to our rehearsal room, Hayes, Yvonne and Reggie got into their cars and drove away. I told Lukas I'd return the trailer to the rental lot after I'd gotten some sleep.

"How are you going to go about looking into this Chuck Townshend fellow?" Lukas asked.

I slammed shut the hatchback of my little white Ford.

"I suppose I'll start by looking for his name on albums at Cat's Records. I'll do that this evening, and then tomorrow I can ask around a bit." I unlocked my door. "I'll let you know what I find out."

We looked at each other across the roof of my car.

"It was a great little tour," Lukas said. "This band's really starting to happen."

"No doubt. I hope we can do this more often."

"Yeah, man," Lukas said. "But I hope we can afford roadies next time." He opened the door of his pickup and dropped behind the wheel. Then he was back out again. "Oh, I meant to ask you how rooming with Yvonne worked out?"

"It was a little rough at first, but we got along all right."

When I reached the old house where I rented an upstairs apartment, Yvonne's car was parked on the street out front, and she was asleep in my bed.

Chapter 11
Muscle Shoals Scenes

By the time Chuck Townshend called two days later, I'd asked around and knew much more about the man.

He owned one of the biggest studios in the small music center of Muscle Shoals, Alabama, housed his production and publishing companies in an adjacent building and had in a long career worked with a wide variety of recording artists—from David Allan Coe to David Bowie, from Etta James to one of Prince's cast-off girlfriends, from the Mills Brothers to Lynyrd Skynyrd. He'd come from Oklahoma to Nashville at first, in the late '50s or early '60s, but hated the rhinestone glitz of the place and abandoned it as soon as he could for the funky anonymity of Muscle Shoals.

The next day I followed his directions south from Nashville, across the back roads of Tennessee and into Alabama. The morning was bright and without clouds. The air was warm enough when still, but the clear chill of autumn could be felt in the wind that roared at my open window as I raced along a series of gently rolling two-lanes. Even though the roadside didn't rise with the friendly swell of North Carolina's mountains, the people in the fields outside the simple houses, the men sitting in front of the courthouse in Pulaski, the women walking on the sidewalks in Lawrenceburg, were the same. I smiled at the steady touch of things so familiar.

At noon we sat in the Tiny Dinette—no tables, just ten stools at a counter and an overflow shelf along the wall—and talked over meat-and-three meals and beer.

"How long have you been up in Nashville?" Townshend asked.

"Let's see. I moved there in the middle of '82, so it's been a little over five years."

"That's a good amount of time. Things ought to start happening for you about now."

"Well," I said. "That'd be nice."

"Are you free of everything? You know, obligations and such."

I felt words hanging in the air around the inquiry—Billy Keith, "Best I've Ever Seen," CBS Records, Bullet Recording, Stallion Records, "Lacy," Mo Biggs. But I wasn't bringing these words to the countertop. Chuck Townshend was. Something in the lanky man's knowing smile made me uneasy. The questions seemed routine, as if the answers were somehow already known.

"Yeah," I said. "My last contracts ended over a year ago. It's just me and the band now."

"Good," Chuck Townshend said. "That's good." He shoveled up a mound of collard greens drenched in vinegar. "Let me tell you what I've got in mind."

* * *

I drove from Muscle Shoals straight to Lukas's house, and we sat and smoked in the little home studio. The first brittle leaves of autumn rustled against the darkened windows as I gave my friend a word-for-word account of the meeting with Townshend.

"And he's interested in the band being part of all this?" Lukas asked.

"Yeah, he liked the band in Tuscaloosa. What he said was that he was willing to give the band first shot at doing the record. And if it didn't work out, he'd bring his guys in."

"But why are we waiting two years?"

"We're not waiting two years, Lukas," I said. "He'll work us into his schedule over the next year and then a record should be out in '89. We'll have time to get better as a band. We'll play on the road as much as we can and build up followings in some other cities. We'll be traveling to Muscle Shoals to record demos of new material and learning to work with Chuck at the same time." I got up and paced the floor. "I think it could be cool."

"Yeah, man," Lukas said. "When can we all go down to check

things out?"

"He wants to book us into a club down there next month. To let his people hear our stuff. He said he'd put us up for the night somewhere, and we could just hang out a day or two."

"Great, man. Let's call the guys."

"Okay, but—" I stopped and crushed out my cigarette.

"But what?"

"I don't really know. Something bothered me the whole time I was talking to him."

"What's that?" Lukas asked. "Don't tell me he reminded you of Billy Keith."

"It's hard to put my finger on. Certain things he said made me feel like he knew me somehow."

"I hope you don't mean like reincarnation or something?"

"No," I said and laughed. "Not knew me, I guess, but knew a lot more about me than he ought to or than he said. Like he'd been following me. But the band seemed like a surprise to him."

"Maybe he knows Billy Keith."

"Probably. But even if he does, I'm sure BK wouldn't have told him all the things he seems to know. This guy has done some snooping—"

Mo Biggs. Townshend was his mystery man.

I stopped pacing and sat down and rubbed my eyes, trying to erase the sudden image of a pale carcass being hoisted onto a gurney and rolled into the darkness.

"Forget it," I said. "Let's call the guys."

*　*　*

It was December before the Muscle Shoals performance could be arranged for the Holiday Inn's lounge. Chuck Townshend said it was a comfortable room where many of the local studio musicians got together and jammed after hours.

I had the feeling that the crowd was almost completely composed of people who worked in the tiny music business community there, but the atmosphere was so different from the usual one the same type of people would have created in Nashville. At The Cannery, the Exit/

In or the Songbird, a crowd drawn completely from Music Row would often be dressed to the nines, cool and reserved, glancing around to see who they might see and who might see them. The people here were relaxed, laughing, casual both in their dress and in the tidbits of conversation I overheard.

When I mounted the stage alone, the applause was warm and sincere. I reached up and adjusted the microphone and then lightly strummed an open G, listening to the tuning in my monitor. Satisfied that all was ready, I kept strumming and looking around the room as if I were lost, as if I'd forgotten something I thought I never would or could. Then, when I felt the audience beginning to pull for me, I fell into a rhythm and sang.

> *The social event of the calendar year*
> *Was circled in red hearts and finally near.*
> *A thrill ran through Kayla and up she jumped*
> > *a-clicking her heels.*
> *Her mother's old dancing shoes still held their shine.*
> *They had cut many a rug in their time,*
> *And on younger feet they would again dance*
> > *the waltzes and the reels.*

"All right!" somebody yelled.

"*Hell,* yeah," from another.

Several people squirmed in their seats, took sips of beer and settled back down, leaning toward me now.

> *Come Saturday night with the bonfires all lit,*
> *The ale in the keg, and the pig on the spit,*
> *Joshua stood off alone as the fairgrounds*
> > *were filled.*
> *But when the fiddles were fondled and the mandolins rang,*
> *He lifted his high lonely voice and he sang,*
> *And it echoed in waves through the misty blue valleys*
> > *and the hills.*

"Lordy! Sing it, son!"

A blond woman at a front table slowly closed her eyes. A crease appeared in her brow, and a smile stretched her lips as I plowed into the chorus.

Songs for the highlands, songs for the sea,
Songs for the lovers who long to live free
From the painful misgivings and the fear of misstep.
Let 'em laugh right out loud
    and dance wild through the crowded jamboree.

As I sang the rest of the song, I scanned the room, glancing now and then at Chuck Townshend.

The tall man sat at the bar. As the lyric passed, he held himself still as stone. In the short interludes between verse and chorus, chorus and bridge, bridge and final verse, he spoke into the ear of a man he'd earlier introduced as the best engineer around. Townshend played airy instruments as he spoke—strummed his shirt, danced ten fingers along the edge of the bar, crashed an invisible cymbal with the long index finger of his right hand.

The engineer said nothing, only stared and worked on his chewing gum.

The band joined me on stage at the end of "Jamboree," and I introduced them to the crowd.

Reggie counted four. Lukas pushed the spread fingers of his left hand into the keyboard, and the low E-B-E sounded like the faraway rumble of a train rolling through mist-shawled mountains. Hayes and Reggie brought the song into the presence of the audience, the guitarist picking out a sparse e-minor line on the low strings, the drummer lightly, almost randomly, tinging a rhythm on the bells of his cymbals.

I looked over the heads in the crowd, my eyes fixed on some unidentifiable point on the back wall. I held my guitar vertically, my right hand around the base of the neck, the headstock pointing toward the colored lights above the stage. I adjusted the microphone again and pulled it to my lips, adding human breath to the soundtrack.

Yvonne stood against me but slightly behind, her left leg grapevining my right, her face turned toward mine in the sudden blue light. One hand held my shoulder, the other my arm. The black bass hung loosely behind her, headstock down.

As the eighth bar passed, she dropped her right hand from my arm, reached back, and on the downbeat of the ninth thumbed her low E and slowly unwound herself from me when I started to sing two beats later.

Faded photograph
In a shirt pocket, travel-worn . . .

A dark and mysterious rhythm took shape. Soft mallets drummed syncopated sixteenth notes on a set of mounted bongos. The kick drum thundered like an anxious heart, skipping the twos and fours and stuttering a sixteenth into the first beat of alternating measures. The low notes of the bass rolled with it, bridging the gap between the percussive and the melodic.

Smiles broke across faces in the crowd, and heads began to nod in time with the music.

I closed my eyes against the sting of sweat pouring from my forehead.

At the end of the second verse, Reggie stood up behind his drums and moved his mallets to a cymbal. Rolling thirty-second notes crescendoed toward a lightning splash.

I opened my eyes and, over these few seconds, watched the crowd in amazement.

As the band followed Reggie's build-up, the people came to their feet, clapping their hands, shouting toward the stage in voices that drowned in the swell of music.

We leaned into our microphones and belted out the first line of the chorus in harmony.

I came for the gold!

Boom-crack-booboomboom-crack-boom-crack-booboomboom...

I howled like the man in the song, suddenly striking it rich after years of digging and believing and digging some more.

When the band settled back into the sultry groove of the verse, the crowd remained standing.

The showcase rolled on like that for an hour, the band feeding the crowd energy and getting it right back. In the end, after two encores, the five of us—Hayes, Yvonne and I, Lukas and Reggie—stood in a line across the stage, bowing, our arms locked around each other's shoulders.

Chuck Townshend, his engineer, and the rest of the crowd still stood on their feet. The room rang with applause and shouts and whistles.

Tears mingled unseen with the sweat that poured from my brow and dripped off the end of my nose with every bow. When I stood looking out over that crowd, I felt the mixture seep through my mustache to salt lips that couldn't stop smiling.

Chapter 12
Catch That Train to Asheville

Yvonne's voice distorted as she screamed through the receiver and into my ear.

"They said they're gonna play it! Turn on your radio! ... There it is! God, it sounds great!"

"What station?" I yelled back.

"KDF! Oh, God! Hurry up, Gabriel!" She started to hum an improvised melody over the chord structure of the intro.

I squeezed the receiver between my ear and shoulder and turned on the stereo. "Hoe-Down" from Copland's *Rodeo* blasted across the public station's frequency, and I hit the button for WKDF.

A split second of silence and then,

I'm running for the station,
And I'm running out of time.
With a rumble and a roar,
My connection blows on down the line.
Crumpled in my hand
Is a ticket to Wonderland.

"Catch That Train" had never sounded so good, not even when we'd listened to it time and time again on the main speakers in Chuck Townshend's Muscle Shoals studio. Maybe it was because I hadn't heard it in a while. Maybe it was because it was on the radio.

I put it with love's mementos
Pressed so neatly in my book.

Then under the weight of the falling night,
I dream I run through woods
To a garden there that grows
Red with every faded rose I never gave away.

I hung up the telephone, not knowing whether Yvonne was still on the other end.

Someday I'm gonna catch that train,
From the depot down on Lovers' Lane....

The song filled the room like a child, showed off for me, drew the whole of my attention to itself. At the beginning of the last verse, I slowly—almost reluctantly—smiled and started to dance.

* * *

A month later, on the morning after a gig at The South End in Memphis, the telephone rang in the motel room. We groaned and untangled ourselves, and I reached for the receiver.

"Mmhmm," I said sleepily, a little angrily.

"You up, cuz?" Cutter laughed. "It's time you were getting up anyway, you slug. I've already talked to the other guys. They're ready to leave."

I sat up on the side of the bed, trying to clear my head.

"What is it, Cutter?"

"They want you to come up here to Asheville."

"They who?"

"WILD-FM and something called the Downtown Association."

"I don't want to come to Asheville," I said.

"Why not?"

"You know why not."

Yvonne's legs slipped around my waist. Beneath her bed-warmed skin, the muscles flexed and she squeezed me tightly.

"It has been seven years, Herr Tanner," Cutter was saying. "I believe it is time to leave your past fixations behind and find new ones for your future."

"Thank you, Dr. Shrinkwrap, but I still don't want to play Asheville."

Yvonne sat up close behind me. With every breath, her breasts touched my back. Her dry hands slid under my arms and massaged my chest for a moment before she pinched my nipples.

"What was that last bit, Cutter?" I asked.

"I said WILD-FM's playing the hell out of your song. And this Downtown Association wants you guys to do an outdoor show on June twenty-third, sort of a first-weekend-of-summer thing. The station'll advertise the crap out of it. Hell, the city's even gonna announce it on the damn water bills."

"What if she's there?" I said.

Yvonne bit my shoulder and tightened her hold on me.

"So what if she is?" Cutter said. "Do this for all of us up here. If Eliza shows up, you can see her and the mister the one time and get it out of the way."

I was quiet. I dipped my index finger in and out between Yvonne's toes until she let loose the body scissors, rolled off the other side of the bed and went into the bathroom. In a moment, I heard the toilet flush and the shower start.

"Gabe?" Cutter said. "What the hell are you doing?"

"Oh, sorry, Cutter." I stood up and then sat back down on the edge of the other bed to turn my eyes from the brightness of the window and to see Yvonne if she walked out of the bathroom before I got off the telephone. "So, why'd they call you?"

"They called Aunt Maggie first, and she said it'd probably be better if they talked to me. You know, my old business background and all." Cutter laughed his laugh.

"Okay, what kind of money are they offering?"

"Well, I don't know what you're used to getting now that you've got a hit record. They told me they could only pay seven fifty. But come on, it'll be a blast. Runion'll turn out in force. You could sell God-knows-how-many CDs and cassettes. The record company'll love it."

"Okay, okay, you've made your point. Go ahead and book it. No, wait! Did you check with Hayes to see if we've got the date open?"

"Done," Cutter said and was gone.

* * *

I traveled home to Runion two days before the performance in Asheville. After eating the supper Mom had waiting, I sat on the porch with her and Dad as the shadows stretched eastward.

"Old man Reese's got his still up and running again this year," Dad said, nodding toward Lonesome Mountain.

I looked and saw near the mountain top the tiny puffs of white rising like smoke signals into the deepening blue of the clear evening sky.

"Surely the law knows he makes whiskey back of that ridge," I said.

"Of course they know," Dad grunted. "Everybody knows."

Mom smiled.

"Well," she said. "He never forgets to deliver his first fruits to Deputy Boyce to be doled out for medicinal purposes. That's the thing."

Like the smoke rising from Lonesome, from the shadowed valley of Big Muddy Creek rose the whistle of a train passing along the French Broad River below Runion.

Dad cocked his head and listened.

"Rain coming Friday," he said.

"What makes you say that?" I asked.

"It's the train," Mom said. "Your dad figured it out."

"Figured what out? The band has to play outside Friday. It can't rain."

"Well," Dad said. "We're going to get rain here on Friday. Don't know what it'll do in Asheville."

"But what's the train got to do with it?"

"Whenever you hear the whistle that clear here at the house, it means the weather'll change third day from then. Since it's pretty now, that probably means rain."

* * *

The thunderheads gray and grow beards of gray showers. They circle the city, closing tighter with every rotation. Storm winds howl in the alleys—lonely, prowling, sniffing at debris. The eye holds just above Pack Square and an electrically charged platform covered by red-and-white-striped tenting.

A crowd of a thousand or more watch the stage then look up at the sky. Watch the stage. Look up. They shift and slosh in the square like water in a barrel.

Please welcome ... Nokturn recording artist . . .

Thunder in my throat.

The music. Shapeless and not loud enough. It oozes from stacks of speakers that topple over and over again into the crowd.

This one is drunk. Half moons of white skin jiggle below the frayed cut of her blue jeans shorts. She asks if I'll ever need a dancer in the band.

An old black man moves almost like something made of rubber, almost like something from a cartoon. His eyes are red, and the stepped-on cigarette bounces on his lip as he mumbles to the girl in the short shorts.

Faces rise in front of me and then sink and rise somewhere else in the swirl and wash of the crowd. My mother and father, fingers in their ears. Brother Butler as a teenager in his green bagboy's apron. Webb Garrison and Libby. Uncle T, glittering. Jay and Wiley. Billy Keith. Mo Biggs, pale and naked, pointing an accusing finger at me. Cutter and Rendy. Bigmama Sadie Butler James, scowling and praying. Mason Queenan, sign-up sheet in hand.

Among the living and the dead, she alone is missing—and yet somehow everywhere at once.

Yvonne bites hard in the soft flesh of my side.

The sky closes.

Rain falls.

The show ends in thunder.

Chapter 13

Neoromantic Nokturn

I awoke almost too late to make my meeting, jumped in the shower, dressed and hurried downtown.

I stepped from the heat of Church Street, through the revolving door, and into the cool atmosphere of the Inn on Printers Alley. As famous as the place was, in all the years I'd lived in Nashville I'd never been inside. But this was where Oswald and Edward Turrenok, the brothers who headed the music conglomerate that owned Nokturn Records, wanted to meet me. Oswald had called three days before to say that the scouts he'd sent to the outdoor show in Asheville had come back with favorable reports. Promotion plans had now been finalized for me, and it was time to put them into action.

I walked down the quiet fourth floor hall and knocked on the door of Suite 442.

Oswald opened the door, took my hand and guided me inside.

Edward sat at a round table in front of a floor-to-ceiling window in the exterior wall, some papers spread before him, the Cumberland River and the historic section of East Nashville behind.

Both brothers wore navy blue dress pants and white cotton shirts with the sleeves rolled up. Edward had a red-and-navy striped tie hanging loosely at his neck. Both men were trim, deeply tanned and of medium height. Both had sea-green eyes and wore their hair oiled and combed straight back. The only striking difference was that Edward's hair was shiny black and Oswald's was the color of sunrise fog.

"Sit down, please," Oswald said, motioning me toward the chair opposite Edward and settling himself into another close beside his brother. "We understand the performances are going well since the release of your single. That is good."

Before I could answer, Edward said, "As we informed you on the telephone, we sent people to see you in Carolina last month. You sold three hundred twenty CDs in just over an hour's performance. That is promising."

I tried to place the accent in the brothers' speech, hearing in it something from central or eastern Europe, perhaps a hint of Bela Lugosi. But it was slight and sporadic, more obvious in the resonance and inflection of the words than in their pronunciation.

"I'm glad you guys're happy," I said and eased myself down into the chair. "We're having a—"

"Gabriel," Edward said. "As you know, Nokturn Records has made its reputation in the world of popular music with the reclusive singer Goddard. However, because we acquired the company through corporate dealings, we can take little pleasure in his success beyond sharing his financial rewards. There is no sense of accomplishment for us. He simply records his master tapes, and we receive them by mail. That is the extent of our personal involvement with him."

"You are our opportunity for more," Oswald said quickly, seeming to know he was heading off my mouthful of questions about Goddard. "We have recently established a management company we call Turrenkey Management. It is our desire to structure your career from this promising beginning, to recreate, if you will, Gabriel Tanner, making him a substantial idol, an icon, exactly in opposition to Goddard, who is insubstantial, a ghost. That is why we have summoned you here this morning."

The Turrenoks sat almost in silhouette against the midmorning light that flooded through the large window. Their cat-like eyes burned in shadowed faces.

I squirmed in my seat.

"Well—"

"As you already know," Edward said, "we released 'Lay Me On the Table' by our other new artist, Chelsea Rambo, at the same time as your train song. Chelsea's persona, her mixture of the hiphop bitch, the debutante, the weightlifter, is exactly right for the current American cultural climate, and her record is performing better than your own.

That much is clear."

"However," Oswald Turrenok took over again, "we feel strongly that your long-range potential is by far the greater of the two. And although your career will require more work, it will ultimately give us bigger bangs for our buck, as the current saying goes. It is due to this feeling that we offer you a management contract." He reached a hand in front of Edward and slid the thick document that lay there across the table toward me. "We are certain that if you completely give yourself up to our guidance, you will scale the heights of the music world."

I looked down at the first page of the contract but didn't touch it. It was a contract slid across a table to me just as Mo Biggs's had been years before. But even though I'd hated how Mo handled me that night, the big man had still seemed like something familiar—a good old boy trying to act out a scene from a movie. These two, Oswald and Edward, seemed alien to me, and I understood that they weren't acting.

"What about the band?" I asked.

"We care little for the band," Oswald said. "You are the creative one."

"But we bill this thing as Gabriel Tanner and Lonesome Star. It's a band. If you sign only me, what happens to them?"

"Without you, the band is no more than a group of random musicians."

Edward shifted abruptly in his seat.

"Again, we care nothing for the band. They are expendable as far as our interests are concerned. That is the fact of the matter, and that is the end of our discussion of them."

I stared at Edward and wondered where he and his brother were going with this. I knew as well as they did that other players could be found, other players as good or better. But other players wouldn't be Lonesome Star. Chuck Townshend had recognized their contribution to my music and used them on most of the new album. I turned my gaze on Oswald. How could anybody who knew or cared anything about my music think Lukas and the others expendable?

Edward heaved a sigh.

"And so. Our operatives in the field have reported to us that you are all music while performing, and that is a good beginning. But unfortunately it is insufficient for the making of the superstar we believe you capable of becoming." He spread both hands flat on the table, stretched the fingers wide, and leaned toward me. "In short, you have no image. Your clothes say nothing. Your movements say nothing. Your entire bloody public life says nothing at all. Only your music speaks, and that is not enough in these days."

I felt my face redden but worked to keep my expression from changing.

"Okay," I said, nodding slightly.

Oswald cleared his throat and, with a restraining hand on his brother's forearm, stood up.

"We intend to recreate Gabriel Tanner as what we have decided to call a neoromantic figure. A contemporary Lord Byron, if you will." He moved around the table toward me. "Let us begin with your physical appearance. The beard is good for the structure of your face, but do not allow it to grow longer than it is at present. It has been said that you might reduce it to a goatee. Consider it." He took a lock of my long black hair between his thin fingers. "Your hair would benefit from being made darker or much lighter. And a few permanent waves should be added. And it must be cut to prevent its looking untidy." He moved behind me and stopped. "You are soft in the middle. The build of today's MTV musician tends to the gaunt. Lose twenty-five pounds. If you cannot accomplish this on your own, we can advance you a small stipend for the services of a personal trainer."

I bit the inside of my lower lip and looked out the window. I imagined I could see through the heat and haze to the mountains around Runion, where this time of year—this early summer lull between planting and harvest—my mother and father would be sitting on their front porch with Aunt Evelyn and Uncle Uart, making plans for the Fourth of July, listening to WILD-FM on their boom box's radio and waiting through song after song that set their teeth on edge just to hear me again.

Edward glanced up from some notes he'd been making, looked over my head, and nodded.

"And so," he said. "You will require an entirely new wardrobe which we shall procure for you in New York City and charge as a recoupable advance to your account at Nokturn. This new wardrobe will consist largely of high-collared white shirts and long dark coats. The shirts will, of course, include ornate collars, breasts, and cuffs, in keeping with the tradition of the Romantic Period you will seek to imitate, to recreate." He loosened his tie a little further and leaned back in his chair. "We have decided to allow you to wear your precious American blue jeans, provided they fit your buttocks properly. We also leave to you the choice of appropriate footwear and eyewear."

"But this is not to be a wardrobe for the stage only," Oswald said. "You will dress yourself in this manner each day and in all seasons. You are not to be seen in public dressed as you are now."

A small smile appeared on Edward's face.

"In case you are unaware, your dry cleaning bills are tax deductible."

I returned the smile and leaned slightly forward.

"You gonna hire somebody to fluff my ruffles and stuff my codpiece?"

Edward slammed both fists on the table.

"This is not a joke, Gabriel Tanner," he said, half standing. "We do not play games where such potential is involved."

Oswald moved from behind me and laid a hand on his brother's shoulder.

Edward settled back into his seat and glared at me for a moment, then began more scribbling on the various papers in front of him.

"It is only that we are quite excited about our plans for you," Oswald said.

"Well, the clothes sound nice," I said. "Sort of like Prince or some of those bands from the sixties—Paul Revere and the Raiders, maybe. I always kinda liked stuff like that." I pictured myself traveling home to Runion in such a getup, stopping at rest areas, stepping up onto the porch at my folks' house, running into Eliza while strolling downtown. "I don't know if I'll wear it all the time, but I can give it a try, I guess."

"Yes, do give it a try, won't you?" Oswald said. "And you are right, of course. The fashion is not new to the world of popular music." He reached down and placed a finger on one of the papers Edward was working on, angled it toward himself, and said without looking up from it, "But the master plan we have devised for you goes far beyond mere fashion."

He paused, but when I said nothing, he continued.

"If you wish to succeed beyond your wildest financial dreams, this change of fashion must become an outward and visible sign of a major change in your lifestyle. You will think the plan we are about to lay before you is completely at odds with your music, but we think you will find that what we suggest will enhance the music you write in the future more than it will conflict with the music you are performing at present."

My palms began to sweat. I leaned back in my chair and sat up again, turned sideways and crossed my legs. Then I cleared my throat, pulled out a cigarette, and lit it.

"You appear tense, Gabriel. Do you drink?" Oswald turned to his brother. "Edward, fix our future star a vodka."

Edward looked at the cigarette and frowned but didn't say anything. He stood up and walked stiffly to a massive oak cabinet with built-in stereo, television and bar. Glass and ice met with a clink. He returned to the table and took his seat.

I looked at the drink he slid across the table toward me but made no move to reach for it.

"We have no beer," he said.

"In your new lifestyle, you must drink, to excess whenever possible," Oswald said.

"I've been doing a lot of that lately, anyway."

"Yes, but beer will not do. It is too ordinary. Choose a liquor. Something exotic, we think. That would be best." He paused. "Something you can make as famous as the martini of James Bond."

"Hard stuff makes me sick," I said, wondering how they knew what I drank.

"Then you must overcome that or learn to live with it. We can arrange for you to attend the most exclusive parties in Hollywood, Manhattan, London, Tokyo, Paris, Monte Carlo. It is important that you be seen at these. You will find that the liquor releases you from your inhibitions, allowing a certain wildness that is essential for our plan and your career. Of course, you will want to use it before every performance as well. And when you are writing. It will open broad horizons to you, I am sure, as it has done for many artists in the past." He paused again and stared at me for a moment. "This is a most important thing. You cannot remain the mundane persona you are."

"I see."

Edward leaned forward and spread his hands on the table again.

"We have composed a list of traits and experiences you must have. The realization of some is, of course, optional, but the appearance of reality in all is essential." Another small smile creased his face. "Shall I rehearse the list with you?"

"I'm not sure I want to hear it."

"Then you are excused, and your career with Nokturn is over," Edward shouted, smacking his hands flat on the table and falling back into his chair.

Oswald lifted a hand to still his brother once again. His pale green eyes searched my face.

"Calm yourself, Edward, and read the list. He will listen."

Edward heaved another sigh.

"As we said, reality in any of these beyond the liquor is optional. It is the appearance of reality that is essential here." He leaned forward again. "You must consider using cocaine. This is, of course, illegal, but we can readily supply you with the best available product from the streets of New York City. It has a wonderful effect. I use it myself quite regularly."

"No shit," I said.

"And you must carry about you a certain air of sexual ambivalence," Edward said, ignoring me, "taking both women and men—particularly boys—as lovers. We can supply these for you from within our companies, guaranteeing them to be tested and free of disease."

I pictured my mother moving through Whitson's Green Grocer and wondering why people are staring at her so. She approaches a checkout line, trying not to appear rattled, anxious to be out of there so that she can get to a mirror. She glances at the scandal sheets on the racks above the candy bars and chewing gum, hoping to avoid the increasing intensity of the stares. And there's her baby, wrapped in the arms of a tall man with the chiseled physique of Michelangelo's "David."

"Women will flock to you out of fascination," Edward continued. "Matters will be helped if you father an illegitimate child or two as well." He smiled. "I am envious."

"This sounds like your neoromantic Byron is just a white mix of Michael Jackson and Prince," I said.

Oswald's jaws flexed and his eyes widened for a moment.

"Perhaps the female in your band, the one you fuck when you tour, could bear you the first," he said. "Yvonne Moon, is it not?"

"Hey, wait a damn minute," I said, standing up and kicking my chair backwards out of the way. It was my turn to slam my fists on the table. "What the hell?"

"We have watched you," Oswald said calmly and moved the chair back into place. "Please sit down again."

I didn't sit down.

"And so," Edward said after a moment of tense quiet. "There is only one final point. You must leave Nashville. You cannot be taken seriously operating from here. You cannot, however, return to your home in Runion. We feel that would be the death of our plans. You must become as rootless as is possible. A nomad." He grabbed the glass of vodka I hadn't touched, stood up, and looked out the window, down toward Third Avenue. He took a slow sip of the drink. "Gabriel, think how exciting it will be for your fans to believe that at any moment in their dull and finite little lives, they might catch a glimpse of you as you stagger down a street in their dull and finite little town. That is something to think about, hmm?"

"And what the hell would a big neoromantic star be doing in a 'dull and finite little town' anyway?" I asked.

Oswald stood close to me.

"We have learned from our work with Goddard," he said, "that the power to mystify and fascinate an audience is the strongest of commodities in the music world. Other artists have it but not the music to perpetuate it, to back it up, if you will. You have the music already, but in the current market place, the music is nothing without the image. Do you understand?" He put a hand on my shoulder. "We offer the image that will allow your music a worldwide market. Tell us you understand."

"I understand," I said. "I understand perfectly."

I turned away from Oswald and stood with my hands gripping the back of the chair I'd sat in through most of the meeting. I read the words at the top of the document that lay on the table in front of me—"Exclusive Management Agreement." The first paragraph listed Turrenkey Management and gave the conglomerate's Madison Avenue address. My name was listed too. My name alone, without an address. Without Lukas. Without Yvonne. Without Lonesome Star. Alone.

Edward finally turned from the window.

"And so. Take the contract to your lawyer. Have him or her study it thoroughly. But execute it quickly, before it is time for your next single to be released. We already have storyboard and director for the video."

A breathy chuckle escaped through my nose at the vision of myself in ruffled garb, traveling through some unidentifiable somewhere, drunk, sick with dry heaves, not a drop of truth left inside me.

"Well?" Edward said, facing me across the table.

"I can't do it," I whispered.

"Bocsánat?"

I found my voice.

"I can't fucking do this!"

Edward slammed both fists on the table so violently that an oily strand of his inky hair came loose and dangled in front of his face.

"Then your bloody pitiful career is over! That is all!" He spun toward the window and stood with his hands on his hips, breathing hard.

"Name me one single fucking recording artist," I said and paused and closed my eyes to calm myself. "One single artist who lives the kind of life you're talking about. What in the hell are you guys on?"

Suddenly Oswald was at my side again, taking hold of my elbow.

"The fact that it is not done will capture the attention of the world, Gabriel Tanner. Reconsider. Take your time. We have thought this through since before we purchased Nokturn, and it will work." He dug his fingers into my arm. "Take the contract. Sign it."

"Listen to me," I said, yanking my elbow out of Oswald's grasp. "I won't even touch the damn thing, much less sign it." I backed toward the door, keeping my eyes on Oswald, listening to Edward's angry heavy breathing. Then I stopped my retreat. "Mr. Turrenok, can't we—"

"I am the calm one," Oswald Turrenok said. "But I am not the good one." His voice didn't waver or grow loud. "You refused me just now. I allow no second chances."

I heard Edward's breath catch, looked and saw his body slump a little bit.

"No, Oswald, please," Edward said. "His mind will change. We will have our artist just as we want him."

"No, Edward," Oswald said evenly, his green eyes seeming to push me back toward the door again. "It is too late. Call Anna. Tell her to make preparations to cease all promotions for Gabriel Tanner and transfer all remaining unencumbered promotional funds to Chelsea Rambo. I will waste no more time here." He stepped quickly to my left, as if herding me out of the room. "Little man. Your compact discs and cassettes have been ordered and shipped or I would stop that as well. But I promise you this. Within a space of weeks you will walk into the music shops to find yourself covered in dust."

I stopped backing up. Lightning struck somewhere just behind my eyes. Fire caught in my throat, and I lunged at Oswald, hitting him square in the chest with a two-handed shove.

Oswald stumbled backwards, fell over the couch, and sprawled in the floor between the couch and the bar. He didn't move or speak, only lay there with wide eyes and a scarlet face.

Out of the corner of my eye, I saw Edward move and tensed again, ready to go after him too.

But Edward had only turned from the window and slumped into his chair. He sat with his face in his hands, shaking his head, and now three or four strands of slick black hair dangled around his ears and wrists.

I turned back to Oswald.

"Did Chuck Townshend know what a bastard you are before he hooked me up with you?" My voice shook.

Oswald took his eyes off me and let his head fall back on the floor.

"Townshend knows exactly what I am," he said in his even tone. "I recognized your talent and paid him handsomely for your project. Yes, Townshend knows me. That is why he removed himself so completely from you and out of my way."

"Damn you," I said through clenched teeth. "God damn you!"

I pulled up hard on the thickly stuffed and pleated back of the couch, pushing out at the same time. But the couch was flimsy, mostly plush padding on a thin wooden frame, and my display of frustration yanked its back legs from the floor. I watched as it stood balanced for a long second and then fell over onto the downed CEO of Nokturn Records.

Chapter 14
A Moonshine Party and the Ride Home

As I rode down the elevator from the fourth floor of the Inn on Printers Alley, all I could think about was being home. Home in the mountains. A place I felt that I understood, a place where I was, if not understood myself, at least left alone for the most part. I pictured myself on a rock ledge I knew on the mountain behind my folks' house, a book or a pad and pencil in my lap, a canteen of spring water beside me, and nothing but the hush of the breeze and the taunting laughter of crows all around. But then the elevator doors rumbled open, and I was passing through the lobby, probably still pale or red-faced from the disaster upstairs.

The band got really pissed when I told them about the whole thing. We moaned and cussed all through rehearsal that evening, but in the end Hayes convinced us that the Turrenoks wouldn't carry through with their threat to pull the record.

"Money's the bottom line," he said. "Whatever thrill they'd get out of you living like that, if they still think there's money to be made, they won't drop us. They may keep pushing for some of these management fantasies of theirs, but they won't just let it all go if we're making a splash right out of the box."

It sounded good, and we started to cool down after that.

I put in a call to Chuck Townshend just the same. When he got back to me, he couldn't believe what had gone on in that meeting. "Harebrained" is what he called their scheme for me as a neoromantic figure for the 1990s. But he believed, like Hayes, that "Catch That Train" was taking off too well to be pulled from the market.

"Despite this bunch of nonsense," he said, "the Turrenoks run about the tightest ship in the business. I'll give 'em a call and see what I can do to smooth things out."

After Chuck's reassurances, I tried to relax and enjoy what was going on with the record. And I tried not to think about what would happen if Hayes and Chuck were wrong.

* * *

The band played MacArthur's on the last Friday night in June, and our schedule didn't pick up again until we played Lexington the next Wednesday. I needed a break after my tangle with the Turrenoks, so I came home to the mountains to stay through the Fourth of July, really glad to get out of Nashville for a few days.

The Fourth was on Tuesday so it must've been Monday afternoon when Cutter called and invited me to come with Rendy and him to Sodom Laurel for what he called a "moonshine party."

"It's just getting underway tonight," he said. "They'll all be pretty coherent for a while, so it should be a good time."

He wanted to come and pick me up at the house, but I told him I'd rather meet him downtown. Then I could follow them and come home when I wanted.

As usual I was a little late. When I got to Runion, their car was parked on Main Street between Ramsey's Funeral Home and the First Southern Missionary Church. They were across the street, sitting on a park bench in the shade of Uncle T's old office building.

I stopped in the middle of Main and waited as they jumped up and crossed over to their car.

Cutter smiled and gave me the finger while pretending to be rubbing his eye.

"Hey, Gabe," Rendy said and blew me a kiss.

A very beautiful girl. Her straight black hair moved in slow motion around her face and shoulders, reflecting the rainbow colors of the late afternoon sunlight and reminding me of Tara Southerland's. Her eyes smiled shiny and black. Her brow and cheeks, her nose and chin, were strong features but somehow soft and delicate at the same time. Lips full, teeth straight and white. Her skin was smooth and dark, and I thought she might have Cherokee or Choctaw in her ancestry.

Cutter's appearance had changed as much as his priorities since he left for college. Except for a few cartoon-like hairs, the top of his head was completely bald. He kept the graying hair that remained trimmed short like Uncle Uart had always worn his. An already iron gray beard that came and went with the seasons was gone this hot summer.

"Let's party!" Cutter yelled out the window as he pulled into the street in front of me.

I watched the two of them through their back windshield. They laughed, they talked, they arm wrestled in the small space between them. They kissed often. Whenever a bend in the road was especially deep or we came to a stop sign, I heard country music blaring from their radio. They'd look back now and then and smile and wave, and Cutter would make a motion for me to keep following.

Finally we turned off the pavement and onto a dirt road that wound its way upward in shadow along the steep sides of a range of wooded hills. Set back in nearly every hollow was a house—a shack really—or a barn, sometimes both, already in the deep shade of sunset. In many of these, weak lights glowed in the windows or bare yellow bulbs burned on the ceilings of porches. More than a few stood dark and overgrown, deserted long ago.

When I could see by the light of the sky through the trees that we couldn't get much higher, the road wrapped around the end of a ridge and came out of the woods into the sunset. Ragged pasture covered the steep slope on this face of the ridge, and strands of rusted barbed wire ran along each shoulder of the bumpy road. We passed an old barn that leaned to its downhill side like the Tower of Pisa, looking as if it might at any minute let go and roll away to the valley below.

After about a quarter of a mile, the dirt track we rode on ended at a small boxy house—square and squat with four main rooms, gray-brown plank siding. Four tall trees surrounded the place. Two on the west against the evening sun. Another on the opposite side and one in back. Several cars were parked beneath the tree on the east side, none looking even close to new. A couple of old buggies and a wagon added to the atmosphere, as did four swaybacked horses that grazed in the patchy grass of the front yard, nuzzling trash and keeping their distance from a crowd of people under the two trees to the right of the house.

We stopped and got out.

"This must be the place," Cutter said.

"What exactly are we getting into here, cuz?" I asked.

"It's a moonshine party, like I said. These folks'll be here all weekend. They'll eat and drink and take part in whatever other sensual or spiritual pleasures come to mind." He caught a loop of Rendy's cut-offs and pulled her to him. "You're gonna hear lots of music and stories. And we'll help them celebrate Delbert Gunter's birthday tonight."

"Delbert's here?"

"He better be," Rendy said. "He's the one that invited us."

As we walked across the yard, I looked at the group of people in the shade of the two tall oaks. I saw Delbert Gunter immediately, right where I expected him, sitting with his fiddle in the middle of a half circle made up of more fiddles, several guitars, a couple of mandolins, a couple of banjos and an upright bass.

He tipped his bow at Cutter and flashed him a wide white smile.

"I got those new teeth for him," Cutter said. "That's how we came to be invited up here." He flipped a salute at the old man. "Just doing my job."

Delbert Gunter shifted in the straight-backed wooden chair and pecked his fiddle with the bow.

"This song come to my mind t'other day for the first time in a long time. Old Granny Gentry used to sing it whilst she was a-battling and a-boiling her dresses and bloomers." He smiled at somebody in the crowd, scratched out a little melody on his fiddle, and started to sing.

Wake up, wake up, you drowsy sleeper,
Wake up, wake up, for it's almost day;
How can you sleep, you charming creature,
Since you have stolen my heart away?

His voice on the old ballad sounded just like I remembered from Saturday mornings in Stackhouse Park with Uncle T. A little nasal, a little ragged in his throat, but strong from his chest.

The sea's so wide I cannot wade it,
Nor either have I wings to fly;
I wish I had feet like a sparrow
And wings like a little dove,
I'd fly away off from the hills of sorrow
And light on some low lands of love.

Hand me down pen, ink, and paper,
And set me down here for to write;
I'll write of grief that bitter and sweet is
And troubles me both day and night. . . .

When he finished singing, he stood up and stretched and smiled widely again.

"I thank y'all for the birthday honors," he said. "Now this old man's gonna lay up under this here tree and listen for a while." He walked gingerly over to the base of one of the oaks, sat down like something falling apart under its own weight and leaned back against the bark. Then he pulled his hat over his eyes and folded his arms across the broad belly of his overalls.

"Let's see what they've got to eat here," Cutter said.

We went up three shaky cinder block steps that rose in back of the house to a new-looking deck of faded yellow-green wood.

Bringing up the rear, I let the screen door bang behind me. But the noise Mom used to scold me about more than anything went unnoticed here, drowned out by the laughter and talk that rang the walls of the small kitchen.

A large mountain woman in a navy blue dress with white polka dots cackled and wiped tears from her brown eyes with a balled-up tissue as she handed us plates.

The table was covered with platters of fried chicken, ham, biscuits and tomatoes, bowls of potato salad and beans and corn. Another table in the corner held pies and cakes.

Rendy took one look at the quick black bodies that zipped from dish to dish and set her plate down. Cutter and I ignored the flies and filled our plates to the outer edges.

The living room smelled of heat, food and hard-living people. In the center, two wooden chairs with straight backs and woven seats—the only pieces of furniture—held a man who strummed a guitar and a bony woman who sang "Jacob's Ladder." Ten or fifteen other folks filled the rest of the room, most of them with plates of food balanced on one hand.

We took a place against the wall by a closed door that probably led into a bedroom.

The front door and a screenless window were open to the porch. Another window that looked out to the west and the last light of day was shut.

A single bare bulb burned in a socket that was mounted on the wall above the doorway from the kitchen. A small ceiling fan turned slowly over the middle of the room, its only purpose seeming to be to make sure there was at least one thing in the room the flies couldn't light on.

We ate our fill and listened to the music, mostly hymns in here. Between performances the only sounds were a couple of mumbled amens, the munching of food, the clink of forks on plates, the hum of the ceiling fan and the flies.

When Cutter and Rendy settled into conversation with people they knew through their work, I decided to go try to talk to Delbert Gunter.

A bonfire now blazed in a rusty barrel that had been set between the two trees. The orange flames glittered on the empty beer cans that already overflowed another barrel closer to the house. Faces took on the glow of fire and alcohol. Wrinkles deepened. Wild young eyes sparkled.

The old musician wasn't by the tree anymore.

I wandered through the crowd for a while, looking for him, keeping quiet, not quite knowing what to say to these people.

Back in the kitchen, I asked the polka-dotted lady who shoved another plate into my hands if she'd seen Delbert Gunter.

"I reckon he'll be headed home by now," she said. "He don't stay around too long these days, especially when folks start to getting loud and all."

I had a piece of cake and went back into the hymn room. There the smell of beer mixed now with tobacco breath and sweat, but the songs remained in the same vein. A thin old man with a white shirt and wiry gray hair was leading the group through "The Sinner-Man."

O sinner-man, where you gonna run to?
O sinner-man, where you gonna run to?
O sinner-man, where you gonna run to
      All on that day?

Outside again, I found Cutter and Rendy and told them I thought it was time I left.

"Goodnight, Gabe," Rendy said and kissed me on the cheek.

"Rendy's on call tomorrow 'til six," Cutter said. "How about we meet over some Stackhouse Park barbecue around four-thirty? I'll get hold of Jay and Wiley too. Just the four of us, okay?"

"Sounds great," I said and looked around the crowd once more to make sure Delbert Gunter wasn't there. "I might stop down by the park tonight to see how the cooks are coming with the pigs."

"Tell Dad and Uncle Galen the womenfolk know they sneak a few beers while they're doing the barbecue," Cutter said and laughed.

With a little patience I squeezed my car out of the line, got turned around without having to ask anybody to move and headed around the ridge and back down the mountain. I swung out of one of the first deep curves and came upon Delbert Gunter in the middle of the road. He hobbled to the left and stood there, flashing his wide new grin, waving me by with one arm and holding his fiddle under the other.

I stopped and rolled down the window.

"Can I give you a lift?"

"Well, I might live a far piece out of your way."

"I can at least carry you down to the main road."

"I reckon you can if you're going that far."

He walked around in front of the lights, squinting and smiling, climbed in the passenger side and lay his fiddle across his lap.

"Much obliged," he said. "The evening's a little hot yet for hiking."

"No trouble at all, sir."

He said he liked those parties, especially when they had to do with his birthday, but he never stayed around much after the drinking started in earnest. Besides, he said, he liked it at home better than any place he knew.

After a few minutes of watching the road he asked about my car—

how long I'd had it, where it had taken me.

"Mostly running between here and Nashville, Tennessee, over the last few years," I said.

"That so?" He fell quiet again. Then, "You know, I've never been out of Madison County no more than two time my whole life."

"Really?"

"Along after my brother run off and got killed in the war, Mother and Daddy up and surprised theirselves and me with a little girl. A little sister. She married in Asheville to a city boy some twenty, thirty year ago. I went there to the wedding. They was at the party tonight. You might've noticed 'em. City folks they look like."

"I'm afraid I didn't notice."

"Well, I won't tell 'em," he said and laughed. "They like being noticed, I reckon."

I could feel him looking at me. My black ponytail hung to the middle of my back at the time, and I kept my nearly black beard trimmed so that to him it probably looked like I'd just been too lazy to shave in a week or so. At least my earring was hidden from him.

"You're sort of a city boy yourself, ain't you?" he said.

"Not really. I'm from around here. I grew up in Jewel Hill."

"Who's your daddy?"

I told him.

"Uh huh. Who's your granddaddy?"

"Grandpa Tanner lived in Montana. The other was Joel James."

"Lord, I knew Joel for a little while years ago. We weren't no more than boys then. He lived for a spell near the head of the Big Muddy Creek up Lonesome Mountain way. Hunted and fished together with him many a time." He chuckled to himself. "Son, we used to rassle of a Saturday, in one side of his daddy's horse barn and out the other. Then go home smelling like roses." He laughed out loud again. "Saturday was bath day anyhow."

"He died pretty young," I said. "I think he was in his early sixties. I don't remember as much about him as I'd like to."

"Well, if you're his grandson that makes you nephew to Dr. T. James."

"Yessir."

"Then if you remember your uncle, you remember your granddaddy. From what I knew of either of 'em they was a lot alike."

We finally reached the main road and I stopped.

"Which way?"

"Off to the left here and then up this side of Lonesome. But it ain't on your way to Jewel Hill."

"You were going to walk all this way?" I said as I pulled out onto the pavement.

"Well, I figured one or another'd come along. They always do."

I followed his directions, quiet for a while.

"I used to come hear you sing in Stackhouse Park on Saturdays," I said at last. "With Uncle T."

Delbert Gunter had been the centerpiece of those Saturdays in Stackhouse Park. He was like a minister to the congregation of mountain musicians. A fiddler he was. A singer of old ballads about kings and princesses and castles, tunes and lyrics passed down through his family since the days before that first great-great-something-or-other booked passage on a leaky nameless little ship chasing sunset and a dream across the Atlantic. Delbert sang songs his grandmother had written about finding her way into Appalachia and founding a life here. And he wrote some of his own songs too, mostly about the old ways of life in these mountains before the intrusion of the big electric world.

"I don't go down there no more," the old man said. "Ain't in many a year now." He pulled a pouch from the bib of his overalls and loaded his cheek with tobacco, folded the pouch neatly and tucked it away again. "That crowd just got to wanting and a-wanting. Now one and then another went off to be closer to some preacher that said he was gonna put 'em on the radio of a Sunday." He rolled down the window and spat. "Closer to Nashville is how they took it. A little guitar picking or a line of harmony on the radio and they think they're I don't know what. Quit their farms. Drive all the way to Asheville or Johnson City for factory work. Buying Cadillacs and singing on the radio. Ain't that something?"

"Nashville can be a hard way to go for some," I said.

"Well, these ain't a-going in the first place. I'll tell you that right now."

I recognized the turn that would take us to the top of Lonesome Mountain.

He pointed that way and leaned his head toward the open window.

"You know where you're going. I'm up near abouts the top." Spit. "Them people up in under them oaks tonight just make music for their ownselves. Most of 'em anyway. There's some has got Cadillacs on the brain." He moved his fiddle off his lap and onto the seat between us. "Music comes from these hills. All around us. You've heard it, ain't you?" Spit.

"I have."

"Music in the hills," he said. "Hills in the heart. Heart in the music. Just so in a circle like." Spit. "Leave that behind and you can't pour water from a boot with the directions wrote on the heel."

I laughed and lit a cigarette.

I could understand that. But where did it leave me? I was from the hills, sure enough. But my music? Couldn't help but be a little bit. More and more those days, I began to recognize melodies and phrases in my songs that harkened back to "Lacy" and reminded me powerfully of these hills. Maybe they were stolen or adapted from something I'd heard growing up. But, then again, maybe they were my original contributions to the circle of music Delbert Gunter was talking about.

But what about Lukas's music? Yvonne's, Reggie's and Hayes's? Where was theirs from? And as for the music the five of us made together, what part of what circle was that music from?

Spit.

"This is it, son."

We were near the top of Lonesome. I pulled over where the road widened as it passed a mailbox with "GUNTER" written on it in white paint. A path ran through grass at an angle away from the road and mailbox to the front door of a cabin that sat against a honeysuckle hillside. Ahead the road veered slightly left, then curved deeply to the right and headed up the hill above and behind the place.

"Much obliged again," he said as he opened the door. He swung both feet out onto the ground, put his hands on his knees and pushed himself up. Then he closed the door and leaned back in across the window frame and grabbed his fiddle. "You know your way to Jewel Hill from here?"

"Yessir."

Spit. He turned back to me, but he didn't say anything, only looked.

"What was the other time?" I said.

"Pardon?"

"What was the other time you left the county? Apart from when your sister got married in Asheville?"

"Well, that's got to do with a widowed childhood sweetheart and a church bus to the World's Fair down in Knoxville. A story for another time." He pushed off the car and let fly another stream of thick juice. "Come see me," he said as he turned away.

"I'll do that," I called after him.

I sat with the high-beams on until he reached his front door, where he threw up a hand and went inside. Every window I could see suddenly lit up at the same time, and the place glowed against the dark hillside. I dimmed my lights and sat there a moment longer, then put the car in gear and rolled slowly on my way, blowing the horn once as I passed above his house.

Chapter 15
Runion Scenes

The morning of the Fourth broke blue, with little dancing breezes shuffling through the tops of the trees. But by the middle of the afternoon when I made it down to Stackhouse Park, the day had grown hot and still. The sun hung above the river, the sky white around it. I guess the temperature was up close to ninety. The smoky smell of barbecue almost completely overrode the smells of new-mown grass, of horse turds and leather—lots of our locals like to bring their ponies to town on big warm-weather holidays.

Uncle Uart told me he'd sent Cutter back to Piney Ridge to get the barbecue grinder he'd forgotten at the house.

I pulled a piece of meat from one of the pigs the men were turning for the last time, wrapped it in a slice of white bread, dashed some hot sauce on it and ate.

Then I floated around the park for a while.

Old men in overalls and long-sleeved gray work shirts sat picking on banjos or sawing on fiddles. Their round-faced hard-singing wives sat beside them, spilling over the sides of wooden folding chairs, dipping snuff and singing alto. Sons or sons-in-law hunkered down on their hams and strummed guitars, each in a white short-sleeved shirt, polyester dress pants of brown or black or navy and loafers with pennies or dimes or nickels in the slots on the tongues. They wore their hair slicked back with a dab of lard and their sideburns long and fat like Elvis's. And these had their wives too, the proper ladies of the homesteads and meeting houses. They were thin with sharp jaw lines, pink knuckles and horn-rimmed glasses, standing by as stiff as if they'd been ironed into their knee-length flower-patterned dresses, singing out with voices as harsh as those of their mothers. And then there were my favorites, the "baby" that each family seemed to have. These girls—unmarried, big-boned and fleshy—smiled and swung their skirts, pressed guitars against their bellies and breasts and wailed like Patsy Cline.

Several of these local musicians I recognized from Saturday mornings spent here with Uncle T or Sundays at the radio station with Jay. A large group of them gathered around a weeping willow at the south end of the main flat of the park. Some had thinned and paled. Others had ballooned and reddened. Two things stood out. No new faces, meaning no young ones outside the usual families, and no centerpiece, meaning no Delbert Gunter.

Another tradition on the wane.

As I hovered in the eastward shadow of the willow, I noticed some sidelong glances my way and realized a few of them must have known who I was—"that Tanner boy that went to Nashville." A strange feeling. I expected to have a guitar shoved at me any minute, to hear a Sodom Laurel or Piney Ridge drawl say, "Pick us one, Gabe." And then the crowd would gather around me.

But it didn't happen. I got no smiles of welcome or nods of recognition, not even from the family babies.

These people hung in limbo between Delbert Gunter and me. But my position as a point along the line between an old man's well lit mountain cabin and the glitter of Nashville gave me no automatic membership in this musical family. I realized I was inspiring more discomfort in them than awe or whatever. I tried to imagine what their reaction might be if I'd been there as the Turrenoks' neoromantic sot. Spooky thought. Then again, maybe I seemed just as foreign as that to these people anyway. Pretty soon the uncomfortable feeling spread to me, and I walked away.

I found Cutter hanging around the pigs, eating, and then we found Wiley up to his waist in the waters just off the park's smaller north flat, there where the Big Laurel and the French Broad mix.

He was about to baptize a pretty redhead. His big right hand held the small of her back while his left nearly covered her face. He leaned her backwards into the water, her long curls first, her ears, his hand. Her body arced, and her breasts never went under. Wiley said something I didn't catch because a pack of firecrackers suddenly went off across the tracks, up by Chunn's Tavern. Then he shifted his right hand up between her shoulders and lifted her gently until she found her feet again.

She sputtered and coughed for a moment and then pulled her darkened hair along the left side of her neck, laid it between her breasts and twisted out the water. Her soaking was complete.

"Hallelujah, sister!"

"Amen!"

"A good dunking, Brother Wiley!"

A rapid series of small splashes very near the couple in the water caught all our attentions.

I looked up and there on the trestle over the Big Laurel sat Jay, gathering up another handful of small rocks and smiling like the devil.

"Are you prepared to get stoned, Preacher?"

Among the group at the side of the river several faces fell open with shock or quickly glared with anger.

Wiley looked up at Jay for a moment. Then a broad smile stretched his pointy face. He shook his head as he gently led the redhead to dry ground.

Within a few minutes the four of us were gathered at a picnic table beside the asphalt basketball court, eating barbecue sandwiches and baked beans and corn-on-the-cob, talking with mouths full of the old days.

Back in high school we'd seemed like separate parts of the same person. We had the same simple dreams, although we didn't talk about them often. Not a one involved work or much of anything to do with being grown up. The dreams we shared were of getting a driver's license, a car and a girl. And of leaving Runion.

Wiley now served as the preacher at the Paint Rock Union Church near Hot Springs and worked in the kitchen at the Stonehouse Café— all the patrons there joked that extra grace needed to be said over food a preacher cooked. He had a vast collection of ties. Around two hundred, he reckoned. He and the redhead he'd just baptized, Rubye, planned to marry in the fall.

Jay was already married to Denise, the varsity girls' basketball coach at Runion High. When old man Buckner, owner/sales manager/

morning man of WHMM, died two years before, Jay bought out the widow. He gave himself the same owner/sales manager/morning man title and kept his old hat of sports announcer only for very biased broadcasts of the girls' basketball games, letting his staff do the rest of the sports both at the high school and the college. In general he ran the station just like the old man had, right down to the "Noon Trading Post" followed by the local obituaries.

"I went to Asheville and bought a copy of 'Catch That Train,'" he said. "I've played it a few times, but I get so many calls from pissed off old biddies that I can't air it much. They're about our only listeners when sports or preaching aren't on."

Cutter had changed the most. Sure, Wiley's life had turned around 180 degrees, but in the Bible Belt such turnarounds are expected and have been commonplace events in the Christian world as far back as the days of Saul-become-Paul. Cutter, on the other hand, had somehow done a three-sixty so that if you didn't count the hair, or lack of it, he seemed not to have changed at all. He still acted like he did when he was sixteen and seventeen, but all his caring for the mountain folks amazed me and everyone else who ever knew him.

We eventually ran out of steam, and Jay and Wiley left to go find their ladies. Cutter stood up too. He stretched his arms above his head, groaned and gave me that devilish grin of his.

"You leaving early tomorrow?" he asked.

I told him I planned to leave around ten o'clock in order to meet the band in Lexington for an afternoon load-in and sound check.

"Good having you home, cuz," he said. Then he walked away, stopping every few steps to speak to somebody or shake a hand.

I sat at that table alone while the sun sank, leaving Stackhouse Park in the blue shadow of Piney Ridge. For a few minutes light stayed on Runion. Brassy brilliance reflected from the windows in town, and higher up and all around the wooded slopes of Lonesome Mountain and its smaller neighbors glowed with the lush green of summer. But as the shadow swelled, twilight climbed to engulf Runion and join the darkening purple of the eastern sky.

When I saw lights and movement on the other side of the river, I knew the fireworks were about to begin. Wanting to watch them from a higher point, I headed for the Riverwalk and town.

Just as I crossed the railroad tracks, I looked up and there in front of me stood Webb and Libby Garrison.

"Evening," I said and looked past them, hoping to see Eliza, fearing that I might see her and her husband.

"Mr. Tanner," Webb Garrison answered.

"Good evening, Gabe," Libby Garrison said.

We didn't talk long, quickly covering the news of work at the mill, Mrs. Garrison's garden, Eliza's younger brother Dennis's progress at Duke.

They asked me about Nashville and said that they'd heard things were going well.

"You've sure got a supporter in that Jay," Libby said. "He still plays that first song of yours at least once a day. I don't hear it on any of the other stations anymore."

"He's just trying to help out," I said. "I guess he thinks I make a lot of money when he plays it." I shoved my hands into my pockets. "I've got a new one out now, but it's on the pop and rock stations instead of the country ones. It's doing okay."

"We better go get a place to watch the fireworks," Webb Garrison said, taking his wife by the elbow. "Goodbye, Gabe."

"Yeah. Bye." I thought I might walk away without more than a scratch, but I couldn't. "How's Eliza?"

Webb Garrison looked away and blew air through his nose, but Libby smiled.

"She's doing well," she said. "Very well, actually. She's got her own business and does the wealthiest women in Asheville. And she's got a darling little house she never gets to spend any time in."

"Say hello to her for me if you would."

"We'll tell her we saw you. She's at Lake James this weekend."

A couple of minutes later I sat on one of the benches outside Uncle T's old dentist office. The fireworks had just started exploding high above the French Broad. But the launchers were set to fire a little north toward Christabel Island and Hot Springs, and I couldn't see them over the building. I looked toward Main Street, thinking I'd go up to the Pizzeria, order a Mountain Dew and watch from one of the window booths.

But from somewhere above and across the street a flash and a spray of green and white caught my eye. As the afterboom echoed among the buildings and shook me inside and I heard the cheers and whistles from the crowd below in Stackhouse Park, my eyes found the window where the fading shower of light still hung like a memory. My insides shook again.

The bedroom window of the apartment on the third floor of the funeral home.

Once more it exploded in light.

I sat and watched that window pulse between dark and light for a long time, even after the show had ended.

Chapter 16
Transitional

It took "Catch That Train" seventeen weeks to climb to number 22 on Billboard's "Hot 100" before the Turrenoks pulled Nokturn's promotional support. After that the song climbed three notches on its own, lost its bullet but held at 19 a second week, then finally turned and spent nine weeks falling off the chart.

On the single's strength, Lonesome Star booked late fall, winter and spring dates, including many new clubs and college campuses in the Southeast and Midwest. We stayed on the road every weekend and sometimes for short tours of a week to ten days, crisscrossing countless times the miles between northeast Virginia and southwest Mississippi, between southern Indiana and northern Florida.

Fans old and new bought the album. Many asked which song would be the next single and wondered when a second album would appear.

I didn't know what to tell them.

We took May off to rest and relax after spring's college work and before sweating out the summer in clubs and at city street festivals. Lukas booked a custom album project into his home studio. Hayes spent the time by his grandparents' pool in Belle Meade and Reggie made a trip home to Atlanta. Yvonne got married and went to Dallas for three days, taking Swede along to meet her mother. I started trying to write some new songs.

On the 17th of May an ASCAP royalty check for airplay of "Catch That Train" and other songs from the album lay waiting in my post office box—$10,046.32. I put it in the bank and bought a newspaper, hoping to find a new apartment in the classified section.

Two days later I found a bigger place on Sixteenth Avenue that a Vanderbilt medical student had just vacated—one half of an old house with high ceilings, hardwood floors and a private entrance in the shade of a tall oak. I moved my stereo and guitars, a desk and chair, a mattress, my hanging clothes and several liquor boxes full of books, LPs, 45s, compact discs, dishes, socks and underwear.

Something in the layout or the smell of the place reminded me of the apartment I'd shared with Eliza when we were married. I thought I'd like that, but within a few days the sense of déjà vu—mixed now with the ache of Yvonne's absence—wouldn't let me think straight enough to write. I moved like a ghost among the stacks of unpacked boxes. One minute I stood in the living room, watching the movement of light that shifted through the oak. The next I leaned against the wall in the bedroom, my guitar in my arms, its strings rusty from the sweat of April's last gig.

With most of my boxes still stacked and no songs written, I threw myself into the summer club and festival work that ran from the beginning of June through the end of July. We returned from our final trip out just after dark on a Sunday. I tried to stay home and rest, but ended up walking down to the Songbird and stayed up drinking beer with Mason Queenan until the wee hours. When the telephone sang out in the morning light, I sat up on the side of the bed with my eyes closed and fumbled for the receiver.

"Hold on," I said and rubbed my face hard with my free hand. Then, "Hello?"

"I've got some interesting news," Chuck Townshend said.

"Oh, yeah?" I yawned. "What's that?"

"I got a call a couple weeks ago from some friends out on the West Coast. They're starting up a new label and looking for product. The Lonesome Star project caught their ears, and they wanted to know if I had anything else like it in the works."

"Good for you," I said and listened to the silence on the other end of the line.

"Gabriel," Chuck Townshend said after a moment, "these are good guys, and not just good on paper like the Turrenoks. You're still pretty pissed about that, I can tell."

"Sorry for the attitude, Chuck. I'm just feeling a little restless right now." I reached for the cigarettes lying on the bedside table. "I've been at this for almost ten years now, and that's over nine years too long to be dealing with big talkers and hare brains." I lit a cigarette. "No offense."

The new Exposure Music sounded solid enough. At least the two women and the man who ran the company had the music business experience Edward and Oswald Turrenok lacked.

"Do you think Nokturn will sell the contracts?" I asked.

"A week ago I wouldn't have thought so," Townshend said. "But then last Thursday I heard that Edward and Oswald had a falling out and split their companies between themselves. Edward got Nokturn. He's not as vindictive as his brother, and I think he'll sell."

"What does Exposure want to do?"

"They'll make an offer to Edward—"

"No, I mean what do they want from us?"

"Well, they're into the music. They liked the video for "Catch That Train," but they were concerned about you not being in it. I told them that was another of the Turrenoks' bad decisions. They want to see the band play live as soon as it can be set up."

I gave Townshend Hayes's number and hung up.

Just another deal, that's what it felt like. But maybe this time something would stick. Maybe the music would get out on the market and stay there. But at thirty-one, the thought that I'd have to follow it onto that market—more van rides, more venues, more interviews— made me tired.

I got up and showered and dressed and left the apartment, bought new strings for my guitars at the music store in Hillsboro Village and returned home. When the strings were on and the guitars were tuned, I walked down the block to Kim's Market and picked up an egg roll and two six-packs of beer to get me though the day.

Chapter 17
Exposure Showcase

Two weeks later, it was a hot August night in Nashville, another Monday, and Memphis blues roared out of the sound system at MacArthur's. People began to pour into the club, and the chaotic murmur of voices slowly rose in competition with the canned music. The stale smell of beer and cigarettes that had hung in the room all afternoon was gone, and I wondered if I'd just gotten used to it or if it always magically dissipated when the club opened for business. Neon beer signs glowed above the bar and along every wall except the one behind the stage. On the television, a baseball pre-game show passed in silence, and club regulars sat at the bar and stared up at it. The instruments waited on stage, polished and mute, reflecting the stage lights and neon—yellows, blues, reds, greens, purples, whites.

I was just downing the last of my third beer, when suddenly I felt a hand on my shoulder.

"Tanner, Al Katt is here from Exposure," Lukas said.

"All right," I said and stood up. "Which one is he?"

Lukas pushed me toward a man in a tightly tailored three-piece suit of navy blue and pinstripes, his thinning gray-brown hair curled into tight kinks. As we approached, Katt stuck out his hand and offered us a half grin.

"Gabriel Tanner, Al Katt, Exposure Music. Great name. You ought to just use that and drop the Lonesome Star bit. Too much Texas in that one, babe. Where'd you come up with it?"

"With Lonesome Star or Gabriel Tanner?" I said.

Katt's half grin slipped a little.

Lukas stepped in and thanked the A&R man for coming from Los

Angeles to hear the band.

"Oh, no prob, man. No prob at all. We think Nokturn really dropped the ball on you guys." Katt turned to me and said, "Love your songs. Great voice too."

"Thanks," I said.

Katt nodded toward the young blond woman standing beside him.

"This is my secretary, Starr Fields. She flies with me to all these showcases, and some say she makes the decisions." He chuckled a little. "Meet Gabriel Tanner, Starr. Is that a great name or what?"

I started to ask again which name Katt meant, but Lukas gave me a nudge of warning.

"Nice to meet you," I said to her. "Thanks for coming."

Katt and Starr turned away to look for their reserved seats.

"Lukas, don't you just love rubbing egos with the big boys?"

"You've got to learn to deal, man," Lukas said. "And slow down on the beer a bit."

I retreated to the stage for one more check of my tuning, then turned and squinted to see past the floor lights. The club had filled up quickly. A few of the big guns from Nashville's Music Row offices sat here and there at the tables, but I knew they'd come only to be seen by anybody who might show up from one of the real music "coasts."

Reggie clambered in behind the drums.

"Gabriel, we need to get started." His voice and manner matched his look—thin and serious. "Let's not keep them waiting."

I nodded and motioned for the stage lights to go down. Then I turned my back to the club's buzzing crowd and stood motionless in the dark with my eyes half closed. I felt the stage shake as the other three came up and took their places.

Hayes picked up his guitar and struck a loud chord.

Yvonne slung on her bass, ran fine long fingers through the spiked white hair she'd come back from Texas with and sounded one quick low note.

Lukas stepped behind his stack of keyboards, pushed his blond hair behind his ears and leaned close to the equipment to be sure of his settings for the opening song. Then he stepped over to me.

"This is it, Tanner," he said in my ear. "It's now or next time."

I smiled. The tension that had gnawed at my insides all day began to change. I felt it focusing itself, tightening, converting itself to energy.

"Ready?" Lukas asked all around as he returned to his keyboards.

With the stage still dark, Hayes's opening guitar chords for "Landscapes" rang like cathedral chimes. On the downbeat of the fifth bar, the lights blazed on, the band kicked in, and I whirled to face the peopled darkness beyond the colored lights.

The glow of video games in the back of the club and the neon beer signs on the wall created an outline around the heads and shoulders of the crowd. From the second row of tables back to the bar, these rhythmically bobbing outlines were filled in with blackness. The faces of the people at the first tables—seven feet in front of me—were an orange-yellow blur in the backwash of the stage lights. But moment to moment, as Hayes or Yvonne or I swung a polished guitar through the beam of the spotlight, part or all of a face, a hand holding a cigarette with its curls of frozen smoke, fingers tapping a knee underneath the table would be sharply etched in blue-white against the blackness.

Look at the landscape behind me.
Look at the landscape behind you.
Different worlds are what we see.
Can you live with what I am?
Can I live with where you've been?
Can love be found on the common ground
Where these landscapes meet?

I tried to dance across the stage during Hayes's guitar solo, but my feet stuck and stumbled under the weight of my hunched shoulders. When I came back around to the microphone, the spotlight reflected from my guitar passed over Mason Queenan's face. I brought it back and held it there.

Queenan squinted and mouthed the word "relax."

I'm a lonesome stranger full of dreams and such.
Beneath haunted moons, through desert lands I've run.

And you've been betrayed by wanting love so much
That in a jungle of emotion
You've dreamed of lying in love by an ocean,
Rolling 'neath a summer sun.
Now I'm struck by the contrast
Between one possible future
And two impossible pasts.

"Landscapes" ended with a swirl on its final A. Over this, Reggie sounded four stick clicks, and the band connected solidly with two sharp jabs at the D that began "Running Toward the Prize."

I took a deep breath and felt my presence of mind escaping toward the darkness where music took over all physical sensation. I could never tell—even after all these years—whether the otherplace was within me or without.

Running, falling, pulling myself up again.
Running, falling, thinking it will never end.
Running, falling, running, falling,
Through the truth and the lies.
Running, falling, running toward the prize.

I turned toward Lukas and smiled as his fingers danced up and down the keys. Yvonne should've been there between the keyboards and Reggie's drums, but I didn't see her. I started to turn to where I thought she'd be standing with Hayes when I felt her against me. The warmth and tightness of her shoulder blades pressed the flesh just below mine, and the sweat-soaked back of her head leaned into the nape of my neck. The feel of her ran like electricity to the far reaches of my body.

At the end of Lukas's solo, everything stopped except for Reggie's boom-crack-boom-crack.

Yvonne released me, and I turned back to the microphone.

So on and on it goes
'Til it feels like something a long time coming

Is blooming like a rose,
Despite the threat of snow.
Reach that higher plain
And don't look back on might-have-beens.
Stand and face the long hard journey's end.

When the band kicked back in and I sang the chorus again, I thought of Eliza and her old belief in a moment like this. Of Mo Biggs and Billy Keith. Of the Turrenoks and Chuck Townshend. Of Lukas, Yvonne, Hayes and Reggie. None of them had seen the whole of the running and falling I'd done over the years. They'd been there through times when the prize I once struggled for had been just out of reach. Or even in my hands and then snatched away. But that prize—the one everybody read into these lyrics—wasn't the prize I wanted anymore, and suddenly I felt the truth of this in a place deeper within myself than ever before.

I howled the bridge.

There's a cabin hidden in the hills of heaven.
It is well lit, it is welcoming and warm.
And an easy chair begs, "Come, sit
By the fire that forged the world,
Where the view goes on forever
And friends are always at your door."

The crowd response between songs—the whoops and whistles and applause—drew me back little by little. By the last three songs my consciousness was able to move easily along the line that stretched from the hidden place where music took me to the sweat-stung eyes and sweat-soaked skin that connected me with the world. All ritual in this event—my being on this stage only as a test to prove myself worthy of a bigger stage—passed away. I was performing without thought of the future, and moment to moment the music was enough.

Before anybody was ready, the last notes of "Catch That Train" faded, and the showcase ended.

Drenched in sweat, I took the beer a waitress offered me and stepped from the stage into the center of the crowd. As I zigzagged through the tables, people stopped me and shook my hand or touched my arm.

"Great show, Gabriel," one gray-haired man said. "Never better."

"It's so wonderful to have you back in town," a strawberry blonde said with a raspy purr. "I absolutely love the new songs."

"Let me know when you're playing next," said another man whose face seemed familiar but didn't have a name attached.

"The band has really improved," Mason Queenan said as he shook my hand. "All the roadwork's really brought out a sound."

I thanked him for the reminder to relax.

"You're still better by yourself, and you don't have to dance during the lead break."

I laughed and waved him out the door, thinking I liked him better than anybody I'd met in the music business.

When the crowd thinned, I noticed Al Katt and Starr Fields standing near the exit. They seemed to be waiting for me, so I made my way over to them.

"Great show, Gabriel Tanner," Al Katt said. "Great voice. Fabulous songs."

"Thank you," I said. An unexpected thrill tightened my chest and took my breath for a second.

Great show, indeed.

In spite of what I'd been thinking during "Running Toward the Prize," I suddenly wanted Katt to invite me and the band out to dinner, a working dinner over which we'd begin hammering out the details of the rerelease of the Nokturn album or the recording of a new one for Exposure. I wanted it for Yvonne. For Hayes and Reggie. For Lukas and the memory of Eliza. I wanted it for the music.

"But now that I've seen you," Katt said, "I see you're not what we're looking for at Exposure."

I felt my face flush red.

"You said you liked the music. Was it the performance?"

"In part. The music was great, no question. But you don't have what the industry wants right now. It's purely a question of image, babe."

I clinched my teeth and took a deep breath that whistled through my nose.

The Turrenoks all over again. Damn you, Chuck Townshend.

"So what can we do to make ourselves what you want?"

"Well, I don't know. It's just my gut reaction, and I can't really tell you what to do to improve. I simply don't think you're going to be able to compete in today's marketplace. You just don't look the part. Maybe lose forty pounds or gain two hundred."

"Katt, you're all fucking form and no content," I said, my voice suddenly rising at the same time the club was falling quiet. "What the hell does that have to do with music?"

"It has everything to do with the business of music," Katt said loudly. "You want fucking content? Here it is, babe, bottom line. The look is everything. The act is everything. You have none of the above. There's your lot in life, babe. Live with it."

My throat tightened. My vision blurred for a moment, and I noticed Starr Fields watching my face and moving slowly behind Katt. My right hand clinched at my side. I could feel the crunch of cartilage, the splatter of blood and mucus across my knuckles.

Suddenly Lukas's hand was on my shoulder.

My breath caught, and I looked my friend in the eyes for a moment. I spun on my heel and headed for the stage, hearing Katt speaking to Lukas.

"Great show, Lonesome Star. Just—"

The sudden crack of skin and bone against skin and bone ricocheted off the brick walls, and I turned just in time to see Katt go down.

Chapter 18
Wrestling with Love

I *stand on Christabel Island, in the middle of Avalon Orchards. Runion is hidden around the next bend upriver, but the west end of the bridge to Piney Ridge is visible. A crowd is gathered beneath it at the riverside, individuals unrecognizable at this distance.*

Near me, people weave in and out of the rows of trees, carrying rough-hewn baskets. Others stand high on ladders leaned into the boughs of the trees, picking apple blossoms.

The air is filled with the humming of bees, with petals falling thick as snow, with the sickly-sweet smell of spring and death.

A body as sudden as lightning rams me from behind and rides me facedown into the inches of petals already beginning to brown and rot on the ground. My eyes and nose and mouth fill with the slimy velvet, and I gag as if drowning. An angel-white forearm stabs across my cheek and wrenches my neck to one side.

I raise myself beneath the weight of the body, and legs scissor my belly.

Darkness falls suddenly, and we struggle on toward the breaking of day.

At last, I twist from under the body and take a firm grip on its jaw and throat, forcing the back of its head into the petals I've breathed all night. Its face—a shadow against the soft whiteness—rises against what strength I have left.

A terse whisper sounds at my ear.

Let me go. Daylight is coming.

Somewhere above, a bird begins to sing—mechanically, monotonously.

* * *

Only halfway awake I slapped my clock-radio off the nightstand.

It flew for a split second toward the closet, but then its power cord caught like a choke collar and yanked it down to the floor with a flimsy crash.

Then I realized my new telephone was warbling instead of the alarm malfunctioning, and while it chirped three more times, I ran through a foggy mental list of family or friends I knew to be expecting or expected to die. Finally I picked up the receiver.

"Mmhmm?"

"Damn it, Gabriel," said a choked voice. "I thought you'd never answer!"

"Yvonne?" I sat up in the darkness, wide awake.

She coughed or retched—I couldn't tell which—but didn't speak.

"Yvonne?" I said again. "Are you okay? What the hell's going on?"

A pained silence struggled through the telephone line.

"Yvonne!"

"Shit!" she said finally. "Shit!" Something—maybe frustration or tears—gagged her for a moment. Then, "I think I'm okay. Nothing broken at least. I'm gonna be black and blue for sure."

"Where are you? Where's Swede?"

"Geez, Gabriel, he's just so drunk tonight. I've never seen him this bad. He just came home from work and went fucking nuts." She winced at some movement. "Shit! Everything hurts like hell."

"Why didn't you just get out or—" I swallowed that. "Where's Swede now?"

Holding the receiver between my ear and shoulder, I fought my way out of tangled sheets and jumped up to look for some clothes.

Yvonne's voice shook and suddenly sounded small and thin.

"He passed out in the shower. The bastard said he wanted to wash me off him." She laughed, a short high wheeze with her familiar edge of musical anger. "He fell like a ton of damn bricks in there, but I didn't see any blood when I checked on him."

"Yvonne, listen to me. If he's in the shower, he ain't gonna stay out for long. You've gotta leave the house right now." I paused for her to argue, but only tinny silence sounded in my ear. "I'll come and get you." I stopped again and thought for a second. "Go outside and get around the corner to Utah. Stay off Nebraska. Head away from town, toward Forty-Sixth. I'll pick you up at the corner or somewhere along Utah as soon as I can. Understand? Are you listening, Yvonne?"

"Yes, Gabriel, of course I understand. Get the lead out, okay?" She hung up.

The green numbers of the clock read 4:05 when I dropped the receiver on the bed and headed for the door. The remnants of the storm that had finally lulled me to sleep only three hours before fell steady and straight through the dreary blue of the street lights outside my apartment.

I wondered where Al Katt was at that moment—in a city emergency room or in first class on a red-eye back to California, an icepack over his face, or sound asleep in some big hotel. I had laughed when Hayes said loudly, "That's one way to get a record company attorney to call you," but I was worried about Lukas and what legal difficulties his attack on Katt might cause him. I gritted my teeth. I should have been the one to knock out the man, and the frustration of not having done so settled in my right hand, which ached and tightly gripped the wheel.

I splashed roughly through the greens and reds and yellows that glistened on rain-soaked West End—constantly scanning around corners for the city police—and at the top of a hill swung onto Murphy Road. On my right, each street was a numbered avenue—Thirty-Eighth, Thirty-Ninth and on until I swerved wildly through the dogleg where Murphy becomes Forty-Sixth Avenue. I passed Nebraska and came to Utah.

I turned right and started moving backwards through the numbers. At Fortieth, I turned right again, and rolled to a stop at Nebraska. Across the street to the left I could see her house, dark like the rest except for the wink-and-shadow-shift of television light through the picture window in front and the white glow from a smaller window partway back on the near side. I pulled onto Nebraska and drove slowly past her house.

She stood in the glow of some late late late movie, still as stone, her face lit by the screen, a fingernail in her mouth.

I drove to the end of the block and turned around. As I came back, both the porch and living room lights blazed on, and she held the screen door open, motioning me inside.

She looked better than she'd sounded on the telephone. She wore sunglasses rimmed with chartreuse frames and a tight, short, electric blue dress.

I stepped tentatively through the door, and she walked over and shut off the television. In the quiet, I heard the sound of the shower still running.

"Amazing," she said. "He's still out like a light in there."

I felt my jaws clench and my breath catch.

Yvonne looked at me.

"Hell, I don't expect him to try to do anything to you, Gabriel," she said. "And I don't expect you to try and kick his ass on my behalf either. You probably couldn't anyway."

"Whatever," I said. "Let's just get out of here. Are you bringing some stuff?"

"My things are in the bedroom at the end of the hall. I'll go pack."

"Why the hell haven't you already—"

Yvonne turned away from me and started down the dark hallway, throwing up a hand and pointing vaguely in the direction of the television as if that were explanation enough.

"Whatever," I said again. "Let's just hurry and go."

I followed her until I came to the dark bathroom. I looked in and, by the glow of the bright living room light, saw that the sliding glass door of the shower stood open at the faucet end. Swede's thick knees were the only parts I could see, so I cautiously walked over and peeked in.

The wrestler still wore his red trunks and black boots. A small knot sagged a little over his left eye. His skin glowed a certain bug-light purple-and-beige, telling of too much time in a tanning bed. A bear of a man, his thick gut and chest were hairy and rotund but far from flabby. The shower stream pounded on his torso as if it were a drum. His mouth drooped open, and he breathed through it heavily. He was dead asleep.

Teardrops streaked the condensation on the glass shower wall, the little window, the mirror, testifying that the hot water had run for a while. But no steam rose at the moment.

I again felt the ache in my right hand, the ghost of a violent desire unfulfilled. The hand wanted to turn off the water and then drag me into the shower on top of Swede, to pound his face to unrecognizable blood, to destroy Swede, to destroy Katt and Townshend, the Turrenoks and Billy Keith, the faceless man who slept with Eliza far away in the dark mountains of home. The fingers curled into a fist. My jaws clenched twice. I backed out of the bathroom, fighting against the pull of violence.

The bright light she'd turned on in the living room spilled into the bedroom from the hall. Framed by that rectangle of illumination, my shadow crossed the floor and all the crumpled bed clothes there, crossed the stripped and askew mattress and climbed the wall.

"You're in my light," she said, grabbing at random handfuls of clothes from the dark closet and dresser drawers and stuffing them into a neon-colored athletic bag.

I stepped aside, out of the doorway, and looked around the small room.

The night stand in the corner on the other side of the bed had a broken lamp hanging off it and a jumbled pile of four novels lying on top. Two covers caught the light. Both showed bare-chested young men hovering over ladies in low-cut formal gowns, a bay in the background on one, a green hill—probably covered in heather—on the other.

A fifth paperback lay only partly on the stand, the rest of it apparently ripped and strewn on the bed and floor.

"I knew he was drunk the minute he pulled in the driveway," she said. "They were doing a show up in Murray, Kentucky, and I guess he lost again. He's a jobber, they call it. He always loses. But I bet he'd found some little man he wanted to impress—" She broke off with a sound that was half cough, half laugh. She sniffed and raised the heel of her hand to her nose. "Anyway, he fixed a sandwich in the kitchen and then he came back here and ate it without saying hello or asking how the showcase went or anything. So, I didn't say anything either. I just sat there in bed reading a story about New Zealand and this man and woman getting ready to fall in love. At least I thought that's what was coming. I only got about halfway through it. It's called *The Bone People*. You ever read it?"

I shook my head, wondering what she meant by saying Swede wanted to impress "some little man."

"It's kind of weird, okay? Not like those other books. Real literature. It makes me want to see New Zealand one of these days. Anyway, he starts yelling his ass off about how he knew I pictured myself fucking the man in the book. I ignored him." She put her hands on her hips and leaned her head back. "I've been feeling one of his rages building up lately. Usually I can make him just mad enough to let it blow. He's a real sucker. It's just that tonight—" She stopped for a moment. "I don't know. It was scary. He grabbed my book. You can see what he did to that."

I looked again at the tattered paper that covered one side of the bed, the night stand, the floor, and thought of a corrupt official's frantic shredding spree. I pictured Yvonne sitting there in bed, naked against the pillows—a lithe fawn, dappled with the ragged bits and pieces of the only romance her misdirected desires allowed in her life. I wanted to grab her and hold her until the tears finally showed themselves, touched my face and chest and slowly subsided.

"At first," she said, "he tried to rip it in half through the spine like you see those strong men do with phone books, but he strained so hard I thought he'd pop a blood vessel in his eye or something. It's like four hundred and some pages, you know? So, then he started ripping up a few pages at a time and throwing them in the air. He was growling like a bear and all red in the face, but he was really trying to keep from crying." She scooted a box out from under the bed and started picking out socks. "I just sat there and watched him go at it, okay? And even though I was scared, I really thought we'd be copulating any second. Then he came after me. I tried to get to the spare bedroom, but he caught me quick and dragged me back in here. He slapped me, choked me, nearly squashed my head between his legs. Can you believe that shit? He kept yelling, 'Fight me! Fight me for real!' The bastard. I thought I was really hurt. Then, quick as he started he just broke off and went to the shower."

Her bag looked ready to burst at the seams.

I listened while she matter-of-factly described what her husband had done to her, as if to her it didn't seem that far out of the ordinary, as if she accepted what had happened as dangerous but still rooted in, and part of, love. I remembered her telling me one time how love felt like a burning knot in her stomach. It was excitement and fear and everything between wound up into a tight burning knot. All her life it felt like that. She never felt the knot with me when we tumbled in and out of bed on the road trips, and that was how she knew she'd never love me. I didn't understand it at the time. But now I listened to her unveil her story in that darkened room where she'd been mauled just an hour before, and I suddenly realized that outside the music we'd made together with the band, outside the twist of motel sheets, I bored her.

"I would've taken you to the moon, Yvonne," I said.

"I know that, Gabriel. That's why I called you." She looked down and struggled with her bag's zipper. "Maybe I'm finally ready to go."

Those words hung in the air between us, almost gleaming with promise but remaining shapeless and undecided.

We stood like that for another moment, still and quiet. Then we froze as the shower stopped and the silence became complete.

Swede groaned, and the little house shook with the hollow thunder of his wet skin rubbing against the sides of the tub as he struggled to stand up. The shower doors banged together, and he groaned again. Wet cloth slapped the floor. The toilet lid fell. He drew a sharp breath, let out one grunt's worth of air, then another, and released the remainder explosively. Boots thudded against the wall and dropped. The lid banged up against the tank and a long sibilant sigh rose above the focused splash of urine in the bowl. Then the dribbling spasms and no flush.

Suddenly his hazy shadow stood in the light that fell through the bedroom door. It shifted slightly. He cleared his throat and said something unintelligible. Then the shadow began to pull itself together, becoming tighter and darker and more and more menacing, covering the floor and the bed and the wall as he stalked down the hall.

In contrast to the threatening shadow, the voice was plaintive, childlike, crying for Yvonne.

She stood perfectly still, facing not toward the shadow as I did but toward the doorway.

Then I fell backwards into the closet.

Swede appeared in the flesh, naked and erect, reaching for Yvonne.

She still didn't move, only stood there with the stuffed bag clutched to her chest.

He started to speak, but his voice seemed to catch in his throat.

Then, as if he felt the other presence, he turned his head and looked directly into the darkness of the closet. He froze for a second, arms reaching out to Yvonne, head turned toward me, eyes glaring.

It was in that moment—standing cloaked against the closet wall—that I found my hand on the barrel of a rifle that leaned there beside me.

Swede turned in my direction. A growl rose from deep inside him, and large hands that had been weakly shaking as they reached for Yvonne grew rigid and rose toward my fear-tightened throat.

I buried the butt of the rifle in the big man's gut. Then, as his airless body doubled over, I yanked up the flat of the stock and nailed his dimpled chin with it.

He reeled backwards, a pained and astonished look on his face. He tripped through the tangled sheets and quilt around his feet, flapped his arms and tried to right himself, but the corner of the mattress caught him behind the knees and flipped him over to land on the back of his neck in the floor on the other side of the bed, momentum slamming him upside down into the night stand in the corner.

The lamp broke again and the romance novels took flight.

My hand refused to release the rifle. I saw myself following Swede into the corner, standing over him and—

"Gabriel, no!" Yvonne shouted and tried to pull the weapon from my hand.

I forced my grip to relax, and she threw the rifle on the bed.

"Run, Yvonne!" I grabbed the bag in one hand and her elbow in the other, and dragged her out of the bedroom where Swede lay crumpled and gasping on the floor.

We flew down the hall and through the living room.

As we burst out the door into a dense rain and the graying of night toward dawn, Swede bellowed her name.

In the middle of the street, Yvonne wrenched her elbow free of my grip and stopped.

It took me a couple more steps to pull up and whirl around to face her.

She stood there, already dripping wet, her throat and hands going white, her mouth working without making a sound.

"I can't, Gabriel," she finally blurted out. "He's hurt. He needs me."

"Yvonne, you're gonna die in there!" I yelled. I leaned toward her and reached out to grab her elbow again. "Now come on!"

"No," she said, backing away. "I wanted to love you. I wanted to go with you like this, but I can't." She suddenly sounded sure of herself. "I just can't." She turned in the middle of the street and started for the house as another pained bellow from Swede shook the neighborhood.

I could feel people watching us through slightly parted curtains.

"To the moon, Yvonne!" I yelled my frustration at her back. "He's gonna blast you to the moon one of these nights!"

She kept walking.

I stood rain-soaked in the street, listening to Swede bawl his remorse, watching Yvonne hurry across the yard. Then I spun around in a circle like a hammer thrower and hurled her bag high in the air toward the house, aiming for its big picture window, hoping the angry sound of shattering glass would make her turn and see me in a new and awful light.

But above the cars that lined Nebraska Avenue, the bag opened and spewed out socks, blouses, shorts and underclothes—the greens and reds and yellows and blues like muted kaleidoscope glass against the gray dawn sky. The clothes settled in slow motion. Some pieces landed in puddles and on the hoods of cars. Some settled on the sidewalk and the yard. Blue panties caught on a radio antenna. All began darkening in the rain. The bag lost its momentum with its contents and plopped empty at Yvonne's heels.

At that she turned.

"I quit, Gabriel. I quit the band as of right now. I gotta get my damn priorities straight." Then she walked up the steps and climbed back into the ring.

Chapter 19
Nashville Departure

I spent two days going out only to get beer and a bit of something to eat, two nights sleeping restlessly in tangled sheets. On the third day I showered and shaved and went out to Liu Lao-lao's Chopsticks in Hillsboro Village to eat lunch. When I'd finished, I walked to the Songbird Cafe and knocked on the door. I wanted to talk to Mason, but the place was locked up. I turned away and walked to the nearest branch of my bank and closed my account.

After renting a small truck, I loaded the mattress, the desk and chair, the dishes and most of my clothes and drove to the Salvation Army Thrift Store on Charlotte Pike. Outside the delivery door in the back of the building, I unloaded it all.

A fellow came out and tried to help, but he was pale and shaking, complaining of having just lost his job because he'd been sick for a few days.

When the truck was unloaded, I shook the man's hand, thanked him and gave him a twenty.

At the apartment again, I opened the back of the car and loaded my guitar and stereo components, the rest of my clothes and the remaining boxes of books and music. Then I swept up the cigarette ashes and popcorn kernels I'd let fall on the hardwood floors, carried out the trash and laid the key on the counter and left.

By the time it was getting dark, I entered the westernmost part of North Carolina, driving through the first low mountains with the windows down and the radio off. Wind and lightning followed me into Murphy. Within minutes after I got into a small motel room for the night, sheets of rain blew by the street lights and hail danced on the hood of the car. I hoped I'd gotten the windows rolled up tightly and thought about going out to check, but I felt sleepy and strangely weak. My head ached. I decided I'd just stretch out on the bed and lie quietly for a few minutes.

*   *   *

A long and narrow room. A ballroom. One wall is filled with tall, paned windows. Shimmering blue-white light faintly falls through them, moonlight maybe, stretching across the floor, revealing the bare hardwood. The light is never still but stays in its elongated rectangles. The spaces between are hard black.

In the closest patch of darkness, vague shapes mill around, and from time to time a body part breaks into the dancing light—a ringed hand, half of a round face, a naked knee and part of the thigh.

The only feature on the other wall is a large, stone fireplace big enough to stand inside.

Eliza leans against the stone, facing it, her head on her forearm.

Movement catches my eye, but I am too slow. The figures have moved through a section of window-light, one dark space farther away—the brim of a cowboy hat, two fingers and a lit cigarette, the headstock of a guitar.

Eliza looks at me, her blue eyes as dark as her hair, a strange smile on her lips.

They move yet another dark space away—a shiny shoe, a large right hand clutching a naked left biceps, a small breast.

A murmuring, like the roll of distant thunder, fills the ballroom.

*   *   *

I awoke feeling feverish and clammy.

The darkness of the motel room came alive with light, and thunder rattled the walls.

I got up shakily, stripped in the stuttering flashes and crawled back into bed, pulling the covers up around my neck.

Rain pounded on the roof and slapped at the windows.

I lay awake, listening to the anger of the storm and trying to clear my head. For what seemed like hours, images from the dream yanked me from the edge of sleep time and again. I couldn't remember if the figures that moved in the darkness were coming toward me or flying from me across the paned blocks of light that cut the room.

But most of all, it was Eliza I couldn't shake. She looked as she had when I saw her last in Runion, smiled as she had sometimes when we'd fought and then shyly begun to make up. At those times we always made love, slowly at first and then with the desperation of trying to hang on. This memory—the feel of her first light touch on my tense body, the warmth of her all around me, the soft fleshiness of her—kept me awake until the sky outside the window began to gray through the storm.

When the woman banged on the door and called, "Maid! Checkout time, in there," I struggled up from the bed and stumbled into my jeans. I opened the door a crack and quickly jerked my face away from the light. Then squinting, I slowly turned back toward her.

"You ain't up yet, hon?" The black of her eyes sparkled even in the shade of the eaves. She was about my age, pretty with her chubby cheeks, small and stocky, wearing a plain blue uniform dress, white stockings turned almost tan by the dark skin of her calves and thick-soled white shoes.

"I think I've got some kind of bug," I said.

"Don't say." She chuckled, a joyous, airy sound that shook her whole body. "I never seen you before, but it's easy to see you ain't feeling yourself. You pale as death, hon." She bent a little to one side and looked past me into the room. "But if you leaving today, you putting me behind."

I suddenly turned away and sneezed.

"I think I'll call the manager and see if I can stay here 'til I'm feeling better."

"Want me to do you?" She laid a hand on the handle of a ratty feather duster and smiled.

"No, thanks," I said, returning her smile with a weak grin. "I wouldn't want you to catch whatever's going around in here."

The manager said I could stay as long as I needed to and gave me the number for a pizza place and a drugstore, both of which delivered.

I slept through the rest of the day without calling either one.

That evening at six-thirty, a shirtless, green-eyed, russet-skinned boy knocked on my door and handed me a brown paper bag from under his red umbrella.

"Mama said give you this."

Inside the bag were a plastic bowl of chicken soup, a spoon and a paper towel, a biscuit, an orange and a 7-Up.

I felt a little stronger after I ate and then better again after a hot shower. I couldn't stay in the room any longer, so I walked over and paid my bill. Back in the room, I checked one last time to make sure I wasn't leaving anything behind. In the bathroom I wrote "Thanks for the soup and kindness, 'hon'" on a fifty-dollar bill and laid it on the lid of the toilet.

I remembered passing an ABC store on the way into town, so I found my way back to it and bought a bottle of Jack Daniels. I put the bottle between my legs and held it there unopened as I left Murphy and drove east into the misty mountains.

* * *

I awoke again to near darkness and the cool wetness of raindrops splattering me from the frame of the car's open window. I rubbed my face hard and wondered how I could've slept long enough for another storm to come up.

A spark of lightning illuminated the rest area at the foot of Balsam Mountain. A burly little man in a cowboy hat came out of the men's room and, under the blue-white light and the trees, became a dappled ghost moving ponderously along the sidewalk and then lumbering through the rain across the parking lot toward an old Buick, his thick hands fumbling with jangling keys.

Mo? I almost said aloud, but caught myself and let my head fall back against the headrest.

I'd wanted only to get home to Runion as quickly and mindlessly as possible, but I'd grown weak and feverish again around Sylva. I remembered coming to a stop at the curb and shutting off the motor. Remembered how my bones turned to cotton in the absence of vibration and motion and speed. The thoughts driving me couldn't overcome that sensation, and I must've fallen asleep immediately. But it was a restless unwanted sleep where the same driving thoughts that flung me out of my sick room in the Murphy motel and through the night had dragged me down into another vivid dream, in which I stood, guitar in hand, on a stage in the back of a gigantic blue bus that thundered over rutted roads. The bus was packed with people, people who were a faceless darkness and a wet heat. I could see all the way to the front and realized that only I knew no driver sat at the wheel. The unguided monster took up an entire Interstate, crushing every tiny vehicle that struggled along in its path. I wanted to scream as it plowed through glass buildings, weathered shacks, burning fields, frozen rivers, and finally flew off the side of a foggy mountain road, plunging down and down and down into the tree tops. But I knew no one would understand the scream when it came. They'd only turn to each other and smile in admiration of the soulfulness in it. The songs were barely recognizable to me. They were mine, but I couldn't remember one moment of creation, couldn't tie one emotion or story to any of them. The band nailed the ending to a blazing set, and everything disappeared in darkness. The crowd went wild. I took it all in, letting the thunderous applause from hundreds of unseen hands soak into my chest, gut, crotch and legs, adding a shower of static sound to each booming beat and flashy riff the band had driven into my back. Then the lights came up, and I stood alone in front of a mirrored wall. Instead of reflecting a man of flesh and blood, the mirror held the image of a creature made of white noise broken by rhythmic pulses of red. But it was my reflection. Somehow I knew the shape it held was mine. My own smoke-rasped voice escaped like steam from its throat. It reached out to cup my face in its hands—or to strangle me—and a spark erupted from that touch and sent a shock through my entire body.

I wondered if lightning struck somewhere near enough to give me the shock that jolted me out of the dream.

I sat for a few minutes more, watching the blue flashes paint pale still lifes of the rest area's building and picnic tables, trees and sidewalks, the few cars, trucks and travelers. I listened to the distant attack and retreat of thunder in the mountain passes, the diminishing drone of wind and rain, the swish of tires through water. The cool splash of rain felt like small kisses on the left side of my neck, on my ear and cheek.

In the rest room, I went to a sink and washed my hands. Still feeling groggy from the unexpected nap, I bent over and splashed my eyes several times with the lukewarm water.

At last I stood and came face to face with my mirrored image, made harsh and pale by my sickness and the fluorescent light. The white noise creature appeared in my mind again.

The look is everything, it said. *I gotta get my damn priorities straight.* I felt my jaws clench. *The act is everything.* A flash behind my eyes. *You have none of the above.* My vision blurred. *Quit.* The skin at the nape of my neck crawled. *Live with it.* I growled and struck.

A web of fracture suddenly appeared around my fist and three thick tendrils shot to the edges of the mirror. I felt the brittle cracking of the glass and the warm blood spurting from my knuckles. I heard the crash of the impact echo like a sharp clap of thunder in the tiled room. When I dropped my unclenched hand to my side, shards of glass tinkled into the sink and onto the floor, and the mirrored image was gone.

Chapter 20
Runion Arrival

A fog had risen behind the storm. In the misty glow that washed over the car, I watched beads of condensation crawl shakily toward me across the hood. The beads gathered size and speed until they jumped onto the windshield and climbed out of sight above my head.

I turned on the wipers and descended into the valley of the Jabbok River. The headlights diffused in the fog, making me squint and catch my breath as I lost sight of everything but whiteness. I slammed on the brakes and geared down, bringing myself to a crawl.

But just as the angle of the road told me that I'd crossed the bridge over the Jabbok and begun to climb the other side, the night slowly cleared. One bright star appeared. Then another. Then another and another. In seconds the sky was flooded with them, and the one that came to me first was lost in the deluge.

Since the rest area, I'd drunk half the bottle of warm Jack but hadn't relaxed and certainly didn't feel any better. I gripped the steering wheel tightly, and my hand throbbed under the bandanna I'd tied across my knuckles. I tried to keep my mind on the road and the driving. I knew every curve and incline on this highway, every creek crossing and village. I slurred over and over to myself whatever was written on each glistening sign that flew toward me out of the darkness.

I was driving fast when the road turned sharply east at Cove. At this speed, in this dead hour, the headlights kicked aside the darkness that had fallen full weight on the Sandy Mush Bald stretch. But the darkness dovetailed behind the lights, leaving me in blackness. The air that roared through the open window cooled as I climbed, and I was thankful for that.

The road forked at Bluff, and I bore right onto 209-A, shooting toward Piney Ridge and Runion. I don't know how much whiskey was left in the bottle, but I knew I was in trouble. In my dream, the blue bus rocketed off a cliff like the ones I was swerving along the edges of. Uncle T had died on this very road. Still I pressed harder on the gas pedal, flying through the ghostly patches of floating fog, not knowing whether they were real or hallucination, taking the insides of the curves and hearing the squalling of my tires echo through the depths of darkness falling away below.

All I can remember was wanting to make the point on Piney Ridge where the lights of Runion can be seen glowing soft on the other side of the French Broad at the dark foot of Lonesome Mountain. If I could get that far, then I'd have made it through the mountains Uncle T hadn't survived. But I was drunk and getting drunker in a hurry.

I rounded a sharp curve and knew there was no stopping the vomit. I slammed on the brakes at the head of a down-sloping straightaway maybe a hundred and fifty feet long, jammed the gearshift forward at the same time as I opened the door and fell out onto the blacktop.

When the retching was finished, I struggled to my feet and found myself alone in the road.

My car was gone.

I staggered in circles but found nothing.

All I could think to do was start walking. I guess I believed that at some point my car would return from wherever it'd gone and pick me up.

But even before I reached the sharp curve to the left that ended the straightaway, I saw the red and white lights glowing in the trees.

It'd nosed itself into the trunk of a pine tree about thirty feet down the mountainside. All the lights were still on, and the motor was still running.

I told it goodnight and walked on.

* * *

A lone fiddle played "Amazing Grace." It wasn't another dream that had come over me. Not exactly. More like a vision.

Delbert Gunter sat beneath a tall oak, his bow swaying over the strings, his face lit with the pink-orange light of sunset. Beyond him, the mountains stood purple in the last light of day.

I rode the echo of that melody up over the ridge and down into the hollow below, through steep-sided valleys, and up another ridge in the Walnut Mountains. From there I could see high Lonesome with Runion and the river sparkling at its foot. The echo fell in that direction and passed over the house and small farm where I grew up. I saw my father mowing the yard and my mother pulling weeds from her flower beds. The echo passed along Walnut Road. I glanced at one spot where three of my high school classmates had been burned alive in a car as they slept off a drunken stupor, and another spot where a short dirt track turned from the pavement and led to a shady dead end where, in the back seat of my parents' car, Eliza, wearing only her bra and socks, had knelt on my naked lap, facing me, her arms around my head and pressing my face to her bosom. The echo rose above Runion, crossing in a blur the roofs of Ramsey's Funeral Home and Whitson's Green Grocer, swooping down over Stackhouse Park and the French Broad River. I rode with the wind up the west bank and onto the top of Piney Ridge, then swung low over Uncle Uart's back pond where Cutter and I used to skinny-dip among the frogs and snakes and sunfish. In back of the Piney Ridge Methodist Church, I hesitated over the graves of Papa and Bigmama James and Uncle T until the fiddle faded away and I heard the voice.

"Gabe?" it said. "Wake up, Gabe."

Then I became aware of the red-lit backs of my eyelids and the stiffness in my body and the pounding in my head.

"I'm gonna have to arrest you if you don't get up," the voice said.

I turned my head sideways and, when the light faded to something more bearable, forced my eyes to slit open. Through my eyelashes I saw Deputy Daggnabbit Boyce sitting on the seat of the picnic table I'd apparently used as a bed.

"You look like hell, son," he said.

I tried to speak, but it felt like my throat was full of dust.

"And you're spooking the Saturday music makers."

Beyond the deputy's wrinkled face, I could see indistinct shapes moving. Far off to my left, maybe somewhere under the trees near the Big Laurel, there was the sound of a hymn being sung in four-part harmony, accompanied by a guitar.

"My guitars," I whispered.

"Come again?" Deputy Boyce said.

I swallowed hard and managed to bring my voice to a hoarse croak.

"I mean, my car's down a bank the other side of Piney Ridge."

"We'll see to that later. Right now, we gotta get you up and out of here."

I don't know how he managed it, but I woke that afternoon in a cell in the jailhouse on Main Street. Not that I was under arrest, Deputy Boyce told me when he brought water and aspirin. I was there to sleep it off so Mom and Dad wouldn't see me in that shape. But they'd certainly hear about it, probably already had, and that was just as bad in a small mountain community. Just as bad or worse.

"We got your car outside," the deputy said. "It ain't really hurt much. Front end's a little caved in, and the radiator's busted. Out of gas too. I'll drive you home when you're ready."

"Thanks," I said and sat up, rubbed my face hard with both hands and tried to pull myself together.

Deputy Boyce sprawled in a wooden chair that sat in a corner of the cell.

"Them guitars of yours are okay. Seems that old Martin's a survivor. Been through two wrecks yonder on that road."

I nodded and leaned back against the cold wall, looking up at the small square of hazy blue afternoon sky visible through the window.

"I reckon the big city done the same number on you it did on ol' T James that time," Deputy Boyce said.

"Yeah," I said. "I reckon it just took longer."

"I loved to hear him tell that story."

I fell asleep again, and when I woke up the next time, it was dark outside—and even darker in the cell. But apart from a stuffy nose and some weakness, I felt all right. The bug I'd picked up seemed to have run its course and taken the hangover with it.

A cool breath of air drifted down from the barred window, and I turned my head on the hard pillow so that I could look up.

Outside, beyond the glow of Runion, stars hung in the black night. While I waited for my jailer to come back and set me at liberty,

I stared at that striped square of sky and tried to remember my first glimpse of the star I'd wished upon and followed so long. Maybe it was dying—or already dead—when I'd claimed it as my own. Or maybe it wasn't mine to claim in the first place. Either way, it had faded and left me here, searching the heavens with the nervous eyes of the lost. I wondered if it had led me to this silent end for a reason, or if it was, even as I followed, no special mote in a stardust of misdirection.

Chapter 21
Homecoming

On the second Sunday in October, the Piney Ridge Methodist held its annual Homecoming service. The varnished wooden walls of the old mountain church rang with words and music as the congregation sang "How Firm a Foundation." The church's pastor, Reverend Tweed, made a few welcoming remarks and announcements to the forty-four people who filled the pews. Then he prayed, after which he paused and looked down at the "Order of Worship" printed in the bulletin.

"We have with us this Homecoming Sunday," he said in his rich mountain drawl, "a son of this church who was long away from us. He was here last year, but when I called on him to sing, he didn't have anything prepared. Well, we all warned him that he better be ready this year. I should tell you that this song is not traditional. It's a song he wrote." He paused and looked at me. "I'm sure it has great meaning for him personally, and after having him play it for me yesterday, I can say that I think it has meaning for all of us. So, while we offer back to the Lord a portion of what we've been given, Gabriel will sing for us all."

I stood up from the front pew, lifted Uncle T's Martin from its case, and sat down on the piano bench my mother had vacated. Ignoring the few stares at my long black hair and the glittering golden ring in my left ear, I settled my guitar in my arms.

"Let us pray," Reverend Tweed said.

While the offering plates were prayed over, I quietly began with a rich E chord and moved lightly into the progression of the song. When my brother Butler and Uncle Uart had lifted the offering plates from the altar table and turned toward the congregation, I strummed the progression louder and hummed the opening bars of "Amazing Grace" with my chord changes. Certain notes in the melody struggled against the chords beneath them. These were moments of tension but not of dissonance, and they felt right.

> *If I die in this place*
> *So far from home*
> *And I never make my living*
> *From my native soil again,*
> *Don't leave me where these strangers*
> *Will walk across my bones.*
> *Take me back and lay me with my next of kin.*

I increased the intensity of my strumming and sang the second verse, in which the singer tells of his first leaving home, a leaving immediately followed by the chorus that expresses the tensions between the excited longing to leave and the prayerful yearning to return.

> *Homecoming dreams are bittersweet to the taste.*
> *Homecoming promises are hope to the displaced.*
> *They echo through my soul with the distant music of "Amazing Grace"!*
> *Let there be a homecoming someday.*

I found my prodigal self in the third verse.

> *I have learned to breathe*
> *Beneath a sea of light.*
> *I've won and lost and paid the cost*
> *To find a future for myself.*
> *But the ties of blood and earth*
> *Still bind across the years and miles*
> *And in my memories the old ways still are dearly held.*

> *Homecoming dreams are bittersweet to the taste. . . .*

When I finished the song I quickly slid off one end of the piano bench, and my mother returned to her place. While I settled my guitar back in its case, she wiped her eyes with a tissue, laid the white ball at the high end of the keys and began the doxology. The people stood to sing, and Butler and Uncle Uart brought the offering forward. I walked to the rear of the church and took a place in the back pew with Cutter and Rendy, Jay and Denise, and Wiley's wife Rubye.

Wiley, having often reluctantly attended this church in his youth whenever he spent a Saturday night with me and my family or Cutter and his, served as the guest speaker and delivered the sermon for this homecoming celebration. He read from Deuteronomy and Hebrews and spoke about the handing down of tradition and faith—from Martin Luther and John Calvin to the James and Clement and Tanner families and his own newborn twins. He even used a couple of phrases from my song, which he must have written down as he was listening.

After the congregation sang "A Mighty Fortress Is Our God," after Reverend Tweed stood with Wiley at the door of the church and gave the benediction and the blessing of the meal, the men slid from their pews, shook the preachers' hands and raced to cars to get the dishes their wives had made for the dinner on the ground.

Rough wooden table tops were brought from the church's furnace room and set end to end on sawhorses and covered with red-and-white-checkered tablecloths. The food spread down the length of the table—platters of fried chicken and baked ham, chicken casseroles and tuna salads, dishes of the season's beans, corn, tomatoes and cucumbers, bowls of potato salad, tins of dinner rolls, biscuits and cornbread muffins, chocolate cake and refrigerator cheesecake and banana pudding, cookies, fresh blackberry cobbler and lemon pie and tea and lemonade and soft drinks and punch.

Uncle Uart Clement took his place first in line, and the feast was on.

"Good sermon, preacher," I said as Wiley and Jay and Cutter and I sat down on the church steps with our heaping plates. "Very literate."

"Yeah," Jay said. "Son, I thought you were one of them Bible-pounding, spit-slinging, hellfire-and-brimstone sermonizers."

Wiley laughed through a bite of a fried drumstick.

"I been to a seminary over in east Tennessee the last couple of summers, and they kind of toned me down a bit. And I figured, you know, this is a Methodist church and all."

"Gabe, I've never heard that song before," Cutter said.

"Nobody had heard it before I played it for Reverend Tweed yesterday."

"When did you write it?"

I swallowed a bit of fried chicken with a sip of unsweet tea.

"I'd been collecting pieces of it in a notebook over the few months of my Nashville days—"

Jay laughed.

"Your Nashville D-A-Z-E, right?"

We all laughed.

"Right," I said. "Anyway, it all came together not long after I moved into the cabin."

"Do I owe anything for quoting you?" Wiley asked.

"Put it in the collection plate next Sunday," Cutter said.

When we finished eating and the other three went off to get their ladies and visit with various people at the dessert table, I walked around the side of the church and into the cemetery. I went straight to the large stone that bore the names of Joel and Sadie Butler James, sat down in the grass at the foot of the graves and lit a cigarette.

The hillside was thick with large and small headstones, some of shiny granite, others of lichen-covered marble. Across the valley stood the old Piney Ridge High School that my mother and her siblings had attended. The large brick structure was largely unused now, except for a section of one floor that housed the community's kindergarten-through-fifth-grade children. Beyond that the French Broad River and Runion lay hidden by the hills, but I knew exactly where they were. Lonesome Mountain rose above them both, its calico autumn dress etched sharply against the blue October sky.

"Mighty pretty view for these sleepers, ain't it?" a voice said from behind me.

I turned around and smiled when I saw Delbert Gunter leaning on his cane a few feet away.

"Yessir, mighty pretty," I echoed. "What are you doing way over here, Mr. Gunter?"

"The food, son. An old coot like me don't get much home cooking up on that mountain yonder."

"I didn't see you out there earlier. Were you at church?"

"No, I couldn't make it in time for the preaching because I was out of peanut butter." The old man laughed and sat down on a nearby stump. "One excuse's good as another, I reckon."

"You didn't walk all this way, did you?"

"Lord no, son. I ain't been able to walk that far in a week or two now." He laughed again and laid one hand atop the other on the handle of his cane. "Our good Deputy Boyce fetched me and the Honeycutt sisters over here in his patrol car. He's around there licking all the bowls clean this minute."

"Oh, I get it. You guys're out on a double date."

"Bite your tongue, pup," Delbert Gunter said. And then he grinned widely and winked.

"Tell me something, Mr. Gunter. Do you remember when I drove you home after that Sodom Laurel moonshine party?"

"I reckon that's why I'm sitting here talking to you like I know you. I don't take up with just any longhair I come across."

I smiled and pulled my ponytail along the side of my neck away from the old man.

"You told me that night about leaving the county once to go to your sister's wedding in Asheville and said there was just one other trip. A story for another time, you said."

"That's right."

"How about now?"

Delbert Gunter looked past me along the hillside.

"Well, I can give you the short of it, I reckon."

"However you want to tell it."

The old man ran his tongue between his cheeks and gums and reached into the bib pocket of his overalls and pulled out a pouch of chewing tobacco. He opened it and dipped his fingers in, pulled out a clump of the dark brown strands and stuffed it into his right cheek, and blew a couple of scraps off his lower lip.

"There was this little girl I got sweet on back in my youth. Mary Lee Haire, she was then. We weren't no more than sixteen or so at the time. Met her at a Independence Day social at the meetinghouse over in Sodom. Lord, but she was a pretty thing. Hair the color of hot weather moonlight and eyes a color of blue I never seen before nor since." He spat a stream of brown juice into the grass on the side of the stump away from the graves. "Well, we got to talking there around the horseshoe pits, and I come to find out she liked fishing. So I worked up a couple of poles from a stand of cane there by the meeting house. I'd brung some line in my pocket and had three or four hooks in a matchbox, so we lit out for a hole in the Big Laurel." Spit. "Well, we didn't do much fishing after all I done to come up with the rigs. I kissed her a time or two there by the creek, and she kissed me back a time or two. Pretty quick we run to a cave-like spot I knowed of, shed our outer garments and committed an uncleanness right there."

I looked at my grandparents' headstone. Between their names and the dates of their births and deaths, an inscription read "Wed Sept 8, 1929." I turned to Uncle T's grave a few feet to the right, at Bigmama James's side.

There was a James family secret Butler had pointed out to Cutter and me on the first Homecoming Day after Uncle T's headstone had been set. The date inscribed for our uncle's birth was "February 14, 1930," little more than five months after Joel and Sadie's wedding. We'd asked Cutter's mother, Aunt Evelyn, about it.

"Your Uncle T was a little anxious to get into the world," she'd said. Then, after a pause, "It wasn't a shotgun marriage. They'd been courting each other for a year or two already."

Life and the living of it hadn't changed so much since then, I thought as I pictured Eliza and me in the back seat of the old LTD, parked in moonlit darkness beside another church and graveyard not far from this one.

Delbert Gunter spat, wiped the back of his hand across his mouth and continued.

"She didn't get with child, so I reckon we got away with it. But it wasn't 'til after, when she drawed pictures in my palm with her fingertip and listened to what all big plans I had for myself—" Spit. "It wasn't 'til then I knowed I loved her." He shifted on the stump, crossed his legs, and laid the crook of the cane in his lap. "Her daddy didn't hanker after no Gunter for a son-in-law, particularly no fiddle-playing Gunter. The first time I come around his place to spark her, he run me off with a shotgun barrel to the seat of my pants. I never stopped running nor hollering the whole five mile back home."

"You ready to go, Delbert?" Deputy Daggnabbit Boyce stood at the corner of the church, munching on a butter cookie.

"A minute, Davis," Delbert Gunter said without turning. "I'm telling this young'un a tale."

"Afternoon, Gabe," Deputy Boyce said. "You ain't been sleeping on no picnic tables lately?"

I grinned and shook my head.

"Don't you let that old man's tale get too long nor too tall," the deputy said and licked the crumbs from his fingertips and took a sip of tea. "I'll be finishing off these cookies, Delbert."

"I'll be there directly," Delbert Gunter said and spat again. He unloaded his cheek and tossed the tight ball of tobacco into a bush by the back corner of the church. Then he wiped his fingers behind one knee of his overalls. "She married a Hot Springs Ledbetter not too long after that. Son, I couldn't count the times I wished we'd come up with a child that day by the creek. Her daddy's shotgun would've been chasing me to the altar with her then." He laughed and pulled a handkerchief from a back pocket and wiped his eyes. "Old Ledbetter finally widowed her ten, twelve year ago," he said and stuffed the cloth back into his pocket. "How I come to leave the county the second time was when she sent me a letter one summer, asking me along on a bus with her and the local Presbyterians to the World's Fair down in Knoxville back in '80 or '82." He stood up and looked toward Lonesome Mountain. "We had a right nice time that day. I enjoyed the trip."

Deputy Boyce appeared at the corner.

"Come on, Delbert," he said, already turning away. "The girls are done in the squad car and waiting. The Falcons and Redskins'll be about started by the time we get back over to their place." Then he was gone again.

"He still thinks with his peter, even if he can't use it no more," Delbert Gunter said and laughed and pulled the handkerchief from his back pocket again.

I stood too.

"Do you still see her?" I asked, stretching. "Mary Lee, I mean."

"No, son, no more than in dreams. She passed on of a heart attack by the end of that year. Only saw her that one day." He fixed the cane in his left hand and wiped his other hand down the bib of his overalls. "Come see me," he said and turned and hobbled around the corner of the church.

I helped my father and brother carry the table tops and sawhorses back to the church's furnace room. Mom, my sister-in-law Patty, Aunt Evelyn and Rendy and Aunt Myrtle loaded leftovers into the trunk of our Grand Marquis.

"Everybody come over to the house," Aunt Myrtle said. "There's plenty of food left for us all to have supper later."

"Our boys took Bobbie and Lydia to watch the football game," Aunt Evelyn said, settling into her car with Rendy. "They'll probably be snoring up a storm by the time we get there."

"Gabe," Aunt Myrtle said. "Let me lock the church door and then you ride with me to the house, okay?"

"Okay." I turned to my parents. "I'll see you over there," I said and watched as they left the dusty gravel lot with Butler and Patty and Aunt Evelyn and Rendy right behind them.

As Aunt Myrtle drove slowly toward the old James family homeplace, the home she'd shared with Uncle T, the air through the open windows gentled my face and smelled heavy with autumn—the sweet ripening of the last two months becoming the dry burning smell of summer's decay. As we passed through wooded sections, a ceiling of orange and rust and yellow boughs hung above the narrow blacktop. Leaves dropped like the first spits of winter snow and blew into the ditches or swirled in the wake of the car. When the roadside opened up, the afternoon sky spread blue and unblemished to the farthest ridges, and the fields on either side lay cut and baled.

"You know, Eliza's still in Asheville," Aunt Myrtle said suddenly. "I see her to get my hair done about every three weeks since she broke me of that weekly habit. She's doing real good. And popular! My lands, she's booked worse than a doctor. She's got her own salon in South Asheville." All of this rushed out as if she were nervous and reading it to a large audience. When I didn't react, she sighed and fell quiet and kept driving.

I knew she was on the verge of saying something she considered a revelation. As she wheeled the car into her driveway, I wondered what it could be. Eliza had a child? Or two? Eliza's husband had effortlessly become fabulously wealthy and was running for the Senate? I closed my eyes and concentrated on the dry smell of driveway dust and autumn leaves.

"Have you talked to her since you came home?" Aunt Myrtle asked.

"No."

I remembered the phone call long ago and the man's voice that answered, remembered our last moments together in the lobby of the Opryland Hotel—my futile attempt to protect her from the drunken cowboy, her assault on the same, the two of us forced apart without a good-bye. "But if you come home," she'd said.

"She's not married anymore, Gabe," Aunt Myrtle said.

"Oh, really?" I turned away and stared at the swirl of color running up the distant front of Lonesome Mountain. I felt my heartbeat rising to my throat and ears. The world around me suddenly seemed far away and thin, like the sound of a transistor radio on the beach when the waves are pounding and the wind is blowing off the water.

"She won't say what happened." Aunt Myrtle let the car roll slowly up alongside the house and stop. "You should call her sometime."

"Maybe I will," I said and swallowed hard, "one of these days." I jumped out of the car before she said anything else, suddenly desperate to plop down on the couch in front of the television and watch football. I wanted to drift off to sleep to the voice of the announcer and the roar of the crowd, the gentle hum of gossip and bursts of cackling laughter from the women around the table in the dining room.

I was able to wait two hours. Then I was dialing the number I'd known since that long ago night at the Dam Dance. I'd ask her mother for her number in Asheville, and when I figured out what I might say, I'd call Eliza.

"Hello?"

I froze for a second and then almost hung up, but I cleared my throat and found my voice.

"Mr. Garrison, this is Gabriel Tanner. How are you?"

"Well, I'm fine. And you?"

"I'm doing pretty well, sir."

"Are you local?"

"Sir?"

"Are you in Runion or Tennessee?"

"Oh, I'm here in Runion. I've been with my family to Homecoming at the Piney Ridge Methodist Church. But right now I'm at my Aunt Myrtle's."

The two of us talked for a few minutes about the weather and the football game that was on.

I relaxed a little. I'd rarely known my former father-in-law to give smiles to anybody except Eliza, but now and again I was sure I heard the spread of one in the man's voice.

"I was wondering if you could give me Eliza's phone number," I said at last.

"Hold on, Gabe," Mr. Garrison said with a chuckle. "She's sleeping right here on the couch."

My gut twisted into such a sudden knot that I lost my breath for a moment. I heard the clunk as Eliza's father laid the receiver down. The football game played loudly in the background, but I still heard Webb Garrison saying, "Baby doll? Wake up, baby doll. The phone's for you." Only the sound of the game was heard for a moment and then another clunk as the receiver was lifted from where it lay. I took a deep breath.

"Hello?" she said, trying to stifle a yawn.

"Hi."

She didn't say anything.

"Eliza?"

"Gabriel!"

I pulled a chair from under the kitchen table and sat down.

"Yeah," I said. "I'm back home."

"I can't believe this. When did you get here?"

"A little over a year ago."

"What?"

I laughed.

"I moved back a year ago August."

"You're kidding. Why haven't you called?"

"I thought you were busy. You know."

"Oh, that. I haven't been busy with that for a while now."

"Okay, enough said. Aunt Myrtle tells me you've opened your own business."

"I have, and it's wonderful." She told me about the salon—where it was, who she had working there, how busy it all kept her. "And what about you?" she said. "What have you been doing since you got back?"

"I'm in school at Runion State. I started back in January and haven't taken a break yet."

"Are you studying music?"

"No, English and Journalism, and I'm working part-time at the local paper too."

"That's great! So you're living at home?"

"I was at first, but then I found this little cabin over on Genesis Road. I've got it on sort of a rent-to-own arrangement with a professor at the university."

"Are you still playing music at all?"

"No, not really. I sang at church today, but that had more to do with others' expectations than my interest."

"That makes me sad," she said. "What about the band you had in Nashville?"

"The band had some personnel changes and such. Kind of fizzled out as a full-time thing. I used to meet them a couple of times every month or so for gigs, but that's fizzled out now too. We still keep in touch though. They're a good bunch of guys."

"All guys?" she said. "I heard that when you played in Asheville a couple of years ago you had a girl in the band."

"Yeah, we had a girl playing bass for us. But she got married and had to quit."

We talked for over an hour, our conversation ricocheting from topic to topic, without doing much more than scratching the surface of her life or mine. This was the conversation we should have had that late night in Nashville. Now we each listened as much to the sound of the other's voice as to the words that were said.

"Can we get together this evening?" I finally asked.

"Oh, Gabriel, I'm busy tonight," she said. "If I'd only known. How about tomorrow? Can I call you at the cabin?"

"Sure," I said and gave her the number. "I'm on fall break, so I'll be there or at the paper."

I hung up the receiver and noticed the quiet around me. I looked through the kitchen and into the dining room, where the women, except for Patty, seemed to sit motionless around the table. My Aunts Myrtle and Evelyn had their backs to me, but their heads were turned slightly, each with an ear toward my conversation. Rendy and my cousins Lydia and Bobbie sat out of sight at each end of the table. Only my mother faced me from the other side. She lifted one dark eyebrow and smiled. I smiled back and stepped outside to have a cigarette.

Before I could settle down again in Uncle T's old easy chair, the telephone rang, and Aunt Myrtle said it was for me.

Eliza asked if I wanted to go with her that night to 45 Cherry, a club in Asheville where a band called the Nighthawks was playing. She said that the club owner's wife was a client, that maybe my band could get back together for a gig or two in Asheville. It would be good, she thought, if I went with her and met the club owner.

I waited half an hour and took the familiar route to her house.

Yellow and red butterflies swarmed in my stomach. My lungs seemed to draw on thin air, and sweat dripped down my sides. The steering wheel felt slick in my hands. I squirmed in the seat, rolled the window partway up and got hot, rolled it down again and lit another cigarette.

How would she look this time? How would I look to her? What would we talk about that we hadn't already touched on over the telephone? Would she be known in this nightclub beyond her association with the owner and his wife? Would people there remember me and "Catch That Train"? Could we sit together in a car as the darkness fell around us and not think about the times we'd rolled anxiously into some hidden parking spot and begun yanking at each other's clothes?

As soon as I pulled into her parents' driveway, she backed out the front door with her purse and an overnight bag. She fiddled with the lock a moment and then stepped away, making sure the storm door closed securely.

I noticed her hair first. Gone was the curly red hair she'd sported in Nashville. She now wore its thick blackness short and straight and parted on the side. Around the nape of her neck and partway up the back of her head it was trimmed close. A lock of longer hair grew from just behind her left ear and lay braided and beaded on her shoulder.

I quickly put the car in neutral, pulled the emergency brake on and got out.

She hopped down the steps and walked quickly toward me. Apart from some changes in style she looked much the same as she had that morning she stood in the doorway ready for work and then left me for what seemed like forever. Much the same as in all my memories and dreams of her since. Her blue eyes were still the palest, oddest shade I'd ever seen and still held their own mysterious silvery light. Her familiar smile appeared like the spark and dance of a struck match. She wore a white t-shirt tucked tightly into beltless faded blue jeans, and as she walked her breasts bobbed beneath the Aztec calendar printed on it.

"You look incredible," I said, walking around the front of the car to open her door.

"Well, thanks. That's nice of you to say." She sank into her seat and reached for the seat belt.

I closed the door and walked around the car, suddenly panicked and at a loss for words.

She'd become a vision to me over the years, something more akin to the afterlife than my past. A restless floating spirit that appeared to me at unexpected moments of the day or night—a thought-glimpse caught in the corner of my eye, a name on the tip of my tongue. The touch of her fingers or lips on my skin in those moments between waking and dreaming, dreaming and waking, the sound of her whispering at my ear or calling from an unbearable distance—these had become as real to me as the wind. And now in the seat beside me she became flesh and voice again.

"You too," she said as I put the car in gear.

"What?" I released the emergency brake.

"I'm glad to see you, too." She rolled down her window. "Oh, I've got some errands to run in Asheville in the morning. Could you take me to my house tonight?"

"Sure."

"Mama and Daddy took my car there to leave it for me. But I'll still come down and call you tomorrow, okay? Maybe we can have lunch or go for a drive."

"I can meet you in Asheville somewhere if that'd be better for you."

"I'd rather come back down here."

"All right." I put my arm on the seat behind her head and twisted around and backed out of the driveway, smiling.

"What are you smiling at?"

I chuckled.

"When I put my arm behind you just now, I all of a sudden thought of that night I bloodied your nose over on Piney Ridge."

"Oh, what a thing to think of!"

From there more and more memories and catching up passed back and forth between us as we rode to Asheville.

We arrived early and for a few moments sat in the car in 45 Cherry's parking lot.

Eliza dug in her purse.

"These tickets say the show starts at ten." She let her hands fall into her lap. "What time is it?"

"A little after six."

"I don't know what I was thinking of to have you rush right over and drive straight up here."

"It's okay. I've enjoyed it."

"Are you hungry?"

"Not really just now."

"Me either."

"Well, is there anything you'd like to do?"

"Want to ride the Parkway up to Craggy Gardens? The fall colors are so pretty in this light."

"Sounds like a plan." I started the car again. "Maybe we can get there before the sun sets."

* * *

We sat side by side on a high stone wall. Our shadows stretched long behind us, and the world swept away in front.

Down the hollow and on the near slopes, the October leaves reflected the gold and rust in the low-angled light. Farther down lay the wide evening-lavender valley, rolling and misting, split somewhere in the middle by the French Broad River.

Eliza leaned toward me and brushed something from under her thigh. She scooted closer in the process and our legs touched from hips to knees.

"So tell me about the girl in the band," she said.

"There's not much to tell really."

"Don't lie to me, Gabriel. That's not what I heard at all."

"Heard from who?" I took out a cigarette and lit it.

The sun blushed redder as it touched the mountains and sank quickly. The sky purpled.

"From some friends who saw the show in Asheville that time. You don't know them."

"And what'd they say?" I flicked my ashes, and they caught in an updraft and flew back into my lap. I blew them away again.

"Just that you two were all over each other," she said.

"Maybe," I said. "It was sort of a part of the show." I squeezed my hand down between our thighs and leaned forward on stiff arms. "The sun's about down."

Eliza wrapped her arms around herself and then unwrapped them and scooted away from me.

"Were you in love with her?" she said.

"I never figured it out. Maybe. Does it matter?"

"Not unless you're still in love with her."

I sat and looked out across the darkened valley now becoming starred like the sky.

"Are you?" she said.

"No," I said at last. "Not anymore."

"I'm getting chilly," she said. "Can we go?"

I was glad when we got in the car and she didn't want to go back to 45 Cherry for the show. I'd spent too much time in nightclubs anyway, too much time in rooms filled with thundering PA systems and bands and drunks and smoke. I'd meet the club owner another time if I felt like it.

She guided me along the Parkway to the exit that brought us down into South Asheville. She pointed out her salon and asked me to stop there.

"Need to pick something up?" I asked.

"No," she said. "I just want to cut your hair."

It was a pretty place, colored in mauve, teal and gray. A pile of brown hair lay in the floor around her chair.

"Let me sweep this up," she said. "I left in a hurry yesterday."

"Hot date?"

"No, not that it's any of your business."

"Hey, you were the one with all the questions about my bass player."

She seemed to ignore that and after sweeping the floor and turning on the stereo she shampooed my hair. The feel of her fingers on my scalp sent chills down my back and, relaxing as it was, I could hardly lie still. Then she moved me over to her chair and wrapped me up with a towel around my neck and a cape spread over me.

"What do you want to do with this?" she asked as she worked tangles from my long black hair.

"With what?" The only "this" on my mind was this moment and what might happen next.

"Your hair. What do you want?"

I chuckled.

"You never used to ask that," I said. "Just did what you wanted to with it."

"I asked you in Nashville that time," she said. "You weren't ready to cut it then." She smiled a little and looked at me in the mirror. "So, how about now?"

"It depends," I said.

"On what?"

I cleared my throat and pulled a cigarette and lighter from under the cape.

"Got an ashtray?" I said.

"Depends on what?" she said again as she set the ashtray stand beside the chair.

"On how much we're gonna be seeing each other."

"If we're not?"

"Then just trim the split ends."

"And if we are?"

"Do whatever you want. You're the one that has to look at it."

Without another word, she gathered a thick black ponytail at the back of my neck and with one long snip dropped the mass of hair on the floor. Then she looked back at me in the mirror, smiled broadly and went on with her work, singing now and then with a line of whatever song was playing on the sound system.

We stopped at a restaurant called Sneakers before I took her home. We talked and ate our dinners, ordered coffee and split a piece of chocolate cheesecake. We each smoked an after dinner cigarette and talked about what to do next.

"Do you want to go ahead and take me home now?" she asked. "We could rent a movie or something."

"I'd rather keep talking to you instead of watching TV," I said.

The small house stood at the end of a white gravel cul-de-sac. The blue of her neighbor's security light lit up her place as well. A stream sang down one side of her house, entered a culvert under the driveway, and fed a pond that took up over half her property. Beyond the pond a railroad gradient rose darkly, the straight line of the tracks silhouetted against the lights of the suburb.

"This is a beautiful place," I said. "How long have you lived here?"

"Eight years or so, I guess. I couldn't stand living in that apartment for long, you know? I'd looked at this place a couple of times and got it as soon as the divorce—"

I stood puzzled for a moment, looking at the shadowed profile of her soft face.

"Oh, you mean our divorce."

"That's what I mean," she said as she turned and unlocked the door. "But I sure didn't mean to bring it up." She pushed the door open and reached inside and flipped a switch.

A lamp came on and lit a living room with a hardwood floor. To the left a partial wall separated this from a carpeted sunken den.

"That way," she said, pointing to the right, "is the kitchen, laundry, two bedrooms and a bath."

"This is great, Eliza."

"Thanks. Have a seat down there." She flipped another switch and an overhead fluorescent light came on in the den. "Would you like some wine or something?"

"Only if you have white. I got sick on red once at a club in Louisville and haven't been able to drink it since."

"I have white. Sit down and I'll get it."

She came back with two fluted wine glasses and a bottle and set them on the wooden coffee table.

"Thanks," I said and poured each of the glasses half full.

She turned on the television and turned it off again and turned on the radio. Then she kicked off her shoes and sat down on the couch and looked at me.

"Oh, I'm sorry," she said, jumping back to her feet. "I forgot you don't like overhead lights."

"It's okay. Don't worry about it."

"I had a lamp in here but it got broken a while back and I haven't been able to replace it. Let me see if I can gather up some candles. That'll go better with the wine anyway, don't you think?"

"Sounds cozy."

She returned in a minute with two squat candles, one red and one green, and two tall slender peach ones in holders. She flipped the switches by the front door and then descended into the sunken den in near darkness.

The light from the neighbor's house came through the den's sliding glass door and played on her movements as she carefully arranged the candles with one at each corner of the coffee table. The pale blue glow highlighted her hair, her forehead and the rounded tip of her nose, the strong lines of her forearm, the swell of her breasts.

The butterflies returned to my stomach as I watched this woman, this ghost of the girl I'd known. Or was the girl the ghost?

"So if you got this after our divorce," I said, "you must've lived here with him."

She leaned back and looked at me, her face unreadable in the dim light.

"We lived here," she said. "But I don't want to talk about that right now."

"You pumped me about Yvonne," I said.

"Who?"

"The girl in the band."

"Oh," she said. "I was just asking, not pumping."

"Well, I'm just asking."

It seemed like a long time that we sat there in the darkness before she spoke.

"We lived here," she finally said again. "He drank a lot, and it was a bad life. Not anything like you and me had way back when. He got violent."

"I've known some guys to do that," I said. "And some girls that like it."

"Well, those girls are crazy. I didn't like it at all, so I had him taken away."

"You what?"

"I filed for a separation, and he wouldn't leave, so I had the police come and get him."

I leaned back beside her in the darkness and stared at her for a moment.

"Sounds like you're even tougher than you used to be," I said and smiled.

"Can I see your lighter?" she said.

I dug it out of my pocket and handed it to her.

She lit it, and the glow rose to her face. She passed the lighter from wick to wick, keeping the flame burning the whole time.

The light in the room grew, but somehow the shadows didn't lessen, only retreated to gather in darker throngs in corners and behind and under furniture.

"Ouch!" she yelled and dropped the lighter. "Damn it!"

"You okay?" I said, leaning forward quickly to pick up the lighter. "The flame get you?"

"No. The damn metal—" She shook her right hand in the air. "It'll be okay in a minute. I don't think it blistered or anything."

"Let me see it."

When she held out her hand, I locked my thumb in hers to hold her steady and looked at the finger in the candlelight for a moment.

"No, doesn't look like there's a blister."

"I didn't think about the metal getting hot like that."

"I should have thought of it, but I was too busy watching you."

A sudden silence fell between us, and in it I pulled her hand to my lips—pulling her closer with it—and kissed the finger.

"Better," she said.

"Good." I unlocked our thumbs and took her hand in both of mine and slid the finger between my lips and massaged it with my tongue.

"Oh!" she said, jerking back a little. "That tickles." Then she relaxed. "Much better."

I began to rub one hand up her arm to her shoulder and down again. I looked at her face and saw that her eyes were halfway closed and her head was slowly tilting to one side. When I felt her arm completely relax, I pushed firmly down on the crook of her elbow, pulling her finger from my mouth and her body toward me in the same motion.

Her eyes flew open at the movement and then closed again as she fell into my arms.

I felt the changes the years had brought to her body. Her shoulders seemed broader. Her breasts softer, heavier. Her arms and legs, neither thick nor fat, felt somehow denser. It was as if the girl I'd known nine years before had been made of air and this woman was made of earth and water.

* * *

The expanse of turbulent gray rolls away beneath where I sit on the high rock wall. In the distance Lonesome Mountain stands with its head and shoulders above the fog.

I can see Delbert's cabin from here, *Uncle T says.* He's lying in the yard, dreaming how a fiddle can sound like rain.

I strain to see but can't.

Where is the rest of the world? The other mountains, the lights beneath the mist.

The rest is the same. *Uncle T flutters the open G strings on his mandolin.* Anything and everything the same in this world. Elvis blasted a hole in the sky with a cannon or that pistol of his and all this gray fell down and settled and that was it.

I look up and squint.

It's hard to tell where it's coming from anymore.

Uncle T looks a lot like me. A certain shape to the jawbone is the same in both of us. The pattern of lines around the eyes the same.

I lie with my back on the stone wall and open my eyes to the gray blankness above.

The mandolin rings again. A fifth added. A seven-note run up the neck.

The way this gray shifts you'll never get back to any exact place you were. *Uncle T's suit sparkles without the sun and the tiny colored points of reflected light dance on his face under the brim of his hat.* So you come back to something different and even though it feels the same ... it's different.

I'm tired. Feeling ashamed of something. I can't tell what.

Here. *Uncle T takes a strip of tin and hangs it over me.* Get a roof over your head.

The tin tilts back and forth. A rumbling sound grows as ball bearings roll from end to end and back again. The tin squeaks. The motion slows. Slows and then stops. The ball bearings come to rest.

I stand at some distance away and somewhat below. I can see Uncle T sitting on the rock wall, his glittering back to me. The mandolin plays. Its song waltzes away toward Lonesome Mountain.

The sheet of tin still hangs motionless in the air, but I can't tell if my body still lies under it.

An echoing shriek, as if the tin canopy is being ripped in two. The scene at the rock wall explodes with a sound like a cannon fired close to my ear.

*   *   *

I bolted upright, still seeing the smoke and ball bearings and glitter of rhinestones rising in the darkness of the room, still hearing the echo of the explosion in the night around me. I swung my feet to the floor and tried to slow my breathing.

A shadow shifted in the gauzy light on the wall just as another metallic screech sounded, and another boom shook the night.

I stood naked by her bed and pulled the filmy curtains away from the window.

A train on the tracks across the pond slowly moved then creaked and banged again. The repercussion of the coupling cars shook and echoed along the train's entire length.

Eliza didn't move.

I took a deep breath and went to the den and put on my clothes, turned off the radio and went back and knelt by the bed.

She startled when I kissed her cheek, then stirred and stretched.

"What time is it?" she said in a warm whisper. But in the darkness, the look on her face was one she might give a stranger. "Where you going?"

"It's a little after two in the morning," I said. "I better get home."

"Oh. I'll see you at lunch, okay?"

I brushed her dark hair away from her forehead and kissed her again.

"Sleep well," I said and rose and left the room.

"Gabriel?" she called after me.

I stopped in the middle of the living room floor.

"Yeah?"

"I'm not that tough," she said, and then the house fell quiet again.

I stood listening for a moment, wondering what she'd meant by that. Then I left by the front door and made sure it locked behind me.

I walked around her car, bending at each wheel and feeling the tread on her tires. I stepped to the edge of the pond and peed, watching the window where she slept.

Marking your territory, Gabriel?

I smiled to myself, dropped into my car and drove away.

*   *   *

Past three o'clock in the morning. I drove up Genesis Road, winding my way toward the cabin in the woods, easing into the driveway and coasting to a stop beneath the kitchen window. Uncle T's old Martin still lay in the trunk, so I got it out and wearily climbed the steps to the deck and slipped through the back door.

In my music room, I turned on a small lamp, looked at my old Guild on its stand and lay down on the daybed without taking off my clothes.

I coughed and heard the sympathetic vibration of the Guild's D string. I looked toward it but didn't get up in response to its call. Its faded and pitted finish testified to all it had been through with me since we moved to Nashville. These days, its strings stretched in silence, untouched, and its womanly curves waited and waited for the return of my passion and warm caresses.

I reached up and turned off the lamp.

My ancient upright piano filled the room with an earthy aroma of dust and old wood and sweat that reminded me of the tiny mountain church in which it had spent half a century or more. How many poundings had its keys taken in revivals back across those years? With what fervor had its strains of "Just as I Am" rung the walls of the old church and wrung the hearts of countless sinners through countless altar calls? After all that passion and soul, it surely felt dead and buried under my distracted and disheartened tinkerings.

"Maybe I won't be away much longer," I mumbled in the darkness. I reached out and lifted the Guild from its stand, laid it on my chest and wrapped my arms around it and fell asleep.

The Fade

Eliza called at ten in the morning and said she'd be in Runion around eleven-thirty. I told her I'd pick her up at her folks' house, but she wanted to come see the cabin. I gave her directions, and, after shaving and showering, went outside to wait.

It felt good to be out of class for a couple of days, even though I had an article to get ready for the *Runion Recorder* by the next afternoon. I fell into the hammock that hung between two trees just off the deck and stretched out, feeling myself both warmed by the sun and cooled by an autumn breeze.

The deep blue sky seemed alive with the calls of unseen crows. The pines rustled above me. A few leaves whispered down from the oaks and poplars. Some small woodland sprite fidgeted in the dry leaves on the left side of the deck. The sound of a chain saw came from farther up Genesis Road, but then it was drowned out by a train passing along the riverbank, its rhythmic rumble and whining whistle ricocheting through the hollers on both sides of the French Broad.

When Eliza arrived, I gave her a quick tour of the cabin, and then we got in my car and drove over to Piney Ridge, making our way toward Bluff on 209-A. We both laughed as we passed the church where Deputy Boyce had found us asleep in the wee hours of a December morning, and we sat quietly together through the curve where Uncle T's car had jumped into the tops of the trees. I pointed out the place where I'd lost my car in a more comical accident on the night I returned for good from Nashville.

"Do you still drink a lot?" she asked without looking at me.

"Not much," I said. "Not since I got home. A beer with Cutter and

Rendy now and then."

"It's hard for me to picture, you know?"

"What?"

"You drinking a lot like that," she said and watched the road ahead for a few moments. Then, "Was there some reason you did?"

A sign indicated that Bluff was five miles away. After winding through that distance, we would pick up 209 and drive north into Hot Springs.

"I had a lot of down time at first," I said. "I lived alone and didn't know many people. That started it, I guess." I paused. "And I missed you, of course."

Again she sat a moment, her face turned away from me as if she were looking up into the colorful autumn woods on the hillside.

"What about Mo Biggs?" she said at last. "I meant to ask about him last night. You had him, didn't you?"

"That's a complicated story."

It's just business, I heard Billy Keith say. *Happens all the time.*

"How so?"

"Well, Mo didn't last long after I moved to Nashville. He stayed in Knoxville, so he kind of just faded out of the picture." I felt my face redden. "You know, out of sight, out of mind."

"I can't imagine that with Mo," she said. "Do you remember how much he called before you moved?"

"Yes, and he called that much after I moved too." I noticed I had a white-knuckle grip in the steering wheel. "But as it turned out, Billy Keith didn't really like Mo much, and I felt like I had to choose sides." I took a deep breath to relax. "I went with Billy. I didn't know what else to do."

"And Mo just let you go?"

"No, not hardly. He complained a lot and finally threatened me with breach of contract if I didn't file bankruptcy, which would have cancelled all my contracts. He wanted me to do that and then sign with him again."

"God, that is complicated," she said. "I'm sorry you had to go through that by yourself."

I wasn't sure what she meant by that, but I wanted to think that she wished she'd been there to go through it with me. She had let my missing her go without comment, so I did the same with what she said.

"I can't imagine filing bankruptcy. Even if it did cancel the contracts, it leads to a lot of other bad stuff."

I could feel her looking at me as I looked straight ahead, my eyes on the winding road.

"You didn't do it, did you?" she said.

"No, I ended up not having to," I said.

"That's good."

"You know, I wish I could say that Mo and I were just as incompatible as music and business are, but it's not that simple." I pulled a cigarette from the pack in my shirt pocket. "I mean, Mo really liked the music. And he really believed in me, I think. But as it turned out, he wasn't very good at the business side of things." I lit the cigarette and rolled my window partway down. "We both had to learn that business way outweighs music in Nashville."

Eliza lit a cigarette as well.

"I was going to ask if you miss the music business," she said. "But I think I already know the answer to that."

"Probably," I said. I told her about the last show at MacArthur's and the way Lukas flattened Al Katt.

"I'd like to meet Lukas and the others some time," she said.

"Maybe we'll plan a trip over there one of these days."

"Did you see the girl bass player before you left?"

"No," I said. I wasn't ready to talk with her about Yvonne. I didn't know if I'd ever be.

She let the lie pass, and we arrived at Bluff. We stopped for lunch at an old store on the winding road between there and Hot Springs.

The place smelled of leather and bacon. The rows of shelves held dry goods and groceries. Behind the counter, two old men made music— one played fiddle and the other mandolin.

I took an Orange Crush from a low red icebox and a Moon Pie from a white metal shelf. Eliza chose a pack of wheat crackers and a Diet Mountain Dew. A plump woman with a nasally mountain twang made a bologna sandwich for me and a tomato and cucumber for her. We went back to the icebox and leaned on it and ate our lunch and listened to the music. Some of the bluegrass tunes I recognized but couldn't guess what they were called. The musicians played a few hymns I could name—"Where the Soul Never Dies," "Have a Little Talk with Jesus" and, of course, "Amazing Grace."

After stopping a couple of places in Hot Springs, where I asked some questions about a series of grave-robbings that had taken place over the past few weeks, we wound up at my folks' Jewel Hill house in the midafternoon. We found Dad mowing the yard for possibly the last time that season and Mom playing "Someone to Watch Over Me" on the piano in the living room. They stopped what they were doing and served us ice water on the porch, but the old gathering was a little awkward for everybody at first, especially Dad.

"Y'all want to stay for supper?" Mom asked as Eliza and I were getting up to leave.

"I've got a piece I need to wrap up for the paper," I said.

"And I need to drive back to Asheville," Eliza said.

My father cleared his throat and spat over the porch railing.

"Maybe Sunday," he said.

Eliza smiled at him.

"That sounds good."

We drove back to the cabin, saying little to each other on the way. But once there, we sat together on the deck, looking over the railing and into the quiet and bright woods, a small metal table and ashtray between us.

"Do you still write songs?"

I sat for a moment and watched two squirrels, one chasing the other, spiraling in a blur up the trunk of a massive red oak.

"Not much," I said. "The last one was almost a year ago."

"I'm sorry about that," she said. "I always liked to wake up and hear you working on a song in the kitchen."

"Really?"

"Oh, yes, that's one of the things I missed the most after—" She stopped.

An uneasy silence hung between us for a moment.

"Well, you know," she said.

I cleared my throat.

"I still write a lot," I said. "Different kinds of stuff." I stood up. "Want some water?"

"Please," she said.

I slid aside the screen of the sliding glass door and went through a corner of the living room and into the kitchen.

I'd been doing all kinds of writing, and much of it was meaningful and rewarding. But I'm a junkie for the elevation and thrill that only songwriting gives me. The progression from creation to performance—when it's right—is breathtaking. Addicting. And I'm an addict. But I'd cut myself off. I was angry with music. Angrier than I'd ever been with Eliza or Yvonne, with Mo Biggs or Billy Keith, with Chuck Townshend or even the Turrenoks. And except for the brief burst of creativity that led to "Homecoming," I'd lost all confidence in myself as a songwriter. My music should have been able to rise above the business and take me with it. But it didn't.

As I filled two plastic RSU cups with water, I looked out the window above the sink and watched her sitting on the deck. The moment, the morning, the whole of last evening—all seemed unreal, and I couldn't shake the feeling that we had come back together too easily, too comfortably. And I thought I could see the same in her unguarded expression.

We would need to be careful.

Back on the deck, I set our cups on the small table and sprawled again in my chair.

"I've just been trying to figure out how long we were apart," she said and took a sip of her water. "Nine years, right?"

"A little over that, I think." Then, "Except for that one weird night in Nashville."

"Oh, Lord, what a thing to remember!" she said and lit a cigarette. She stood and walked over to the edge of the deck and blew smoke at the trees. "That was a weird time, for sure."

I lit a cigarette and went to stand beside her.

"You don't seem very different from when we lived together in Runion," I said. "You seemed tense that night in Nashville, but now you seem like yourself again."

"I hope that I'm smarter than I was," she said. "Either of those times."

"I'm sure you are," I said.

"You seem different."

"Really?"

She blew more smoke at the trees.

"You seem kind of restless," she said. "Not fidgety or nervous. Maybe kind of haunted in a way."

I thought about that for a moment.

"You're probably right," I said. "I've got a lot that I have to live with."

"Such as?"

"Well, let's see. I can think of a lot of things. but I've got three things in particular." I blew smoke rings into the clear golden air.

"Well?" she said.

I snuffed out my half-smoked cigarette and grabbed our waters and brought them back to the deck railing.

"The first is Mo Biggs," I said. "I told you this morning how the business with Mo took a bad turn." I paused. "What I didn't tell you is that Mo is dead."

"What?" Her eyes widened. "When did this happen? How—" She stopped.

"It was New Year's Day almost seven years ago now. He had a heart attack. I saw him the day before as I was going home to Nashville from being here at Christmas. He didn't look good."

She turned and leaned back against the railing, quiet for a long moment.

"I'm sorry about that," she said at last. "But people die. Why is it something you have to live with?"

"Part of it is the heartache and stress I caused him." I told her about my last meeting with Mo and how he died. "I have to live with knowing I did him wrong and not getting the chance to make it right or even say I'm sorry."

The sun dipped below the treetops on its way to setting behind Piney Ridge.

"I don't think you have as much to regret in all that as you think you do," she said. "But I'm sorry he left that way." She snuffed out her cigarette. "What's the second thing?"

I had to think a moment. Then, "It's that my dream didn't come true," I said. "And that I still want to be a star. I have to live with that never happening."

"Who says you can't still make your dream come true?" she said.

"Well, I'm thirty-two years old, and I live in Runion. As good as life gets from here on out, I'm afraid that deep down I'll always wish that things had been different." I turned and leaned my back against the railing beside her. "Maybe that'll fade as I get old, but right now it doesn't feel like it."

She crossed her arms over her breasts and rubbed her palms up and down her sleeves.

"Maybe the way you think about it will change, you know?"

"Maybe," I said. "I hope so."

"Okay, the third thing," she said, continuing to rub her arms from shoulder to elbow.

"This one has to do with you," I said.

"Uh-oh," she said and smiled at me.

"I think about what happened to us and why, and I'm embarrassed about that."

"Why are you embarrassed?"

"It's the sense of failure, I think, and the time wasted and lost." I took a sip of my water, and the coolness of it felt good on my tongue. "I walked away from our wedding vows and our marriage. I left you and everything behind for nine years, and I don't have a damned thing to show for it."

She looked at me without any particular expression in her eyes or words on her lips.

"I think about all the mornings that I missed watching you sleep and about all the other things that make a life together. And about what my leaving put us through on our own."

So far we'd hardly talked about her second marriage, and although we'd made a couple of tries to learn about the other's love life, we hadn't told each other much.

One reason that I didn't seek out Eliza—or even news of her—in the year that I'd been home was that for a long time I hadn't sorted out my feelings about Yvonne. Through the winter after I left her and Nashville, we talked now and then, mostly when I was lonely or when she was having a rough time with Swede. After a couple of calls, we talked like old friends, but always a tension hummed below the surface of our conversations. We both sensed it, I think. Maybe that's why we quit talking. When spring break came and I spent the week with Lukas, I didn't contact Yvonne. I drove by her house that Tuesday afternoon, but the place was dark. A last shudder of violent emotion made me speed away once and for all.

I wasn't ready to tell Eliza any of this.

"I hit some good licks in those nine years, and I guess I got farther than most do. But none of my little conquests justifies what was lost."

The sun set behind Piney Ridge, and the October chill was taking over the twilight air.

"I'm getting cold," she said. "Come inside and play me a song, okay?"

In the music room, we undressed each other slowly and made gentle love on the daybed.

* * *

She left around seven-thirty, and I sat at the small table in the living room, working on my article. I was doing the final editing when I noticed that I was humming softly to myself. A haunting melody in a minor key, delicate and old-sounding. I tried to place the tune and couldn't. I thought at first that it might be part of what I'd heard Mom playing that afternoon, but this had a simpler, more driving sound to it than the melodic line of the old Gershwin tune. Then I thought that it might be an old mountain hymn or ballad, something I'd heard, perhaps, from the fiddle and voice of Delbert Gunter. That felt more likely but still not right.

"Must be mine," I said aloud and looked up from my writing and sat for a few moments staring at the reflection in the sliding-glass door.

A man at a small table. Papers scattered in front of him. All lit by a small reading lamp. Shadows and stained knotty-pine tones.

Gabriel Tanner.

I shuddered so violently at Mo Biggs's voice that my pencil leapt from my fingers and skidded across and off the tabletop.

I'll tell you what.

I knew the voice was in my head, yet I couldn't help straining my eyes to look into the dark corners of the room and beyond my reflection to the dark deck.

You can know your heart, Mo Biggs's boggy-sounding voice said. *You can know your mind.*

His voice, but not any words of his that I could remember.

I tried to steady my breathing.

Eliza had said I seemed haunted in a way. Maybe she was right—she usually is about such things. Being alone in the cabin that evening was different from being alone there only two nights before. When I hadn't felt her absence. When I'd learned not to dwell on all that had been lost.

You can know yourself as wise and kind . . .

Now I'd been dwelling on these things and sitting in near darkness, writing about the midnight robbing of graves in an old Appalachian town. No wonder my mind could turn to such ideas and imaginings.

. . . and still be frightened of things you find in . . .

"Dark corners," I chanted three or four times in response, but Mo's voice fell silent. Then, feeling just the slightest touch of a lost thrill, I wrote on the back of a page of notes,

Dark corners . . .
Where the rattling bones
Mark the danger zones—
Dark corners . . .
We've all got 'em.

"All right," I said and got up to fetch my guitar.

* * *

Every place—and every life—makes its own music.

The coasts vibrate with crashing waves. The plains sigh with endless wind in grass. The lowlands hum with heat. The snow-covered western mountains sing with their own melting. And dotted here and there across this land, the big cities chatter and blare like nightclubs filled with drinkers and jazz.

The music of my place on this earth comes alive in the way an echo runs its hollers and hillsides, in the way old tools and election days and week-long revivals still resonate in stone and wood.

Listen . . .
The wash of the river . . .
The whisper of a breeze in autumn leaves . . .
A chorus of crows high up on the mountainside . . .
The pealing coronets of sunlight filtering through a stand of pines . . .

And from somewhere down the river—or from that dark holler yonder in the wilder mountains of Piney Ridge—or from up around the nearest bend in Genesis Road—comes the flutter of a mandolin, the cry of a fiddle, the rasp of a voice: "Amazing grace, how sweet the sound. . . ."

ॐ ॐ

ACKNOWLEDGMENTS

My thanks first, and always, to Leesa Cody, whose love of me and the music remains astounding and inspirational, and to our sons, Lane and Raleigh Cody, for both of whom music is a passion.

I appreciate all who have supported my life and music-making over the years: all my Cody, Reeves, Plemmons, and Harrell relations (both living and late), Sam and Sharon Barnett, Tony Kiss, Brian Maloney, and a host of others in Madison County and Asheville, North Carolina, and in Nashville and Johnson City, Tennessee.

For all the musical experiences and friendship over the years, I am grateful to many music-makers and bandmates: the late jb (Jim Baird), Mark Burchfield, Dale Burton, Mark Chesshir, Terry Davis, David Ecrement, Gene Ford, Steve Grossman, Dave Jacques, Ben Ledford, Kirk McWilliams, Danny O'Lannerghty, Mike Radovsky, Harlon Rice, Bruce Soesbee, Jobie Sprinkle, Jim Stapleton, and the late Jackie Street. Thanks also to other musical and family folks who have contributed in both large and small ways to the life and music of this story: Becky Chesshir, Ashley Cleveland, Tom DuVall, Eugene Epperson, Dixie Gamble, Faith Hill, Kevin Hornback, Jim Isbell, John Jarvis, Cathi King, Phil Madeira, Gary Morris, Joey Plemmons, the late J. D. Reeves, the Reeves Sisters (Dot and Ernie), the late Earl (Richards) Sinks, and the late Ron Weathers.

Thanks are due to teachers and readers who have guided my writing over the years: Jennifer Atkinson, Rick Boyer, Renni Browne, Rick Chess, Schuyler Kaufman, P. B. Parris, the late Jeff Rackham, and A. D. Reed.

I appreciate the support of my friends, colleagues, and students in both the Department of Literature and Language and the broader community at East Tennessee State University.

Finally, I am deeply grateful to A. D. Reed of Pisgah Press for believing in this book, improving it with his editing and insight, and making it a reality.

About the Author

Michael Amos Cody spent the early years of his adult life as a songwriter in Nashville, after which he earned his PhD in English from the University of South Carolina. He now teaches in the Department of Literature and Language at East Tennessee State University. In recent years, he has returned to music, releasing the albums *Homecoming* and *Wonderful Life* and performing live in a variety of venues. His short fiction has appeared in The *Tampa Review*, *Yemassee*, and other publications. *Gabriel's Songbook* is his first novel.

Also available from Pisgah Press

Mombie: The Zombie Mom   Barry Burgess
$16.95

Letting Go: Collected Poems 1983-2003   Donna Lisle Burton
$14.95
Way Past Time for Reflecting
$17.95

Musical Morphine: Transforming Pain One Note at a Time   Robin Russell Gaiser
$17.95

MacTiernan's Bottle   Michael Hopping
$14.95
rhythms on a flaming drum
$16.95

I Like It Here! Adventures in the Wild & Wonderful World of Theatre   C. Robert Jones
$30.00

LANKY TALES   C. Robert Jones

Lanky Tales, Vol. I: The Bird Man & other stories
$9.00
Lanky Tales, Vol. II: Billy Red Wing & other stories
$9.00
Lanky Tales, Vol. III: A Good and Faithrful Friend & other stories
$9.00
The Mystery of Claggett Cove
$9.00

Red-state, White-guy Blues   Jeff Douglas Messer
$15.95

Buried Pennies   Peter Olevnik
$14.95

Reed's Homophones: A Comprehensive Book of Sound-alike Words   A.D. Reed
$17.95

Swords in their Hands: George Washington and the Newburgh Conspiracy
$24.95   Dave Richards
Finalist in the USA Book Awards for History, 2014

Trang Sen: A Novel of Vietnam   Sarah-Ann Smith
$19.50

Invasive Procedures: Earthqukes, Calamities, & poems from the midst of life   Nan Socolow
$17.95

Deadly Dancing   THE RICK RYDER MYSTERY SERIES   RF Wilson
$15.95
Killer Weed
$14.95

To order:

IP

Pisgah Press, LLC
PO Box 9663, Asheville, NC 28815
www.pisgahpress.com

CPSIA information can be obtained
at www.ICGtesting.com
Printed in the USA
FSHW022139290321
79868FS